"*O*ne of the brightest lights in our genre.
Her writing is truly scrumptious."
Teresa Medeiros

"*S*he writes with a captivating blend
of charm, style, and grace that never fails
to leave the reader sighing and
smiling and falling in love."
Julia Quinn

"*C*all her 'the historical Jennifer Crusie' . . .
James gives readers plenty of reasons to laugh."
Publishers Weekly

"*S*he's a gift every romance reader
should give herself."
Connie Brockway

"[*J*ames] forces the reader
into a delicious surrender."
USA Today

"*R*omance writing does not get
much better than this."
People

By Eloisa James

PLEASURE FOR PLEASURE
THE TAMING OF THE DUKE
KISS ME, ANNABEL
MUCH ADO ABOUT YOU
YOUR WICKED WAYS
A WILD PURSUIT
FOOL FOR LOVE
DUCHESS IN LOVE

Coming Soon

DESPERATE DUCHESSES

ELOISA JAMES

Pleasure for Pleasure

AVON BOOKS
An Imprint of HarperCollinsPublishers

AVON BOOKS
An Imprint of HarperCollins*Publishers*
10 East 53rd Street
New York, New York 10022-5299

Copyright © 2006 by Eloisa James
ISBN-13: 978-0-06-078192-7
ISBN-10: 0-06-078192-0
www.avonromance.com

First Avon Books paperback printing: December 2006

Avon Trademark Reg. U.S. Pat. Off. and in Other Countries, Marca Registrada, Hecho en U.S.A.
HarperCollins® is a registered trademark of HarperCollins Publishers Inc.

Printed in the U.S.A.

10 9 8 7 6 5 4 3 2 1

Acknowledgments

I wish to thank novelist Carola Dunn for generously sharing her expertise in arcane Regency minutiae. Dr. Jean-Marc Passelergue of Baugé, France, gave the Earl of Mayne the perfect motto, and Sylvia Clemot of Rueil Malmaison, France, generously provided my Sylvie with excellent French. As always, my research assistant, Franzeca Drouin, was a treasure of information, though all errors are (regretfully) my own.

This book is dedicated to the bon-bon lovers who frequent the Eloisa James Bulletin Board, sharing their laughter, creativity, and passion for the Earl of Mayne. Love you, guys!

1

An extract from the widely proclaimed memoir:
The Earl of Hellgate,
or Night Scenes Amongst the Ton

Dear Reader,

As I would loathe to shock and dismay you, I must beg all ladies of a delicate disposition to put down this volume on the moment.

I have lived a life of Immoderate Passion, and have been persuaded to share the particulars in the hopes of keeping any susceptible gentlepersons from following in my steps . . .

Oh Reader, Beware!

May 24, 1818
15 Grosvenor Square
London residence of the Duke of Holbrook

There was no way to introduce the subject with delicacy, at least none that Josie could imagine. "None of the novels I've read elaborate on the wedding night," she told her sisters.

"I should hope not!" her eldest sister Tess said, not even looking at her.

"So if we're going to discuss Imogen's wedding night, I'm not leaving."

"It wouldn't be appropriate for you to join us," Tess said, with the rather wearied air of someone who has said the same on two former occasions. After all, of the four Essex sisters, Tess, Annabel, Imogen, and Josie, there was only one left unmarried: Josie.

"We'll give you all the details you need on the eve of your marriage," Imogen put in. "I don't need the talk. I am a widow, after all."

They were seated around a small table in the nursery, having a light supper. Josie's chaperone, Lady Griselda, was technically dining with them as well, but since she had spent most of the evening huddled in an armchair reading the Earl of Hellgate's memoirs, she hadn't taken more than a bite, nor contributed to the conversation a whit.

They were eating by themselves because Imogen had heard it might cause misfortune to see her groom on the night before the wedding, and since Imogen was marrying their guardian, the Duke of Holbrook, they couldn't eat in the dining room. Technically, Annabel's son Samuel was a member of the party, but since he was all of four months old and dreaming of a red shiny ball, an occasional longing snort were his only contributions.

"If my season continues as it's begun," Josie said, "I shan't be married at all. One can hardly obtain one's entire education in the ways of men and women from the pages of novels."

"Tess, did you know that Josie has made a list of efficacious ways to catch a husband?" Annabel asked, taking a final bite of syllabub.

"Based on our examples?" Tess said, raising an eyebrow.

"*That* would be a remarkably short list," Josie said. "Lady is compromised, gentleman is forced to marry her, marriage ensues."

"I was not compromised by my husband," Tess said, but she was laughing.

"You married Lucius only after the Earl of Mayne jilted you at the altar," Josie said. "It wasn't precisely a long courtship period. All of ten minutes, as I recall."

The smile in Tess's eyes suggested that those ten minutes had been sweet, and Josie didn't want to think about that because it made her feel jealous. If she, Josie, were jilted at the altar, there'd be no secondary candidate waiting in the next room. In fact, given her disastrous performance on the marriage market, the altar was likely a prospect she should discard.

"It's true that I was compromised," Annabel said, "but Imogen is marrying Rafe for pure love and after a long courtship."

"I suggested we elope," Imogen said, grinning, "but Rafe said he'd be damned if he'd follow in Draven's footsteps and allow me to direct all the wedding traffic to Scotland."

"He was right," Tess said. "You're going to be a duchess. You couldn't marry in such a hurly-burly fashion."

"Yes, we could have."

"But think of all the pleasure you would have denied the *ton*," Josie said. "The prime enjoyment of the season so far has been watching Rafe stare at you longingly from the side of the ballroom. Now, are we going to discuss your wedding night, or not? Because there are marked gaps in my knowledge."

"There are *no* gaps in my knowledge," Imogen said, "so—"

"I knew it!" Josie said. "You and Rafe anticipated the night, didn't you? Oh, the shame!" She threw a dramatic hand up to her brow. "My sister lies prostrate under her guardian."

"Josephine Essex!" Tess said, suddenly turning into the eldest sister who'd raised them all. "If I hear you say such a coarse thing in the future, I shall—I shall swat you!"

Josie grinned. "I was merely demonstrating that the gaps in my knowledge do not have to do with mechanics."

"Anything else will have to be learned on the fly, darling," Annabel said. She had gone over to the crib and scooped up Samuel. Now she was comfortably snuggled into a deep chair, feet up and casually crossed at her slender ankles, cuddling the baby. He was used to such manhandling and slept on.

Josie knew that she should do a better job at curbing the wild flares of jealousy that periodically gripped her. Yet all she had to do was look from one to another of her three sisters to feel the pinch as sharply as frozen toes while skating. All three of them were slim. Well, Annabel wasn't precisely slim, but she carried her curves splendidly. All of them were (or soon would be) happily married. Two of them married titles, and if Tess's husband didn't have a title, he was the richest man in England and anyone with common sense would agree that such wealth trumped a coronet.

"I'm serious," Josie said, pulling her mind back to the subject at hand. "Annabel, you're only here for the wedding, and Imogen is leaving on her marriage trip directly. What if I have to marry quickly? You won't be here to give me advice."

In the back of her mind, Josie knew that she might have to do something drastic to find a husband. No one was wooing her in the normal way of things, so she might have to compromise someone in order to get the deed done. Which would require an immediate wedding. "When Annabel was about to marry Ewan, Imogen told her that she should kiss her husband in public."

"Goodness, do you remember that?" Imogen said, looking faintly surprised.

"You said," Josie reminded her, "that Draven didn't fall in

love with you because you refused to kiss him at the race-course. Whereas Lucius did fall in love with Tess because she allowed intimacies in public."

Tess was laughing again. "I'll have to inform Lucius precisely why he's so fond of me. It was all that kiss at the race-track!"

"Hush," Imogen told her. "That was just a stupid idea I had last year, Josie. You mustn't take it so seriously."

"Well, I do take it seriously," Josie said. "That is, I would if anyone showed the slightest inclination to kiss me in the open air, or the closed air, for that matter."

Annabel looked up from kissing Samuel's head. "Why so bitter, dearest? Has no man presented himself whom you admire?"

There was a moment of silence in the room, as everyone realized that a letter or two had gone astray between London and the Scottish castle where Annabel lived with her earl.

Characteristically, Josie took the bull by the horns. "I'm not exactly the toast of the season," she said grimly.

"Oh darling, the season has scarcely begun, hasn't it?" Annabel said, tucking the baby's blanket around his little shoulder. "There's plenty of time to lure any number of men."

"Annabel."

She looked up at the tone in Josie's voice.

"I'm known as the Scottish Sausage."

If Josie were writing one of the novels she loved to read, she would have said that there was a moment of stricken silence.

Annabel blinked at her. "The—The—"

"It's partly your fault," Imogen said, a sharp note in her voice. "*You* introduced Josie to your revolting neighbor, Crogan. When Josie rejected his advances he wrote a school friend named Darlington. And most unfortunately, Darlington appears to specialize in cruel set-downs."

"Has the tongue of a snake," Tess said flatly. "No one

loathes him, although they should, because he's so clever. But he hasn't shown any cleverness here, just garden-variety malice."

"You can't mean it!" Annabel cried, sitting up straight. "The Crogans?"

"The younger one," Josie said morosely. "The one who sang all those songs in the tree outside my window."

"I know you didn't want to marry him, but—"

"He didn't wish to marry me either. He felt it was beneath him to wed a Scottish piglet, but his elder brother threatened to throw him out if he didn't court me."

"What?" Annabel said, confused. She was trying to think about her neighbors, the Crogans, and not about Samuel's warm little body under her hand. "How could he possibly insult you, Josie? We had him to the house only once, and I refused to allow him to take you to the assembly!"

"I overheard his brother urging him to marry me," Josie said.

Annabel's eyes narrowed. "Why didn't you tell me? Ewan would never have let that little toad write insults to his friends in London. As it is, I'm sure he'll kill the man. He almost did it last year."

"It was too humiliating."

But Annabel had known her little sister for eighteen years, and she could recognize the slight flush on her face. She said with a little gasp: "Josie, you didn't have anything to do with young Crogan's illness, did you?"

Josie tossed her hair. "He probably ate something that didn't agree with him, the disgusting little turnip."

"He lost two stone in a matter of a fortnight!"

"That wouldn't hurt him. And he deserved it."

"Papa's colic medicine for horses," Imogen told Annabel.

"It wasn't Papa's," Josie said. "It was mine. I created it myself."

"Josie and I have already discussed the inadvisable

approach she took to the problem," Tess said, looking up from peeling an apple.

"Inadvisable? She could have killed the man!"

"Absolutely not," Josie said indignantly. "When Peterkin gave it to the stable boy, it only made him sick for a week."

"I rather think the younger Crogan did deserve it," Imogen said. "After all, he instigated all the unpleasantness Josie has suffered in London."

"What did he call you?" Annabel asked. And then: "Ewan is going to kill him. Absolutely kill him."

"He called me a Scottish piglet," Josie said flatly. "Darlington made the term into the more alliterative Scottish Sausage, and the sobriquet has stuck." Even she could hear the stark despair in her voice.

"Oh, Josie, I'm so sorry," Annabel whispered. "I had no idea."

"I did write you a few weeks ago, but perhaps our letters crossed as you were coming from Scotland," Tess said.

"It's too late now," Josie said. "No one will dance with me unless he's forced to by Tess and Imogen."

"That is simply not true," Imogen said. "What about Timothy Arbuthnot?"

"He's old," Josie said. "Old and widowed. I can certainly understand that he wants a wife for those children of his, but I don't care to play the role."

"Timothy is not old," Tess said. "He can't be more than a year or so into his thirties, which is, may I point out, the same age as all of our husbands."

"Besides," Imogen said, "thirty is a watershed year for men. If they're going to develop intelligence, they do it around then, and if they don't, it's too late. So you mustn't hanker after men in their twenties. That's like buying a pig in a poke."

"Don't mention pigs," Josie said through clenched teeth. "I don't like Mr. Arbuthnot. There's something waxy about his face, as if he got up in the morning and had to push his nose into place."

"What a revolting description," Annabel said. "While we need to turn this unfortunate situation around, obviously Arbuthnot isn't the one to do it."

"There's no way to turn it around," Josie said. "Unless by a miracle I suddenly became slim, everyone thinks of sausage when they look at me."

"Absurd," Annabel said. "You look beautiful." They all stared at Josie for a moment. She was wearing a dressing gown, as they all were. Josie scowled back at them.

"The problem with you," Annabel said, "is that if one doesn't know you, you look like one of those sweet Renaissance madonnas."

"With round, maternal faces," Josie said glumly. She hated her cheeks.

"No, with beautiful, glowing skin and a sweet look. But you're not at all sweet by nature."

"True enough," Imogen said, eating a last seed cake. "You do have the most marvelous skin, Josie."

"Unfortunate that there's so much of it," Josie said.

"Nonsense. I've told you many times, as has Griselda, that men are very fond of figures like ours," Annabel said. "Griselda! Wake up and tell Josie how delicious your figure is. And mine, for that matter."

"The three of us do not have the same figure," Josie said. "Your figure curves in and out, Annabel. Mine just flounders about."

Griselda looked up. "This book is incredible. I am almost certain I know who Hellgate is."

"Your brother?" Imogen asked idly. All of London was reading Hellgate's memoirs—and most of London had decided that Hellgate was really the Earl of Mayne.

"I don't think so," Griselda said, having clearly given the matter serious thought. "I'm only a third of the way through, but I don't recognize a single woman whom Mayne has courted."

"Courted is not exactly the word for his interactions with women, is it?" Josie remarked.

"One needn't be exact about such things," Griselda said, unruffled by this slur on her brother's character. "We all know that Mayne is not a saint. But although the writer is extremely clever, I don't recognize the women."

"Is it true that Mayne is in love?" Annabel asked. "I can hardly believe it. Remember when we first met him, the night we arrived at Rafe's estate?"

"You staked him out as your property," Tess said, smiling.

"Well, then *you* engaged yourself to him at the first opportunity," Annabel retorted. "There was no respect for my prior claim."

"One might say that almost all the Essex sisters tried to claim him in one way or another," Imogen said, giggling.

"Least said about *your* efforts the better," Tess put in.

"Well, there was nothing illicit between Mayne and myself," Imogen said. "'Tis a tale quickly told. After sleeping with half the women in London, he refused to bed me, and that without a second thought."

"My brother is a man of honor," Griselda said. She raised her hand at the hoots of laughter around the table. "I know, I know . . . his reputation is not the best. But he has never deliberately injured anyone's feelings, nor taken advantage of a woman in a vulnerable position. And you, Imogen, were in a vulnerable state of mind."

"There's always the possibility that he is simply burnt to the socket," Josie said. "That's what makes me think that Hellgate is Mayne. Yes, perhaps he has a vivid reputation, but it's all due to the past. Your brother hasn't had an *affaire* in years, Griselda."

"Two years," she said with dignity.

"You see? Apparently Hellgate talks of repentance, and

I expect Mayne is indulging in the same sort of thinking. I wish you'd let me read the book, Griselda. I am certainly old enough."

"I beg to differ," Griselda stated, adding: "Mayne is in love, and we should allow his peccadillos to rest in the past." She opened her book and began reading it again.

Annabel was frowning to herself and rocking Samuel. "Griselda's right. While it's vexing that Mayne somehow managed to slip by all four of us and marry a stranger—and I do wish to hear all about his exquisite Frenchwoman—the important person is *you*, Josie."

Josie almost jested about refusing to marry if she couldn't have Mayne, but she choked it off. Spinsterhood was too real a possibility to be spoken out loud.

"It's all a matter of dressing," Annabel announced. "You must go to that wonderful woman of Griselda's."

"I already have an entire new wardrobe, thanks to Rafe."

"I took her to my *modiste,* Madame Badeau," Imogen said a bit doubtfully, "but—"

"She gave me a marvelous corset," Josie said. "At least when I'm wearing it I don't feel as if I'm swelling in all directions like an unmoored balloon."

"I don't like that corset," Tess said flatly.

"Unfortunately, neither do I," Imogen said.

"Well, I'm not giving it up," Josie said. "I can almost wear Imogen's gowns when I'm in it; can you imagine, Annabel? If the *ton* laughs at me now, imagine what they would say if I wasn't wearing the corset." That's how she thought of it: The Corset.

"What's so miraculous about this particular corset?" Annabel asked. Samuel had woken up and was having a late night snack.

Josie looked away. It was bad enough that she, Josie, was saddled with breasts that she privately thought were far too large: like melons when oranges were the appropriate size.

But Annabel had no compunction at all about feeding Samuel in front of them all, and her breasts were even larger.

"It's a contraption made of whalebone and lord knows what else," Tess told Annabel. "It goes from Josie's collarbone all the way past her bottom."

"How on earth do you sit down?" Annabel asked.

"It's miraculously designed," Josie told her. "There are let-in seams around the hips."

"Is it comfortable?"

"Well, not particularly," Josie said. "But *ton* parties are not precisely comfortable at the best of times, are they? I find them invariably tedious. I can't dance well at all, and that seems to be the only pleasure one might take in them."

"You danced more gracefully before you began wearing that object," Tess pointed out.

Josie ignored her. "Madame Badeau designed a number of gowns that fit perfectly over the corset."

"That's just it," Tess said, "they fit the corset, not you."

"I like it," Josie snapped. "And since I wouldn't be caught at a ball without it on, you might as well stop insulting me."

"We're not insulting you," Imogen said. "We just think you might be more comfortable with another sort of undergarment."

"Never," Josie said.

Griselda shut the book again. "I simply cannot imagine how Hellgate had time for anything other than dalliance. Why, I'm only on the seventh chapter and his behavior is beyond scandalous."

"I think the true wonder is that Hellgate wasn't compromised and forced into marriage," Josie said. "Daisy Peckery's mother allowed her to read it, and Daisy said that Hellgate bedded any number of young, unmarried women."

"Another reason why a similarity between my brother and Hellgate should be dismissed at once," Griselda pointed out. "Mayne has only slept with married women."

"A wise decision on his part," Josie said. "From the reading I've done, together with my observations of the *ton* in the last month, I would say that any man engaging in indelicate behavior around a young, unmarried woman is extremely imprudent. All sorts of marriages result from the most innocent, if foolish, kinds of dalliance."

"I can attest to that," Annabel put in. She had married her husband after a scandal broke in a gossip column.

"In fact," Josie added, "by my estimation a woman who does not have a solid offer would be extremely foolish *not* to engage in a measured amount of imprudent behavior."

Suddenly she realized they were all looking at her.

"No one has made the slightest approach to me," she pointed out. "My remarks were intended to be purely theoretical."

"I was remarkably fortunate to find myself paired with Ewan," Annabel pointed out, frowning at Josie. "Other young women have not been so contented with a choice made rashly and under difficult circumstances."

"I understand that," Josie said. But inside she felt all the frustration of a theorist who has worked out a brilliant theory—and been given no material on which to practice. She could hardly create a scandal when men wouldn't go anywhere near the Scottish Sausage.

And yet even sausages had to get married. More and more, she thought that she would have to obtain a husband in a less-than-honorable fashion. Of course, she didn't mean to share that salient fact with her sisters.

Annabel turned to Tess and Imogen. "So how long have you two been aware that Josie was planning to create a scandal?"

Imogen popped a grape in her mouth. "I should think she came up with the idea about a year ago, didn't you, Josie?"

"Actually," Tess corrected her, "I would place Josie's

resolution about the time she first began reading all those novels printed by the Minerva Press."

Josie gave a mental shrug. So her plans were known to the family—and now to Griselda, who was looking up from her book, rather startled.

"There is a trifling detail that you have overlooked," Josie said.

"And what may that be?" Annabel asked.

"It takes two to create a scandal, and since no man will even dance with me, I think the Essex family is likely to be free from the taint of a contrived marriage."

"I certainly hope so."

"I should amend that: yet *another* contrived marriage," Josie said. And then ducked when Imogen threw a grape at her.

2

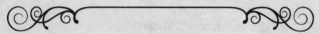

From The Earl of Hellgate,
Chapter the First

Perhaps others who embark on a life marked by Sins of the Flesh realize in their infancy that they are born to a life of notorious liaisons. I, Dear Reader, was raised in blissful ignorance of my future infamy.

In fact, it wasn't until the tender years of my youth, when I in all my innocence visited the Court of St. James—oh, I loathe to set down the words—that I met a duchess. The episode of the green stockings is known to some, but I can tell you now that . . .

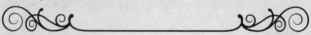

St. Paul's Cathedral
London

It was a serious wedding, plump with pomp and circumstance. Imogen made her way up the aisle of St. Paul's Cathedral to be greeted by no less than the Bishop of London. She was exquisitely gowned in cloth of gold; the groom committed the forgivable solecism of taking her hands during the ceremony, and smiling down at her in such a way that tears came to the eyes of many an unhappily married soul. And even some of the happily married ones.

Garret Langham, the Earl of Mayne, watched his closest friend, Raphael Jourdain, Duke of Holbrook, stand at the altar with a sense of deep satisfaction. The day was when he might have scoffed at a man with Rafe's look of abject adoration. Rafe resembled nothing so much as a lovesick cow, or rather bull. Which was just fine, because Mayne felt the same way. Before long, it would be he standing before the bishop, swearing to love and to cherish, as Rafe was doing.

His heart quickened at the thought, and he could almost feel his own features taking on a look of imbecilic adoration. After all, Sylvie was *his*. He'd never understood that before; never guessed how powerful it was to know that the woman you most love in the world has agreed to be yours.

He glanced at his left. She was standing beside him. Sylvie de la Broderie. Even her name sent a shiver of delight up his spine. She was dressed, as always, with exquisite correctness. Her gown was a rosy pale pink that somehow didn't swear with her pale red-gold hair. He could just glimpse her elegant retroussé nose. Little curls fell down her neck from under her jaunty, unmistakably French bonnet, adorned with a flutter of tiny ribbons. Like her bonnet, Sylvie was unmistakably French.

Mayne's mother was French, and he loved nothing more than speaking the language. It all felt right: he had finally, at long last, found a woman whom he adored, and she was French.

"It's providence," Rafe had said lazily the night before. They were toasting his wedding with water, since Rafe didn't drink.

"And my sister adores her," Mayne had said, unable to stop categorizing Sylvie's perfections.

"Good old Grissie. You must find your sister a husband now that you're contemplating domestic bliss. You're so unnaturally cheerful that I can hardly stand your presence."

"Well, you won't have to bear me for long," Mayne had retorted. "Wedding trip, eh? There's a newfangled notion."

"Are you saying that you won't wish to take your Sylvie to a remote location, preferably on the slowest boat available?"

An image flashed into Mayne's mind, of himself peeling back Sylvie's long gloves, revealing a sweet delicate wrist and . . .

Rafe had laughed at his silence.

Mayne knew that he was dangerously smitten. All he had to do was glance down at his fiancée's gloved fingers to feel a stirring in his groin. The very thought of peeling off those gloves made him more fraught with passion than he'd been in years. Likely, he thought with a flash of amused contempt for himself, since bedding his fifth or sixth matron.

Yet Sylvie was different from all those women he had bedded, from the first to the thirtieth. She was even different from the only other woman he'd truly loved, the one matron who had not given in to his skilled seductions, Helene, the Countess Godwin. The countess was seated a few rows behind him. They rarely spoke to each other, and her happiness with her husband shone from her eyes. Mayne's bitter disappointment (though he was ashamed to admit it) had hampered him from the kind of cheerful relationship he enjoyed with most of the society ladies whom he'd bedded.

Of course, that life was over. Sylvie was a virgin, innocent in the ways of the body, even if she had a practical French approach to the bedroom. In fact, she'd told him in her enchanting French accent that she doubted she would make him happy in the bedroom. A little smile curled Mayne's mouth. Those were naive words, though one would never think to use that term of his sophisticated, sleek fiancée.

Now he glanced down at the curve of Sylvie's cheek, her pointed chin, the slender fingers holding her prayerbook, and was struck by a wave of gladness. Of course she would make him happy; she had such small acquaintance with desire that she knew nothing of it. And for some dark reason, her innocence made him happy.

Women had always fallen into his arms with dismaying ease, turning their lips up to his before he asked for the privilege, their eyes following him about the room before he knew their names. But Sylvie had to be introduced to him three times; she kept forgetting his name. They had never shared a passionate kiss, even after becoming affianced: she had a strong sense of propriety. It wasn't as if he *wished* to kiss her into silence.

Well, he did wish it.

But no one would want Sylvie to be silent: her flow of enchanting, laughing conversation enlivened every minute. In fact, once he finally had her in bed with him, and married, he could imagine her ravishing commentary on the night when he showed her, slowly and tenderly, all the delights that a woman experiences in the arms of a man.

"Ironic, isn't it?" he had said to Rafe the night before. "Here I am, with my reputation—"

"Spawned by the devil to cuckold unwitting husbands," Rafe had put in.

"With my reputation," Mayne had repeated, "and Sylvie de la Broderie agrees to marry me."

"A chaste goddess, by anyone's terms. Though I never knew a woman's reputation was important to you."

Mayne suddenly remembered that Rafe's affianced bride, Imogen, hardly enjoyed the reputation of a snowy dove. "It isn't. But I find some cynical enjoyment in the fact that Sylvie's reputation is so irreproachable."

"I suspect that everyone in London is sharing your bewilderment. Or they would be if you weren't so damned good-looking."

"Sylvie is not a woman to be swayed by something so unimportant."

"Thank God, Imogen isn't either," Rafe had said, making a face.

"You're not so bad. Now you've lost your gut."

"I'll never be a fashion plate. Whereas you always have that look about you, Mayne. I expect that's why she took you. You look French."

Mayne had opened his mouth to protest—surely Sylvie loved him for his character, for his tenderness toward her, for his passion, always held in check—but caught back the words. Sylvie was his. He had gone down on one knee and offered her an emerald ring that had been in his family for generations . . . and she had said yes.

Yes!

He didn't need to boast, even to his closest friend, about the affection that Sylvie felt for him. Such emotions were best left unvoiced. Sylvie was an aristocrat, from the tips of her delicate gloved fingers to the jeweled heel of her slippers. The daughter of the Marquis de Caribas, who luckily escaped with his estates intact from the carnage in Paris, would never insult herself or him by naive murmurings. He loved her, and she knew it.

She accepted it, with a tiny bend of her head, as her due.

And he . . . he was almost afraid that what he felt went beyond love. He trembled just to be standing next to her, bored his friends by speaking about her whenever she wasn't near, found himself watching her whenever she was.

As if she felt his eyes on her face, she looked up and smiled. Her face was a perfect triangle, from her delicately flaring eyebrows to her high cheekbones. There was nothing superfluous about her, nothing loud, nothing inelegant. "Stop looking like that!" she whispered to him in her enchanting French lisp. "You make me feel quite odd."

Mayne grinned at her. "Good," he said, bending over so that he breathed it into her ear. "I want you to feel quite odd."

She gave him a reproving little frown and turned back to her prayer book.

At the altar, Imogen looked up at Rafe and said clearly, "I do." Relief was clear in every lineament of Rafe's body. He bent his head and kissed his bride, ignoring the bishop, who was still reading out of his prayer book. Mayne grinned. That was just like Rafe; up to the very last moment he was worried that Imogen would realize what a poor bargain he was.

"Why should she marry me?" he had demanded, the night before his wedding. "God, I want a drink at times like these."

"Well, you can't have one," Mayne said. "Normally, I would assume that she's blind and desperate. But since she shows no signs of infirmity, and she's clearly not desperate, being one of the richest young widows in the *ton,* not to mention beautiful, I can only conclude that she's lost her wits."

Rafe ignored him. "She says—" the raw emotion in his eyes caught Mayne by surprise—"she says she loves me."

"As I said, she's cracked," Mayne said, instinctively trying to lighten the conversation. "Perhaps she's taking you for the title. She wants to be a duchess. In fact," he said, warming to the task, "I'm fairly sure that Imogen said as much to me. Wasn't *I* supposed to marry her at one time? Of course, a duchess is better than a countess."

"Least said about you and Imogen the better," Rafe growled, and there was a note of deep warning in his voice.

But it had to be said, clearly, before the wedding. "We never even kissed, not really," he told Rafe. "I kissed her twice, to make her see that our friendship was nothing more than tepid."

"I should kill you for those two kisses." There was a swirl of danger in Rafe's voice.

"She didn't enjoy them, and neither did I."

"Damned if you haven't made hay with all my wards. You were engaged to Tess, and stood her up at the altar—"

"*Not* my fault!" Mayne put in. "You know perfectly well that Felton asked me to leave."

"Jilted one of my wards, kissed another one twice—"

"I've had nothing to do with Annabel," Mayne said hastily. "Nor Josie either."

"Well, on that subject," Rafe said. "I want you to help me with Josie. Not with your usual shenanigans."

"I'm almost a married man." At least, he would be as soon as he could talk Sylvie into setting a date.

"Josie is having a difficult time on the market. And it's only going to be more thorny once Imogen and I leave on our wedding trip."

"What's happening to her?" Mayne was genuinely surprised. "I would have thought she'd take like wildfire: she's intelligent, witty, and damned beautiful. And didn't you and Felton give her a dowry, besides the horse from her father, I mean?"

"She made an enemy of some neighbors of Ardmore's in Scotland, a couple of ne'er-do-wells by the name of Crogan. Apparently, one of them was courting her up there, wanting the dowry but not her. Well, once she learned the truth of it, she—she—"

"She what?" Mayne asked, trying to picture Josephine Essex growing violent. "Struck him?"

"She dosed him with a medicine that cures colic in horses," Rafe said flatly.

"Colic in *horses*? Dr. Burberry's Colic Juice?"

"Apparently it's something she created herself. Stop laughing, Mayne! The lad was near death for a week, apparently, and lost over two stone in weight."

Mayne was bellowing with laughter. "That's Josie! Did I tell you about the time she arranged for Annabel to be thrown from a horse so that Ardmore could rescue her?"

"Apparently this Crogan was an ass. Josie says he should be grateful for the slimming program."

"You've unleashed a poisoner onto the innocent male population of London," Mayne said with relish. "If she doesn't like one of her suitors . . ." He snapped his fingers.

"Crogan said he wasn't attracted to her because she was too fat."

"Fat?"

"She does have a generous figure."

"So what?"

"Crogan took revenge. He wrote to several friends of his. Oh, he didn't say anything about the colic medicine; no man wants to confess that he's lost two stone because he was unable to leave the privy for days. He called her a prime Scottish hoglet."

Mayne's lips tightened and every impulse toward laughter disappeared. "Ugly. But who would pay attention to the opinion of some Scottish farmer?"

"He was sent to school at Rugby."

"Darlington!" Mayne said.

"Precisely. Darlington. Apparently Crogan was a schoolboy acquaintance."

"That's very bad luck."

"It's Darlington's wit that's the problem."

"Darlington generally limits himself to scandal of the sexual kind. Surely Josie has not embroiled herself in that sort of thing? Why, she's only been on the season for a few weeks."

"We're six weeks into it," Rafe said. "You simply haven't noticed."

"Sylvie loathes being bored, and I'm afraid that Almack's is nothing if not tedious."

"Josie hasn't created a scandal. But Darlington has swept up a storm of gossip on behalf of his despicable friend Crogan by putting a wager in the books at White's that the man who marries Josie will have a liking for pork."

Mayne said something under his breath.

"Men of sense have paid no attention to it, of course. But young men tend to be fairly shy in their matchmaking, and there's a sour group of young bucks watching whoever dances with Josie and then making fun of him. The truth is that she's lost the boys of her own age, the ones who should be courting her."

"Give me their names," Mayne said between clenched teeth. He'd spent so much time with the Essex sisters over the past two years that he felt as if they were his own wards. Or his own sisters.

"It spread before we even knew of it," Rafe said. "If Josie had laughed in the face of curiosity, or carried herself with dignity, it would have faded into nothing. But . . ."

"They've turned on her." Mayne had seen this sort of thing happen before.

"She's invited everywhere. But she isn't asked to dance, and she has no suitors of her own age. I have no doubt but that there are many men who would like to have greater acquaintance with her—as you say, she is beautiful and funny—but they are not braving the eyes of the *ton*."

"Fools," Mayne said.

"I need you to help while we're gone."

"This isn't as simple as when you asked me to accompany Imogen to Scotland. What the hell can I *do* for Josie?" His voice was rough because he was angry. The very thought of anyone insulting Josie, with her shining eyes and funny, cynical little remarks made him so enraged that he felt breathless.

"Be her friend," Rafe said simply. "Her sisters have not allowed her to go anywhere alone. Tess and Felton have been going to Almack's every week. Annabel will attend our wedding ball, though her babe is hardly four months old. Her husband told me he would like to return to Scotland, but just that Annabel flatly refuses to leave until the season has drawn to a close."

"Next year will be different," Mayne said slowly, remembering the many seasons he'd drifted in and out of balls.

"The pariah of one year can be the belle of the next. Why the *hell* didn't I know about this?"

"You've been with your lovely Sylvie."

"Sylvie can help Josie. She has a French air of disdain that Josie can copy."

"Do you think that her sisters haven't tried to teach her to look confident? Why, Imogen drilled her in holding her chin up and not looking miserable until I felt as if Josie were being kitted out for the Royal Fusiliers. But it's not working."

"These things never last more than one season. Remember how everyone made fun of the Wooly Breeder one year? That was Darlington as well. As if the poor girl was to blame for her father making so much money sheep-farming. The following season she came back as if nothing had happened, and people were tired of the game. She married respectably."

Rafe sighed. "I tell you, Mayne, I bloody well can't wait until this season is over. I've never seen a girl so miserable. It's enough to make you rethink the whole idea of having daughters."

"Wards are bad enough, are they?" Mayne said with a grin.

The door opened, and Lucius Felton walked in, followed by Rafe's brother Gabriel. "Forgive us for interrupting," Lucius said with his usual imperturbable gravity, "but Brinkley asked us to make our own way to you."

"You're just in time," Mayne said. "I'm about to lecture Rafe on the trials and tribulations of the wedding night. It's been so long since the man was bedded, I'm afraid he's forgotten the process."

Lucien smiled and seated himself. "Somehow I doubt that."

"As do I," said Gabe with an uncharacteristic chuckle.

And Mayne, looking at Rafe and seeing the smile in his eyes, came to the same conclusion.

* * *

Not everyone in St. Paul's Cathedral felt the same mixture of anticipation and wild affection that the Duke of Holbrook's wedding inspired in Mayne. Josie, for one, felt nothing other than abject misery. But since that was becoming a way of life for her, and she was well aware how utterly despicable it would be for her to diminish her sister Imogen's pleasure, she pasted a smile on her face.

It was a smile she was getting very good at. She'd practiced it in the glass at home. She curled the corners of her mouth up until her lower lip pouted out a little bit. Her mouth was probably her best feature, although she had no doubt but that anyone who saw her smiling would think of nothing but her round cheeks.

Imogen, of course, looked absolutely exquisite. Of the four sisters, Imogen looked most like her, in a cursory kind of way. They both had dark hair, and the same arching eyebrows. *Meant for laughing,* her sister Tess had told her years ago. But Imogen's face was slender and heart-shaped, whereas her own was pie-shaped and round. *Pie-shaped.*

Josie wrenched her mind away. Tess said she should think about her best features, but to be honest, she was sick of thinking about whether she had good skin or not, when the only thing she really wanted was to see a few bones sticking out under that skin. Imogen was looking up at Rafe in a way that made her even sicker. With jealousy.

At least she was woman enough to admit it. Tess squeezed her hand and Josie glanced at her eldest sister. Her eyes were filled with tears. "Isn't it wonderful?" Tess whispered. "Imogen looks so happy, finally."

Josie felt a bolt of guilt. Of course, she wanted Imogen to be happy. Poor Imogen had had a horrible few years, what with eloping and then losing her young husband within a few weeks. Josie tipped the edges of her smile even higher. "Of course," she whispered back. Tess's husband Lucius was looking down at Tess with precisely the same adoration with which Rafe looked at Imogen.

She didn't even want to look to her right, because the Earl of Ardmore always had that look in his eyes when he looked at Annabel, even when Annabel grew round as a lighthouse. That had made Josie like Ardmore even more than she had before: he seemed just as in love with Annabel as he ever was, even though Annabel's little son was only a few months old and she hadn't lost all the weight.

Too bad most men weren't like him.

But that was veering into a dangerous thought, the kind that led to tears, so Josie looked back at the altar. The bishop was taking an unaccountably long time with his sermon, blathering on about love and forgiveness and such-like topics. The importance of marriage as an institution within which a man and woman loved and respected each other.

For goodness' sake, Imogen and Rafe had already chosen each other. They didn't need the lecture. But the bishop wandered on to the importance of marriage as an institution that cherished harmony in the family and the home.

I would marry anyone, Josie thought desperately. The thought of the little book she'd carefully created over the past two years, a list of all the ways by which heroines in novels made their admirers ask for their hands in marriage, sickened her now. The reality was so much worse than she'd pictured. She had no admirers.

She never thought that a man would have to undergo ridicule if he even danced with her. It wasn't that she was left at the side of the room. Her eldest sister, Tess, if not Griselda and Imogen, would never allow it. She no sooner was returned to her chaperone than a friend of one of her brothers-in-law would bow before her. But she saw through them. They were dancing with her as a favor, and although she quite liked some of them, they were *old*. They were funny, and complimentary, and one of them—Baron Sibble—even seemed to like her for herself. He asked her for two dances at every single event, and even Tess could not have demanded such devoted service.

"Young men are fools," Lucius Felton had told her on the way home from her first ball, when not a single man her age asked her to dance. "I was a fool as a youth."

"Like this?" she had asked, sobbing so hard that she could hardly speak.

There was a moment's silence. "Never like that consciously," he said finally. "But Josie, young men are like sheep. They follow each other's lead. There were quite likely young men in the room tonight who would have asked you to dance, but they can't quite brave the ridicule."

"I just don't understand why this happened," she had whispered, broken-hearted.

"It's Darlington," Lucius had told her. "Unfortunately, he is dictating fashion this season."

"Why would he care about me?" she'd cried, from the depths of her heart. "I've never met him, have I? Do I know him?"

"Perhaps it's because he's English and you're Scottish. There are Englishmen who resent the fact that your sisters have made excellent marriages amongst English aristocracy."

"That's—That's not my fault!" It was the eternal cry of the unjustly accused.

"You are not the only one," he added gently. "Cecilia Bellingworth will have a difficult time shaking the label Silly Billy, and that's merely due to her unfortunate brother not being right in his head. Darlington didn't make up that label; I'm not sure who did. But who will be brave enough to marry her?"

"I'd rather be silly than fat," Josie had said flatly.

"No, you wouldn't," Lucius had said. "And you are *not* fat, Josie."

But Lucius Felton had no idea of the depths of longing

Josie felt to be thin. To dance around the ballroom, gowned in a diaphanous costume gathered with fragile ribbons under her breasts and floating around her like a cloud of pale silk . . . The whole world could see that Miss Mary Ogilby never wore a corset; why should she? She was as slender as a reed. But Josie wore a corset. If she could, she'd wear three corsets, one on top of each other, if only they could rein in all the flesh that seemed to pop out wherever she looked.

Not that she looked.

She'd had the mirror taken out of her bedchamber months ago and felt life was better without it. No diaphanous gowns for her. Imogen's *modiste*—the very best in London—had pointed out that seams were needed to construct *an agreeable shape*. The words were emblazoned in Josie's memory.

Well, thanks to that *modiste,* she had an agreeable shape, presumably. She certainly had a lot of seams. The dress she chose to wear to Imogen's wedding was designed to hold her in and cover her up in as many ways as possible.

Josie wrenched her attention back to the altar. Finally the bishop seemed to be droning to a halt. Not that Imogen showed any sign of listening to him. She was just looking at Rafe, looking at him in such a way that Josie actually got a lump in her throat. Beside her, Tess was blotting away tears with a handkerchief her husband must have given her, since it was twice the size of her hand. Josie gritted her teeth. If she cried, there was no one to give her a handkerchief.

Her eyes would turn red.

They would swell and her skin would turn blotchy.

They would—

Rafe leaned down, cupped his new wife's face in his hands, and said quietly, but so that Josie could clearly hear him from where they stood in the first row, "All my life, Imogen."

In the end, Lucius Felton had two handkerchiefs, which was just like him.

3

From The Earl of Hellgate, Chapter the First

. . . She removed her stockings with the greatest delicacy imaginable, Dear Reader. I was transfixed at the sight of her ankle, slender, exquisite. In one rash moment I laid my heart—and my lips—at her feet and worshipped that dear part of her body as it so clearly deserved . . .

The Duke of Holbrook's wedding fete
15 Grosvenor Square

Lord Charles Darlington was feeling rather morose. There was no doubt that life was difficult when cravats were so expensive, and the *ton* so tiresome. Of course, there were pleasures in life, although small.

The pleasure of a well-turned retort was one. One might think that Darlington was something of a monster, but he was not. He knew perfectly well that he was a trivial person, and he never failed to promptly acknowledge the fact, as did his friends.

"You are excessively tedious tonight," Berwick remarked. "At this rate it would be almost more interesting to prance around the dance floor, listening to some chit giggle at me." Young girls had a tendency to fall into nervous laughter faced with Berwick's sulky good looks, although his lack of a fortune kept him (in Darlington's opinion) from becoming fatheaded.

"If I sparked wit for you it would be a misuse of precious resources," Darlington retorted. "Do you suppose that anyone realizes we are here?"

Berwick looked around the crowded dance floor. "Not a chance of it. The butler of Holbrook's practically whispered our names—that is, the names we gave him."

Wisley and Thurman trotted up to them like eager little spaniels. "By Jove, you did get in, Darlington!" Thurman bellowed. "I bet Wisley here five guineas that you couldn't get yourself invited to Holbrook's wedding fete."

Darlington preferred not to mention that he had received no invitation. It was the first time that he had been cut from an important event. Hang it, he *was* the son of a duke, albeit the third son. Why his mother had to keep turning out males when there wasn't an estate to keep them in handkerchiefs, he didn't know. But now he carelessly adjusted the line of his coat (a blush-colored superfine wool that he found immensely soothing to the eye) and said, "Of course I had an invitation, you idiot."

He did too. He had an invitation addressed to one of his brothers.

"Well, she's here," Thurman said cheerfully. "The Scottish Sausage. Except I'm thinking we should come up with a new name. How about the Scottish Saucepan? How do you like that, eh?" He beamed.

"Like what?" Darlington said, an edge to his voice.

"Scottish Saucepan! It came to me in the middle of the night. I hadn't drunk my chocolate before bed, you see, and I couldn't sleep, and I was thinking about what a clever turn of the tongue you had, and there it was! Came to me in the night, like—like that writing on the wall they talk about in the Bible."

"Thurman, you are an utter ass," Berwick said.

Thurman looked mildly offended. He was an English sausage, if sausages came in a peculiar bell shape. He had a dimpled double chin and glinting, small blue eyes. He'd been called an ass so many times that he likely took it as a compliment.

"Don't you think it has a Darlington ring?" he demanded. "He's rubbing off on me. All that cleverness, I mean."

Darlington turned away. He would be very happy to see the last of Thurman, if only he didn't need an audience. He was honest enough to know that about himself.

"Let's see what she's wearing tonight," Thurman persisted. "You know all the lads down at the Convent will ask."

"My wife tells me that if she hears of me at the Convent again, I'm barred from her company," Wisley said, speaking for the first time. He was a slender man with a discontented mouth traced by a faint mustache that never grew thicker nor thinner. They had all been at Rugby together, and of the four of them, Wisley had done the best. He had married for money, and even Thurman, who had more money than he had need of, admitted that Wisley had fallen on his feet. His bride was fairly pretty; only the most severe of critics would note that her brows met in the middle. Or that her skin was olive. Darlington, who *was* the severest of critics, had kept his opinion to himself.

"Which would be the tragedy?" he asked now. "To be barred from your wife's company, or from the Convent?"

"It's like those old games where there are two doors and one leads to a lion," Berwick commented.

"I don't see that," Wisley said languidly. "My wife is no lion, and the Convent, while a perfectly respectable pub, is growing a bit monotonous."

Darlington eyed Wisley. Unless he missed his guess, Wisley's wife was drawing him away from the group. He knew perfectly well that she didn't like him. Every time she saw him, her face took on a closed, calm look that spoke of deep hatred.

He should probably let Wisley go free, off to a life of mind-numbing domesticity.

"Well, *I* would never give up the Convent for a wife," Thurman announced.

"Your wife, should you ever have one, will likely be paying a subsidy to the place to keep you occupied," Berwick said acidly.

"My wife will madly adore me," Thurman said, sounding truly huffy for the first time.

The worst was that Darlington could see that he believed it. What was he doing with a pack of fools like this?

Berwick shrugged. "'Tis a tedious subject, but I would warn you, Thurman, that in my experience the only women who engage in mad adoration—other than of themselves, of course—are invariably plain."

"I could make any woman adore me!" Thurman said shrilly. "It's all a matter of how you treat her."

"But women are so monstrously attracted to beauty," Berwick said.

Darlington thought he really ought to intervene. His carefully hewed little circle was disintegrating around him.

"Wicked women are," Thurman said. "But good women, the ones one has to marry, those women are interested in commercial transactions."

Darlington recognized that as something he'd said, once upon a time. "I prefer the wicked kind," he said now. "They're so much more interesting to talk to."

"But you can't marry someone who's interesting to talk to," Thurman pointed out, absolutely correctly. "And Darlington, you need to marry."

Darlington sighed. It was wearisomely true. If only to stop his father's imminent apoplexy.

Thurman never knew when to shut his mouth, and so he

kept going. "I really thought you wouldn't be invited to-night, and you know, if the Essex sisters shut you out, you'd have a demmed hard time finding your way back into society. Those women left Scotland, descended on England like a swarm of locusts and married every title on the market."

Berwick frowned at him. "Keep your voice down. You're at a wedding ball for one of them, you ass."

"No one's listening," Thurman said, looking around. The ballroom at the Duke of Holbrook's town house had ceilings so high that even the chatter of hundreds of overexcited members of the *ton* just floated upward and resulted in a pleasant buzz. The orchestra at one end sounded like the dim hum of caged bees.

"I suppose I should find a wife," Darlington said, feeling ineffably depressed.

"I certainly mean to," Thurman said. "I require beauty, a sufficient dowry, and a docile disposition. Oh, and an impeccable reputation. After all, I bring the same to her."

"What a fortunate woman she will be," Berwick said. "And you, Darlington? What will you require?"

"A sensible view of life," Darlington said flatly. "That, and a great deal of money. I am very expensive."

"Shall we meet in an hour or so and exchange notes?" Berwick said, something of a genuine smile lighting his eyes. "I must say that I am thoroughly amused."

"Will you be looking for a wife as well?" Thurman demanded.

"I believe not," Berwick replied. "I was on the edge of that decision, but luckily I have been delivered from penury in the nick of time. And everyone knows that penury is the final step before marriage."

"So you got some money from somewhere, did you?" Thurman said. "Is that why you've been out of a town for a fortnight? Did your father die? Can't say I heard that. And you're not in black."

"Tsk tsk," Berwick said. "I *do* have a black armband, albeit edged in a charming shade of purple. My adored and loathsome Aunt Augusta succumbed to some sort of malady while in Bath. Naturally, she left all her money to her beloved nephew."

Darlington felt even more depressed, but exerted himself to suitably compliment Berwick on the pleasures of financial stability. Unfortunately, there were no aunts, loathsome or adored, in his family tree. And even if there had been, he was the least likely to be chosen as an heir; his brothers were all eminently respectable in comparison.

Thurman's little blue eyes were shining as he taxed Berwick about his income. Then Darlington noticed that at some point Wisley had slipped away without a good-bye, likely to his wife's side. He wouldn't come to the Convent that night, or ever again. Darlington knew that.

The days of the little circle of friends from Rugby were over. Wisley was gone. Berwick was rich, and Darlington couldn't bear the idea of Berwick picking up a tavern bill. Thurman was a fool, but Berwick was not.

If he didn't change his ways, he'd be left with Thurman to spout his own witticisms back at him, and reflect his bad temper.

Darlington shuddered faintly. "The search is on, gentlemen," he said. "Wives."

Thurman and Berwick stopped talking about canal stocks in mid-sentence. Berwick raised an eyebrow. "The season just grew far more interesting," he said softly.

"I expect I'll choose the right wife by the end of the evening," Thurman said.

"It may take me slightly longer," Darlington said. "I have such trouble choosing cravats some evenings. If I dread making mistakes in the selection of a pink versus yellow cravat, who knows how difficult it will be to choose a wife?"

"Wives are like cravats in that you must simply determine

market value, and make your decision accordingly," Berwick said. "There are only a handful who can support you in the manner to which you will rapidly become accustomed."

"Damned if you aren't going to be a magnate by the time you're thirty if you keep being this intelligent, Berwick," Thurman said.

Berwick smiled.

"You *are* a magnate!" Thurman gasped.

"Dear, dear Aunt Augusta," Berwick said, his usual thin smile somewhat more vivid. "Apparently no one had any idea just how interested she was in all those northern industries. Why, she funded an entire coal mine. Said she liked the shiny black color of it."

"My God, once that news leaks, you're going to be the talk of the *ton*. Every mama's dream," Thurman said.

Darlington did what had to be done, what had to be done by any man whose friend has been suddenly elevated into the highest reaches of society, or at least as high as one can go without discovering nobility in the family tree. He slapped Berwick on the back, swallowed his rage. And then: "I have been thinking for some time that we have outgrown our little gatherings at the Convent."

Thurman gaped at him and Berwick's eyebrow shot into the air.

"The whole business of the Scottish Sausage is growing tedious. I'm having thoughts of morality, which just goes to show that I'm growing stupid in my old age."

"You ain't old," Thurman said.

"I shouldn't have done it," Darlington said. "It wasn't as clever as the Wooly Breeder, though God knows I probably shouldn't have done that either. I can't believe I did anything prompted by Crogan, who has to be one of the more repellent fools on the earth. In truth, I did it for the pleasure of herding about all the witless men who call themselves gentlemen, and damned if I didn't make myself as witless as the least of them."

"Witless? Everyone knows we're the clever ones," Thurman bleated.

Darlington didn't know why he'd spent so much time with such a cretin.

Berwick was as intelligent as they came, and he didn't show a flash of emotion at this sudden parting of boyhood friends. He bowed, as elegantly as any magnate. "It's been a pleasure," he said, a marked lack of interest in his voice.

They had banded together on a whim, and it seemed they would part with as little ceremony, albeit years later. Darlington nodded at him, and nodded to Thurman.

He turned and walked a few feet before scanning the room for a wife. But what he really wanted wasn't money, a single woman as rich as Berwick's Aunt Augusta.

He wanted intelligence. Someone who was amusing and would talk to him, rather than reflecting back his own empty jokes. It was unfortunate that the task of finding her seemed Herculean.

He left behind a couple of dumbfounded men.

"Damned if he didn't mean it," Berwick said. "I think he means to marry." And then, after a moment's contemplation, "The poor sod."

"Perhaps he'll take the Scottish Sausage," Thurman said, an edge in his voice showing that he didn't take to being snubbed by the man he'd bought so many rounds for. "*She* can afford to pay his tavern bills, by all accounts."

"Her brother-in-law's as rich as Croesus," Berwick said.

"She's one that won't be looking in his direction, though," Thurman said. "The Sausage won't be able to marry until next season, if then. Remember the Wooly Breeder?"

Berwick shrugged. The truth was that whereas a year ago

he hadn't any prospects of marriage, now he was set to become a prime candidate. And he didn't want his chances of gaining the very best to be marred by any unpleasantness resulting from their mockery of the Scottish Sausage.

"Do you suppose he really means it about not coming to the Convent tonight?" Thurman asked.

Berwick looked at him. Sometimes the man's stupidity was truly astounding. "He's dropped us, you ass."

"What?"

"He's dropped us. Darlington. He's gone off and he's not coming back to the Convent. He'll find a rich wife, I suppose, or get his father to buy him a pair of colors. Either way, he just said good-bye."

Thurman gaped at him. "He said good-bye because he's going to look for a wife. We'll all meet in a few hours and discuss how we did."

Berwick's mouth quirked. "He's gone. Wisley went first; he just didn't have the manners to comment about it."

"Wisley?" Thurman looked around wildly as if the man was standing silently at his shoulder. Then he turned back to Berwick, blinking rapidly. "Nonsense. We'll all meet at the Convent tonight, or tomorrow, and enough of this nonsense. We always meet at the Convent."

Berwick wouldn't be there, but he didn't see any point in arguing over it.

"Let's find the Sausage," Thurman urged. "I'm sure her dress is bursting at the seams over the excitement of her sister's wedding."

Berwick shrugged again. "All right." Privately, he thought the whole subject was tedious. Thurman had been the one to nourish the gossip, to repeat over and over little unpleasantries about this Scottish girl. The rest of them didn't really care, and Darlington had even reminded them of Crogan's repulsive behavior at school.

But they'd done it, for lack of anything else to do, as much as anyone. And because it was a suitable follow-up to the Wooly Breeder.

The whole thought process gave Berwick an unpleasant feeling in his stomach. Had they really made something of a *career* out of ruining young women's marriage prospects?

Unpleasant, that.

He walked after Thurman, who kept wedging his large body into groups of people, searching for the Scottish Sausage. After a time Berwick walked in the opposite direction. There are times in a man's life when he finds that he's ashamed of himself. Berwick had felt it before, and he never liked it.

Thank God for Aunt Augusta, he said to himself.

Just then a tight-lipped woman stepped in front of him. "Mr. Berwick," she said majestically, "I trust you remember me? I was a good friend of your dear mother's."

After a second's chill panic, Berwick remembered her name. "Lady Yarrow, what a pleasure to meet you again."

She pulled a thin, dyspeptic-looking girl from behind her like a fish on a line. "My daughter, Amelia. I'm quite certain you met as children; in fact, you probably gamboled together on the lawn of Yarrow House when your mother came for tea."

Berwick was quite certain that never happened. From his few memories of his mother, he guessed that she would no sooner think of taking her second and thus worthless son with her on a social engagement than she would take holy orders.

Amelia eyed him. He bowed. And then he suddenly understood.

This was the beginning.

4

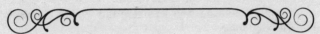

From The Earl of Hellgate, Chapter the Second

Believe me, I know the anguish this depraved and wicked story must be causing you, Dear Reader, but my confessor assures me that I must tell all in order to keep other youthful sinners from my path. This duchess—so young in years, so old in depravity—opened a door that led into some sort of a service closet. There did she charge me with the task of making her the most happy woman in Court . . .

Under my direction, circulation of this newspaper has increased tenfold," Mr. Jessopp said, his back so rigid with anger that he couldn't even feel his stays. "Nay," he corrected himself. "It's improved hundredfold. What's more, I've brought up the tone. Twenty years ago *The Tatler* had a reputation for scurrilous investigatory practices, sending men out to bribe butlers." He curled his lip to indicate his opinion of the practice.

"It's not as if the place ain't rife with butlers carrying away a bit of the ready," Mr. Goffe said. Jessopp's partner was leaning against the fireplace, sucking on a rancid pipe.

"I don't go to them," Jessopp said, explaining it again. "They come to *me*. There's a difference."

Goffe shrugged. "Whatever you say."

"Anything happens in London, particularly amongst the *ton*, is mine for the asking."

Goffe took his pipe out of his mouth. "Then how's about handing over Hellgate, and let's stop this demmed wrangling."

"Hellgate is Mayne, everyone knows that."

"The story may refer to Mayne's exploits," Goffe said. "You have to give the devil his due. But it was never the Earl of Mayne who sat down and wrote that up. For one thing, he's got no call to. For another, he don't need the ready. And it's not a gentlemanlike thing to do. We need the author of those memoirs!"

Jessopp's own well-annotated copy of the *Memoirs* was over on the table. But here was another instance where he and his partner had a difference of opinion. "I think it was a gentleman doing the writing," he said stubbornly. "I read it over with that in mind."

"Well, if you know all the doings of the *ton*, name the man," Goffe said. "Go ahead."

Jessopp thought about how much he hated his partner while he decided how to reply. "I don't know who wrote it yet. You know that. But there are turns of phrase that could only have been written by a gentleman. Even that bit about how he named all the women after a Shakespeare play: that isn't the sort of thing an average man would dream up."

"We need to know for certain," Goffe said. "For God's sakes, don't get us embroiled in a lawsuit, but we need the answer to this one, Jessopp. If your regular little rodents haven't told you—"

Jessopp moved in instinctive protest at this characterization. He had wide circles of friends, who were kind enough to bring him information.

"Whatever," Goffe told him. "Yer friends have failed you this time. That means we need to go back to the old days, if you ask me. We need a rattler, the way we used to have. One of *The Tatler*'s own rattlers. That's what we need."

Jessopp curled his lip. "We've moved beyond those days. Now people come to us. We leave that sort of sneaking corruption to the scandal rags."

"We are a scandal rag," Goffe told him, unmoved. "What's more, we're a scandal rag that's passing up one of the biggest scandals around. If that book was written by someone in the *ton*, then that's a story that *The Tatler* needs to break. We own the *ton*."

Jessopp couldn't help seeing the truth of that.

"The *ton* has a right to know who's hiding behind the name Hellgate," Goffe continued. "Mayne will thank us when we ferret out the truth of it. Who's depraved enough to take someone else's strumpets and turn the tale into a triple folio, sold in leather?"

"If the author is a depraved member of the *ton*," Jessopp said, "that reduces the number of suspects to around seven hundred."

"It's not the biggest story of this year," Goffe said. "It's the *only* story of this year. Take our whole budget, Jessopp. Just get that name, and get it fast. If someone else breaks the truth of it, we're done. They all buy us because they can trust us to dish up the dirt, for all you want to call it by prettier names. That dirt is paying for our breakfast sausage."

Jessopp reached out and curled his fingers around his copy of Hellgate's *Memoirs*. "You have your uses, Goffe," he said slowly.

"Damn right I do," Goffe said, relighting his pipe.

5

From The Earl of Hellgate, Chapter the Second

'Twas a small space, just large enough for the two of us. My heart sank, as there was no place to lie down. A moment later I was introduced to the sweet art of standing fare. She curled her legs around me with all the strength and wiliness of a circus performer. My hands gave her support as if I were made for the chore (and indeed, I think perhaps I was). Then she rode me, Dear Reader; she took me where she pleased.

The Earl of Mayne sauntered up to Josie as if he'd seen her only yesterday, although she'd been in London for two months, and he'd never bothered to say hello to her. She found that intensely irritating. He may be old enough to be her older brother, but he didn't have to act with a brother's carelessness.

She resisted the impulse to stick out her tongue at him. There were limits to how much of an older brother he likely wished to be.

"Miss Essex," he said, bowing as if she were the queen.

She didn't waste time with pleasantries. "You called me Josephine on the trip to Scotland," she pointed out.

"Josie, actually. And how are you?"

"Fine," she said flatly. She liked Mayne, and felt hurt that he had never bothered to see how she was doing in her first season. Even when she became notorious . . . he must have heard about that. "Aren't you going to ask me to dance? Because generally your sister Griselda has at least five men arranged who are required to ask me to dance."

"She must have forgotten to give me my marching orders," he said easily, handing her a glass of champagne. "Drink this, *chérie*. You look as if you could use it."

"Why?" she asked a little wildly. "Because I'm standing here at the ball given for my sister's wedding, waiting for my prearranged dances to begin? Because I'm—"

"Because you're growing hysterical," he observed. "How interesting. I never knew you to be hysterical before."

She took a deep breath. "Well, I'm very sorry to tell you that I am remarkably tedious company."

"We all are when we're wallowing in self-pity," he said, without a trace of sympathy in his voice.

"You don't know what it's like."

"Thank God I don't. There's nothing more monotonous than Almack's on a hot Wednesday night. Nothing but sweating jackasses and flushed young women trotting about in too many ribbons."

Josie didn't know why she'd even wanted Mayne to care about how she was doing. He was a fool, just like the rest of them. She started to look about, because if he wasn't her designated dancing partner, there was sure to be another old codger limping along in a moment. But then she remembered something. "You're engaged to be married! I saw you in the church."

His eyes lit up and for a moment Josie forgave him for not caring about her debut. "I want to introduce you to Sylvie.

I am persuaded you will be enchanted by her," and he took
her by the arm and started towing her across the floor.

"Isn't she French?" Josie asked, hanging back so that he
had to walk slowly. Anything was better than standing around
looking like a marooned cow missing her herd. "I'm sorry,"
she said, coming to a halt, "I don't remember her surname. I
wouldn't want to meet her without knowing her name."

"Her name is Sylvie de la Broderie."

She had to smile at the way Mayne said it. He was so—so
adorably beautiful, in a rakish, French kind of way. All that
exquisitely tumbled black hair, falling precisely in the most
popular of windswept styles. And cheekbones you could cut
with. She could see why Annabel and Tess had nearly come
to blows over who was going to marry him. "What's Miss
Broderie like?"

"She's very intelligent. She paints portraits, in miniature.
They're exquisite. She has the skill of a natural *artiste,* and
her father gave her the best tutors in Paris, at least until they
fled to this country in 1803. Her father . . ."

He kept talking about this paragon he'd discovered, pulling her across the room again. He talked just the way that
Rafe talked about Imogen, which annoyed Josie.

"But what does she look like?" Josie said, stopping him
again.

"Look like?" He blinked at her. "She's beautiful, of
course."

"Of course," Josie said, skipping a little to keep up with
him. She knew all about Mayne's reputation for seducing
beautiful women. By most accounts he'd had a hundred affairs, though none of them lasted over a fortnight. Not to mention that everyone was saying that he was the model for the
Earl of Hellgate.

A moment later Josie was curtsying before Miss de la
Broderie, and one thought was foremost in her mind. Everything about Sylvie de la Broderie was exactly as Josie most

longed to be. She was slim, of course, and dressed in a gown that was clearly French. Imogen kept telling Josie that clothing construction was all in the seams. Well, Miss de la Broderie's gown didn't have any seams. It was made of a sheer material that swept down her body and then swished out around her toes. All around her bosom was exquisite embroidery in silver-gilt thread. A beautiful little twisted tie ran under her breasts and fell down the length of her body.

But it was her face that Josie kept looking at. Mayne was marrying a woman with a perfect face. It was the face of all the heroines in the romantic novels that Josie loved. Sylvie had huge eyes and a laughing mouth, and one beauty mark, just above her crimson lips. She looked—well, she looked utterly confident. Why shouldn't she be?

Josie curtsied, feeling as dumpy as a bowl of yesterday's porridge.

"I am enchanted to meet you," the goddess said with a ravishing French accent. Mayne stood beside her with a gaze of helpless adoration. Without even glancing at him, Miss Broderie waved her fingers in his direction and said, "Mayne, *chéri*, leave us if you please. I should like to make Miss Essex's acquaintance."

And just like that Mayne was gone.

Josie must have shown her astonishment on her face, because Miss Broderie suddenly smiled at her. "You think I am too peremptory with my fiancé, yes?"

"Well, of course not," Josie said. "That is—"

"Men must be treated with the same courtesy that one treats a good strong farm animal. Firm, yet kind. Now my dear, I have heard all about your disasters."

Josie swallowed. Of course she had. Everyone had.

Miss Broderie leaned over and said, "Shall we visit the ladies' retiring room? I assure you, it is quite my favorite place, and in this house there is a beautiful one."

Josie blinked at her. Over Miss Broderie's shoulder she

could see Timothy Arbuthnot bearing down on them. Timothy was one of her most faithful dance partners; she frequently reminded herself that his four orphaned children did not disqualify him from matrimony. Although his lack of hair might.

Miss Broderie shot a look as well, and then before Josie even knew what had happened, they were slipping through the door into the ladies' retiring room. Josie never went to those rooms on her own. She knew what went on there. The ladies sat around on little spindly chairs that made her feel like an elephant and talked about who was expecting a proposal of marriage from whom.

When they weren't gossiping, they were staring in the mirror while powdering their noses, or adjusting their hair, another of Josie's least favorite activities, right along with being mocked, or sympathized with. Although she had to say that none of the debutantes she'd met had been unkind, and in truth, they had no reason for malice. She presented no threat whatsoever to their marital ambitions.

Luckily, there wasn't anyone in the retiring room when they entered, but a second later Josie's luck ran out because her sister Tess strolled out of the privy chamber. "Josie, darling!" she said, giving an equally large smile to Miss Broderie.

Josie sat down while the two of them curtsied and generally summed each other up. She'd got to know the ritual. Women eyed each other and then quickly decided whether they considered each other worthy. Since Tess was beautiful and married to the second richest man in England, she rather thought that she would pass Miss Broderie's inspection. And since Miss Broderie was just as beautiful, and engaged to Mayne, it was a friendship made in heaven.

"I have longed to meet you in private," Miss Broderie was saying. "After all, we share quite a bit, have we not? If I am not mistaken, you are the only other woman whom the Earl of Mayne asked to marry."

"It was only a matter of a few days," Tess said hastily. "He didn't mean anything by it."

"Of course," Miss Broderie said. "I completely understand." She sat down beside Josie. "Please, Mrs. Felton, won't you sit with us? I just met your beautiful little sister."

Josie suppressed a snort. She hadn't looked in the mirror but she knew just what she'd see there: a rigid, plump girl with a face like a moon. The only good thing about her was her posture, and that was because her corset laced from the middle of her shoulders all the way down to her hips.

Tess sat down and took Josie's hand. "I can think of nothing I'd prefer than sit for a bit. When they talk about carrying a child, no one mentions how much it makes your feet hurt!"

Now they would start chattering about babies, and such; after all, Miss Broderie would likely be having a baby as soon as she married. Lord knows, Annabel was *enceinte* within a month. But Miss Broderie looked no more than politely interested.

"I have heard that there are some discomforts involved in the—the procedure," she said, waving her hand.

Josie couldn't help giggling.

"How have I spoken incorrectly?" Miss Broderie asked.

"It's charming, Miss Broderie," Josie said quickly.

"Please, you must both call me Sylvie. After all, I am marrying a man who has so many . . . *ties* . . . to your family." Her eyes were twinkling. "I am practically an Essex sister myself, don't you think?"

Tess giggled at that, and Josie laughed outright.

"You'd have to be Scottish instead of French," Tess pointed out.

Sylvie shuddered. "Never. I am the French part of your lost family stick."

"Family *tree*," Josie said.

"Precisely. And as the French branch on that tree, I

propose that we do something about Josephine's unfortunate situation. Mayne told me about it and—"

Just like that, Josie stopped laughing. Mayne had talked about her? To Sylvie?

"I have heard of something like it in Paris," Sylvie was saying. "It was some years ago, you understand, before Father became disenchanted with all the unpleasantness there—" and with a wave of her hand, she referred to the troubles that had presumably taken the lives of many of her acquaintances.

Josie had to get out of the room. It was bad enough that her sisters and Griselda considered her a pitiful case, and that her brothers-in-law had given her a dowry, just to lure a husband. It was—*enough.* "I'm sorry," she said stonily, rising from her chair. "I must have forgotten—"

"Sit, please," Sylvie said. Her voice had ten times the authority of Josie's former governess. "Life is, you understand, young Josephine, full of these humiliations. Absolutely ripe with them. You must learn to swim the wave, do you understand? Turn everything these fools are saying back on themselves."

Tess had obviously fallen under the enemy spell because she pulled Josie back onto her chair. "She's right. The whole situation could switch in the blink of an eyelid."

"I would wake up to find myself the most marriageable woman in London," Josie said, hearing the grating desolation in her voice and not knowing how to hide it. "I find that truly hard to believe."

"I believe that most things in life are within our control," Sylvie said. "Now, is there any particular man whom you would wish to marry, Josephine?"

"You might as well call me Josie," Josie said ungraciously. "And—well, I just want—"

"Josie has a list," Tess said. "Do you remember what's on your list, darling?"

"Why bother? There's no question of narrowing the field of my admirers."

"A list is an excellent idea. I myself had just such a list when I selected Mayne," Sylvie said.

"You did?" Josie asked. "May I ask what was on your list?"

"A great deal of money. A title, because I was born into the French nobility and it is too late for me not to care about such things."

"Do you sympathize with the revolutionaries?" Josie asked with some fascination.

"My feelings are divided. In the beginning my father was young and idealistic. We moved to Paris and he became Napoleon's finance minister. But then the corruption . . . the nepotism . . . We fled in the night. My mother never shared my father's hopes. She loathed the revolutionaries because they killed, and so brutally, many people whom she loved. Luckily, my father saw the direction of the wind, and brought us all here a year or so before war was declared again. But of course, there were those people we knew who did not survive."

Tess made a sympathetic noise.

"The people had little to eat under the old system," Sylvie said, with a little Gallic shrug that said volumes. "But this is a gloomy subject, and will make us all more miserable than we deserve to be."

Tess grinned at that. "So there is a degree of deserving misery, then?"

"Of course! These foolish men who have spread rumors about our Josephine, they are deserving much misery. Much. Do you know them, Mrs. Felton?"

"You must call me Tess; after all, we are nearly sisters," she said with a mischievous smile. And then sobered. "The ringleader is a man named Darlington, and I have never met him, to the best of my knowledge. Apparently, he is a second or third son, I don't remember which, to the Duke of Bedrock."

"Bedrock's surname is Darlington?" Sylvie said. "A charming name for such a one as this."

"I've seen him," Josie said. "He's very good-looking, all yellow curls and blue eyes."

"I suppose we could have someone seduce him," Sylvie said thoughtfully. "Men are so amenable in the first days of love. I have noted it innumerable times."

"It's a shame that Annabel is married; she would take to the task immediately," Josie said.

"Another sister?" Sylvie asked. "Do you realize the legendary reputation the four of you have gained amongst the *ton*? I heard about you the very moment I arrived for the season. Four exquisite Scotswomen who took London by storm and scooped up all the available bachelors."

"I'm afraid that our happiness in marriage may in itself have led to Josie's uncomfortable experience," Tess pointed out.

"The contrast is just too great," Josie said, striving for a careless tone. "Between myself and my sisters, I mean."

"You are just as beautiful," Sylvie said. "It is simply your misfortune to follow such remarkable successes. You must expect a certain grumpiness amongst those Englishmen who were not chosen by your sisters."

The door opened and Josie's chaperone, Lady Griselda, poked her head in. "Oh darling," she said, "there you are! Timothy Arbuthnot has been looking for you with a veritably desperate air."

"I like it better here," Josie said. In truth, it was the first time all day that she had felt happy.

Griselda raised a delicate eyebrow. "In that case, I shall join you, if I may." She smiled at Sylvie. Obviously, Josie thought rather grumpily, Mayne's choice of wife pleased everyone.

Well, who could not like Sylvie?

She was laughing with Griselda now. Griselda had apparently encountered Lady Margaret Cavendish, whose hair—according to Griselda—had changed color. "She's yellow as a marigold," Griselda was saying. "Actually the color of burnt marmalade, if you know what I mean."

"And what hair had she last week?" Sylvie wanted to know.

"Brown," Griselda said decisively. "I can't imagine how she did it."

"They have all sorts of potions that will dye one's hair," Josie said. "Don't you remember how Papa used to encounter dyed horses at shows occasionally, Tess?" She didn't add that their own father was quite adept at dyeing a horse black, in order to make him a more attractive candidate for sale.

"We are discussing who should seduce this objectionable person," Sylvie said, "this Darlington, and now of course I know precisely who should do it."

"Do what?" Griselda said.

"Make Darlington fall in love," Sylvie said. "You, *chérie.* You are the one."

"What?" Griselda blinked at her future sister-in-law.

Josie almost giggled. Apparently Sylvie was not a good judge of character. Griselda was certainly beautiful enough to seduce Darlington or anyone else, given her pale blond curls and lush figure. But after being widowed some ten or eleven years previous, Griselda had not indulged in even the slightest indiscretion. Her reputation was, in her brother Mayne's rather acid summary, a thing of snowy wonder that made her a terrible foil to his exploits.

"You must seduce this Darlington," Sylvie said patiently. "We need the man silenced, and I'm sure it won't be difficult for you. Why, Josie reports that he is good-looking. And yellow-haired. The two of you will be exquisite together."

"I don't wish to have anything to do with that poisonous

viper," Griselda said. "And I know precisely what he thinks of me. He told Mrs. Graham that I was unattractively chaste."

"Then he meant precisely the opposite," Sylvie said. "If you were not quite so chaste, you would be enormously attractive. And Griselda, surely you do not need us to create some compliments for you?" She waved at the glass, and all four women instinctively looked at Griselda's reflection. *"Guardez!"*

Josie had to smile. Griselda had reached the age of thirty-two without a single wrinkle, nor any sign that she was much over Sylvie's age. Her hair fell in perfect ringlets, and her figure was wound in something soft and silk and utterly entrancing. In short, she looked like a china shepherdess, only not nearly as hard nor as cold.

Tess leaned forward. "Though it is vastly improper of me to say it, Griselda, I think that Sylvie has a wonderful idea. All you would have to do is make him fall in love with you. He's not a complete devil. You might find him amusing. Felton says that Darlington graduated with a First, which is remarkable for a gentleman. Likely, he's bored."

Sylvie was waving a fan gently before her face and nothing could be seen but her mischievous eyes. "I think that I have seen the gentleman in question, dear Griselda."

"Hmmm," Griselda said.

"You must have noticed his shoulders."

"As Tess mentioned, this is a remarkably improper conversation," Griselda said, obviously remembering her role as chaperone.

"I am quite used to impropriety," Josie said. "Not a one of my sisters found her husband without a scandal."

"I certainly don't want a husband!" Griselda said.

"Of course you do," Sylvie stated. "Every woman wants a husband; they are so necessary to one's comfort, like a flannel night rail in the winter. Necessary, but tedious to acquire."

"And you did tell Imogen that you were considering marriage," Josie added.

"Well, I certainly wouldn't marry a man like Darlington."

Sylvie's eyes rounded into a shocked expression. "We never suggested such a thing! Never! Of course, you will want to marry a man with a sweet and modest disposition. Otherwise not even an optimist could see you sharing breakfast with him after a year or so."

"My own Willoughby was remarkably modest," Griselda remarked. "But my ability to watch him eat calves' head pie for breakfast lasted precisely one day, as I recall."

"I expect I would have been just the same," Sylvie said with a little shudder. "But I mean to begin as I shall go on, and therefore I shall inform Mayne that we shall never breakfast together. That way he will not be disappointed by my absence."

Josie thought that was a bit mean, but after a moment she realized that Mayne probably didn't care about breakfasting. She wasn't stupid, nor naive. What Mayne wanted was to sleep in the same room with Sylvie, not eat there.

"I suppose I could contemplate a flirtation with Darlington," Griselda said.

"Just long enough to reduce him to a state of slavering adoration," Sylvie said reassuringly. "Then you can shake him from your skirts like so much dust."

Josie liked the sound of that.

"This is not the sort of solution that had occurred to me," Griselda said, looking thoughtful.

"Indeed," Tess said with a gurgle of laughter. "Griselda and I and Josie's other sisters have been pursuing irreproachably correct ways of ameliorating the situation. Really, Josie, you do have a number of admirers now."

"Old men," Josie said impatiently.

Sylvie raised an eyebrow. "Dearest, young men are invariably tedious. I think you don't realize what a sacrifice

Griselda makes by even contemplating a brief flirtation with a man not yet thirty. Without experience, they have nothing to say."

"Darlington always has something to say; that's his stock in trade," Tess observed.

"But he is unlikely to have made many mistakes, and mistakes are what make a man truly interesting."

"Has Mayne made mistakes?" Josie asked with some curiosity.

Griselda laughed, but Sylvie said, "Without question. He has the look of a man who has mistakenly found himself in far too many beds, for one thing. He has clearly put too much value on variety. I shall insist that as my husband, he show far more prudence."

"But do you mean that he will . . . he will continue to—" Josie stopped. There were limits to what a young unmarried woman was supposed to voice, after all.

"Oh, undoubtedly," Sylvie said, fanning herself. "Although he is currently playing the role of a sentimentalist, and doing it with a great deal of relish, I must say."

"He told me last night that he was ravished with love for you," Griselda said.

"Charming," Sylvie said, with a markedly unsentimental cheerfulness. "As I said, a temporary wash of sentimentalism. Which will lapse with time, as it always does. And since he is half French, I expect it will transform itself nicely into cynicism. I think cynical men are so interesting, don't you?"

"*You* should be starting a flirtation with Darlington," Griselda pointed out. And then added hastily, "If you weren't affianced to my brother, of course."

"Alas, I cannot come to Josephine's rescue for that very reason. How long do you think it will take you, dearest Griselda? I shouldn't think more than a week or so, do you?"

Griselda had a light in her eye that suggested just a hint of rivalry with her beautiful sister-in-law, or so Josie thought.

"I expect I can make significant inroads on his affections this very night," she said. Then she stood up and surveyed her gown in the mirror. It had a classical drape, winding around her breasts and making the most of her curves. With a few deft pulls and twitches, suddenly a great deal more bosom was showing.

"An excellent thought," Sylvie said.

"I can manage this endeavor without instruction," Griselda said, with the faintest edge in her voice.

Sylvie instantly looked utterly cast down. "I didn't mean in the faintest, smallest way to imply that you were anything other than utterly *ravissante*!" she cried, her accent suddenly far more French. "Don't be angry with me, dearest Griselda. I'm so happy to be your sister that I rushed in where I should not have walked!"

Griselda smiled at that and turned around to give her a kiss. "You are your own fascinating self," she said. "And besides, I do need advice. How shall I make an approach to him? Under the circumstances, he is unlikely to draw near me."

Tess's eyes lit up. "My husband can introduce you!"

"Too obvious," Griselda objected.

"I have read a number of novels in which young women drop various items of clothing, thereby attracting attention of a nearby gentleman," Josie said. "A fan would be easiest."

"I don't want to drop my fan," Griselda said, looking alarmed. "This is my favorite and I should hate to have the sticks bent or broken."

"Sacrifices must be made," Sylvie observed. "In a good cause."

"In that case," Griselda retorted, "I'll drop *your* fan. You can give me mine back at the end of the evening."

Sylvie showed no sign of offering up her fan. It was the same delicate pink as her costume, and sewn over with matching seed pearls. "Are you certain that you wouldn't wish to drop a shoe?" she inquired. "You are wearing ravishing slippers, if you don't mind my saying so, Griselda. And you could perhaps manage to show some ankle at the same time. Men are so foolish when it comes to ankles."

"Why is that?" Josie asked. Sylvie seemed to be the sort of person who actually answered questions, and since her ankles were one of Josie's best features, she had often wondered whether she should accidentally expose them more often.

"A woman's ankle, slender and perfectly turned, is a thing of beauty," Sylvie said. "I myself wear all my skirts a trifle short, as should you, Josie darling."

"I need the longer skirts to balance my hips," Josie said.

Tess groaned. "Madame Badeau told you that, didn't she?"

"She is correct," Josie stated.

"Madame Badeau makes excellent designs," Sylvie said peaceably. "I myself have a ravishing pelisse that she made for me. But I am not certain that I entirely agree with her tactics as regards your costumes, Josie."

"As I have repeatedly said myself," Griselda put in.

Josie groaned inwardly. They appeared to be about to reenact a battle that had replayed itself since she first visited Imogen's *modiste,* Madame Badeau. "It is *my* figure," she pointed out, "and my costumes in question. Without Madame Badeau's corsets, I would swell in all directions."

Even now Josie could feel the reassuring pressure of whalebones around her body, holding all her extra flesh in place. True, it was uncomfortable, and it made her feel rather like a wooden puppet at times, especially while dancing.

"I do not agree," Griselda said. She appealed directly to Sylvie. "Josie is convinced that she must wear this horrendous contraption that Madame Badeau espoused. As you can see, she barely sits with ease."

But to Josie's relief, Sylvie didn't jump to Griselda's

support. "I expect that Josie finds the garment rather comforting."

"I do," Josie said with emphasis. "I shall wear it whenever I am seen in public. Can you imagine if I took it off? They would stop calling me a Scottish sausage and say that I had swelled into—into a sausage patty!"

"They will lose interest," Sylvie said. "Particularly after Griselda diverts Darlington's attention to herself."

"I do believe that I shall drop my shoe," Griselda said. "A fan is too obvious, almost pedestrian. And these are *very* nice slippers. I'd forgotten how much I like them."

They all looked to the ground. Griselda's slippers were cream silk embroidered with pale blue, very small fleur-de-lis. Her stockings were the same color, with pale blue clocks.

"I am so happy to be entering your family," Sylvie said. "I could not bear to be sister to a woman who did not understand the importance of shoes."

Griselda smiled at her and dropped her skirts. Her eyes were more excited than Josie had seen them in ages, and she had a little smile hovering on her mouth. She took a miniature pot of color from her reticule, rubbed it on her lips, and then made a playful pout before the mirror. "I feel quite different. Rather wicked, I suppose."

"But surely you have not enjoyed your widowhood entirely alone?" Sylvie said, looking rather appalled.

"No, no," Griselda said, "there have been small attachments here and there, but I have never deliberately planned anything of this nature."

Josie just stopped herself from gasping.

"Therein lies the difference between the two of us," Sylvie said. "For you are half French, and I am fully French. Consequently, I cannot imagine embarking on any sort of romantic adventure without a good deal of planning. I would owe it to myself."

Griselda laughed. "You sound so sophisticated, Sylvie,

and yet I have observed you with my brother. The two of you are remarkably chaste, are you not?"

"I am always chaste," Sylvie remarked. "I have yet to see the reason why I should allow any advance in intimacy on the part of a man. I'm afraid that planning does tend to reduce one's tendency to be reckless."

Griselda paused in the door.

Sylvie grinned at her. *"Avance pour vaincre!"*

"I shall report on my conquest later this evening," Griselda said. "Josie, may I remind you that you have several dance partners waiting for you, when you choose to emerge."

Tess was tucking an errant curl high on her head. "I must return to the floor as well."

"Lucius will be looking for you," Josie said.

"It is an excellent thing to have a husband looking for one, rather than the other way around," Sylvie said. "I shall emulate you."

Tess smiled at her. "I have been remarkably lucky in that regard."

6

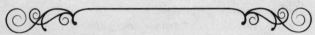

From The Earl of Hellgate, Chapter the Third

I fear it will reveal my arrogance if I say that I did fulfill the command of the duchess—shall we term her Hermia? My skills I consider to be God's providence and gift, for the duchess informed sometime later that *God had pricked me out for women's pleasure* . . . and I have devoutly followed His directive ever since.

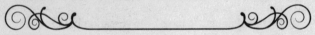

Thurman walked up to the Sausage as if he'd been introduced. In a way, he felt as if they were old acquaintances. Surely if he, Thurman, actually talked to the Sausage, Darlington would come to the Convent to hear his tale. He could send him a message, telling him that he had a story Darlington couldn't miss. Thurman felt panic at the idea of not having Darlington at his side. Not having Darlington's witticisms and cutting observations to pass the time.

"I'm a friend of Darlington," he said by way of invitation.

The Sausage blinked at him and then looked away, staring at the wall over his shoulder. "I would rather not be reminded of your friend's ill-bred phrases."

"Ill-bred? He ain't ill-bred," Thurman protested.

She still didn't look at him. But: "Despicable Darlington," she said mockingly. "I vow the phrase is quite appealing."

Thurman scowled. What he should do is dance with the piglet. That way he could make a great story out of how she trod on his feet with her little hooves and squealed in his ear. "Would you like to dance?"

She glanced at him for a second and then turned her entire head so she was staring at the wall again. "Absolutely not."

"Why not? You're desperate, aren't you?"

"You're some sort of fiend," she said. "Why on earth are you being so impolite? To the best of my knowledge, we've never met."

The disgust in her voice gave him a thrill of power. It wasn't just Darlington who could come up with cutting phrases. He could too. "I don't mind being a fiend as long as you don't cast me into a swine," he said.

"You are swine," Miss Essex said, glaring at him instead of the wall. "Oink, oink, Mr. Whatever Your Name Is. Why don't you trot back to whatever vulgar little pen you came from?"

Somehow his little jest hadn't come across with the same aplomb that Darlington achieved. She was looking at him so that he—*he*—felt uncomfortably aware of his rounded stomach. Everyone knew that weight in a man was a good thing. Made him strong and long-living.

But Thurman had the same quivering sense of failure that he used to have when he was called before the class to do the multiplication tables. Miss Essex had a powerfully nasty gaze. In fact, he hated her.

She wasn't done talking. "You are the sort of man who pinches maids," she was saying. "I can't imagine how you found your way into this ball."

Thurman felt that in his gut: he was sensitive about the

fact that his family's wealth came from running a printing press. He always laughed it off as his grandfather's intellectual fling, but he knew his claim to the title of gentleman was fragile.

"You are the sort of woman who will never be so lucky as to be pinched," he said, tasting Darlington's acid tones on his tongue. He could be as cutting as Darlington. He moved a little closer. He really loathed this plump Scottish girl. If he had his way, fat Scottish girls would never be allowed into a *ton* party at all. "You'll never be lucky enough to be tupped either," he said.

Then he just stood there, watching her. To tell the truth, he was rather surprised at himself for voicing such a thing in the midst of a society affair.

She got a little red in the face, so she must have known what tupping was. "You are—filth," she said.

Her voice was shaking. He rather liked that. She turned and darted away, and Thurman didn't move. He could feel rage swelling in his chest the way it used to when the schoolmaster flogged him for not knowing his tables. It was all tangled together in his mind: Darlington was gone, the Convent was gone, what would he do at night? Without Darlington, people would think he was stupid. It was all the Sausage's fault, because Darlington didn't drop him until he had those thoughts of morality.

That was *her* fault.

The Sausage's fault.

7

From The Earl of Hellgate, Chapter the Fifth

I fear that in telling the next episode of my life, I
may endanger the reputation of the sweetest and
most virtuous lady to have come to my attention.
I beg of you not to attempt to discover her name,
no matter the temptation. I shall simply call her
my darling Hippolyta. If she reads my poor offering, I would say to her what lies buried in my
heart:

**I have seen only you,
I have admired only you,
I desire only you.**

Josie turned away, rather blindly, and walked straight
through the crowd, heedless of anyone who might see
her face without its rigid smile. That was a horrible, disgusting swine of a man. Without warning, Mayne loomed before
her.

"Hello there," he said, grinning at her. Then his face
changed in a flash. "What's the matter, Josie?"

She swallowed hard and before she knew what was happening, Mayne was leading her out onto a marble terrace

that lay white and shining in the light of the torches placed at its edges. He walked her to the broad balustrade that lined the terrace, turned her around and then stood directly in front of her so that no one could see the tears snaking down her face. "What happened?" he demanded.

The torches were throwing glinting lights onto Mayne's tumble of black curls. His eyebrows were drawn into a perfectly straight scowl. "It was a horrid man," Josie said, hiccupping ungracefully, although it didn't matter because it was Mayne. "He said—He said—" But she couldn't say what he said, because Mayne was so beautiful and it was all so humiliating.

He had a large white handkerchief in his hand. "Steady on," he said, patting her cheeks dry. She tried to smile at him but her mouth wobbled. She turned away and leaned over to look at the borders below. The bushes were all in shadow.

"Who was it?" Mayne asked conversationally, but Josie heard the clash of steel in his voice.

"Is that sweetbrier or southernwood?" she asked. "It smells enchanting."

"Josie."

She turned back and shook her head. "I don't know. Some acquaintance of Darlington's." She took the handkerchief from him and wiped her eyes again. Mayne was looking thoughtful, like a man who was about to pummel half the male population of London.

"What did he look like?"

"I hardly noticed. The room is poorly lit, and he is nondescript, really. It's not that important," she said shakily. "I know what they think of me. I know—" Her eyes filled with tears again and she groped for the handkerchief, forgetting she had it. It fell to the ground, and without thinking she bent to pick it up. And stopped with a small *oof* as her corset almost sliced her in half.

Mayne plucked it from the ground with an easy sweep.

"What on earth?" he said, and then glanced about. "We're far too public here."

"Could we possibly leave the ball altogether?" Josie said. "I—I am not having a pleasant evening." But then she remembered his fiancée. "Yet Sylvie will wonder where you are."

Mayne's whole face lit up when he smiled. "May I say how happy I am to hear you use her first name? And of course I shall take you away. Sylvie is, as I'm sure you recognized immediately, a singularly self-sufficient woman. She actually came to the ball with another party. My only fear is that she has little use for me at all, and she certainly won't notice if I disappear."

"That can't be true," Josie said. If Mayne were her fiancé—though the thought was inconceivable, because of course he was far too old—she would never let him out of her sight. The thought made her feel a little queer in the stomach, so she allowed Mayne to tuck her hand under his arm and concentrated on making her smile as rigid as her back.

They walked through the crowd at a leisurely pace. They were only stopped once, by Lady Lorkin, who put a thin hand on Mayne's arm and crooned something to him.

She glanced once at Josie, but didn't bother to greet her. Mayne bent toward her and she breathed something in his ear. Her eyes were bright and avid, like a child who sees a puppy running free on the lawn.

Mayne laughed a low, intimate kind of chuckle and murmured something. Then he gently removed Lady Lorkin's hand from his sleeve and they walked on. After that Josie noticed the way women kept turning to look at Mayne, their eyes dancing over him in a manner that made her acutely aware of how prized he was. And yet Sylvie, who had won him, didn't mind if he disappeared for a while. It was an odd fact of life, she had to suppose.

"We should find Griselda," Mayne said, looking about.

"After all, she is your chaperone and I must tell her that we are fleeing."

"No!" Josie said, remembering suddenly that Griselda was presumably carrying out Sylvie's order that she seduce Darlington. "Absolutely not."

"Why not?" Mayne said. "Isn't my sister a good chaperone?"

"Of course she is. I simply wouldn't wish to bother her," Josie said weakly.

"There's a great deal that I do not understand about you, Miss Josephine Essex," Mayne said. "I suppose I can send her a note. A young lady should not trot away from a ball without informing her chaperone, you know. The chaperone might well assume the worst."

"Not if I'm with you," Josie pointed out.

"While your confidence in me is touching, I can assure you that there is many a mama in the room who would not wish her daughter to gallivant out of a ball by my side."

"Don't be foolish, Mayne. I'm the woman least able to be compromised at this ball."

He raised an eyebrow but scratched a note on his card and told a footman to give it to Griselda. "Where would you like to go?" he asked once they were seated in his carriage. It was a gorgeous little vehicle, a dark glossy red picked out with his coat of arms on the door.

"Anywhere."

Mayne was eyeing her in a peculiar way. "It would be thoroughly improper, but—"

"No one will believe I'm doing anything improper." She said it flatly, because it was true.

"In that case," Mayne said with a wolfish grin, "welcome to my parlor, young lady." He rapped on the roof, shouting "Home, Wiggles!"

"Wiggles?" Josie said, feeling better the moment the carriage started to move away from the ball. *"Wiggles?"*

Mayne grinned at her. "Presumably the son of Papa Wiggles . . . one day the proud father of William Wiggles, Wilfred Wiggles, and perhaps even a Wilhelmina Wiggles."

Josie smiled back, rather wanly. "Your house?" she asked. "Do you live in this vicinity?"

"All of two blocks away," Mayne said, and even as he spoke the carriage slowed. "You will be unchaperoned, but I assure you that my house is absolutely awash with servants."

"More to the point, you're in love with Sylvie," Josie said.

"That fact will likely curb any fiendish plans I have for your ravishment," Mayne agreed.

She scowled at him. "Don't you dare make fun of me, Garret Langham."

"I didn't mean to."

She stared at him a moment, eyes narrowed, but his face looked genuinely surprised. "I know that I am not to anyone's taste when it comes to ravishment. There is no possible way anyone would ever think that you had such plans—*you,* the man who has slept with every beautiful woman in London—so we can dispense with worries about my reputation."

A butler was holding the door open, and Mayne swept her up and into the house without a word. "Ribble, we'll have champagne in the turret. Veuve Clicquot-Ponsardin, old and cold, if you please."

"The lamps aren't lit, my lord," said the butler.

"Not a problem, Ribble. I'll see to it."

Josie was struggling out of her pelisse. Mayne scowled at her again and then snatched it from her shoulders, handing it to a footman.

"Do you have a turret? How lovely!" she said, trying to avoid questions about why she was so awkward.

"Would you like something to eat?" he asked.

She shook her head.

"I'm feeling peckish, so you'll forgive me for eating something, I trust. I'm afraid that Rafe made a mistake by asking Fortnam and Mason to cater his wedding ball. Did you see the sandwiches stamped with huge H's for Holbrook?"

Josie shook her head again. She never allowed herself to eat in public, thinking it would simply fuel the talk about her waistline.

"Stamped in liver paste," Mayne said, taking her arm and heading up the stairs. "Looked as terrible as they tasted. Bring us something delicious for a light supper, Ribble, if you would."

They walked up the stairs, past the main floor and through a small door. Mayne pulled a tinderbox from a small shelf, and so Josie saw the room in the flickering light of a small flame. The ceiling was domed and painted deep blue with faded gold stars. The walls were paneled, and painted with curious winding vines on which grew an occasional rose. The only furniture in the room was a small chaise longue, two cozy chairs, and a tea table. High on the walls there were small windows, eight of them for each of the eight sides. Moonlight filtered down into the room in a lazy kind of way that made the vines on the wall look charmingly mysterious.

"Oh, this is lovely!" Josie said, clasping her hands. "It's utterly magical."

Mayne was lighting one of the Argand lamps attached to the wall. "You've discovered its secret," he said, laughter running through his voice.

"It must be the only turret outside the Tower in the whole of London," Josie said. "How on earth did it survive the great fire?"

"Oh, this house isn't that old," Mayne said. "My grandfather had a daughter whom he loved very much, by the name of Cecily. Aunt Cecily was born early, before she should have been. Apparently she was lame from birth and had weak lungs as well. She loved nothing more than to read books. She fancied herself a princess, you see, and this was the perfect chamber from which to be kissed into wakefulness."

"She was absolutely right. Was she wakened?"

"Unfortunately, Cecily died before I was born."

"I'm so sorry."

"There were no other children in the family for years, until finally my father arrived. He loved her more, he said, than his own mother, because he spent hours and hours of his boyhood here, listening to her tales of knights, dragons, and fanciful monsters. You see, she had some of her stories painted on the walls."

He held up a lamp, and sure enough when Josie looked closely at the twining vines, a small unicorn with a curious smile was dancing up the vine, and hanging insouciantly from one hand was a small boy. "My father," Mayne said, touching the little imp. Josie recognized that mop of wild hair and the aristocratic nose, even in a youthful version.

Josie longed to ask when his father died, but didn't dare.

"He died some ten years ago," Mayne told her.

"Oh dear," she said, taking his arm.

"He told me many of Cecily's stories," he said. "And Griselda remembers even more than I do."

He put the lamp down rather abruptly on the small table. "Are you able to sit down in that contraption you're wearing?"

Josie felt a flood of pink coming up her neck. "Yes, of course," she said, striving for a casual tone. But she could hardly mention the word *corset* in front of him.

"Is it a corset?" he asked.

"That's none of your business!" she snapped, sitting on the edge of her seat. She couldn't sit back; the corset was let in with clever little grommets around her bottom so that she had just enough space to sit elegantly, as long as she kept her legs close together.

Mayne threw himself into the chair opposite her. He was all broad shoulders and strong legs, and he looked utterly comfortable. "How can you stand that?" he asked with some curiosity. Before she could answer, there was a scratch at the door and he shouted, "Enter!"

Josie bit her tongue as footmen brought in champagne and a tray of food. In fact, she waited until she had a glass of cool, apple-bitter champagne in her hand to give her courage, and then she said, with just the right air of sophistication, "Ladies never discuss their undergarments with gentlemen, Mayne."

"But you and I are friends."

"We are not friends!"

"Yes, we are." He was grinning at her, and there was something in his eyes that was very hard to resist. "I assure you that you are the only lady of my acquaintance ever to ask me to take part in a farce like that you arranged in Scotland. You must be a friend, because I'd be afraid to make you my enemy."

"You mean when Annabel's horse bucked?"

He threw back his head and laughed. "Annabel's horse didn't just buck, you little witch! You put something under that poor nag's saddle to make it dance in the air."

"It was in a good cause," Josie protested, feeling a smile curl her lips. "I merely thought that if Ardmore was scared for Annabel's life, he might realize that he was in love with her."

"He had realized that all on his own," Mayne said. "A man comes to that sort of insight slowly, believe me."

Josie felt the champagne slide down her throat. It was reckless, delicious, sitting here in a gorgeous little jewel-box of a room with one of the most desired men in London for company. It made her feel sophisticated. As if she, Josephine Essex, weren't the least desirable debutante on the market. She pushed the thought away and drank more champagne. "How did you realize you were in love with Sylvie?" she asked boldly.

His face changed the moment she said Sylvie's name. Naturally, she felt a fierce pang of envy; who wouldn't? To tame a man of Mayne's reputation, and to tame him so thoroughly that his eyes almost changed color when one's name was mentioned . . . what a feat.

"I walked into a ball in Terence Square," he said. "I had no intention of going, to be truthful. Lucius was out of town, and Rafe was rusticating in the country. I had just returned from our trip to Scotland—and if my sister lost her breakfast one more time in my company, I had vowed to disown the family and flee to Moscovy. At any rate, I came straight to London, and of course there were a hundred invitations. I'd lived so long in those benighted rags that Rafe calls clothes that I felt like being splendid. Do you know what I mean?"

Josie shook her head. For her, going to a ball was an agonizingly tedious process of strapping and lacing and wiggling into clothes that felt too small. Being worried that she would sweat in them, that she would have to bend over, that she wouldn't be able to survive without a trip to the privy.

She could feel Mayne eyeing her corset again, but thankfully he didn't say anything.

"As it happened, the Queen was receiving that afternoon. So I went to the Drawing Room. There was the usual flock of debutantes waiting to be received, and there, just in the middle, was an exquisite woman. I knew immediately that she was French, of course. It wasn't her voice, but the way she carried herself. There's nothing *common* about a Frenchwoman, do you know what I mean, Josie?"

Josie had probably read a few too many French romances for her own good. "Do you mean that Frenchwomen aren't loose?" she asked dubiously.

"Oh, they misbehave with true *joie de vivre*. But they never look at a man with an invitation in their eyes," he said, stretching his feet out. His legs went so far across the small floor that his feet almost touched her slippers. "They wait for a man to approach them, or they shrug them off. Do you see the difference?"

Josie thought about the eager way that Lady Lorkin's eyes had skated over Mayne's face. She took another swallow of champagne. It was a vastly improper thing to say, but: "Lady Lorkin, one must assume, is not of Gallic origin."

She was rewarded by a snort of laughter. "Not a bit of it."

"Are you carrying on an *affaire* with her?"

The laughter died in his eyes immediately. "I am affianced to Sylvie."

"I didn't mean to imply—"

But he wasn't angry anymore. "I did have a tryst with her, some three years ago now. I'm afraid that she may have built it into a treasured memory."

"Yes, I can see that."

He looked faintly embarrassed. "I feel like an ass even saying such a thing in front of a young lady."

"I may be young, but I'm not stupid. And if you remember, one of my sisters was engaged to you, so I'm fully aware of your scandalous background."

His eyes fell and he was studying his boots again. "I should never have stood up Tess at the altar—"

"Not only that but you almost had an *affaire* with my other sister," Josie interrupted. She was feeling blissful, for the first time since the season began. She grinned at him. "You spell nothing but trouble for the Essex sisters. We shall all be very glad when Sylvie ties you up nice and tight at the altar."

"Unfair!" he protested. "All the Essexes have married without a protest from me. And I did not have an *affaire* with Imogen."

"I know that," Josie said smugly. "Though not for lack of trying on her part."

He looked startled at this but said nothing.

"Why *didn't* you allow her to seduce you?" Josie asked, holding out her glass so he could fill it again. "Imogen is very beautiful. She was widowed, so there wasn't a husband to worry about. What on earth stopped you?"

"Do you think that I just gallivant around London, sleeping with any woman who throws me a lure?"

Josie thought about it for a moment. "Yes."

"Well, I don't."

"If you'd had world enough and time . . ." she said mischievously.

"No, you little devil, that scrap of poetry won't work. Marvell says his lady might remain coy if they had world enough and time—"

"The coy Mayne," Josie said, interrupting him again. "Ah Mayne, how the *ton* has misjudged you! Why, you'll hardly credit it—" she opened her eyes wide—"but they seem to think you are the greatest seducer of women ever to grace the *ton*."

"Well, I'm not," Mayne said sharply, draining his glass and filling it again.

He seemed a bit peevish, so Josie dropped the subject. There was nothing worse than being nagged about one's bad traits. It was so much more pleasant to pretend they didn't exist. Like overeating. She was going to eat one of those delicious sandwich squares, even given that she had sworn that very morning never to eat again.

She leaned forward from the waist, carefully, reached out for a sandwich and bumped Mayne's hand. He was smiling at her, and suddenly Josie knew to the bottom of her toes why all those London ladies made fools of themselves over him. He must be well over thirty years old, but his eyes had a devilish smile in them that made her feel—

She dropped the sandwich as if it stung her.

Mayne was already sprawled back in his chair, but he bent forward and picked it up for her. "I'm afraid of what would happen if you tried to lean farther forward," he remarked.

She scowled at him and edged back in her chair.

"So are you going to tell me what you're wearing?" he asked, eating half the small sandwich in one bite.

It was all so easy for him. Women falling at his feet, and not a bit of guilt no matter what he ate. It just wasn't fair. "No, I am not going to talk about my undergarments."

"You look absurdly uncomfortable," Mayne cheerfully observed.

Josie ate a bite of her sandwich. It was wonderful, a burst of salmon flavor with a touch of cucumber. "Your chef is marvelous," she said when she finished.

Mayne leaned forward, grabbed two more for himself and one for her. "Don't forget your champagne," he said. "Champagne was designed by God to go with smoked salmon."

There was a moment's reverent silence while they both ate. Then Mayne emptied the last of the champagne bottle into Josie's glass. "Have we drunk all that?" she asked, slightly alarmed.

"No, it was half empty when opened," he said sarcastically. "If you won't talk to me about your undergarments, will you talk to Sylvie about them?"

"Certainly not!" Josie squeaked, picturing his slender fiancée.

"One of your sisters, then?"

"Naturally, Imogen took me to her very own *modiste*, a

Frenchwoman," she added pointedly. "Madame Badeau. I have entirely new clothing for the season, and while you may not approve, I assure you that Madame Badeau is the very best *modiste* in London."

Mayne's eyes narrowed and he was staring at her again. Josie would have straightened, except she couldn't be any straighter than she was. She drank her champagne and then broke the silence. "I might as well say what I'm sure you're thinking," she said, putting her glass down on the table with a little click. "The only thing that gets me into this gown at all is my corset. It works miracles. I love it." She finished the last sentence bravely.

Mayne wasn't looking at her anymore; he was cutting the string around the cork of a bottle of champagne that Josie hadn't seen before.

"Are we going to drink more?" she asked, with a little gasp.

He shrugged. "Why not? At this point, we've missed most of the party. I shouldn't like to return you to Rafe's until we are quite certain the crowds are gone and no one will see us. I don't suppose you've drunk much champagne in the past?"

"I had a glass once before," Josie said, looking lovingly at the bubbles in the bottle. "It's much more interesting than I thought."

"Don't develop a passion for it," he advised her. "Look at Rafe and how long it took him to become sober."

"Oh, I won't."

He lifted his glass and held it up to hers. "To the future, Josie?"

"Why do you call me Josie, and I call you Mayne?" she asked, taking a deep draught of champagne. It was making her feel brave and reckless.

"You can call me whatever you like," he said with a shrug.

"Then I'll call you Garret. We *are* friends, after all, and I think that a gentleman who has the gall to question a lady about her undergarments should be on intimate terms with her, don't you think?" A thought struck her and she plunged straight into another question. "Do all those women whom you slept with address you as Garret, or Mayne?"

He was grinning at her, a lazy, beautiful grin with a touch of the devil in it. He looked like nothing in the world so much as a slightly wicked Bacchus crafted by a master sculptor. It made her feel audacious. After all, it wasn't Lady Lorkin in this chair. It was she, Josie, the most scorned debutante of the year. "I love champagne!" she added.

"I begin to think I should ring for a sobering cup of tea," Mayne said. And then: "No, you little witch, I have never asked the women with whom I had *affaires* to address me by my first name. It isn't done."

"Why not? If I were going to—to unclothe myself in front of a person, I would certainly wish to be familiar enough to call him by his first name!"

He laughed at that. "There's more intimacy involved than unclothing," he pointed out. And then looked a bit appalled at himself. "I shouldn't have said that."

"We're talking about bedding," Josie said impatiently. "You can pretend I'm your younger brother, if you wish."

He eyed her. "I don't wish."

"Well, my point is that if I were ever to take my clothing off before someone, I certainly wouldn't do so in an atmosphere of such formality."

Mayne was staring at the bubbles in his champagne, turning the glass so the golden wine caught the light. "Most ladies undress with the help of their maids and then slip under the covers."

Josie thought about that. It sounded like a very good plan to her. That way one's husband would never be unnerved by the sight of one's flesh. "Where does the gentleman undress?"

"Of course, ladies and gentlemen never share a bedchamber," he said, looking through his glass at her now. "No one could imagine such a thing; that sort of intimacy is left for the lower classes. No, the squire strides into his wife's bedchamber, admirably covered in a striped dressing gown of sturdy linsey-woolsey. Then he drops his dressing gown . . . "

Josie had a sudden vivid image of what Mayne would look like without a dressing gown, or anything else.

". . . but not before he turns down the lamp," Mayne finished. "No promiscuous looking among the aristocracy. Absolutely not."

"And she never uses his first name?" Josie said, wrenching her mind away from the gutter.

"Never. In fact, she says little, in my experience." Mayne rested his head on the back of his chair and gazed at the ceiling. "And this is truly something you should *never* repeat to your intimates," he said. "I should not tell you, but I will anyway. The truth is that I can't imagine why women go to such lengths to anger their husbands by having *affaires,* when most of them don't particularly enjoy the intimacies themselves."

"Then you," Josie said, thrilling with the daring of this desperately improper conversation, "must not be very good at bedding women. Perhaps Imogen had a lucky escape." She grinned at the low growl that came from his throat. "Tess and Annabel gave Imogen a wedding night talk," she told him. "And this time they finally allowed me to stay because I was supposed to be getting married this season."

Mayne's jaw clenched. "And they said something about *me*?" There was stark disbelief in his voice.

"Why on earth would they be interested in you? You should be careful that all this adoration from foolish women like Letitia Lorkin doesn't go to your head."

"Josie, you witch"—and it didn't sound like an endearment anymore—"can you kindly inform me precisely how my name came up during this oh-so-delicate conversation?"

"As I said, *you* didn't come up. But the fact that many men are unable to make women happy in bed did."

"Don't tell me your sisters were worried about Rafe." He sounded horrified; it was likely a question of insult my friend, insult me.

"No. But—" Josie stopped. It was one thing to be indiscreet with Mayne, and it was another to reveal that Imogen's first marriage had not been entirely satisfactory in that respect.

He didn't say anything, just stared at his glass. "I seem to have no problem providing a suitable experience."

Josie sipped her glass a bit more cautiously. She was feeling definitely tipsy. It was agreeable, but a native cautionary streak was advising her to stop drinking.

"Bravo for you," she said.

He looked at her, and she felt the impact of his wild black eyes to the bottom of her toes. " 'Twas I who found it unsatisfactory," he said to her. "And I can't tell you in what respect, because it's not the kind of thing you talk about with virgins." Saying the word seemed to startle him and he snatched up the bottle. "Damn it. I'm three sheets to the wind," he growled. His voice had darkened to a champagne-drenched growl. Josie thought it was the most sensual thing she'd heard in her life.

"Why'd you keep doing it, then?" she asked, watching him through her lashes so he wouldn't know how curious she was.

But he didn't even glance at her. "I haven't," he said. "Haven't had a woman, if you'll excuse the vulgarity, since Lady Godwin, and—" He stopped.

Josie knew who Lady Godwin was. She was a brilliant musician who wrote waltzes with her husband. Lady Godwin had created that bewitching waltz that she had danced around and around Rafe's ballroom, in the days before this horrible season started. Now Josie couldn't dance a waltz because she didn't want anyone putting a hand on her corset. A man could feel every spike through the thin silk of her gowns.

"You mean," she said carefully, "the countess?" Was that misery in Mayne's eyes?

"The very one. If you'll believe the foolishness of this, I fancied myself in love with her. Hell, I *was* in love with her."

"How dare she reject you?" Josie cried. "I shall never think well of her again."

He grinned at that. "She stayed with her husband, you little witch. She loved him, more than she loved me, and since she didn't love me even an iota, that was easily done."

"Sylvie is far more beautiful," Josie said stoutly.

"Yes." And, after a while: "Sylvie is a painter, did I tell you that? Both of them artists."

"I wish I had a talent for something like that."

"What do you have a talent for?"

Josie shrugged. "Nothing ladylike, nor artistic either. I can't even embroider, and all I really like to do is read."

"Reading is an estimable pursuit."

"Not what I read," Josie said with a burst of reckless honesty. "I like to read books published by the Minerva Press."

He laughed at that.

"They're really very good."

"Adventures, escapes, damsels in peril—why Josie, I hardly know you! Aren't you the one who's afraid of riding, even though you love horses?"

"It's impolite of you to mention it."

"Well, I'm about to get even more impolite," he said, with just the faintest slur in his words. "You need to take off that blasted corset. Don't slay me, but you never looked like that before."

"Like what before?"

"Now you sound like my mother," he told her. "My mother could—"

"What did I not look like before?" she interrupted. "You might as well finish. I am ready for a grossly uncomplimentary remark." She wasn't, really, but it sounded courageous.

"When we were on the way to Scotland, I noticed several times that you had developed a really lovely figure," he said, waving his glass in the air.

"Oh," she said, taken aback.

"When I first met all four Essex sisters, you understand, you had a perfectly charming little figure for a girl of your age—damn it all, what *is* your age?"

"I was fifteen when you first met me," Josie said with dignity.

"Bit lumpy, back then," Mayne said, "but all girls are. On the way to Scotland, I remember telling myself several times that you were developing the kind of figure that was going to break men's hearts and make them grovel in your wake. You didn't quite have it yet, and you certainly didn't know how to walk."

"Then I got fatter."

"No! Then you showed up wearing this contraption that makes you look—you look—well, you look stuffed."

"Like a stuffed sausage."

"Take the damned thing off."

"What are you talking about?" Her blood was pounding through her veins.

"Take it off," he said. He stood up, and to his credit, he wasn't even unsteady. "I'll help."

"You must be drunk," she said with horror. His face didn't appear to have the cruel ravishing power of the heroes in her favorite novels, but how would she know? He was standing before her looking helpful and just slightly drunk.

"For God's sake, Josie," he roared, "I don't want to seduce

you! How can you think such a thing. I'm thirty-four, in God's name. Thirty-*five* in two days. And you're what? Eighteen?"

"Almost nineteen," she said, tight-lipped.

"Well I am almost thirty-five. And in the course of my long and misspent life, I have never yet taken up cradle-robbing. Finally, as I think you are quite aware, I am in love with Sylvie!"

"Then what—what do you want?"

"If you won't talk to Sylvie, and your own sisters colluded in stuffing you into this despicable garment, then I'll have to show you myself."

"Show me what?"

"Show you how to walk so that you make a man slaver at your feet, of course. Isn't that what you want?"

"Of course that's what I want!" she cried. "But I can't—I can't unclothe myself."

"Not all the way," he said, pained. "You just need to take off that cravat thing and put your gown back on."

"It's not a cravat, it's a corset! And you're drunk."

"So are you," he said, laughing a little now. "We are both drunk in the starlight room. That's what my aunt used to call this: the starlight room. When she was very ill, toward the end of her life, she would lie on this couch all night and watch the stars on the ceiling, and the stars through the window. Sometimes my father would stay with her through the night."

"It must have broken his heart when she died," Josie whispered.

"He always said that without her, he wouldn't have known how to love. My grandparents were as stiff as if they'd been carved from wood."

Josie's eyes filled with tears. "That's so lovely. My sisters taught me how to love, because my mother died before I was born."

His eyebrow shot up. "Before?"

"Well, on the same day. But she never even held me, so I think of it as if she was gone before I arrived."

"I suspect that Lady Godwin taught me how to love," Mayne said. "Damned annoying that is."

"Annoying why?"

"Because she dismissed me without a second's thought. But I couldn't stop thinking of her." He shrugged.

"You love your sister," Josie pointed out.

"Of course I do. But I meant a truly passionate love." He shook himself and suddenly his eyes snapped into focus, staring down at her, and before she knew what had happened, he'd pulled her to her feet and nimbly turned her about. Then he was unbuttoning her gown down the back.

Josie felt as if the champagne had dulled her responses. This particular impropriety had never been covered by her governess, Miss Flecknoe. Mayne didn't want to seduce her. He thought she looked like a stuffed sausage. So did it matter that he was about to see her corset?

"God almighty," he whispered as the dress fell open.

He'd seen her corset.

"What in the hell *is* this thing?" He sounded almost angry. "It looks like the underpinning of a ship."

"It's a special corset they sell in Paris for larger ladies," Josie explained, feeling a burning flush rise up her neck. "Would you *please* button my gown back up?"

But he was pulling at the strings.

"You can't just pull at me," Josie said, breathless. "You have to unhook at the top and bottom. And then you can start to unlace, but you have to do it slowly. Very slowly."

"Why?" he asked, and she heard the sound of a little hook being torn apart.

"Don't do that!" she cried, agonized. And then: "Because I might faint if it opens too quickly."

"Damn." He said it flatly.

She didn't faint, even though the pressure released so quickly that she swayed forward. He grabbed her, large hands holding her shoulders. He steadied her, and then pushed her gown forward over her arms. As it fell to the floor, the corset followed. Of course it didn't fall with a gentle swish, the way her gown did. It clanked because the whalebones were capped with special little tips of lead, so they wouldn't dig into her skin.

The tighter, the better, Madame Badeau had said, showing her how her maid should brace herself against the bed and force the lacings closed. And then she'd said the magic words: You won't be able to eat while wearing this, of course.

In Josie's mind, that had been the moment when The Corset, as she thought of it, moved to sacred status. The Corset would give her a successful season. The Corset would stop her from eating, and give her a slender, refined shape, and give her a husband.

It hadn't worked out that way. And besides, Josie found herself perfectly able to eat while wearing it.

Mayne was staring at the ground, where the corset had fallen. "It looks like a bizarre kind of chrysalis that hatched a butterfly," he said, picking it up by one of its many straps. "What in the devil were you wearing this for, Josie?"

He wasn't even looking at her, but Josie slung her arms across her thin chemise and tried not to think about all her unbounded flesh. "It made me thinner," she snapped.

"You don't need to be thinner," he said. Then he glanced at her. "Are you cold? Put your gown back on."

There was a moment's silence and then Josie said in a stern little voice, "I can't, not without the corset. It won't fit." That was one of the gifts of The Corset. She was able to wear gowns that were almost—not quite—the same measurements as those worn by Imogen.

Mayne tossed the corset to the side, where it fell with a dull clang and a tinkling of lead-covered tips. "I'll get you something to put on," he said. Before she knew what happened, he was out the door.

Josie spread her arms. It was . . . glorious to have the corset off. Glorious. She was wearing a chemise of the lightest lawn. It felt like air, billowing around her.

8

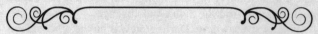

From The Earl of Hellgate, Chapter the Sixth

For some time my Hippolyta made me the happiest of men, and though her interest turned to another, I still dream of the luscious fruits of our friendship. I think I may say that we were both at the Countess of Y—'s garden party in '07. You will recall the fashion for omelettes eaten in the garden that raged that year. Well . . .

Griselda's first husband had been handed to her on a platter by her father. "I've had an offer for your hand in marriage," he had said.

"Who?" she had gasped, thinking of Lord Cogley, with whom she'd danced the night before.

"Willoughby," Papa had said, impatient as always. "I accepted him. Decent family, very nice settlement, you're not likely to do better."

"But—" she had cried. And cried.

It was over.

Ever since poor Willoughby had died, facedown in a plate of jellied fowl, Griselda had looked to men for an occasional, discreet amusement. Only twice, if the truth were known. And neither of those *petites affaires* lasted over one night. She considered those two a judicious distraction from the round of visits, balls, and events that made up her life.

One more flirtation . . . and then she would put her mind seriously to the question of matrimony. She was frightfully aged: almost thirty-three, although she would rather expire than admit it. And she didn't look that age.

Finally she saw him. Darlington was on the other side of the room, talking to Mrs. Hotson and her daughter. Griselda paused thoughtfully for a moment. Mrs. Hotson was, of course, famed for the large amount of money her husband had made investing in some sort of machinery that produced lace, of a crude nature and fit only for undergarments. Not Griselda's undergarments, naturally; she prided herself on wearing chemises as beautiful as her outerwear. Just because there was no one but a maid to see did not mean that a woman should relax into slobbery.

Darlington was quite handsome. He had those tossed curls that all the men were affecting these days, from the Bishop of London (who should have known better than to have curls peeking out from under his hat) to her own brother Mayne. Mayne's were, at least, natural, and Darlington's appeared to be as well. There was nothing more unappetizing than the thought of a man patiently waiting while a servant crimped his hair. Darlington was lean and tall, and beautifully dressed, for all she knew that he didn't have a penny to his name. Well, perhaps he had a penny or two. One had to think that the Duke of Bedrock wouldn't toss off his youngest son to live in the gutter.

But Darlington needed to marry well. He was obviously trying to interest himself in Letty Hotson. Letty was standing next to him, her mouth slightly ajar, listening closely as he bent his head to tell her something. Even from across the room she could see the trace of self-loathing in his face, almost hear the detached sound of his voice. Dear me, Griselda thought, I shall be doing the man a favor by extracting him from that company. If there was one thing she knew about, it was marriage between incompatible persons. He and Letty would never share an intelligent conversation.

A moment later she was standing beside Mrs. Hotson, complimenting her on her daughter's dress; Letty was swathed in lace from head to toe. And two minutes after that, Griselda was strolling away with Darlington's hand under her arm, having cut him from the herd.

"Aren't you going to regale me with a clever phrase about Letty's lace?" she asked a moment later. "Lacy Letty?"

"I am too busy trying to ascertain why you wish to speak to me, Lady Griselda," he said. "I fear that my sins have come home to roost."

"Calling Josie a sausage was indeed a sin," Griselda said, and her voice came out harder than she meant it to be.

"I vow never to do so again."

She turned to look at him in surprise.

"I've been an ass, and I'm sorry."

He had queer gray-green eyes with thick eyelashes. The odd thing was that he actually did look rueful. Why on earth hadn't she thought of speaking to him before? Perhaps she could have cut off poor Josie's miseries after the very first ball in which they heard giggles about the Scottish Sausage. "You've made her season a horrendous trial," Griselda observed. Again her voice was more critical than she meant it to be, given that she was supposed to coax him into a flirtation and then extract a promise of better behavior.

It was a trifle disappointing to realize that she could simply walk away right now and consider their flirtation at an end.

"If you had asked me to close my mouth, I would have."

"Why?" she asked, and then: "Not that there should be any reason for stopping behavior so cruel and—" She stopped.

"Ill-bred?" he put in, with an odd twist of his lips.

Griselda felt like saying the truth, so she did. "Aye, ill-bred. It is ill-bred to mock those who are less fortunate than you."

"You're right in every particular."

"Although," she added, "obviously you are not truly ill-bred."

"One would hope not," he said, but there was something sardonic in his voice that suggested that he, at least, felt that a father's title as duke did not necessarily constitute good breeding. "May I ask you to dance with me?"

Griselda knew she probably should go back and report victory. If she hurried, she might even find Sylvie, Tess, and Josie still in the ladies' retiring room. Rather oddly, Sylvie seemed to enjoy herself far more in seclusion than she did circling the ballroom floor. Earlier, Griselda had seen her circling the floor with Mayne, and Sylvie had looked almost—*almost*—bored.

But Griselda was never bored on the dance floor. "I shall dance with you, but only if you treat me to a taste of this oh-so-precious wit that I hear about."

He shook his head. "I've decided to stop making my reputation at the expense of others."

"It's all very well to eschew unpleasant comments about defenseless girls," she said tartly, "but surely you're not planning to enter a monastery?"

The strains of a waltz began, and he smiled down at her as she put a hand high in his. "I thought perhaps I would become a truly boring person now. One of the ones whom everyone looks up to."

He was a beautiful dancer. "I see precisely what you mean. There *is* something about you of the Puritan. I suppose you have a sweet and modest disposition, and you've merely been pretending to be wicked these past few years."

"Precisely. I have had to put away my ardent desire to

become a bishop, but perhaps I shall still give up the world and its vanities."

"I shall have to test you," she said, giggling a little. "You know all good men go through some sort of temptation." His arm was warm and strong around her waist as they danced.

"In the desert, I believe," he said, looking around in a way that made her break into laughter. She caught the startled eyes of a friend, Lady Felicia Saville. Felicia had never quite recovered from a bout of lovesickness she suffered over Mayne, and Griselda tried to avoid her as much as possible. But now she gave her a laughing smile. She was dancing with one of the handsomest, most intelligent young men in the *ton,* and she was enjoying herself.

"There's no desert in England," Griselda observed.

"That's a good thing."

"Why?"

"Because I've heard tell that people go quite unclothed in the desert." His eyes danced with laughter. For a moment she thought *he* was trying to seduce her, but that was ridiculous. "Consider Lady Stutterfield in that state, for instance." He nodded toward a rawboned woman who moved by in a stately fashion, clothed in great quantities of starched taffeta.

"Perhaps it is just as well that England has no desert," Griselda agreed.

"One never knows, of course, when the earth's magnetic poles will change their position and turn this country into a sandy wasteland," he observed. "I learned very little in school, but I do remember that."

"I'm quite certain that I've heard it said that you took a First."

"Firsts are so easy to obtain these days," he said. "Especially if one is partial to gossip, as I am. History is nothing more than a large collection of such tales, and my First is in that subject, which should qualify me in your esteem."

"History is made up of gossip? I thought it was made up of grand events and grander people. And dates. My governess quite despaired of my ability to keep dates in my head. I could never see the point of it."

"Neither can I," he said companionably, and she could tell he meant precisely what he said. "But think about gossip. What do you most prefer to gossip about?"

"People, I suppose."

"Yes, but people doing things. I think that there are three truly interesting sources of gossip. One is eccentrics, and another is financial failures. One can practically sum up the history of the world in those terms. Alexander the Great? An eccentric, and then a financial failure. Napoleon, Charlemagne, our own English Henry IV . . . all make interesting history, and each of them is either an eccentric, a financial failure, or both."

"You haven't told me the third category," Griselda observed.

"Shouldn't you like to guess?"

She thought for a moment. "Adultery . . . or possibly murder. But on the whole adultery is so much more interesting to discuss; murders have a dreary similarity at the base."

"One could argue the same of adultery, but I won't," he said, laughing. "You see, Lady Griselda, you would have had a top First, if only the universities weren't such fools about allowing women to attend."

"I'm sure I wouldn't want one."

"Why on earth not?"

"So that I could predict at what year England would turn into a desert? And pray, sir, what possible use would that news be to me?"

"You could prepare the *ton* for the eventuality of waltzing with no clothes," he said.

He *was* flirting with her. Really, she thought that as a

woman who was ten years older than he, she would have to carry this conversation all by herself. But he was surprising her. First he swore to cease his talk of sausages, and now he was engaging in a flirtation.

"I'm afraid," she said in a melancholy type of way, "that I would have to leave the *ton* if that became the normal way of things."

"Couldn't stomach it?" he said sympathetically. "Whenever I have to visualize something of an unpleasant nature, I think about muffins."

"Muffins?"

He twirled her around the bottom of the room and their legs brushed together. "Muffins are very helpful in these situations," he said gravely. "For example, if I think of Lady Stutterfield without her support garments, not to mention all that taffeta, I might feel faint. So I think of a hot, buttered muffin and I feel much better. On the reverse side, if I think of you, Lady Griselda, without your garments, I also feel faint, though for different reasons."

"So you think of muffins?" she asked, her eyes caught by his intent ones.

"Dry, horrid muffins," he said.

"I think you show a remarkable attachment to nursery food." She drew back as the music came to a close, and curtsied.

"Will I see you tomorrow in the park?" he asked.

"Shall you be there, pursuing a marriageable young miss?" she teased.

"Yes," he said baldly.

She was a bit surprised, but then realized that Darlington was presumably the sort who could flirt with a willing, presumably available widow and blatantly pursue a wife at the same time. She kept smiling and withdrew her hand. "Perhaps I shall see you there," she said.

"Lady Griselda—" he began.

But she turned away with a dismissive flutter and a polite smile. While he was a most enjoyable man to share a waltz with, she had no particular desire to watch him hook poor Letty Hotson and her dowry of lace.

9

From The Earl of Hellgate, Chapter the Sixth

There we were, with our omelettes quite besmiring our garments—Dear Reader, remember your promise to me that you will make no attempt to discover the identity of my Hippolyta—and she said to me, in the prettiest manner imaginable, "Dearest Sir, will you not aid me in removing this unsavory breakfast from my person?" Reader, may I say that it was a meal I shall never forget?

The door opened, and Josie slapped her arms back in front of her breasts. They were far too large; she couldn't say how it happened, but in the last year, her breasts had grown enormously. At least you don't gain in your legs, Imogen had told her when they were looking at her reflection without The Corset. That was true. Her ankles and legs were fairly slim, compared to the rest of her. It was her hips and breasts that were vulgarly rounded.

Mayne handed her a gorgeous flowered dressing gown, keeping his eyes on the far wall. She slipped her arms through the sleeves. It was a sensual delight: smooth, sleek silk in a dark violet color, covered with arabesques and wild curls of Indian leaves. "This is so beautiful," she said, tying the sash. "Have you traveled to India?"

"Good lord, no."

"Clothes matter a great deal to you, don't they?"

"Absolutely." He turned around. "You look better in that robe than you do in a gown that doesn't fit you."

"My gown does fit me," she said with dignity. "With the corset."

He handed her glass of champagne back. "Now. You sit down and I'll give you a lesson in how to walk."

"So as to make a man slaver," she prompted, sinking into a chair. It felt wonderful to be out of the corset. She crossed her legs and relished the sensation of being able to curve her back. The champagne slipped down her throat in a now familiar rush of apple bubbles. A queer rush of affection bubbled with it, for this exquisite dandy of a gentleman who was taking such time to show her how to succeed on the marriage market.

"Precisely." Mayne reached down and grabbed her discarded dress. He gave it a speculative shake.

"What on earth are you doing?" she asked. He was wrenching off his coat. "Why are you undressing?" She might have been naive, but even she could tell that this was no scene of seduction, in which he managed to take off her clothes under a ruse, only to strip himself naked.

"I think I could show you best if I put the dress on," he said, frowning in an adorable fashion. "Thank goodness, it has short sleeves. I'm afraid my arms are unfashionably burly from working with horses."

And before she could say anything, he stripped off his shirt as well. He wasn't even looking at her, so Josie just sat, transfixed. He would never be able to put her dress on, any more than she could. He was all smooth, sharp-cut muscle, beautifully defined. She thought men had mats of hair on their chest; she'd seen hair curling from the shirts of men working in her father's stables. But Mayne was smooth, smooth except for the muscles standing out under his skin.

Now he looked utterly unfamiliar. The sleek, exquisitely groomed Mayne, in the moonlight filtering through those small overhead windows, looked wild, like Bacchus, the god of wine. He would be perfectly at home in a shadowy wood, vines wound in that mop of curls, a sleek mat of hair beginning at his waist.

Without noticing, Josie had frozen in her chair, not making a sound, as if a wild animal stalked her chamber without seeing her. She felt a blend of attraction and fear, of amazement and shock.

A second later the attraction turned to helpless laughter.

Mayne picked up her pink dress and in one swift movement ripped it down the back. Then, before she could utter a protest—one of Madame Badeau's special creations! Made of the finest silk, with an overskirt of rose gauze and trimmed everywhere in tiny white glass beads!—he pulled the sleeves briskly up his arms. She could hear a faint ripping sound, but really, did it matter at this point?

"Now," he said, stopping to have a swallow of wine. "Here I am."

"There you are," she said, laughing helplessly. His muscled arms stuck out of her little pink cap sleeves with all the incongruity of a tiger wearing an apron.

"Pay attention," he said severely. "As I said, here I am. Miss Lucy Debutante."

Josie leaped to her feet and dropped into a curtsy. "What a pleasure to meet you, Miss Lucy." She couldn't help noticing how much easier it was to curtsy when you were wearing a dressing gown, and had no corset to poke you in the back of the legs.

Mayne dropped a very credible curtsy as well. Then he strode to the side of the room. "All right," he said. "Now watch me carefully. Lucy is young and unknowing, but she's been a *coquette* from birth. That means that she instinctively knows that men wish to see a woman's hips sway when she walks. Do you understand?"

"No," Josie said. "My governess, Miss Flecknoe, taught me to walk with a book on my head." She put on Miss Flecknoe's mincing voice. "Ladies must walk upright, without unnecessary wiggling of the torso."

"Miss Flecknoe is an idiot," Mayne said. "Wiggling is precisely what you do, in a refined manner, you understand." He put a hand on his pink-clothed hip and began to walk across the room toward her. Somehow, like magic, his walk took on the sleek stroll of a female predator, a woman so confident of her appeal that her hips swayed like a ship encountering a swell of water.

He turned around and giggles burst from her mouth. Of course her poor dress came nowhere near meeting in the back. In between the gaping seams was a broad expanse of smooth skin.

"Stop chortling, witch," he said over his shoulder. "It's your turn."

"My turn?"

Somehow Josie found herself next to him. "Let your hips sway," he said. "You have lovely hips; I could see them even when you turned yourself into a sausage."

"I don't—" Josie said, but weakly. Perhaps the corset would have to go.

She walked beside him, across the room, but it didn't work. She didn't feel like a *coquette,* for all she put a hand on her hips and swayed. She was trying not to think about how wide her hips would look, going back and forth like that. And then she realized that what she'd really like would be Mayne's body in a female form, because his hips were absolutely flat and of course that was why he looked so sensual when he pretended to be a woman.

He stopped short with a little exclamation. "You're not giving this your attention, Josie!"

"I am," she protested. "I really am. I'll try again." And she ran back to the wall and, under his gaze, walked toward him, trying to waddle from side to side. Because that's how she felt about it: as if she were waddling. If waddling would make men slaver, or even ask her for a dance that hadn't been arranged by one of her sisters, she was eager to do it.

Mayne's eyes narrowed and she could read failure there.

"Maybe I simply . . ." her voice trailed away.

"You're not *feeling* it. Have you ever kissed anyone, Josie?"

"Of course I have!" And then she realized what he meant. "You mean, kiss a boy?"

"I was thinking more along the lines of kissing a man," he answered, amused.

She shook her head. Who would want to kiss her? Was he blind? He must have read that in her face.

"There's the problem. You don't have any sense of yourself because you—you don't have any sense of yourself. Have you—" But he checked himself. Whatever that question was, it clearly couldn't be asked, even under the influence of far too much champagne and moonlight.

Then he was there, in front of her. He was wearing a pink dress with cap sleeves. The glass beads painstakingly sewn on by Madame Badeau's seamstresses glittered in the moonlight. He should have looked absurd, but instead, Josie felt as if Bacchus himself had indeed wandered into this strange little turret room and was there, with a deep wild invitation in his eyes.

Although what he was saying didn't sound inviting.

"I'm going to kiss you," he said briskly. "Someone has to do it the first time, and it might as well be me because I'm very good at it. But Josie—" He caught her around the shoulders.

"Yes?" She knew her eyes were round.

"I'm in love with Sylvie, you know that."

She scowled at him. "I take it you think I might fall in love with you because of a kiss."

His smile was crooked.

"Don't worry. Since we are being frank, I shall tell you that I have no intention of falling in love with anyone who is as old as you are." His smile disappeared. "My sisters have done nothing but throw men of your age at me since the season began, and while it was most kind of them to dance with me, I . . ."

Her voice trailed off. He actually looked a little hurt, but perhaps that was just her imagination, because he said easily, "You want to marry someone your own age, which is absolutely appropriate. Although I would recommend that you look for someone who has actually reached their majority."

"I have a list," she told him.

He grinned at that. "What's on your list?"

"I shan't tell you all of it, as it's private. But I did decide that twenty-five was quite old enough, after Imogen pointed out that Rafe fit nearly every item I had written down."

"Someday, I would love to see that list," he said, his eyes gleaming with amusement. "But now the night grows toward dawn and your sisters will be wondering where I've taken you."

Josie shrugged. Her skin was prickling all over and she was acutely aware that the two of them were alone, both half-clothed. "Imogen has presumably left with Rafe on their wedding trip," she said. "Tess has gone home with Felton, and Annabel had already left the ball when I encountered you. She has a new baby and she misses him after a mere half hour, or so she says."

"Motherhood takes some women like that," he said. "Like an illness."

He took a step closer and tipped up her chin. "You have beautiful skin, Josie, did you know that?"

"It's my best feature," she muttered, mesmerized by his eyes. They were looking at her in such a way, as if . . . as if . . .

His hand cupped the back of her neck and fingers curled into her hair. "Your hair is beautiful too."

"Brown," she said, trying to break the spell of his liquid voice.

"Bronzed in the sunlight," he corrected her. "There was one afternoon on the way to Scotland when you sat in the carriage window and the sun played with your hair for hours: it was all bronzed deep tones, bewitching and soft."

Josie knew she would never feel the same about her hair.

Then he bent closer. This is it, Josie thought. She knew what to expect, of course. She'd seen Lucius Felton brush kisses onto Tess's mouth. She'd seen the Earl of Ardmore drop kisses onto Annabel's hair, and her shoulder, and wherever the poor deluded man could drop a kiss. She'd even come around the corner of the corridor once and seen Imogen in Rafe's arms, and he was kissing her, and their bodies were touching.

But it wasn't at all what she thought.

Mayne's mouth didn't brush her adoringly, the way Felton's had Tess. Instead his mouth came down on her like a crushing weight, hard and demanding. She had no idea what was being demanded, and had to stop herself from struggling. No wonder Mayne's affairs lasted only two weeks, she thought dimly. The man doesn't know how to kiss!

He was probably as bad at the whole of bedding as he was at this.

But it would never do to make him feel bad, not when he'd been so kind as to try to—whatever it was he was trying to do. Give her her first kiss so that she could walk better, and if that wasn't a stupid notion, she'd never heard one.

The hand he had in her hair did feel rather nice, as if he was coaxing her to do something, to do what? His tongue too . . . he was running his tongue along her lips. A strange thing to do. Josie filed it away in her mind as yet another substantial reason why the Earl of Mayne had remained unmarried until the ancient age of thirty-five.

And then suddenly it all changed.

How or why, Josie didn't know.

All of a sudden, she could smell him. He smelled wonderful, a spicy male soapy smell. She looked up at him and his eyes were heavy, and suddenly she could feel his thumb rubbing against her neck, and it all felt very queer. As if—As if she'd just taken off her corset.

"That's my girl," he said against her mouth. His voice was dark as the room, dark as a wine god's own purr. She opened her lips to answer him. And that was the biggest surprise of all. Because in one smooth movement he pulled her up and against his body, and at the same moment his tongue came into her mouth.

She went rigid with surprise. It wasn't clean. It wasn't hygienic. Surely it wasn't—

But she lost the thought in a haze of sensual feelings, because somehow her arms were around his neck and curled in his hair. And those breasts that she so despised were pressed against his chest and it felt exquisite, like torture and pleasure at once. And he was in her mouth, speaking to her without words, his hands holding her tight so that she couldn't move back. Except she didn't want to. All she wanted was to be crushed against his big, solid body, feeling small and sensual, and all the things she never felt.

Which was exactly what he meant her to feel.

As if the thought and the truth of it came in the same moment, a pulse of liquid flame swept over her body, weakening her knees, making her feel as if she couldn't stand without him. He was driving into her mouth, fierce, demanding strokes, and she knew why women wept when he left them.

As if he could read her thoughts, he pulled back and stared at her. His eyes had darkened, or perhaps the room had darkened. They didn't look blue anymore but black, and for a second she thought she heard the breath rasp in his chest.

"Well," he said finally. "Josephine Essex, that was your first kiss."

She opened her mouth, but nothing came out. She just stared at him, arms around his neck, her mind a dark, muddled place of desire—aye, she was not so stupid as to not recognize it. Then she took her arms down, and fought to regain her mind as well.

There was something odd in his eyes. "Was it acceptable?" That growling purr was gone from his voice now.

"Absolutely," she said, her hands trembling as they tightened the knot of his dressing gown at her waist. "Will"—she cleared her throat—"Will I be able to walk correctly now?"

"I hope so, Josie." He said it almost as if it were a prayer. "I-I believe so."

She managed a little smile at that. "You have a lot of faith in your powers of seduction, Lord Mayne. I suppose it comes from years of practice."

"One is always capable of being surprised," he said, rather obscurely. And then backed away. "Let's see if I've made an ass of myself, shall we?"

So she turned away from him and walked to the opposite wall. He hadn't made an ass of himself. She could feel it in every movement of her legs, in the brush of her breasts against his dressing gown. When she turned around to walk to him, she was ready.

She stopped for a moment, in the pleasure of performance. Smiled at him, at the beauty of his eyes, and the way his hair, even now, looked as if it had come from the hands of a master. He looked a bit pole-axed, so she smiled again.

These smiles were a world away from the grimaces she'd used as masks in the last weeks of the season. She could feel the plumpness of her bottom lip, the smile in her eyes, as if she were seeing herself from the outside.

And then she started to walk toward him. Plump full hips curved naturally, beautifully, to a waist marked by a man's silk sash. Her breasts swelled above, and for the first time in her life she knew that they were right for her body: balancing her hips, carrying themselves proudly, beautiful in their generosity.

"Not quite," he said. "Watch me again."

She thought she saw what he meant this time. Even in the absurdity of that muscled body, and the frail pink gown, she could see that he was slightly rolling from the hips. Rather than walking the way she normally did, by putting one leg briskly in front of the other, Mayne was swaying forward. There was a swing in his gait, a promise, a ridiculous promise given the bursting fabric—but she saw what he meant.

He was on the other side of the little turret room. "Again," he commanded.

She walked toward him slowly, listening to her body, walking almost on tiptoes because it felt right and because her legs were still trembling a little from the kiss. She walked to just before him, and paused.

"Garret," she said. And raised an eyebrow.

"I think—you have mastered the art," he said. His voice was strangled, dark, and she loved that.

So she tightened the cord around her waist even tighter, and sure enough, his eyes dropped to her breasts.

"Josie!" he said sharply.

She grinned at him. "You *did* say that men would slaver at my feet, didn't you?"

"Not old men like myself," he said, with a reluctant bark of laughter.

"I believe I shall stop being doctrinaire about age. Look how much I have learned from you."

"Nothing that you couldn't have seen in the eyes of men of any age," he said. His voice had that low rumble again.

She smiled at him, a little crooked smile. "We'll see whether I'm able to bamboozle these men with my new walk."

"And no corset."

"No corset," she said, sighing.

"None of which has anything to do with the beauty of your face," he said, turning up her chin with his hand.

"It's too full," she whispered.

He rubbed a slow thumb down her cheek. "Not all women were designed to be angular. Your cheek has the slightly sulky, round beauty of a Madonna."

"Annabel said that too," she said, feeling a little breathless.

"Your eyelashes are sinfully thick," he went on. "And your mouth—" He stopped. "I'll leave your mouth to the tremulous twenty-year-olds whom you desire so much."

Josie digested this while looking at him. Of course he'd swept through the *ton* like fire through straw. Thinking of the discontented, skittish faces of most of the matrons whom she'd met in the endless round of debutante balls comprising the season, she would have been surprised if there was one among them who didn't fall on her back at his approach. It gave her a peculiar sinking feeling, as if she were in danger of committing some sort of folly that she hadn't thought possible.

"Garret," she whispered.

His straight black brows snapped together and he dropped her chin. "Better not call me that in public, little witch," he said, turning away. She watched him quickly pulling the pink dress forward. His skin was brown and the curved muscled shape of it made her feel queer. In danger. So she flashed back: "I hope you're not afraid that people will think I'm hankering after you?"

He pulled on his shirt, and to her faint—but quite obvious—pulse of disappointment, a flutter of elegant white linen fell to his waist.

"God no," he said, turning and giving her a wry smile. "I'm afraid they'll think I'm hankering after *you*."

Josie's heart beat loudly in her ears. "Well, that would never happen." His jawline was just faintly shadowed with beard. He looked like a black-browed pirate, although even as she watched, he tamed the shirt, cramming it into the waist of his trousers.

"Don't watch me," he muttered to her, pushing the shirt down so it didn't leave a bulge in his knit pantaloons.

I'd like to do that, Josie thought to herself. But she was sure the thought didn't show in her eyes. "It's interesting," she told him. "Who knew that it was so hard to control a shirt?" He wrenched on a jacket. It sat perfectly across his shoulders, turning him in an instant from a bold, derisive pirate to a sleek earl whose midnight blue jacket echoed his insolent blue eyes. Suddenly, instead of radiating a dangerous sensuality, he looked like an assured member of the world's greatest aristocracy.

Josie sighed. It was a painful transition to watch, the more so because of her vivid knowledge of all the women who had seen Mayne turn from private to public, from hers to no one's, and that in the turn of a coat.

"Well," he said, "I'd better sneak you back into your house. Shouldn't be too difficult."

Not for someone with his experience sneaking in and out of houses, Josie thought. But she kept it to herself.

Her hair was down her shoulders and tumbling down her neck. She bent to pick up the corset, but he laughed and snatched it away, tossing it against the wall. "You're not wearing that again. You go out tomorrow and buy yourself gowns that celebrate the body God gave you, rather than shaping you into a different one, do you hear?"

Even pale with exhaustion and champagne, hair tousled, jaw shadowed, he was the most beautiful thing she'd ever seen. "I will," she said, filing the memory away. She walked past him.

"Go to that *modiste* Griselda uses," he said, catching her hand.

She looked up at him inquiringly. "Don't call you Garret. Don't use my corset. Do use Griselda's *modiste*. Do walk as if I were a man in skirts. Do consider men over thirty, but allow the younger ones to slaver at will."

Mayne stood looking at her, feeling as if he'd been knocked off balance. Josie was so beautiful, with that cloud of witchy hair around her shoulders, her beautiful curved, laughing mouth and her intelligent eyes. "Christ, you're breathtaking," he said.

He could see in her eyes that she didn't believe him. There was no question, though, that a decent gown would take care of that. If she would only prance into a ballroom wearing his dressing gown, the male part of the room would fall to their knees. He kept having to make himself stop looking at the way her breasts swelled seductively under the heavy silk.

"Will you be coming to the Mucklowe ball at the end of the week?" she asked him.

What was there about Josie that made a lump rise in his throat every time she looked anxious? "Mucking around with the Mucklowes," he said, putting a hand on her back to lead her down the stairs. "I suppose I'll be there, if Sylvie wishes to go. She has eclectic tastes when it comes to the *ton*."

Josie reached the bottom of the stairs and waited for him. "It would be wonderful if you could be there."

"If you want me to, I'll be there."

Her face eased into a smile. Those crimson lips of hers were dangerous. And he was a man in love with another woman.

"Sylvie and I wouldn't miss it," he assured her. And then took her back to her house. It was amazing how easy it was to return her to her room without being seen.

All those *affaires* of his had taught him something, he thought as he wandered back down the street toward his house, having sent his carriage trundling off before him. There was a thick fog settling as dawn came up, and he felt like walking. The trees looked blurred and furry, as the fog drifted in, until he found himself moving along in a small room walled by cloud.

It was a remarkably lonely feeling, as if he carried a small patch of ground with him, and all the rest of the world was unpeopled.

10

From The Earl of Hellgate, Chapter the Sixth

I told her that I would like to pass all my Nights with her, and she responded that she had only Days to give. I taxed her with being ungrateful to never have lent me a single one of her nights, but wasted them in the solitude of her bedchamber. She said . . .

G riselda took the news that Josie intended to visit her *modiste* that very morning and order an entirely new suite of clothing extremely cheerfully, although she had to miss a promise to ride in Hyde Park. Josie noticed that she was extremely vague about who she had promised to meet.

"I'd much rather come with you," she said. "You know I've loathed that corset contraption that Madame Badeau fashioned for you. Yes, the corset forced you into gowns that were approximately the same measurements as Imogen. But neither one of us, darling, has Imogen's body. And frankly, although I have never said so quite so openly, I believe that the two of us are blessed."

"How can you say that?" Josie asked, more amused than anything else. This morning she seemed to have a new acceptance of her figure. It wasn't perfect, but it no longer felt repulsive.

Griselda was wearing a fetching morning gown of light lawn scattered with posies. It came a little short, in the French style, and showed an enticing pair of slippers. She looked beautiful.

But of course, Josie reminded herself, Griselda's figure wasn't as plumpy as her own. There was nothing stout about Griselda. She was—

"You and I have precisely the same figure," Griselda was saying. "And Josie, as I have told you from the moment you entered this house, our figure is one adored by men."

"So much so that they've called me everything from a piglet to a sausage," Josie pointed out.

"Crogan was an unpleasant fool, forced into courting you by his brother. And I do believe that Darlington was responding more to your corset than to your figure. You *had* no figure with that corset."

Josie was starting to think the same herself. "Do you think it's too late?" she said, her voice growing rather thin as she said it.

"Absolutely not."

"Wait a moment!" Josie said. "What happened with you and Darlington? Last night?"

A smug little smile danced on Griselda's lips.

"You did it," Josie breathed. "You seduced him!"

"Well, not in the strictest meaning of the word," Griselda said, a frown creasing her brow. "I certainly hope that you didn't form the opinion that I am in any way *easy*, Josie. That was a most improper conversation. I'm afraid that Sylvie is French, you know."

"I know that."

"The French like nothing better than to talk of naughty subjects," and that was obviously all Griselda was going to say of it, because she was gathering her reticule and her shawl. "We must go now. Madame Rocque grows more sought after every season. We shall have to pay her at least double to give you a gown on the spot. But I ordered an evening gown from her three weeks ago. If she has it ready, she can simply adjust it for you."

"I'll never fit into your gown," Josie protested.

"Of course you will. Oh, you're a little slimmer in the waist," Griselda said, "though who could tell when you were all sewed up in that corset?"

"I'm not—" Josie said, but found herself talking to the wind.

Madame Rocque's establishment was at number 112, Bond Street. Josie had never seen anything quite like it. The antechamber was made up with all the intimacy of a lady's boudoir. Everything, from the silk-covered walls to the delicate chairs, was buttercup yellow. A dressing table hung with yellow silk stood to one side, and laid reverently over a chair was an exquisite gown, the kind Josie would never dare to wear. It had no seams, and Madame Badeau had said that seams were essential for someone like her.

She wandered over to gaze at the gown. It was just a swath of ruby-colored net, sewn with the smallest glittering beads that Josie had ever seen. It looked outrageously expensive, and supremely comfortable. Why shouldn't it be? The bodice was nothing more than a wide vee that appeared to plunge to the waist.

"You would be splendid in that gown," Griselda said, appearing at her shoulder. "Isn't it wonderful the way Madame has a few gowns made up so that one can actually see them? I personally find looking at a costume far more inspiring than choosing one from an illustration."

"Do you mean that she had the gown made up solely so that we could see it?" Josie asked.

"Likely she has a regular customer to whom she offers a lower price if they allow their garment to be viewed for a time before delivery," Griselda said. "I do believe that I shall try on that costume. Unfortunately, it is not appropriate for a debutante."

"*You* will?" Josie asked, fascinated. Griselda wore gowns that enhanced her lush figure. But in the years she'd known her, Josie had never seen Griselda put on a gown that was transparently seductive.

Madame Rocque swept into the room like an admiral's ship leading a small flotilla of clucking attendants. "Ah, my dearest Lady Griselda," she cried, dropping into a deep curtsy.

"Madame Rocque," Griselda said, returning the courtesy.

Seeing that, Josie sank into a curtsy worthy of a queen. Madame Rocque's sharp black eyes darted around her body. "Ah!" she said with a sharp intake of breath.

Josie braced herself. Now Madame Rocque would start talking of seams and corsets.

"Finally, I have a young lady whom I can make look more like a woman and less like an insipid fairy," Madame Rocque crooned. "Although, she is a very young lady."

"Her first season," Griselda said. "And I'm afraid it has not started on a salutary note, Madame. Thus, we turn to you."

"You should have come to me immediately," Madame said severely. She clapped her hands and sent several of her attendants running off in all directions.

Then she led Griselda and Josie into a smaller room that had the same sense of being a gentlewoman's private boudoir. "May I bring you a glass of champagne?" she asked. "Sometimes, to make a change of this nature, some Dutch courage is helpful."

Josie was wearing one of her gowns from last year, since none of Madame Badeau's seamed constructions fit without the corset. And she had left the corset in Mayne's turret. Suddenly she realized that both women were looking inquiringly at her, and Madame Rocque was holding out a glass of something that looked like champagne. "Oh no," she said hastily. "I couldn't possibly. I would be most grateful for a cup of tea, Madame, if it wouldn't be too much trouble."

Madame nodded to one of the girls who trotted away. Then she began prowling around Josie, around and around, running a line down the center of her back, touching her shoulders, her neck. "Miss Essex," she said after a moment, "I must see you in your chemise, if you please. No gown."

Josie was resigned. Madame Badeau had also examined her figure in a chemise only. Whatever Madame Rocquet said, it couldn't be worse than the clucks and cries of the distressed Madame Badeau on seeing her uncorseted. A moment later she stood before Madame Rocquet, clothed only in a chemise of the finest lawn. Every line of her body was visible, Josie knew, although with practiced ease she avoided glancing into the three-way glass to one side of the room.

Madame Rocquet prowled around and around, not saying a word. Then suddenly she started speaking to Griselda. "Deep colors would be best, of course, but in the first year . . . no."

"I thought the same thing," Griselda said, sipping a glass of champagne while she sat in one of the comfortable chairs to the side. "That crimson gown in the antechamber would be lovely."

"Too bold, too sophisticated," Madame Rocquet muttered, touching Josie again on both shoulders. She seemed to be measuring her without a tape, rattling numbers to a girl who stood ready to jot them down. "Now for you, Lady Griselda, that dress would be exquisite. But I have made no fortune selling you sophisticated clothing either. For you, the costume of a chaperone, albeit, since I make them, one of the most exquisitely gowned chaperones in London."

"I have been a chaperone for the past few years," Griselda said, "but as it happens, I did think that gown might suit me, Madame."

Madame looked over and met Griselda's eyes. A small, knowing smile curled her mouth. "Indeed?" she said, returning to those quick, brief touches by which she was measuring Josie. "I am most happy to hear that. Now this young lady cannot wear crimson, but I think we might choose violet. Violet and periwinkle. No pink, no white."

"White makes me look like a bleached elephant," Josie said. Of course, she had bought a number of white gowns from Madame Badeau, but they were for wearing with the corset.

"Nothing I design will make you appear to be a circus animal," Madame said. "I do not think white for you, because your skin is of a lovely sort, the cream of the dairy, this. We accent it, we do not kill it. Now . . ." and she fired out a rapid list of instructions to one of the girls. "I have a gown that we might try. When would you like to appear as your new self?"

"The Mucklowe ball," Josie said before Griselda could open her mouth. "Would that be possible, Madame? It's the end of this week."

"I shall manage, I shall manage," Madame muttered. "I shall create something exquisite."

"I want to look slender," Josie said, feeling a wave of bravery.

"Poor Josephine has had a difficult time this season," Griselda said to Madame.

Madame stopped in her flutter of measurements. "Not—the Scottish Sausage?"

Josie swallowed. It seemed that everyone in the world knew.

"There was a mention of it in a gossip column," Madame said, "but no description. I promise you that once you appear in one of my creations, no one will ever think of sausages again in your presence. You do not wish to appear slender, Miss Essex. No indeed."

Josie chewed her lip. This was just what Annabel, and Griselda, and finally, Mayne, had told her.

"You want," Madame said, pausing impressively, "to appear *seductive,* not like a dried-up little stick from a tree!"

Griselda was nodding and clapping.

Then Madame's attendant came in with a gown and she snatched it up. "For you," she said to Josie, "I would make this up in a deep blue-violet. Just young enough, the color, to pass for debutante, and yet not so insipid."

Josie stared at the gown. It was made of soft gathered swaths of silk, so slight they looked almost like net. They came across both shoulders and then crossed under the breasts. "You see," Madame said, whipping the gown around, "in the back this darker color becomes long sashes that fall almost to your feet."

"I can imagine it in a tawny yellow color," Griselda said.

"Perhaps," Madame said. She threw the gown over Josie's head. "This is only a sample that I made up for my own satisfaction. I prefer to work with cloth rather than on paper, if you understand."

The gown seemed to fit. It felt sinuously comfortable, luxurious and sensual.

"You must look," Griselda said, smiling at her from the side of the room.

Josie swallowed, turned, and looked in the large glass to the side of the room.

"Yellow is not what I would choose," Madame was saying. Clearly there was no going against her opinion, even in the smallest details. "As I said before, I—"

But Josie wasn't listening. The glass showed a young woman whose rounded body breathed sensuality, whose hips and breasts were in perfect proportion—and both looked as if they were made to be fondled.

"They'll be at your feet," Griselda observed.

"You were right," Josie said in a stifled voice. "You were right all along, and I didn't listen to you."

"You were infatuated by that corset," Griselda said rather smugly. "Now, Madame, we need at least four evening gowns, and of course an assortment of morning and promenade gowns. Have you other gowns to show us, or perhaps sketches of those that aren't made up?"

11

From The Earl of Hellgate, Chapter the Eighth

And so began, Dear Reader, a new period in my misbegotten life. It was the first time that I had entangled with an actress; I shall protect her name by calling her Titania, after the immortal Shakespeare's creation. She was truly a queen of love; and she expressed herself in prose as well as kisses. One letter that I will always treasure was sent to me after, dare I say it, we spent an entirety of three days and nights without leaving our bed . . .

Lord Charles Darlington went to Hyde Park driving the little phaeton that his father had given him for his birthday.

"If you'd gone into the Church as I told you to," his father had said, his jaw working furiously, "the Church would have taken care of you."

Charles had snorted. "Just think how much fun I would have had, riding in all those funeral processions for free."

"You'll be the death of me." Since that was usually the end of any given conversation with his father, Charles had turned to leave, but his father had one parting shot. "For God's sake, get yourself a wife and stop infuriating every person who matters."

Driving up and down the paths in Hyde Park, and around and around the great walk looking for an exquisite little cream-pot of a widow who wouldn't consider marrying him wasn't the way to find a wife. But it did give him time to realize just how many young girls first blushed when he glanced at them and then shot panic-stricken looks at their mothers.

It was becoming bitterly clear to him that he'd turned into a toothy bastard when he wasn't looking. It would have been nice to blame it on bad company. He caught sight of Thurman waving furiously at him from a racing vehicle twice, but both times he cut sharply in the opposite direction. But the truth was that he'd done it himself, out of the bottomless pool of anger and venom he seemed to carry around with him.

And if that wasn't a precise confirmation of his father's many summings up of his character, he didn't know what was. He'd taken all his rage and directed it against young girls whose only fault was to be born to a wool merchant or eat a few more Scottish pasties than the rest.

At least, he thought to himself, self-loathing is a break from making cynical, supposedly witty remarks.

Lady Griselda was nowhere to be found. Obviously, she didn't mean it when she said she would see him in Hyde Park. In fact, now that he thought about it, it was obvious that Lady Griselda—who was, after all, Miss Essex's chaperone—had only flirted with him so he would stop calling Miss Essex such unpleasant names.

Why he didn't see that last night, he didn't know. But somehow it hurt more than it should have after a ten-minute banter. He drove home in a furious mood and dashed off a note to Lady Griselda Willoughby. He used stationery that was as luscious and expensive as she was.

She used him; he'd use her. He'd threaten her.

I feel my newfound ethics slipping away. Encourage me tomorrow evening.

He paused. If he were truly daring, he would simply fix an appointment at a hotel. But she would never come. Never. Of course she wouldn't. A lady of her reputation and stature likely had never entered a hotel. Well, the hell with that.

Ten o'clock at Grillon's Hotel, he wrote, and signed it, *Darling.*

Then he looked at his portfolio and pulled a one hundred pound note from the payment he'd just received from his publisher. If he needed to, he could always join the Church and learn to go on his knees for a living. He'd rather go on his knees before Griselda, he thought.

There was something about her that turned him into a raging bundle of lust. She was all cheerful, delicate femininity. She smelled like clean living and faint perfume, like women who spent their mornings relaxing and their nights dancing. Who never screamed at their children, nor their spouses.

Thank God, Willoughby, whoever he had been, was long gone. She would never sleep with him if her husband had been alive; he knew that with a bone-deep knowledge. She wasn't a woman to play false.

But she might . . . she just might be a woman who would have an *affaire*. Who would be enticed by a mixture of bribery and desire—for she liked him too; he had seen it in her eyes—and might be enticed into something rash.

He sealed the pounds in an envelope and sent over a servant to Grillon's with a request for their very best bedchamber for the following night. To the best of his knowledge, there was nothing happening except a soirée given by the Smalepeeces, which couldn't be anything other than tedious, and Mrs. Bedingfield's musical evening. Griselda would never go to that, if only because she was chaperoning Miss Essex. No one would go to a musical evening unless they attended in the mad hope that a single gentleman would accidentally find his way there. Lady Griselda was far too experienced in the ways of the *ton* to consider the possibility.

Darlington was not the only man riding in Hyde Park that day who wished for acquaintances who didn't appear. Harry Grone had grown old, somehow. These days he liked nothing better than to warm his toes at his fireplace and think about the glory days. But here he was, trundling around the park, gaping at the sparks and dandies.

Because out of the clear blue sky, the glory days were back. They *needed* him. *The Tatler,* them as had pensioned him off and said they weren't doing his sort of journalism any longer. But now, out of the blue, they needed his sort of expertise.

The job came with a nice budget, so Grone had decided to take a carriage into Hyde Park and see what was what. He always called it surveillance in the old days. Now he'd lost his touch, he'd be the first to admit that. He couldn't put a name to many a young man's face he saw.

But it was all in the brains. And his brains told him that it wasn't book-learning that would tell him who Hellgate was. If there were a clue in that book, someone else would have found it. Jessopp, more like. If there was anything known about the *ton* that Jessopp didn't know . . .

No, it was going to take his special brand of journalism.

In the end, he had to ask someone to point out the man he sought. But once Grone found him, he couldn't stop a grin of pure satisfaction. There was a face as foolish as a turnip. Took after his father, you could see that in a moment, from the puce waistcoat to the high-perch racing carriage that was absolutely improper for the park. An idiot. Just what he hoped for.

Grone rapped on the roof of the hackney and directed the

driver to return him to his lodgings. That was enough of a trip for a man of his age. Once home, he got out of the carriage and tossed the driver a coin, biting back a curse as his right knee twinged. Early to bed tonight . . . because tomorrow he was taking out a bag of gold sovereigns and going to start what he did best.

Sweetening the pot.

12

From The Earl of Hellgate, Chapter the Eighth

My Titania sent me this letter written on blush paper, in a delicate purple ink:

Carry me off into the blue skies of your love, roll me in dark clouds, trample me with your thunderstorms . . . but love me, love me.

Sylvie de la Broderie found that races, racehorses, and racetracks were productive of two things only: boredom and dust. She didn't like either. Dust she could tolerate under the right circumstances, although she couldn't bring those circumstances to mind at the moment. A picnic, perhaps. She wasn't very interested in the out-of-doors, but picnics could be quite agreeable. And to tell the truth, she'd had something of a picnic in mind when she agreed to allow Mayne to accompany her to the races.

But Epsom Downs racetrack was a great distance from a charming linen tablecloth spread under a gracious willow tree, perhaps next to the Seine . . . Sylvie stifled a sigh. It was cruel to think that such a beautiful life as she anticipated in Paris had been interrupted. Frenchmen were so much more understanding of one's inclinations than were Englishmen. The English had no imagination. If he had had even a scrap of imagination, her fiancé must have known instantly that the racetrack was no place for her.

Instead, Mayne was briskly pointing out all the benefits of their position. They had seats in a box belonging to his friend, the Duke of Holbrook. Sylvie approved of that; she thought that dukes were good friends to have, and Holbrook had easy ways that spoke of an ancient title. Sylvie was a snob when it came to families: the older the better.

She had that from poor *Maman*. Once again Sylvie thought how pleased she was that *Maman* had been carried away by that terrible cold just before Papa made such a drastic decision as to move them all to England. True, Papa had been absolutely right. She and her sister Marguerite might well have suffered the same fate as so many of their dear friends, crowded into the Bastille—but Sylvie wrenched her mind away from that thought. She could not, she literally could not, contemplate what had happened to all the gay, exquisite people her papa had known. Albeit she had not yet debuted when they lived in Paris, but her *maman* had always discussed the goings-on of society with great freedom, so she felt that she did know them.

When Papa wrenched them away from France and settled Marguerite and her in this rainy cold spot, she had been only ten. Poor little Marguerite was merely a year, and far too young to know what she had lost.

The racetrack was extremely noisy. One had to assume that such things existed in Paris as well, but as far as she remembered, her *maman* had never mentioned such a thing. She could ask her father, but he was at their estate in Southwick, occupied with the dogs. Papa seemed to spend most of his day letting dogs in and out of the house. It was no way for a French aristocrat to behave, particularly one with a houseful of servants.

Sylvie sighed. The only enjoyable thing about the race-course was that English gentlewomen were taking the opportunity to dress themselves with *élégance*. In the box next to hers, Lady Feddrington was wearing a bonnet that looked like nothing so much as an entire meringue, tied up with a ribbon. It wasn't entirely successful, but it had a notable streak of originality about it. And she was waving a fan with a sweet little amber fringe; Sylvie decided that she would quite like to know where it came from. She glanced to her right. Mayne was scowling down at a book they'd given him on entering.

"When does your animal run?" she asked, to be gracious. She had to ask it twice, but he was quite apologetic once she got his attention. That was one thing she liked about her future husband. He was invariably polite.

"I am running two horses," he said, "an elegant little filly named Sharon and the lazy sorrel gelding who just trotted in last."

"Oh dear," Sylvie said, "you should have told me that your horse was running by us, Mayne. I would have paid attention."

"I told you he ran in the fourth race."

Apparently he thought that she was counting these tiresome rounds? Sylvie noticed that Lady Feddrington was wearing diamonds as large as daisies in her ears. Rather gauche, or could one put it down to flare? It was so hard, sometimes, to decide between the two. Certainly Lady Feddrington had an adorable *visage,* with her pouting lips and wide set-apart eyes.

"I might go to the stables and see how my jockey is doing," Mayne said. "It can be quite dispiriting to lose so badly, and I want him to keep his heart up for Sharon's race. Would you like to accompany me?"

"To the barn?"

"If you would be interested."

There was no question of that. Mayne had a great deal to

learn about ladies, obviously. "I shall pay a small visit to Lady Feddrington," Sylvie said, giving him a gently corrective smile. In time, he would learn the appropriate places to invite his wife. An enclosure designed for animals was not one of them.

She stood up and waited while he collected her pelisse, her reticule, and her fan. She carried her parasol herself, as she was determined that not even one ray of sunlight would strike her face.

"Lady Feddrington," she said, as Mayne opened the small door between their boxes, "I trust I do not intrude. We met two nights ago at the Mountjoy fete."

"Miss Broderie," Lady Feddrington said with just the right amount of appreciation to soothe Sylvie's slightly disturbed spirits, "I am enchanted to see you. Please do come and relieve the tedium of this afternoon."

That was precisely the right thing to have said in front of Mayne; it meant that she did not have to point out the same herself. So Mayne took himself off, and Sylvie plumped down next to Lady Feddrington. Within a few minutes they were bosom friends, speaking on the intimate level that Sylvie most enjoyed and which she constantly strove to achieve. In fact, Lady Feddrington—or Lucy, as it turned out—was such good company that Sylvie quite forgot that she was in such an objectionable place as the racetrack.

"I feel just the same," Lucy confided sometime later. "Of course, I do my best to support Feddrington in moments like these. He has a large stable and works himself into a disagreeable state of anxiety over large races. In fact, I have to insist that he leave me in the box by myself, because I find that I do not enjoy close proximity with a man in a lather of anxiety, if you'll excuse my frankness. But *you* will never suffer as I do, dearest Sylvie. One cannot imagine Mayne in a lather over anything!"

Sylvie agreed. One of her primary reasons for choosing

Mayne had been his impeccable appearance at every moment. He was almost French that way. Well, considering that his mother was French, his elegance must have been inherited from his mother. Although given that his mother had retired to a nunnery, Sylvie found her elegance slightly hard to imagine.

The important thing was that Mayne's attendance at her side had not been all it could be. "He was distraught," she told Lucy. "I prefer an escort who is more attentive. Mayne actually showed a slight surliness when I did not notice that his horse had lost a race."

"They're always like that," Lucy said comfortingly. "I have been married for three years now, and I am, perforce, an expert on the subject. And darling, you will be the same, for I believe that Mayne's stables are even larger than Feddrington's. They grow increasingly agitated in the weeks before a large race, such as the Ascot. Feddrington even wakes up in the middle of the night at times, if you can countenance it."

"You don't!" Sylvie said with horror, before she caught the words back.

Lucy giggled. "Do you mean share a bedchamber?" And, at Sylvie's little nod, "Of course not!"

"You *must* forgive me," Sylvie said, flustered. "It's just that I have many things still to learn about English nobility."

"I feel as if I've known you forever," Lucy said, bending her head closer, "so I shall tell you something truly indiscreet, hmm?"

Sylvie loved indiscretions.

"When Feddrington is nervous and can't sleep in the night, he visits my chambers," Lucy confided.

"He has the temerity to wake you up?" Sylvie said, blinking at her. Her father would never, under any circumstances, have woken her *maman*. *Maman*'s chambers were sacred to her sleep, and even her maid knew better than to enter the room until eleven of the clock, and then only if she carried *une tasse de chocolat*.

"I have yet to break him of the habit," Lucy said, sighing. "I have impressed upon him that my sleep is more important than his horses, but I don't seem to be able to convince him. Men are invariably selfish in these matters, you know. I have found it best for the happiness of the household if I simply acquiesce. Of course, I have made it clear that such things will be tolerated only if the race is truly one of the largest, such as the Ascot."

Sylvie was appalled. She tended to avoid thinking about the issue of marital intimacies; her *maman* had unfortunately passed away before clarifying these things. But Sylvie knew instinctively that this was not an aspect of marriage that would please her. Under no circumstances would she engage in something so distasteful in the middle of the night. Perhaps . . . one evening a month. She had decided that would surely be enough to satisfy Mayne. After all, she had chosen a man with a reputation for finding his own pleasures; while she was rather looking forward to the idea of having *enfants,* she did not consider marriage to be a contract ensuring that she provide all the entertainment.

"Mayne is so in love with you," Lucy said, giggling again. "He must be positively ardent."

"He behaves precisely as he ought." Now she thought about it, Mayne would never be so impolite as to try to wake her at night. Never. Her poor friend Lucy's husband was obviously incommodious and, though it pained her to think it, ill-bred.

"Oh!" Lucy cried. "Here is my dear friend Lady Gemima. I asked her to join me this afternoon."

Coming toward them was a woman wearing an exquisite

promenade gown of periwinkle blue. "She has the most lovely costumes," Lucy sighed. "She's not married, you know, but she's enormously rich so she just does precisely as she pleases." She lowered her voice. Lady Gemima was greeting Mrs. Homily, a red-faced matron who had been trotting up and down in front of the boxes like a terrier smelling a rat. "She was engaged four years ago, but then the gentleman died. I do believe he was a marquis. She put on mourning for a year, and then declared that she would never marry. She is the only daughter of a younger brother of the Duke of Smittleton. He was a colonel in the army, stationed in Canada, and as I understand it, he made a positive fortune in shipping. So of course then he was given his own title. One would think that she would be bad *ton,* unmarried as she is, and raised in Canada. But she's not."

Sylvie could see that for herself. Lady Gemima wasn't precisely beautiful. Her face was a trifle long, and her mouth too coolly intelligent. But her hair was an extraordinary striped, tortoiseshell color, and as she came into the box and curtsied to Sylvie and Lucy, Sylvie saw that her eyes were green and fringed with thick lashes of the same color as her hair. Her clothes were obviously French. Sylvie rose with the sense of having at last met someone who was, as her papa would say of boxers, at her weight.

A few moments later she confirmed that opinion. Lady Gemima was uproariously funny. She no sooner sat down than she had them in stitches, telling them exaggerated tales of the kind of exploits that an unmarried woman obviously shouldn't know about.

"Am I horrifying you?" she asked Sylvie at one point. "I believe you're engaged to the Earl of Mayne, so I thought you were probably unshockable. If not, you soon will be."

"I am," Sylvie said, although it was quite untrue. She was rewarded with one of Lady Gemima's warm smiles.

"I didn't think you were one of those tiresome debutante

types," she said. "Lord, but I'm tired of young women. Men are so much more interesting."

"I don't agree," Lucy said.

"Neither do I," Sylvie said. "I find men of all things tiring and inevitably troublesome. There is nothing more pleasant than spending the afternoon in this way."

"Well, of course, amongst *ourselves*," Gemima said. "But I am bored by endless conversations about reticules. You can't even discuss a petticoat without it being a bit too risqué for someone."

"I heard the funniest thing about petticoats the other day," Lucy said, giggling again. "Lady Woodliffe told me that she ordered all her petticoats in pale gray silk so that they would suit whatever garment she wore. She intends to stay in half-mourning for her darling Percy the rest of her life."

"Ridiculous," Gemima said. "Considering that the man died in the arms of a strumpet, by all accounts. You'd think she'd be wearing pink ruffles." Her lifted eyebrow was so funny that Sylvie kept laughing. "But you do know, don't you, that the oh-so-righteous Lady Woodliffe was seen coming out of Grillon's Hotel last spring?"

"No!" Lucy gasped.

"Indeed. I heard it from Judith Falkender, who's a very reliable source. Of course, she may have been trying to catch her husband in the act."

Sylvie wrinkled her nose. "Why would she bother? And what is this place, Grillon's?"

"Oh, it's the only hotel in London worth visiting," Gemima told her. "All the ambassadors stay there. I stayed there for a fortnight a year ago, just to see if I would like it, but even though I took a whole floor, there really wasn't enough room for all the people it takes to put myself together. You'd like it, Lucy. Are you still interested in all things Egyptian?"

"No," Lucy said. "I stripped the ballroom of all those odd statues and things. Feddrington is quite displeased because they cost so much, but I gave them all to the British Museum and now he's happy because they're going to name a room after him."

"The Room of Feddrington Monstrosities," Gemima said, laughing. "I thought it was a bit much when you had those death gods overlooking the ballroom."

"They added atmosphere," Lucy said, shrugging off her criticism. "And look how well it turned out. The director of the museum almost fainted when I showed him Humpty and Dumpty. That's what I called them," she told Sylvie. "They were great monstrous things, around ten feet tall."

"I'd love to go to Egypt," Gemima said lazily. "I'm thinking of starting to travel, you know."

"Alone?" Sylvie asked.

"Well, since I dislike the idea of taking a husband merely as an umbrella stand," Gemima said, "I expect I shall travel alone. Although to be quite honest, that would be merely a figure of speech."

Lucy laughed. "You don't know Gemima yet, Sylvie. She has the largest household of anyone I know. How many personal maids do you have at the moment, Gemima?"

"Three," Gemima said, "but only because I'm so very difficult. If one poor woman had to deal with me, I'd have to give her a hardship allowance."

They all laughed, and for a moment the pale English sunshine turned the whole racetrack into a delightful place, full of women with brains, temperament, and beauty. "I *am* enjoying England!" Sylvie said, delighted.

Mayne was dodging around crowds of chattering men to return to Sylvie when he caught a glimpse of her laughing in Lady Feddrington's box and sighed with relief. Thank God, that little French face of hers wasn't looking at him with an expression of gentle disappointment. She was laughing harder than he'd ever seen her laugh, so hard that her parasol had actually slipped to the side. Then Lady Gemima turned her head so that Mayne caught her profile, and he saw the reason. Everyone he knew adored Gemina, except for a few carping Puritans. He could leave Sylvie with Lucy Feddrington for at least another half hour.

He turned around and headed back toward the long, low stables where Sharon was waiting for her race. There was something odd about Sharon this morning, something he couldn't quite put his finger on, but that didn't feel right. His jockey had sworn up and down that Sharon was absolutely herself.

"Mayhap a little spooked by the crowds," Billy, his stable-master, had said.

But Mayne wondered. He started plowing back through the crowds, head down, when he heard someone call his name. He looked up and there was his sister, Griselda, and next to her, Josie. She looked none the worse for all that champagne; it must be her youth. He had a distinctly heavy head himself.

"Darling," Griselda said lavishly. She seemed to be in extraordinarily high spirits. "We want to see your horses, of course. We were on the way to the box, but now you can take us to the stables."

Josie was smiling at him without a trace of shyness. Shouldn't she be the least bit shy after last night? Well, why should she?

"I'm not sure you should come to the stables," he told Griselda. "There's so many ruffles on that costume that you might frighten the horses."

"Nonsense," Griselda said, waving her parasol about in a manner guaranteed to strike fear into the heart of a skittish thoroughbred.

Mayne tucked Griselda under one arm and Josie under the other. Josie wasn't wearing the corset. In fact, she was showing a rather delectable figure, although her costume was rather oddly designed, with seams leading here and there that hardly accentuated her better features.

She looked up at him and said something he couldn't hear, so he bent his head to her.

"We went to Griselda's *modiste* this morning," she whispered in his ear.

"I trust that you bankrupted Rafe," he said back, loving the way her eyes were shining with excitement.

"I expect so," she said impishly. "We didn't inquire into such pedestrian details."

He gave a mock groan. "It's a good thing he's on his wedding trip. You could—" But he bit it back. What on earth was he thinking, about to suggest that she charge her clothing to him?

She looked up at him, eyebrow raised, but now they were in front of Sharon's box. The filly looked very small for such a large box.

Griselda was perfectly happy to peep over the top, and made clucking noises at Sharon, rather as if the filly were a kitten who might be coaxed into purring. Sharon ignored her. But Josie opened the box and went straight in.

"*Don't* mess your slippers," Griselda cried. "You know that animal likely—" She waved her parasol to illustrate her point.

Billy gave a snort that expressed precisely what he thought about a lady who didn't know that he cleaned the stall the moment one of his horses did something of that nature. Josie ignored her, going to Sharon's side. She was saying something to Sharon in that dark little voice she had, and of course Sharon started arching her nose into Josie's arm and making little snorting noises. Mayne leaned against the wall of the stall, raising his hand when Billy thought to take Sharon's head.

Josie had stripped off her glove and was running her hand

here and there on Sharon's side. Billy moved forward again but Mayne shook his head.

She raised her eyes and looked at him, and Mayne knew. "Feel here," she said quietly. His fingers came after hers, nibbling down Sharon's shining side, just to the left of her backbone. She had been beautifully groomed; Billy must have worked on her for hours.

Josie's fingers stilled and then moved to the side so he could feel. There were hard little nubbins under the skin. They rolled under his fingers. "What the devil is that?" he asked.

"It's not serious," Josie told him. "My father's groom used to call it—" She hesitated.

Billy was there now, his dirty blunt-tipped fingers in the same place, his face dark. "The devil's nuts, that is," he said. "I missed it until this young lady found it. I should throw in my job, I should."

Josie shook her head at him. " 'Tis all I did, as a child. My father's stables were very large, and he put me in charge of minding the horses' health from the time I was twelve."

"What do we do for these nuts?" Mayne asked. It didn't seem to bother Sharon terribly when he touched them. A tiny ripple crossed her skin, as if a breeze passed over the shining surface of a lake.

"She can't race with it—" Josie began, but Billy interrupted her.

"You knew it too, me lord. You axed me just an hour ago was Sharon all that she could be, and I said yes. And she's not, is she?"

"You'll want to check the other horses," Josie said. "It can spread through a stable like wildfire." She nodded toward the horse blanket hanging to the side. It was a splendid throw, embroidered with the earl's crescent and the words COEUR VAILLANT.

"It's spread through blankets?" Mayne asked.

"You might want to stop embroidering the blankets with your crest and put the horse's name on instead. It stops the spread. But it can jump from horse to horse on a curry brush as well."

Mayne nodded, seeing in his mind's eye the way his gelding loped to the finish line this morning. "Damn it, I should have known about this."

"There's only the five horses of ours in London," Billy was saying to himself. "And this is only a week or two old, because I would have seen that, I would have."

"I'm sure you would have," Josie said soothingly. "It's only because I don't know Sharon at all that I could see she was in a bit of discomfort."

"I am sorry, Garret," his sister said from the aisle outside the box. "You must be very disappointed not to be able to race her."

"Not as disappointed as the punters will be. Sharon's odds were three to one. I'd better escort you back to the boxes; Sylvie will be wondering what became of me. Billy, will you take care of scratching Sharon from the race, please?"

Billy nodded. "I'm that sorry I missed it, yer lordship."

"We both missed it," Mayne said.

Josie gave Sharon a last pat on the nose. "We were never able to come up with anything that takes the nuts away; it seems they simply have to run their course. But I do have a comfrey bath that seems to give some comfort. I'll send you the recipe, Mayne."

Billy closed the gate behind them, thinking that he was a lucky sod to have a master like that, and no one would know from the way Mayne looked that his heart was set on Sharon winning the race. And she would have, if she'd been fit to run.

"I just wanted you to win so much I didn't see them devilish nuts," he muttered to Sharon. "It's the devil's own luck."

"There'll be another race for Sharon," the young lady

said, leaning over the gate and giving Sharon a last scratch. "She's a beauty, and she wants to race, you can tell that. I expect that's why you didn't notice her condition. She's such a game one that she would have run her heart out, whether they vexed her or not."

"Aye, and she would have done that," Billy said, cheering up a little. He watched the young lady as she went. She was hanging onto the master's arm and talking up at him. By the time they turned the corner at the end of the aisle, she had him laughing.

It wasn't every young lady who knew what nuts were, and had a recipe for a horse bath. Of course, men being what they were, the master probably didn't recognize that.

Josie was scandalizing Griselda by telling her how much she missed spending time in the barn.

"A *barn*!" Griselda screetched, clutching Mayne's arm and generally acting as if she might be kicked by a bull at any moment. "I can't imagine why you'd wish to be in a barn."

"They have a peaceful sort of smell," Josie said, "as if nothing bad could happen in the world."

Mayne found himself nodding. "It's harness dressing: grain and axle grease."

"And new rope," Josie said to him. "New rope has a wonderful smell. But mostly it's hay. Well, hay and tired horses."

"You have always spent far too much time in the barn," Griselda told Mayne. "I remember mama being quite worried that you would end up looking like a stable boy." She smiled at Josie. "Our mother was terribly happy when Garret suddenly developed an interest in his clothing."

Mayne thought about the great red barn on his estate, that same barn he'd spent so many hours in as a child. He hadn't spent an afternoon there in two years, likely. He was always in London, and even during the autumn and winter, he went to Rafe's or another friend's estate. His stables, for him, were a matter of buying horses, sending them off to his estate for training, and then having them shipped to the racetrack in question. Not that he didn't visit, because he did so often. But he wasn't part of the life of the barn, the way he had been when he was a boy.

"Time was," he said wryly, "when the black cat couldn't have another set of kittens without my knowing precisely the number."

Josie grinned. "Kittens, pshaw! I knew the number of mice that our little tiger was catching. She always wished to show me their carcasses before she ate them."

Griselda shuddered. "You might keep that detail to yourself, *if* you please."

13

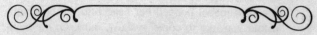

From The Earl of Hellgate, Chapter the Eighth

Dear Reader, you have not forgotten your promise to resist the impulse to identify the names of
the dear women who were kind enough to share
their company with me, have you? There is no
need to tax your memory by investigating beautiful actresses who have played Titania in the
past century . . . I will clasp her name to my bosom until death do us part.

All of us.

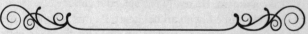

Griselda plucked the note off the salver Brinkley offered her. A smile spread over her face. She discounted
the feeble attempt at bribery immediately. She had read
genuine shame in Darlington's eyes when he promised not
to mock Josie again. But this invitation . . .

It deserved consideration.

She sat down and stared at the rose-colored walls of her
bedchamber. If she did this—this horrendous, delicious,
tempting thing—it would be for the last time. While she had
two small little trysts in the ten years since her husband died,

she had allowed each man precisely one night. But they had been older than she, cheerful bachelors who understood the rules and abided by them. She had remained the best of friends with both gentlemen. But Darlington was *young*. Terrifyingly young.

And she had made up her mind to—

"Grissie!" Annabel popped her head into the bedchamber. "Would you like to come upstairs and keep me company while I see to Samuel? He's due to wake from his nap any moment, and you said you'd like to be there."

"And when did I give you permission to call me by that revolting nickname?" Griselda said with a mock scowl.

"You didn't," Annabel retorted. "But now that I'm a married lady, and you're no longer my chaperone, I'm taking the liberty."

Griselda hopped up, hastily thrusting Darlington's note into her sleeve. "How did Samuel sleep last night?" she asked as they walked to the nursery.

"Like a dream. He really is a splendid child."

Griselda agreed, with all her heart. At this advanced age, she had suddenly been struck by an acute longing for a baby. And she was willing to take a husband to attain one.

So . . . But she shook the thought away because Master Samuel crowed with delight to see them coming.

"Go ahead," Annabel said, laughing. "You pick up the little rascal." He was kicking his chubby knees and smiling with a madcap grin that was designed to make everyone in the vicinity love him . . . and it was manifestly successful.

Griselda scooped him up, never feeling the note slip from her sleeve. She was too busy cuddling Samuel, and tickling him, and generally making it clear to him that she was a very, very important person.

So it wasn't until Samuel began making squawking noises that indicated, in all likelihood, that while he liked her, she wasn't the person who produced milk, that she turned around. And found Annabel seated in a comfortable rocking chair and grinning at her. This was an entirely different kind of grin from that on her son's face.

"Griseldaaaa!" she sang, waving a little slip of paper in her hand.

Griselda plumped Samuel into Annabel's lap and snatched at her note. "Give me that!"

"Grillon's Hotel," Annabel said, laughing aloud. "The place where my reputation died a painful death. Why, if I remember you correctly, no lady ever enters Grillon's Hotel. 'I've never entered such a place!' " she said, imitating Griselda's voice.

"And I never did enter such a place until your sister Imogen constrained me to do so," Griselda said, ripping the note and tossing it into the fireplace.

Annabel pointed commandingly at the seat across from her. "Sit down this minute, you wild widow, and regale me with the tale of who on earth is asking you to Grillon's. Who is Darling—" But the words faltered on her tongue. "It's Darlington!"

Griselda fell into the chair with rather less than her usual grace. "It is indeed."

"But no one meant that you should trade your virtue for cessation of his nasty talk," Annabel said. "Oh, Griselda, you didn't think that was what Sylvie meant when she directed you to seduce him, did you? Because she only meant it in the sense that you should flirt with the man, and entice him into changing his mind."

Griselda had to smile; Annabel looked so horrified. "I know that," she said. "It's just that Darlington . . ."

"He's blackmailing you. The scoundrel!" Annabel's eyes narrowed. "He's not blackmailing just *you,* Griselda, he's blackmailing all of us. That's what he means by his 'morality slipping,' doesn't it? He actually thinks to blackmail you into entering Grillon's Hotel and carrying on an *affaire* with him. Rafe may be away on his wedding trip, but my husband will beat Darlington into smithereens, and Tess's husband will ruin him financially." She looked as if she were about to leap out of the chair, nursing baby or not, and send Darlington to his doom.

"So I gather you think that I shouldn't go to Grillon's?"

Annabel gasped. "You can't possibly be considering it! Absolutely not, Griselda. That's a sacrifice that not one of us would ever wish you to make, including Josie. In fact, it would probably make Josie ill just to hear of this. That horrid, impudent little mushroom of a man."

"But I don't think he's *little*," Griselda said. "He's at least as tall as Rafe."

"I didn't mean—" Annabel snapped. And stopped. "Griselda Willoughby," she said slowly, "you tell me what is happening here."

"Well, you are a married woman," Griselda observed.

"Manifestly so," Annabel said, dropping a kiss on the fuzzy head of her son. "And as such, Griselda?" She paused, eyebrow raised.

Griselda looked down at her ankles rather than meet Annabel's gaze. Her stockings were really quite beautiful. "Don't you think these are exquisite?" she asked, pulling up her skirts a tad and swinging her ankle in the air. The silk was so thin that they gave her legs a golden sheen, like canary wine.

"Griselda," Annabel threatened.

"I'm thinking of having a tryst with the man," Griselda said, watching Annabel carefully under her eyelashes to see if she looked horrified at the thought.

But she didn't. In fact, she just looked fascinated. "It's nothing to do with Josie, then?"

Griselda shook her head. "Darlington promised to say nothing of Josie in the future, and I believe him. He had the air of a man who has finally realized he made himself loathsome."

"Well, why on earth would you wish to have an *affaire* with someone who is loathsome?"

Griselda laughed. "It seems that marriage has left you unaccountably naive, dearest."

"I have never been naive," Annabel said, deftly switching Samuel to her other breast. "I gather that Darlington has some attributes that are . . . enticing?"

Griselda smiled.

"In that case," Annabel said, "I shall entertain Josie while you frolic in Grillon's Hotel."

"I am rather old for him."

"Robbing the cradle?" Annabel said cheerfully. "And why not?"

"He can't be more than twenty-four."

"That's nothing. Look at how many marriages have a twenty-year gap in favor of the man."

"It would be my last such indiscretion," Griselda said.

"I know, darling," Annabel said. "Because you should marry now, and have yourself a little Samuel." Samuel let out a great burp, so she stood up and plopped him into Griselda's arms.

"I suppose . . ." Griselda said.

"You're a born mother. Of course you suppose. Is Darlington a possibility?"

"Certainly not! I just told you that he's less than thirty. One doesn't marry men of that age. One might dance with them—"

"Or meet them in a hotel," Annabel put in. She curled back in the chair, watching as Griselda snuggled a sleepy Samuel.

"I can't go to a hotel," Griselda half whispered, looking appalled.

"Where did you meet your other indiscretions?"

"I was living in my own town house, of course."

"Has chaperoning us put a damper on your personal life?"

"Oh, no! It's been wonderful. Before you girls appeared, and Rafe asked me to chaperone you, my life was . . . quite silly, I'm afraid. It has been eye-opening, to say the least, to see three of you fall in love. And I'm quite sure Josie will find the right person as well."

"Do you have anyone in mind to marry?"

Griselda shook her head. "I fully intend to take the matter seriously in hand, after . . ." Her voice trailed off.

"After one last unmarried indiscretion!" Annabel said, giggling madly.

"Hush! You make me feel like the veriest light-skirt," Griselda said.

"Wait! I think I know who Darlington is! Does he have blond hair and hollowed cheekbones—a rather madly dissolute look? *Griselda*!" Griselda was looking distinctly guilty, so Annabel laughed so hard she almost choked. "You're right. The man is utterly delicious—and completely off-bounds. Just the person to meet in Grillon's Hotel."

14

From The Earl of Hellgate,
Chapter the Fourteenth

By now, Dear Reader, my limbs were yet young, but my sensual appetites were growing tired and old. I began to thirst for something I could find in no place, a tenderer and sweeter emotion than I had known so far. But alas, I was not to find it . . . instead, a young lady whom I shall term Helena . . . have you discovered my foibles yet, Dear Reader? Do you know why I name these ladies as I do?

Eliot Governor Thurman had been having a difficult week. Neither Darlington, Wisley, nor Berwick had appeared at the Convent, though he waited there until two in the morning. In one blow, he'd lost all three of the people he counted his friends.

There'd been others at the Convent whom he had believed to be friends, but when Darlington didn't appear, they gave him their shoulder. By midnight he was well aware that without Darlington's comments, and Berwick's wit, and Wisley's acid little nods, he was worthless. To these supposed friends, he'd been nothing more than an open purse.

With all his heart he hoped that Darlington wouldn't find a wife. Who'd want him? Penniless and sharp-tongued as they come.

He was wandering disconsolately around his rooms, wondering if invitations would stop, once it was clear that he was no longer part of the entourage surrounding Darlington. He couldn't give up the life of the *ton* now. A ball would have no flavor if he was not around Darlington. Part of the most exciting gossip in the room.

He kept drifting from room to room, wondering what to do with himself. It had been miserable at the Convent. He wasn't a man who hungered for silence or private thought. He wanted to roar with laughter, thump the table, and order another round that he would gladly pay for.

Finally he decided that he had to go to Lady Mucklowe's ball on the morrow. Darlington would be there. He couldn't stay at home and have Darlington think that his feelings were hurt. No, he would go to Mucklowe's ball and—he fingered his cravat in the mirror over his mantelpiece—he would go to Mucklowe's ball and he would find the Scottish Sausage.

She was the reason why Darlington had dropped him. She was the reason Darlington had started thinking about morality and didn't want the comfort of the Convent anymore.

He wouldn't do it so as to tell Darlington later either. He'd do it for himself, because he was just as clever as Darlington ever was. In fact, maybe he'd do something really witty, like make the Sausage think that he was courting her. As if he would ever do such a revolting thing. But he could trick her into it with a few compliments. Maybe he'd even kiss her, so that she would look at him with stars in her eyes, thinking that a man of substance had finally decided to court her. And then he'd spurn her. And finally he'd go to the Convent and gather his own group of friends, tell them what he'd done and how funny it was.

He could see her plump cheeks right now, quivering with the pleasure of his kiss.

Perhaps he could find her in Hyde Park, and start his courtship now.

"Cooper!" he howled.

His man came running out of his bedchamber.

"I'm going to the park. Order my carriage; I'll wear the puce waistcoat. With the sage-colored costume."

Cooper opened his mouth but caught his master's eye. Thurman was in no mood to be told what colors did and didn't go together. Darlington dressed with a casual flair and often put together colors that weren't as conservative as Cooper's choices. Now that he, Thurman, was going to be a leader of the *ton*, he must needs develop a style of his own.

It wasn't until Thurman was knotting a cravat with a casual violence that crushed most of the starch that he realized precisely what he meant to do.

He meant to be the new Darlington.

Darlington had retired, suffered a change of heart, turned pansy, weak-kneed, however one wanted to say it.

He, Thurman, hadn't lost his nerve, and he never would. He'd been standing in Darlington's shadow so long that people didn't realize that he could be just as clever, if he wished. That was clear at the Convent last night. They thought no one but Darlington had a witty comment to make.

They were wrong.

Either he'd use the Sausage or he'd find some other thing to be clever about. It was that simple.

15

From The Earl of Hellgate, Chapter the Fourteenth

I know you are literate, you are well-read, you are all that is admirable ... I have endowed each of my all-precious ones by the names of characters in the incomparable Shakespeare's most beloved play ... a work that, like this memoir, is about dreaming and beautiful women ... If the incomparable Bard wrote *A Midsummer Night's Dream,* then I, poor I, am writing of *Midsummer Nights' Affaires* ...

The best suite at Grillon's Hotel had a large bed and a number of charming seating arrangements. There wasn't a hard-backed chair in the place. Darlington wandered about, touching the marble mantel to make sure there was no dust. The hotel was the opposite of the Bedrock estate, where he was raised. Bedrock Manor was made of a pinky-golden stone, and stood on a hill, so that in the summer the grass all around burned brown, and it took on an almost Italian aspect, like a Tuscan house dreaming in the sunshine. It hurt to think about those days, running about in the vale with his two brothers, never knowing that there was nothing for him, that it was all for his brother Michael.

They don't tell you, when you're sprouting, that you're nothing more than a spare in case the eldest doesn't make it. They let you run free around the estate, in and out of stables, up and out of trees that would never belong to you. Because not even one tree would belong to you. They give you only two choices: go into the army and kill people; go into the church and bury them. Well, three choices. You could fix on a way to support yourself that disgraces the family honor, at least from the family point-of-view.

It's my failure that I didn't find a respectable third way, Darlington thought to himself. Instead I sank into a rage that apparently lasted for years. Father would never have considered raising me to a business, and yet no one—but no one—seemed to have noticed that doing nothing leads to no income.

He shook the thought away.

An appropriate third way was obvious, always had been. Prostitution. Marry for money, marry well, marry a dowry.

To kill, to bury, or to screw.

Really, there wasn't any choice about it at all.

She was just late enough so that he thought she wasn't coming, and that the suite was to be wasted. It was after eleven when he heard the discreet knock on his door. He was sprawled in a chair, but he leaped up as a footman ushered in a heavily veiled female form and then left.

His heart bounded, and he walked over to her, laughing. "Is there anyone under these veils?"

"Oh no," came a demurely smiling voice. "There's no one here but I."

"And you are the Ghost of the Lady of Shallot, I suppose," he said, lifting off one veil only to discover another.

"Was the Lady of Shallot the woman who dashed about on her horse wearing no clothing?" Griselda demanded when he had tossed aside her third veil.

"That's Lady Godiva," he said, grinning down at her. He was clutching her hands with all the enthusiasm of a vicar greeting a sinner come to mass. "If you'd like to put on a performance, I'll be happy to be your steed."

He saw the moment the jest made sense to her, because her eyes widened. Then a naughty chuckle erupted from her throat. "I'll have you know that I am a very proper widow," she said severely, "and no one speaks in such a manner to me."

"You aren't a widow tonight," he said. She had turned and was wandering about the room, so he came up behind her and wrapped his arms around her.

"I'm not?" Her hair was the sulky yellow of a peach, and tied up in elegant ladylike ringlets that hadn't even been disturbed by her veils.

He nipped her in the ear. "You're not," he breathed in her ear. "I think you're actually Lady Godiva, and you wandered into my room by accident."

Her body was still, and he couldn't tell if she were the sort who would welcome imagination, or whether she was a woman of rigid common sense.

"And what am I doing, wandering into a gentleman's bed-chamber?" she asked. His heart began to pound in his ears, because her voice was inquiring.

He ran his hands from her shoulders down the front of her pelisse, and then quick as a wink undid the twists that held it together. As he drew it off her shoulders, he said, "Well, you lost your clothing, of course."

She turned around and smiled at him, and it was as if a perfect Dresden shepherdess leapt into vivid life, wrinkling her nose at him. "How did that happen?" She sauntered over to the table where the champagne stood, wrapped in a cold wet towel. "I should tell you, Darlington, that I rarely lose my clothing."

He was there, pouring champagne. "I somehow know that," he said, handing her a glass.

"This will be my third such encounter," she said, waiting until he had a glass as well. "And my last."

He raised an eyebrow.

"I've made up my mind to marry."

These weren't flirtatious smiles, but the rueful sort shared by campaigners on the eve of leaving for a battle. "I as well."

"You do need to marry," Griselda said, sipping her champagne. She looked delightfully concerned for him.

He leaned over and dropped a kiss on her lips. "So do you."

"I?" she asked, and one perfectly arched brow flew into the air.

"Surely Willoughby has been dead ten years," he said. "And Lady Godiva has only found herself wandering three times?"

"For one night only in each case," she told him. "An inflexible rule. I always think it is so helpful for everyone if we are quite clear from the beginning."

"One night," Darlington said, feeling a pang of regret that nearly felled him to his knees. He only had one night before he must begin his marriage campaign. But none of that mattered in the face of the ravenous desire he felt for Griselda.

She glanced around the room, and he decided to lay down a rule of his own. "I have never married, but I've heard that such encounters take place under the sheets."

"Indisputably," Griselda said, her face not revealing a thing about her marital relations.

"And I imagine that affairs among the nobility often have the same lack of vivaciousness."

"If one considers setting vital to . . . vivaciousness."

"One does," he said simply. "Tonight Lady Godiva rides in the open." And just to give her an idea of what he meant, he pulled off his jacket and threw it to the side, pulled off his shirt and sent it flying in the same direction.

He knew he was desirable to women. True, he'd made love to very few. He had no stomach to make love to a sour-smelling lass who'd give herself for free in a tavern, little money to pay one who might smell better, and no heart to flirt with a maiden to whom he couldn't offer marriage. But that didn't mean he hadn't seen their eyes follow him, seen a certain interest in her face when a woman surveyed his chest or glimpsed his forearm.

Griselda's eyes rested on his chest, but he couldn't tell what she was thinking.

"If we only have one night," he said softly, "then I think that Lady Godiva should begin her ride, don't you?"

But she was not a woman to be hurried.

He took down her hair, pin by pin, and made a delicious discovery. Those ringlets, the lady's claim to propriety and beauty, were only for show. Down tumbled her hair, and it was thick as silk and straight, until it reached the end where it formed perfect little ringlets.

"I've never seen anything like it," he said, pulling them and admiring how they curled back into a perfect spiral.

"My maid puts in the curl," Griselda said.

"How does she do that?" He was entranced, wanting to know every detail. "Do you stand there, naked, flushed, warm from the bath?"

She laughed at him. "I sit, respectably clothed in my dressing gown, and she wields a hot iron behind my shoulders."

"I'm your maid for the night." He took his time removing

her gown, unlacing her corset, finally pulling off her chemise.

Surely she would insist on the lamp being turned down?

But she didn't. She didn't even glance at the light. Under all that clothing, she was as ripe and delicious as a peach, her breasts falling into his hands with an abandon that made his laughter catch in his throat, laughter that couldn't make its way to the open air because he was in the grip of a lust so fierce that he'd never felt the like.

He was intoxicated by her long sweep of corn silk hair, with its little jubilant twists at the ends. He brought it over her breasts, and then pulled her in front of the mirror. They stood there together, she a study in creamy skin and silky hair, and he a harder, golden version of the same. "We look—" he said, and cleared his throat.

Griselda tipped her head back against his shoulder and watched him.

"I thought ladies were terrified by nakedness." He was kissing her neck and talking between kisses.

"I've always liked looking at myself," she said, watching his hands on her body in the mirror. "I like looking at you as well."

He ran a hand down the curves of her side. She loved the intent look on his face.

"Willoughby was not fond of mirrors."

"Hmmm," he said, obviously only vaguely listening. It was half a caress, his touch, and half a shaping.

"Our wedding night was something of a fiasco."

He raised his eyes.

"Neither of us had any experience in the area," she said, laughing. She'd never told a soul about the night. It felt enormously freeing.

"Poor Willoughby," Darlington said. "None at all?"

She shook her head. "Not that I know of."

"What happened?"

"We couldn't make it work. Not really. His belly was in the way, and it was mortifying for both of us, and so he kept losing his—his interest, as it were."

"Poor sod!" Darlington said, horror in his voice.

"We tried again a few days later and it was more successful." Darlington was beautiful: a muscled, young stallion of a man. Her two previous lovers had been cautious men in their forties, men who slid gently under the bedcovers and expertly, charmingly, made her as comfortable as they themselves were.

Darlington was another matter. She turned around so she could see him better, and found herself fascinated by the hollows in his hips, by the tight arch of his behind, by the golden sheen of his skin.

"Are you always like this?" she finally asked.

"Like what?"

"Naked. When you're with a woman."

His eyebrow shot up. "Have you seen me wandering through ballrooms without my waistcoat?"

"No, foolish one. I meant when you're engaged in intimate activities."

"Well, as to that," he said. And pulled her against him, a shock of skin to skin. "I haven't found myself in many intimate situations, and that's the truth."

"You haven't?" She blinked up at him, wondering.

He shook his head. His hands slid down the planes of her back, making her feel deliciously smooth . . . feminine.

"Why not?"

His hands dropped away. He turned and picked up his glass. "No money to pay for the privilege, no living to back up the indiscretion . . . how could I?"

It seemed he had a code of honor, this man whom half of London considered despicable.

"How did you afford this room?" Griselda asked.

He turned. "Mad use of funds," he said. "Every person deserves a last madness before they settle into domestic slavery, don't you think?"

"Domestic slavery?"

He drained his champagne. "How else could one describe marriage?"

"Companionship," she said. And thinking of Annabel's, Tess's, and Imogen's marriages, "Passion, friendship, love." She added, "Children."

"You're an optimist," he said. "I see marriage as a fiduciary transaction. I will bring to the marriage little more than my skills in bed. My father made that clear to me at an early age. Under those circumstances, I've always found it hard to indulge an impulse to dally with a woman."

"Because it took on the flavor of practicing your marriage-bound skills," she said, sipping her wine and trying not to ogle the long line of his thigh.

"The taint thereof," he corrected her. "But I do believe that I'm finally old enough to face my fate, coward that I am."

She walked toward him, feeling her hair soft on her back. He had his back turned to her, so she ran her hands, palms flat, up the strong planes of his back. He shivered, but said nothing.

" 'Tis a dismal way of looking at marriage," she said, curving her hands around the muscles of his shoulders.

"Reality so often is disappointing."

"Not tonight." Then she came squarely up against him and felt his intake of breath through her body as well as his.

"I believe that we are in an altogether different realm than marriage."

"I maintain, sir, that a marriage can be passionate."

"I beg you to relinquish such unpleasant thoughts." He turned around.

And what he was doing with his hands . . . well, it was enough to make every thought in Griselda's head fly away.

An hour or so later Griselda was boneless, weak, satiated. "It's time to leave," she said, battling her own inclination to sink back into the bed. She bent over to pick up his dressing gown, but Darlington made a noise like a growl, a deep urgent noise in his throat, and she hesitated. And then he was wrapping his arms around her again.

She could feel his arousal, and her own blood sped into a throbbing melody in response. Some dazed part of her mind was measuring this evening against her other experiences and finding them to have no correlation. No other man had shown interest in more than one polite, cheerful coming together in which both parties were mutually satisfied.

"I don't—" she gasped.

"Lady Godiva," he breathed into her ear, "ride me." He picked her up as easily as one might swing a child in the air, carried her across the room, and then he was sinking back into one of the large armchairs, his face alive with laughter and wicked pleasure, a sinful pleasure that had everything to do with her body and his, and nothing to do with beds.

"Shouldn't we return to the bed?" she asked.

"Bed?" He was laughing aloud now. "I'd like to make love to you in the outdoors."

She felt herself blushing, and he was pulling her forward, lowering her. It was an odd way of proceeding. He stopped, hand between her legs. "I like to watch you," he said silkily. "Your eyes almost close, but not quite, did you know that? And when you breathe so quickly, your breasts move. Your cheeks are pink, you know." And all the time his clever, clever fingers were dancing between her legs.

"Charles," she sobbed, and finally, finally, he let her fall forward, onto him. And then he stopped talking and made a hoarse noise in his throat.

She knew instinctively how to ride. It must be a skill that comes to Lady Godivas in time of need, because she found herself throwing her hair back so that it fell to his knees, arching her back and laughing.

He wasn't laughing anymore. His face was rigid, his teeth clenched. "Ah, God, you're so—" But the words disappeared somewhere and he just concentrated on shaping her breasts with his hands until he really couldn't take it anymore, so he ran a thumb across her rosy nipples. Her eyes drooped and suddenly he was helping in the race, thrusting upwards with all his force.

And then she was crying out, falling forward into his arms, and he was clutching her tight, that lovely damp back, as tight as he could, wrapping his own lady in his arms so she couldn't ride away from him.

16

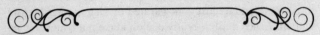

From The Earl of Hellgate,
Chapter the Fourteenth

At the time I met Helena—in the ballroom at Almack's, Dear Reader—I thought I had sipped the cup of passion to the dregs. In short, I thought to marry. For surely marriage is the counterpart to the inertia of old passions, the weariness that comes from seeing one's former lovers in all four parts of the ballroom.

Yes! Such was the extent of my depravity . . .

Lady Mucklowe knew exactly what it took to make a ball into a tremendous success: a single stroke of genius. A few years ago she had created the most talked-about event of the season by inviting Lord Byron to read aloud his favorite love poem. That had ensured the presence of every wanton woman in London, as she later boasted to her sister. Wanton women cheer everyone up: gentlemen in the hope that such a woman might do them a favor, and gentlewomen in the realization that they had someone interesting to talk about.

Tonight she was confident that her place as the reigning queen of the interesting party would be confirmed. "I'm not sure I understand, Henrietta," her husband said fretfully. Henrietta Mucklowe told herself for the fortieth time that if she had been lucky enough to have a more interesting spouse, she wouldn't have such imaginative parties. Because if Freddie weren't Freddie, they might actually have something to talk about at home, and she wouldn't spend most of her time dreaming about fantastic entertainments.

"Masks, dear," she repeated. "The footmen will be giving one to everyone as they come in. And they must wear them; it's a requirement of entrance."

Freddie looked nonplussed, so she explained, "Like wearing knee britches into Almack's. You can't get in without them."

"What about York, eh?" Freddie asked. Occasionally he did have a pertinent point. "You can't just tell a royal duke that he's got to wear a mask or be done with it."

"Perhaps he won't come."

"Saw him today." Freddie grunted as he readjusted the garters on his stockings. "He told me he wouldn't miss it after that other ball you gave."

"Byron was a very good idea," Henrietta said, with a nod of self-congratulation.

"Not that, the pheasant last year. Cook's a genius."

"That too," Henrietta said. If one had to snare a royal duke by food, she was willing to do it. "You have to wear a mask, Freddie."

"A what?"

"A mask!"

"Oh. All right."

Another marital disaster averted, Henrietta made a brief tour of the downstairs. Hundreds of masks, all stitched from black silk (for men) or rosy silk (for women) waited at the entranceway. Candles were lit and footmen stood ready to replenish them. Three hundred bottles of champagne lay waiting, stuck haphazardly in pails of cold water. All ready. The house hummed gently, an empty tidewater pool about to be filled to the brim.

And then, abruptly, it all began. She heard the high, excited tones of Countess Mitford at the door. Within an hour there was a snarl of carriages that stretched for blocks in every direction. The butler was holding up marvelously, not allowing anyone in without a mask firmly attached to his face. In truth, as soon as people entered the house and saw that everyone was wearing masks, and gained a sense of the possibilities, there was no complaining.

Chaperones grew rigid with alarm, but it was too late. Daughters strained forward like young whippets eager to race. Mothers clutched their arms, whispering instructions, but every girl in the room knew that the rules were off for the night. Anyone might dance a waltz if she were masked. Any girl might dance with the worst rake in the room, if they were both masked. How could she know who she danced with? How could she be responsible for her actions? And yet, each person had the prickling sense that the most important person would surely find him.

Wives held their heads high and glanced roguishly to the left and right, looking for their lovers. Husbands trotted off to the card room, knowing that for once their expression wouldn't betray their hand, or moved in a slow prowl toward one of the two ballrooms, searching for a memory, a girl they once loved, a youthful evening.

There was no one who greeted the masks with more joy than Miss Josephine Essex, formerly known as the Scottish Sausage.

She handed her pelisse to the footman without blinking an eye. In the past month she had almost had to wrench her sheltering, comforting pelisse from her body, so uncomfortable was she with her figure. But that very afternoon

Madame Rocque had delivered the first of her evening gowns, and Josie was wearing it. Rather than being seamed to follow the lines of a corset, this gown was wrapped to fit Josie's own body. It was a kind of indigo violet, far too dark for a debutante, but Josie didn't care.

"My goodness!" Griselda had said that afternoon. Which was enough. Josie dressed more happily than she had in her life.

True, when she looked at herself in the mirror, wearing only the smallest corset designed to support her breasts, she had an agonizing pulse of anxiety. She could actually feel silk swishing around her unbounded hips. Surely she looked too large, too undisciplined, too bulky?

But then she took a deep breath and walked toward the glass, walking the way that Mayne had taught her. Even thinking of his lithe muscled body wearing the rags of her pink dress made her giggle. And watching the way the dress gave her a woman's shape—a shape she'd had all along—made her eyes narrow.

He was right.

Mayne was the veteran of a hundred *affaires,* if all the stories were true. How had Imogen described him once? As having a Lucifer-like exhaustion. Josie couldn't help grinning at herself. His mouth had lost that dissolute droop when he was bound up in sparkling pink silk and undulating across the floor toward her.

Now she adjusted her rosy mask—luckily, a color that went perfectly with her gown—and glanced around for Griselda.

Griselda was wearing the daring crimson gown that Madame Rocque delivered for her. Actually, in some ways Josie hardly recognized her chaperone. When they first met, several years ago, Griselda was the quintessential pretty, English gentlewoman. She dressed with the exquisite propriety of a widow interested in two kinds of reputation: that of sexual propriety, and that of good taste. She was a merry, adorable person who showed little interest in the opposite sex, other than a fervent wish to discuss their foibles. In point of fact, while she generally had a beau or two hanging in her train, they were often foolish young men, good for nothing but bleating poetry and providing an arm on the way into supper.

But somehow, in the last few months, Griselda had changed. Josie couldn't quite put her finger on it. Yet as she glanced back, she was fully aware that her chaperone would be the least chaperonelike woman in the room. Madame Rocque's crimson dress was fashioned in such a way that swaths of dark crimson came over the shoulders and crossed—but they didn't actually meet until almost Griselda's waist. Now *that* was a gown that a debutante could not wear.

But, of course, Griselda was a widow. "I will certainly not wear a pink mask," she was saying. "I'll take one of the black ones, if you please."

The footman seemed to be bleating something about Lady Mucklowe's instructions, but it was of no use. Josie could have told him that. Within two seconds Griselda was happily tying a black band around her eyes.

"You look wonderful," Josie whispered to her. "That black makes your hair look positively silver."

"Silver!" Griselda squealed.

Josie laughed. "I didn't mean it that way. It looks like moonlight. I do like the fact you didn't put ringlets in your hair tonight. They wouldn't suit the gown."

"I thought it was time for a change," Griselda said with some satisfaction. "Now, darling, just because we are wearing masks is no reason for improprieties."

Josie opened her mouth but Griselda held up her hand. "Josephine, I am not a fool. I am as aware as you are that many a marriage is made under the threat of a lost reputation, and likely a few fathers will burst out of these doors demanding that some reprobate offer marriage by the morrow. But you, my dear, have no need to resort to subterfuge. Just wait and see."

"I don't mean to engage in subterfuge—" Josie began.

But Griselda interrupted again. "Only once has one of your sisters knowingly done such a thing, and that was in the case of Imogen's first marriage. I'd ask you to think about that marriage carefully, Josie. Were Imogen and Maitland happy?"

"Obviously not."

"I rest my case," Griselda said magnificently. She twitched her shawl so it fell to her elbows and provided a frame for her gown. "Shall we enter?"

They paused for a moment on the threshold of the first of Lady Mucklowe's two ballrooms. A footman sprang forward and offered them glasses of champagne. Before Josie could even stretch out her hand, three gentlemen bowed before them.

"I am," one of them said magnificently, "the Prince of Purpalooseton."

In the flurry of laughter that followed the revelation that Lady Mucklowe had decreed that no one was to use his proper name, Josie became aware of one important thing. Those three gentlemen had not sprung to their side only because of Griselda and her crimson bodice. Within a moment they were joined by two more gentlemen, and for the first time in her life—and with a feeling of dizzy pleasure that was all the more intense for being so new—Josephine Essex found herself flirting simultaneously with four men. Griselda waltzed off in the arms of the Prince of Purpalooseton, but she herself was too happy to dance.

Plus, she knew quite well she was a terrible dancer.

Sometime later she found herself in an animated circle, discussing the most sought-after book in London, *Hellgate's Memoirs*. "I may not know who wrote it," said a gentleman in an orange waistcoat, his mask sitting rather rakishly on his large nose. "But there's no question whose memoirs we're reading. The moment I read the chapter about the woman he met at Almack's." He lowered his voice. " 'Tis Lady Lorkin and Mayne, obviously."

"Absolutely not," said a tall, willowlike man with a fair mustache. "The memoirs are a disgrace, but that chapter could not possibly refer to Lady Lorkin. I thought the pertinent point was the *water spaniel*."

"How so, sir?" Josie asked.

"Water spaniels," he said. "Don't know a woman who can abide the breed. Always in the water, aren't they, and then they shake themselves, and then hey! Presto! The lady is wet. Splattered with water. Wet."

"An obscure point," the orange waistcoat said. "What's that got to do with Mayne or Lady Lorkin?"

Another gentleman strolled up to the circle and joined them. Josie glanced, and then looked again. There was no mistaking those shadowed cheekbones and straight eyebrows, mask or no mask. Nor, for that matter, his clothing. Mayne was wearing a garnet-colored jacket that fit his muscled body as if it had been sewn on that evening.

She gave him a huge grin. For a moment she had forgotten her transformation, but then his eyes raked her body swiftly. He had an eyebrow arched, and it didn't take women's intuition to know he approved of her current gown as much as he loathed her former corset.

"Must be a woman who loves dogs," the willowy man was burbling on. "Even wet ones. I say that Hellgate is Charles Burdiddle. Mind you, we shouldn't be discussing such a risqué subject."

Josie had no idea who Charles Burdiddle was. She glanced at Mayne. "We're discussing an infamous piece of literature, sir," she said to him. "The Earl of Hellgate's *Memoirs*. Unfortunately I have not had an opportunity to read them, but I have heard enough about them from my sisters to understand that Hellgate appears to have considered intimacy a challenge rather than something to be defended against."

"Intimacy outside the bounds of marriage is always a challenge, not a defense," Mayne said. His voice had all the liquid, Luciferian exhaustion of a man who is tired of saying the proper thing.

"But women so rarely think so," Josie pointed out. "In fact, it strikes me as a thoroughly male point of view. Did no one consider the idea that perhaps the memoirs are utterly false, and written by a woman?"

"That would be a remarkable deception. I believe there are ladies hoping desperately to be the next *mistake* that Hellgate commits," the willowy gentleman said with a sarcastic edge to his voice. "Particularly if he would consent to do so in a three folio sequel, handsomely bound in leather."

The orange waistcoat drew in his breath and said, "There is a young lady present, sir!"

"She doesn't appear to be shocked," Mayne observed.

"In the case of a less-than-fascinating man," Josie said, "a woman should always defend against intimacy."

"A woman should defend her virtue in every instance," the orange waistcoat said. "Once a woman succumbs to the kind of disreputable behavior depicted in Hellgate's memoirs . . . well, she is nothing more than a thing unworthy. Stained! The woman described under the *nom de plume* Helena, for example. Shameful!"

"Tsk tsk," Mayne said. "You speak, sir, as if one's past were irredeemable. As if one could never compensate for mistakes of the heart."

"One cannot. Scandals of that nature dishonor the soul. There is no recovering from them. Whoever Helena may be, she will never regain the true heart of womanhood: her sanctity and purity. She is *stained*."

"He doesn't seem to agree that stains come out in the

wash," Mayne said aside to Josie. "Perhaps Helena was his wife. Will you dance?"

"Of course." And she turned toward him with the new, lithe freedom that came with wearing no corset, with a confidence bred from the hundred admiring glances thrown her direction in the last half hour.

"You wouldn't dance with me," pouted the willowy man.

"Count yourself lucky," Mayne said. "I know what a terrible dancer she is, and so I've already braced myself—and my toes."

"No one who moves with such grace, such elegance, could be a poor dancer," the orange waistcoat said mournfully, as Josie left on Mayne's arm.

Which she was pinching as hard as she could. "How dare you say such a thing? Now no one will wish to dance with me!"

"In that dress, they would dance with you if you were using a cane. In fact, I'm only worried that you'll be stolen from me as we dance."

Josie giggled. It was wonderful to feel seductive and beautiful, and be here, laughing on the arm of the man whom she thought (privately) to be the most handsome man in the *ton*.

"Mind you," he said a moment later, after she trod on his foot again, "you *do* have two left feet. What's the matter? Didn't you pay any attention to that dancing master Ewan lured up to the north country?"

She blushed a little. "I can't help it. I'm horribly awkward, in truth. I don't enjoy dancing very much."

"I'll come find you later, when they've turned to waltzes," Mayne said, dancing her out of the circle and off the dance floor. "You might want to just stand about and allow your suitors to ogle your bosom rather than dance with them. At least until the waltzes start."

"I'm even worse at waltzing."

"Well, you'll have to merely accept admiration," Mayne

said cheerfully. "I should probably try to find Sylvie, although I suspect that I know her location."

"Where?" Josie asked, glancing around. "What's she wearing?"

"Yellow," he said. "And a black mask."

"Griselda demanded a black mask as well."

A tall man with appreciative eyes and a lock of brown hair falling over his forehead paused beside them. "Skevington," Mayne said, "may I entrust you with Miss Essex? I thought I'd poke about and find my fiancée, and of course Miss Essex's chaperone is lost in the crowd."

Skevington had a quite charming smile. "Nothing would give me more pleasure," he said, bowing.

"Skevington over-dresses," Mayne said, waving at the man's embroidered waistcoat. "But it's not a mortal sin."

Josie smiled up at her new companion. "'Tis far worse to be over-opinionated."

"To be over-enthusiastic is surely a mortal sin," Skevington said. He showed no pique at the slur to his waistcoat, and Josie liked him the better for it. "At the risk of showing great over-enthusiasm, Miss Essex, may I request a dance?"

"In truth, I would prefer to walk from this room," she said.

Skevington had a lean, intelligent face with kind eyes. They left Mayne, and Josie did not glance back, just walked with her new sultry sway and hoped he was watching.

Then she couldn't bear it and turned her head.

He was gone.

17

From The Earl of Hellgate, Chapter the Fifteenth

**I asked Helena to marry me, Dear Reader. She
refused. She called me her pearl, her golden one,
her cherished dream, and yet she rejected my
hand.**

Thurman thought masks were a rotten idea. How could
he build a reputation if no one knew who he was?

He'd caught sight of Darlington; his features were unmistakable. Darlington was leaning against the wall of the ballroom, and by concentrated attention, Thurman was able to
see that he was watching Lady Griselda Willoughby dance
with Mr. Riffle. He had to grin at that. Darlington was losing his twig if he thought that Lady Griselda would marry
him. True, she had one of the neatest estates on this side of
Hampshire, but she would never interest herself in a loose
screw like Darlington.

Wasting his time, Thurman thought. But he had no time
for Darlington. Darlington was yesterday's news, and he
was bursting with the ambition to make himself into Darlington's successor. He was already in a good way to doing

it. Last night he'd gone to the Covent Garden Theater and surreptitiously written down a number of clever remarks. Then this morning he'd gone to St. Paul's and hung around the middle aisle, where all the clever inns of court men came to gossip, and he'd picked up even better scraps and fragments. He had them all snugly written down, and he'd already used two to great effect.

Of course, no one knew who he was, so he'd have to think of tonight as something of a practice run. But that was all right. It took timing to get a jest right. When he first came in, he'd told Lady Mucklowe that the only happy marriages these days were to be found among the servants. That line garnered laughter in the theater the previous night, but somehow it didn't work with Lady Mucklowe, who stared at him, and said, "Young man, I am relieved that I do not know who you are; I should dislike having to reproach myself for inviting you."

Thurman was relieved by her ignorance as well. But after that, two jests that he'd heard in St. Paul's had gone over very well to little groups, and one of the men had said, "By Jove, that's quite clever!"

He had an excellent line to do with courtship in mind, and so he prowled around until he found a large circle of people standing just inside the windows leading to the garden. Thurman didn't really approve of that; his mother had been adamant that night air might give her darling son a chill of the lungs, and he had always listened to his mother. But driven by an ambition stronger than self-preservation, he strolled up to the circle.

With the mask, it was all very easy. He simply walked up as if he belonged there. He found that the circle was clustered around a young lady who was sitting on the library table in such a way that her ankle was perfectly visible.

It was a nice ankle, Thurman saw with a glance, but it stood to reason that the young lady was not all that she could be. Manners are a lady's best defense against impropriety, his mother used to say, shutting her lips tight.

Likely *this* young lady wouldn't mind a racy joke or two. Thurman took in the ravishing nature of her dress, her vivid chestnut hair, luminous white skin, and lips the color of spring raspberries. She was laughing with a deep, husky chuckle that made it clear she was no chaste maiden.

They were all talking about some Shakespeare play being put on at the Hyde Park Theater. "I shouldn't want to see it," Thurman put in. "The very name Shakespeare sends shivers down my spine. Memories of Rugby, you know."

"I was frightfully idle when I was at school," Skevington said (for Thurman recognized him due to his height). "I'm afraid I couldn't recite more than a line or two to save my life."

Of course, Skevington went to Eton. "Gentlemen know whatever they need without books," Thurman said, "and if one's not a gentleman, then whatever one learns is bad for him."

The girl turned her head and looked at him. She had large eyes, thickly fringed with lashes. Christ, she's beautiful even with a mask on, Thurman thought, though normally he wasn't one who paid much attention to these things. A bit too fleshy for his taste. He let himself eye her rather boldly, because after all, she was clearly not a lady.

"I think I'd like to go into the garden," she said, sliding off the table without waiting for a gentleman to extend his hand. Another sign of her lack of training.

So they all drifted into the garden, she carrying them along like the petals of a flower. Thurman was thinking that he really ought to go find another group to practice his lines on; he had a good one saved up about a mother's love, when Skevington said something that made him stiffen all over.

He had the girl's arm, and he was walking just in front of them. A couple of the fellows had drifted off, and only three of them were trailing after. "Miss Essex," Skevington said, perfectly clearly, "would you like to return to the . . ."

But Thurman didn't hear the rest over the roaring in his ears. It was the Sausage: it was. She'd done something to herself. She'd changed herself.

She'd stopped being a sausage and become this—this ravishingly insouciant girl whose curves were practically making Skevington kiss her toes.

He stopped short and watched Skevington draw her back to the house. All of a sudden the frustrations of the last few days crashed into his mind again. The Scottish Sausage was about to become the toast of the season; he could see that.

She was still the Sausage, though. Now that he looked at her, she was as plump as ever—plumper even. Disgusting. Mother always said that women should eat like birds; they didn't need the same strength that men do.

Someone should tell her that she couldn't just swan around like that, thinking that no one would notice that she was even fatter than before.

He might even be the very person to do it.

18

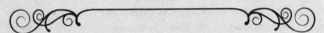

From The Earl of Hellgate, Chapter the Fifteenth

She mocked me by taking me in the private gardens behind the town house of the Duchess of P——. No, not the formal gardens, Dear Reader, the Duchess's private walled kitchen garden. She took me there and it's with a heavy heart and a sense of sin that I recount to you that she danced in her folly . . . danced on the flagstone paths . . . danced without her gown, without her chemise . . . as bold under God's sky as any sparrow.

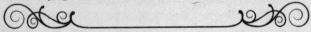

Within ten minutes Griselda had lost Josie. And that was annoying, not because she felt any particular urge to chaperone Josie too closely, but because Josie was wearing a dazzling gown, delivered that very afternoon by Madame Rocque, and Griselda would have loved to judge its reaction.

Josie's eyes had shone like stars when she realized that the ball was an impromptu masquerade. "No one will know I'm the Sausage," she had breathed in Griselda's ear.

"No one would ever think such a thing in that gown," Griselda had said back. Josie was all curves and beauty and youth. Her seductiveness struck one in the face, at least if one were quite as tired as Griselda felt. She was conscious of muscles that she didn't know she owned, and they were all twinging.

By two hours later she was even more tired. Josie was a tremendous success, and Griselda had every belief that most of her newfound suitors would hotly pursue her on the morrow, mask or no mask.

"Superb planning," the Duke of York boomed as he passed Griselda in the corridor, his hand plumply encased in that of an actress from the Adelphi Theater. She knew who he was, of course; the duke was wearing his commander-in-chief uniform, fringe and gold braid everywhere, with his ceremonial sword dangling at his side. Apparently he thought she was his hostess, Lady Mucklowe.

Far be it from her to correct him. "I'm gratified to hear it, Your Royal Highness," she murmured, curtsying so deeply that her knee almost touched the ground. York hastened off after the actress, his stays visibly creaking as he trotted along. Behind him billowed a cloak with yards of deep gold fringe, gold frogs, and a red taffeta lining.

"Do you suppose that he has the Order of the Bath embroidered on his undergarments?" came a husky voice at her ear.

Her mouth curved into a welcome smile without conscious volition, and her heart started beating quickly.

"One has to assume that someone is making those garments," he said, his hand warm on her back. She was walking with him before she realized what she was doing. "Smalls, by order of His Highness."

She gave a gurgle of laughter.

"I know what you're thinking," he said into her ear. "Smalls that aren't so small, eh?"

"You, sir, should be out looking for a wife."

"I could say the same to you of a husband. Alas, I can't tell one heiress from the next."

"You managed to find me without any trouble."

"I saw your hair the moment I entered the door."

Her heart was beating quickly. "This is not what we planned!"

"Life is full of tempting surprises. You look ravishing, enticing, and a wee bit fatigued."

Griselda bit her lip. It was because she was all of thirty-two.

"God knows I am," Darlington continued. "Muscles ache in areas that I don't generally think about." He whispered in her ear, "My ass. Who knew that was so exercised by our activities last night?"

"I did," she murmured back, unable to resist. She could feel herself turning pink.

Now she knew where they were going. After all, she'd been to Lady Mucklowe's parties before. Slowly but steadily, he was steering her through the second ballroom and toward the French doors, and then (she would guess) out into the garden. "I'm not going into the garden with you," she said, digging in her heels.

"I wasn't asking you to," he said, unperturbed.

"I'm not going anywhere in private," she said, panicking. He was too luscious, and she was too weak, or perhaps it was the other way around. She had to look for a spouse, and so did he. "I saw Cecily Severy," she hissed at him. "She's wearing dark lavender."

"An old maid pressed in dark lavender," he sang, dreadfully off-key but perfectly audible.

"Hush!" she said, choking back a laugh.

"Was surprised to marry someone not of her gender. *I've never seen such a thing!*"

Griselda was giggling hopelessly.

"Here, take back your ring!" he caroled. And then, putting on a commanding voice: *"I won't,* her groom cried, *you must surrender!"*

They were in the corridor, and before she could tell him that ditties were supposed to rhyme and actually be funny, he pulled her against him.

"Oh," she said, and the laughter died. He was kissing her desperately, and yet the taste of laughter was in his mouth, because it always was.

"Surrender," he growled at her.

"No!" she said, her breath coming in quick gasps. "I'm a chaperone—I have to see what Josie's—I have to—"

"She's fine," Darlington said, his tongue curling a burning line on her throat.

But Griselda took a deep breath and pushed him away. She straightened her mask with unsteady fingers. "I do not kiss at balls, ever," she told him. "I do not engage in this kind of behavior. I'm sorry, but our . . . our tryst is over."

She turned to leave, but he stopped her. "Take me to my fate."

"Who shall it be?"

He shrugged. "You choose."

"Cecily Severy," she said after a moment. "'Tis markedly improper of me to say so, but she's a very kind woman, and a lovely one."

"She lisps."

"We discussed that already."

He pulled her close again, but not too close. "She's scrawny," he whispered. "Do you know I haven't been able to think of anything but you all day? I can't go from your body to one of those scrawny debutantes."

"The first thing you are going to do," Griselda said, pretending she didn't hear him, but actually filing away the words as memories she could treasure later, "is bring my Josephine into fashion."

"I owe you that," he said.

"You owe *her* that. And yourself," she added.

She led the way into the first ballroom and stopped in the door. It was a welter of ruby and saffron and peacock blue silks, dotted as if with pepper by black masks.

"Christ," Darlington muttered, just low enough so that she could hear it, "this is enough to persuade me to take up Brummell's mode of dress."

Griselda had just glimpsed Josie in the corner. "I want you to meet Miss Essex." She thought Darlington uttered a little groan, but she wasn't sure. No one likes to be presented with his crimes.

And as they came up to Josie, she couldn't help grinning. Griselda had no idea how or why the transformation had happened, but when Josie decided to accept the nature of her God-given body, she had done so with a vengeance. Rather than wear her hair down, like so many debutantes, she had scooped it all on her head, great curlicues of shining hair held in their place by diamond clips given to her by Tess. The dress delivered by Madame Rocque was really too risqué for a debutante, Griselda thought. She should have put her foot down.

It wrapped Josie's body like a kiss, all dusky violet with a low neck marked by the smallest ruffle standing up around the bodice. Rather than attempt to give her the sticklike figure that the current fashion demanded, Madame Rocque had clothed her in a way that showcased her woman's body. Next to her, all the floating gowns caught up with ribbons under tiny pert breasts looked boring.

Josie looked sultry, dangerous, erotic—and at the same time, young, fresh, and beautiful. She was like sin packaged and made young again.

"Christ," Darlington said, stopping dead.

Griselda had a sudden pang. What was she doing, introduc-

ing Darlington to Josie? Of course, he would—he would—
But he didn't look like a man transfixed by lust. Instead, he
was frowning down at her.

"What in the hell did you do to that girl?" he whispered.

Josie was flirting with four gentlemen at once, handling
them with the aplomb of a woman who'd been on the market
for several years, and who had spent her entire life being
feted for her beauty.

"Nothing," Griselda whispered back. "Behold the lovely
girl whom you labeled a sausage!"

"Not fair," he said. "You're not playing fair, Lady Godiva,
and I'll have to take a forfeit." His voice darkened, and she
squirmed away.

"None of that!"

"There's something different about her. She's not stuffed
any longer."

Griselda bit her lip.

Darlington shook his head. "I'm no good at this sort of
female thing. But you can't blame me for not seeing *that*," he
said in her ear. "If she'd looked like this in the first month of
the season, I could have called her a sausage, a cow, or the
entire herd, and not a man would have paid attention to me."

"Now I want you to dance with her," Griselda said, beating down an impulse to drag him in the opposite direction.

He glanced over. Josie was playfully rapping one of the
gentlemen on the knuckles. "I don't want to. She's in fashion, Griselda. That's Skevington at her right. Hell, maybe
she'll marry him. He's got a sweet little estate, and a title
coming when his uncle cocks up his toes."

Griselda blinked.

"You don't want me to take her away from Skevington.
He looks entranced."

"Josie doesn't," Griselda remarked.

"A problem of a different nature. But she will not be

entranced by me either." And he pulled Griselda gently but firmly in the other direction.

"Why wouldn't she be entranced by you?" Griselda asked, feeling queer as she asked it. But she might as well be straightforward. "Josephine has a very large dowry."

"My father informed me of that before the season began," he said, making swiftly for the door to the ballroom. "In fact, he was under the distinct impression that I would be able to get even more money out of Felton than has been offered. It is unfortunate that I have a low tolerance for boredom."

"Josie is not boring! She is one of the cleverest, most witty young women I know."

"They're the worst kind," Darlington said. "It's exhausting to have to reply to pert comments made by a woman in her early years. They expect so much."

"But you, of all people," Griselda protested, "should be able to snap back a reply."

"In that respect I am rather an amateur," Darlington said. He slowed down now that they were in the hallway.

"Where on earth are we going?" Griselda asked. She was trying to think of a clever remark to make, and she couldn't think of a single thing to say.

"A place I discovered the last time I was in Lady Mucklowe's house, for the Byron reading, ages ago."

"I missed the reading," Griselda said. There was something terribly exciting about holding hands in the middle of a crowded party. Of course, no one would possibly know who she was. Not only did she have the mask, but her hair was not in its usual ringlets, and she was wearing a thoroughly scandalous gown. She didn't even feel like herself.

Everyone would know who Darlington was, though. There was no disguising those curls and his lean, lithe figure.

They were half running down a corridor now, obviously a

passageway reserved for servants. "Charles," Griselda said, trying not to pant. Only old women panted. "Where are we *going*?"

"The kitchens, of course," he said. And there they were, in a low-ceilinged kitchen, paved in flagstones. It was full of servants, darting to and fro, preparing for the supper that would be put on at two in the morning. No one even glanced at them.

"Come on," Darlington said, and pulled her between a chef, two cooks, and four scullery maids. "The back door."

They were outside. It was oddly quiet, with just a muffled roar from behind the closed door, as if the ocean were contained on that side.

"How very, very lovely," Griselda said. It was an old garden, with high brick walls separating it from the larger formal gardens that stretched behind the house. The old red brick was overhung with white burnet roses that could be dimly seen from the light pouring from the kitchen windows.

Griselda began to pick her way down the uneven little walk between beds of early carrots, lettuce, and some bluish-purple leaf that she couldn't identify.

Darlington followed her. "An enormous crop of horseradish," he said, glancing to the right.

A large red cat gave them the arrogant, slant-eyed glance of a born mouser, jumped the wall and disappeared.

They walked all the way to the end of the garden where the roses hung, their stems tangled into a mat as heavy as horse blankets on prize thoroughbreds. In the very back there was a little wooden bench.

"This garden seems so familiar," Griselda said slowly. "I know! Didn't Hellgate have a tryst in a kitchen garden? Oh, Darlington, was it you? I have been beginning to believe Hellgate is modeled on my brother."

"Absolutely not!" Darlington said. "I have never done anything indiscreet in a kitchen garden. You called me Charles a moment ago."

"A momentary indiscretion," she said, "should never be followed up by more of the same."

"But I want more of the same."

"Life is full of wants."

He was cupping her face in his long fingers. "Hush," he said, and his face came toward hers in that one moment before she closed her eyes and gave in. Thoughts were flying around in her mind like trapped birds: *She shouldn't! They shouldn't! They might be seen!*

"I'm going to take off your mask," he murmured against her mouth. There was something almost angry in the way he was kissing her. It was an insistent, possessive kiss, the kind a man gives when he wants to say something without words.

Griselda broke away, gasping.

But without saying a word, he drew her back, slowly, giving her time to say no. But she couldn't. All she did was raise her face to his, and open her mouth to his, and say "Charles." That was enough, though. Somehow they found their way onto the little wooden bench.

"We can't—" she gasped.

"We won't," he said, eyes gleaming. "It's not dark enough. But I'm going to kiss you senseless, Lady Godiva." He bent his head and said it against her lips. "I'm going to kiss you until you forget that little plan you have to find yourself a husband tonight."

"I—" she gasped, but his hand closed on her breast.

Griselda was the kind of woman who never found herself at a loss for words. She had a reputation justly deserved, for words of kindness at the right moment, suitably spiced gossip in appropriate circumstances, and a chuckling laugh that covered most other eventualities. Now she couldn't seem to bring a rational phrase to her mind.

"You must stop," she said finally. She was arching herself into his hand like a wanton cat, and yet an itchy, almost tearful feeling was coming over her at the same time.

He let his lips drift to her forehead, and kissed her there, and on her eyebrows, and on her nose.

"Why are you so affectionate?" she asked. "I don't even know you."

She felt the shock of what she'd said go through his body. "I feel," he said a moment later, "as if I know you very well. Last night—"

"Gentlemen have these sorts of small trysts all the time," she said, not harshly, but trying to be clear.

"I haven't," he said. "Perhaps I shall, once I'm married and my wife and I tire of each other." There was a dreadful weariness in his voice that broke her heart.

"You won't!" she said, running a hand along his cheek. He had pushed his mask up to the top of his head, where it was making his thick blond hair stand on end. "Your wife will come after you. She'll never let you out of her sight."

He pressed kisses on her eyelids, so she closed them, wishing that she couldn't smell him so well. Because he smelled better than the roses, better than the drifting scent of thyme and rosemary.

"True, nonetheless," he said.

"Not so. Why, all three of the young ladies I've chaperoned have made happy marriages. Josie is the only one left."

"And you. You have to find a spouse as well. For yourself."

She didn't want to think about that, so she leaned toward him again, and he took up her silent invitation.

19

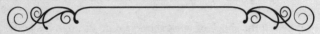

From The Earl of Hellgate,
Chapter the Fifteenth

My Helena now wears another man's ring, sleeps
in another man's bed, calls herself by another
name. But may I venture to hope that some small
part of her heart remains mine? Some small
part of her heart remembers dancing free . . . until I caught her, of course. Even then the dance
continued. She knew . . . she knew at the time,
Dear Reader, that she was to be married.

Ah, dear Helena, should you chance to read my
poor Memoirs, think of me!

Mayne finally found his fiancée tucked away in Lady
Mucklowe's study, chatting with a circle of young
women who were sharing a plate full of small pasties and
what looked like three bottles of champagne. They'd all
taken off their masks and were laughing like hyenas when
he walked into the room.

He was conscious of a feeling of acute annoyance. Why
in the hell did he have to constantly search for Sylvie? Why

couldn't she stay in the ballroom? She was never in sight.

Though to be fair, she didn't engage in any sort of impropriety. Not Sylvie. Her touch-me-not air was so strong that sometimes he found it incredible that she had agreed to marry him.

The thought brought a smile to his lips. It didn't even waver when she looked up at him with an unmistakably displeased expression.

"Mayne," she said.

"Darling," he said, picking up her hand and kissing it. "I've been searching for you. I was hoping to take you into supper." Little Polly Cooper, who was suffering through an infatuation for him, giggled madly.

Lady Gemima grinned up at him. "Are you taking her away, Mayne? Because we're finding your fiancée absolutely delightful." Mayne never knew quite what to think about Gemima. She was beautiful, of course. But she was so intelligent that it was rather disconcerting. She had a way of making a man aware of his own faults without even mentioning them.

Sylvie's eyes were sparkling as they walked out of the room. "I am making some friends here in London. I am so happy about this!"

He glanced down at her. "That's wonderful, Sylvie. Gemima—"

"Oh, do you know her?" Sylvie dropped his arm and clasped her hands before her. "I find her of all the most interesting. So original. And her gown was by a male *modiste*, can you imagine? His name is . . ."

She chattered on. Mayne's mind wandered. He hadn't seen Josie in a while. He'd seen his sister dance by with a fair man who looked faintly familiar, but he couldn't place him with a mask. He'd rounded a corner and come across Annabel kissing her husband, Ardmore, which was just like her. And she'd given him her usual impudent grin.

He didn't think it was a mistake to worry about Josie. He had a funny feeling that she might not avoid improprieties as she ought. After all, her sisters had found themselves extraordinarily happy marriages by behaving in less than proper ways. Josie had almost certainly registered that fact.

Then he noticed with a start that Sylvie had stopped talking and was looking up at him.

"I'm sorry, my dear," he said. "My mind wandered for a moment."

"Your mind often wanders when I speak to you of important things," she said with a bit of a snap in her voice.

He was surprised. Had she been speaking of something important? "Please tell me again. I promise to give it all my attention."

Sylvie pouted, but then gave in and smiled at him. "I was telling you of Mrs. Anglin's indiscretion. A most important topic, as I'm sure you'll agree."

"Absolutely."

"Everyone is saying that *she* appears in those memoirs that everyone is talking about! Apparently she is portrayed as a character called something odd, Mustardseed or the like. Perhaps I should read the memoirs, but I read so slowly in English."

"That's an unlikely suggestion," Mayne said. "Mrs. Anglin hasn't the *joie de vivre* for that sort of high jinks." Plus, though he didn't want to say so to his fiancée, he was perfectly capable of recognizing his own life when it was written down in lamentably bad prose. To his memory, Mustardseed was Mrs. Thomasin Symonds.

Sylvie shuddered visibly. "I shall never touch her hand again ungloved, I assure you, after what I was just told. How she could lower herself!"

"There weren't that many details, were there?" Mayne asked. He had thrown the book away unfinished, but all he could remember was a lot of talk about throbbing chests and hushed voices.

"Too many," Sylvie said. "I found it all most distasteful, at least as Gemima was describing it."

Mayne looked down at her and marveled once more at his fiancée's perfection. She was like a white, white rose whom no one had touched, or soiled in any way. She rarely allowed herself to be touched without gloves. She would never treat him to a vulgar scene in which she burst into tearful protestations of love for another man. She would never allow a younger version of himself (or Hellgate) to lure her into a stranger's bed.

She was his, and only his.

The very idea of it sent a bolt of passion through him.

"Shall we walk in the gardens?" he asked, hearing the huskiness in his own voice.

She glanced up at him, but appeared to see nothing amiss, because she nodded. "I am not in the least hungry," she said. Like a bird, Sylvie appeared to eat only crumbs, and then only at the oddest times. He had never actually seen her eat a meal, for example. She tended to move things around her plate and then place her tableware on top, as if concealing the contents.

He strolled all the way to the far end of the garden. Most of the revelers had poured back into the house. It was at least two in the morning now, and the garden was dark and mysterious.

"I'm not sure I like it here," Sylvie whispered.

"It's quite safe."

"I know I am safe with you," she said, smiling at him. "It's one of the things I like about you, Mayne."

"Won't you call me Garret?" he asked. "At least when we're alone?"

But she shook her head. "Absolutely not. It would only

lend itself to the impression that we share a degree of inadvisable intimacy. Why should we present that illusion, when it is not the case?"

A solid argument.

"Perhaps we might be slightly more intimate," Mayne said, his mind sliding quickly away from the memory of kissing Josie. He hadn't realized it at the time, but that was a deeply disloyal kiss. Sylvie would dislike it, if she knew.

She frowned at him and her tone was slightly—just slightly—frosty. "How do you mean, sir?"

"This," he said softly, and bent to kiss her. She was really quite small. He took her delicate face in his hands. It felt like the face of a child. She spoke through his kiss, as if his lips weren't on hers.

"I am not enjoying this."

"Oh," he said, straightening up.

There was a tiny frown between her brows. "I am not in favor of intimacies before marriage," she told him. "I thought we were in agreement on this front."

"But a kiss," he said hopelessly.

She raised her chin. "I am not the kind of woman who takes pleasure in courting disgrace in a garden, Mayne."

"You wouldn't be—" But there was a look in her eye that made it adamantly clear that she meant what she said.

The truth was that she couldn't be as inviolable, as untouchable, as goddesslike as she was, if she were a light-heeled wench who would collapse into his arms with a giggle, the way so many other women had done in the past.

And he didn't want that. He hadn't had an *affaire* in almost two years now. He felt as if slowly, slowly, he was regaining a sense of himself, a cleansing from the dozens of tawdry little evenings when he walked home with perfume on his coat and tears on his sleeve. He had come to a stage in his life after which he wanted to share his life with one woman, and one who would be his alone, as he would be hers alone.

They turned in silent agreement back to the house. "I'm thinking of putting my stables in order for the next racing season," he said.

"Didn't you tell me that you meant to do that a month ago?" Sylvie inquired, not unkindly. "Do you need to hire someone?"

He'd forgotten that he'd told her . . . of course, he'd been thinking constantly about it for months. "It's not an easy decision. I'd have to be there."

"One should never allow a secondary to hire important staff," Sylvie said rather vaguely, waving to a friend who was also going into supper. "Shall we sit with Miss Tarn, Mayne? She speaks French so divinely. She tells me that she's had a private tutor for three years. I can't think why more English people don't bother to learn French properly."

But Mayne was on the edge of an important decision. He was the type of man who would never bring himself to say such a thing, but he felt it might—would—change his life. Certainly, it would change Sylvie's future life.

"No," he said rather brusquely. "We need to talk, Sylvie. I never seem to find you alone."

"That would be quite inappropriate," Sylvie said, waving at Miss Tarn and mouthing *no*. He glanced to the side and saw she was wiggling her eyebrows to indicate some sort of silent disapproval of himself. Or was it mockery?

"We will be man and wife someday," he observed.

"It sounds so horridly Puritanical when you say 'man and wife.' I'll never be a wife, not in that pedestrian kind of way. I'm a lady first. And you're a gentleman, not a *man*."

He sighed. "A small table, please," he told the footman bowing before him. "No, we will not be joining anyone."

A moment later they were seated in such a way that Sylvie could see the entire room, and her reticule, shawl, and fan were arranged to her satisfaction. Then she turned her eyes to him. "Mayne," she said, "what on earth is the matter?"

He felt a little of the uncertain clutch on his heart lessen. "I've made a mess of my life, Sylvie." He said it flatly, without any drama.

"In what sense?" she asked, an enchanting little wrinkle appearing between her brows. "Have you lost your estate?" She put a hand over his. "I have a great deal of dowry, Mayne. It is yours."

It almost made him feel teary. It must be because he'd been alone so long, and finally he had someone to talk over these issues. And she was so generous.

"Don't worry!" she said. "My father, also, he has much funds, as you say in England. He will not allow a daughter of his to go without these funds."

"It's not money. I almost wish it were."

"What then?"

"My life has slipped away in a series of tawdry little *affaires* and meaningless friendships. I haven't done anything. I never took up my seat in Lords. I'm hugely wealthy, to be honest, Sylvie, but I had little to do with that either. My friend Felton advises my man. I scarcely know what I own, anymore."

"Is that Lucius Felton?" Sylvie asked. And, at his nod: "A very wise thing to do, on your part. Mr. Felton is a genius in such things, is he not?"

"My estate runs itself," Mayne said, out of the quiet desperation he'd felt for more than a year. "I haven't taken up my seat in Lords because, frankly, I'd be a flat loss on the floor. I've no interest in enclosure acts or sending pickpockets to the Antipodes."

"But what is wrong with this life?" Sylvie asked, looking at him with frank, curious eyes.

"What life?"

"*This* life," she said. "It's hard to put in English. But the life of a *galant*."

"The life of a gentleman with nothing to do but enjoy

himself," Mayne translated. "I'll tell you what such gentlemen do, Sylvie. They flirt with other men's wives, and sometimes they bed them. They involve themselves in foolish bets over carriage rides and boxing matches."

Sylvie nodded. "Yes, those things. And they manage their estate, and are kind to those beneath them." (Sylvie's father, after all, had supported the revolution, at least at the beginning.) "They have children and make certain those children are raised to be intelligent members of society, who know their place and what they should do in life."

"That must be my problem," Mayne said. "I don't know my place. Nor yet what I should do in life."

Sylvie's little brow knit. "You should do . . . what you're doing now. You are a good man, Mayne, with friends and substance. What more do you want?"

"I want to make something," Mayne said helplessly. "Construct something."

She stared at him, and then her mouth fell open. "You mean like that very odd marquis, the one who constructed a windmill on his estate to catch the wind?"

"No. Although if I had an inventing bend of mind, I would be happy to retire to the country and make windmills."

"That would not do, so I am pleased to hear that you are not one of those. I would prefer to have nothing to do with inventors. They are extremely strange people, by all accounts. Of course, sometimes it is a useful trait. My father's blacksmith was excellent at making pipes with strange bends in them."

Mayne looked at his hands.

"Perhaps when we have children you will feel differently," Sylvie said. Her voice was so sympathetic and yet nonplussed that Mayne couldn't help but smile at her. He leaned over and dropped a kiss on her nose, even though she strongly disapproved of public displays.

"You're very dear, do you know that?"

"No, I am not. I am very fortunate. I like being precisely what I am: a lady. I like to go to balls, and talk to my close friends."

"That's true enough," Mayne said, taking her hand. "I can never find you because most of the time you are ensconced in the ladies' retiring rooms, chattering away."

She smiled at him. "That is where all interesting things happen at a ball."

"Would you ever be happy spending a great deal of the year on my estate?" he asked, knowing the answer.

Her smile did not falter. "Never. But Mayne, if you decide that living in the country will make you contented, I am perfectly able to take care of myself. Your house here in London is in an excellent location. Once I have renovated it to the French style, it will be very comfortable. And then I have so many friends. I believe I shall be quite happy at—how do you call them in England?—house parties. Yes, that's it. I would much dislike to think of myself as a shackle on your ankle."

"A poetic simile," Mayne said wryly. "I should miss you."

"But we face a great many years together. I am certain that we shall like to live in different places for periods of time. I have often observed that the best marriages are so. I would much dislike it if either of us were unhappy, Mayne."

"Where will the children be?"

She raised an eyebrow. "Why, where children are supposed to be. In the country, in town, wherever they wish to be."

Mayne laughed. "They won't express wishes for some time."

"I dare say," Sylvie said. "I know nothing of children, you understand, Mayne. But our children will be perfectly amiable, I am sure."

She was so cheerful, so genial, so courteously willing to

live apart from him for their entire lives. And from their children too, he had no doubt. And yet: he looked at her again. Sylvie was no ogre. There was the beautiful little pointed chin, and wide, friendly eyes with an inquisitive, intelligent gleam to them.

"Don't you wish there was more to life than this?" he asked again, rather desperately.

And saw those beautiful eyes fill with concern. "I do not." She said it with certainty. "May I speak frankly?"

"Of course!" He took both her hands.

"I come from a country where many people, young women of my mother's age, were brutally killed for nothing more than being who they are. They were born to rule, not to work. Born to a life of pleasure, rather than toil. I was lucky enough that my father became a friend to Napoleon rather than an enemy—at least until he saw the truth of that regime—and yet I see the horror of it, in my mind, you understand? I know what happened in the Bastille: the cruelties, the loss, the terrible loss of it."

Inside his palms, her hands curled into fists. "How can you ask me if I want more than this life? I am so lucky to have this life! I sit here, dressed with such elegance as my friends and relatives once enjoyed, eating exquisite food, in no danger of my life, and in no fear, and you ask me if *this is enough*?"

There was a moment's silence between them.

"Oh God," he said, "I'm so sorry, Sylvie. I'm a bastard to have even asked."

But she caught herself up. The fierceness faded from her eyes, replaced with her inimitable self-possession. She slipped her hands from his and smiled at him, that intelligent, assured smile that had first attracted him. "I am very happy. It would be unthinkable for me to be otherwise."

"I see that. I expect you are the best possible person for me to talk to on this matter."

"It is often so with friends. I find that when I talk to a friend, and learn her perspective, my view of the world shifts."

"Friends," he said. "But surely we are more than friends, Sylvie?"

There was nothing in her smile that was more—or less— than friendly. "To be friends is the greatest love of all between people. This lovers business—pah! It goes in the night. I have seen it so. *You,* Mayne, of all people, know that this emotion does not last. I decided long ago to have nothing to do with it, and I have found it a wise decision."

He leaned toward her and ran a finger down the curve of her cheek. "I love you, Sylvie. I feel that passion for you."

"Our friendship will take us beyond the point when you feel that for me. Perhaps I should not say so, but I have been told that there are certain similarities between your past and that of this Hellgate. I do not in any way wish to diminish or discount your feelings, but according to these *Memoirs,* it seems you have felt this passion on a regular basis . . . for one or two weeks only?"

He was grinding his teeth. "I did not write those *Memoirs.*"

"Of course not," she said, shocked. "But you did have many of the relationships that lie at the heart of the account, did you not?"

She read the look in his eyes. "You must not feel terribly!" she cried. "Because we speak frankly to each other, we need not feel hurt when, after a few weeks of these intimacies, you are not so passionate anymore. We will not cry over the inevitable. I shall never make you a scene because you gain interest in another woman. You have always been discreet in these things, Mayne. Everyone says that of you. You are the consummate gentleman."

"I had hoped . . ." he said. But he wasn't sure how to finish the sentence.

She raised a hand. "You needn't ever worry that I shall disgrace you. While I understand a gentleman's desires, I do not share them. It is not for me, this life of sneaking in and out of bedchambers." She gave a delicate shudder. "To be blunt, Mayne, your children will be your own, and I shall create no scandals."

Should he thank her?

But she had turned away and was waving toward the next table. "There is lovely little Josie! Have you noticed how delightful she appears this evening? A new *modiste* can change a woman's life, and your sister has done an excellent job of drawing away Darlington . . ."

She chattered on, but Mayne wasn't listening. He was staring at a tasteless lobster patty and thinking that in balance, perhaps it would have been better if he was wholly French rather than only half. At least if he were on the way to the tumbrel, he would have been caught up by events, taken by death.

Oh for God's sake, he thought. Don't be such a melancholic sap.

He looked up and caught Josie's eye. She was sitting with Skevington, who showed every sign of a man who would be calling on Rafe within a week with a generous settlement in mind and a ring in his pocket.

"Mayne," his sister Griselda called. "Don't you have a horse running in the Ascot?"

He nodded. Although poor Sharon still hadn't recovered from the devil's nuts, and had been scratched as of that morning. If he'd been more observant of his stables, he could have prevented that. It should never have been allowed to spread through his horses. He had only one unaffected.

"Shall we make up a party? Sylvie," she called, "shall we make up a party? They have the prettiest boxes at the Ascot. You must see them. The Feltons have a box the size of the royal one, and Tess told me yesterday that they will have to miss the race. It would be a pity to let it sit empty."

Sylvie wrinkled her nose. She hated the dust and the bother of racetracks, she'd told him once.

"The Ascot is not like a normal race," Griselda said. "The Queen will be there. And the Duke of Cambridge, with his new bride."

"All right," Sylvie said, not happy, but accepting it. Then she waved excitedly in the other direction.

"Who is it?" Mayne asked.

"Darlington."

Mayne scowled.

"Never fear," she said as Darlington wove his way through the tables toward them. "Your sister has stopped him in his tracks."

"How do you mean?"

"He won't insult Josephine again." Darlington was a tall fellow, with a face that Mayne had to suppose women found interesting. On the whole, he looked decent, for all he had the reputation for having a snake's tongue. Not that Mayne would ever forgive him for mocking Josie. He looked at him with murder in his eyes, and Darlington recoiled slightly, but bent over Sylvie's hands.

Before Mayne realized it, she was asking him to join their party for the Ascot.

"Bloody hell," Mayne said as soon as the man walked off. "We don't need that blackguard with us."

"You don't understand," Sylvie said, patting his hand as if he were five years old. "It's always better to have someone just under your eye if they're a bit of a problem. With Griselda keeping him busy, Darlington wouldn't dare to make an untoward remark about Josephine."

"Josie has taken care of that herself," Mayne remarked. "No man in his right mind would call her a sausage. She looks ravishing and Skevington is groveling at her feet."

"We'd better invite Skevington as well," Sylvie said. "If

we have enough people, perhaps we'll have a small soirée in the box, and it won't be as tedious."

Mayne loved races. He loved the pounding excitement, the crowds, the swirling energy, the horses, the smell of the stables . . . The only racehorse he had who hadn't caught the devil's nuts was a nervy filly named Gigue. She had an oyster-gray coat and sensitive ears. If he'd spent more time with her, or he had a better trainer, she might even have won tomorrow. She loved to race, loved to slip past the other horses with a flip of her tail.

But she hadn't had the training she needed, he knew that. She needed someone to work with her, day after day. It would probably be better if it wasn't him, but he still needed to be on the estate, watching, making sure it was going well.

He pushed his lobster around his plate a bit more while Sylvie invited two more passersby to join them in the Feltons' box.

Josie smiled at Mayne from the far table. He managed a smile, but it was a flat one. She narrowed her eyes at him. So he turned back to his lobster as if it were a cream trifle that he longed to eat.

20

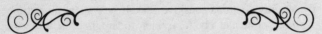

From The Earl of Hellgate,
Chapter the Sixteenth

I was now determined to find a wife, Dear Reader. The passions I had lived through were making me old before my time: too much passion and too little tranquility. But such is the fate of my life that when I sought tranquility, in the bosom of the Church . . . yes, I fear to say it! But the truth must be told. Dear Reader, I took myself to the Church one morning and threw myself at the altar, when a soft and delicate hand lifted me, and a gentle voice said, "Sir, what ails you?"

Sylvie knew the moment their carriage entered the grounds of the Ascot that this was an event she would enjoy. Mayne had gone early in the morning, of course. He was endearingly serious about this horse he had running, and Sylvie had tied a pink ribbon about her wrist that clashed slightly with her costume, just so that every time she noticed it she would remember to watch the race with Mayne's horse in it.

"How on earth will we know when his horse is running?" she asked Griselda. "I believe its name is Gigue."

"Oh, there's a book sort of thing," Griselda said absently. Sylvie loved that about Griselda. While Mayne made her feel prickles of guilt because she wasn't interested enough in his horses, his absurd *crise existentielle*, his absurd declarations of passion for her . . . Griselda understood precisely the importance of these things in relation to a new promenade dress.

In fact, Sylvie thought to herself, without Griselda, Mayne might not be as desirable a *parti* as he was. Although she hadn't encountered another man who fit as many of her requirements as did Mayne. But there were moments when he was gruelingly tiresome.

All men are, Sylvie reassured herself.

"I wonder whether this hat is better slightly farther back on my head," Griselda said, surveying herself in a little gilt mirror. She was wearing a hat as large as an entire wheel of Stilton and an enchanting promenade dress that was the precise pale blue of a delphinium.

"I like it as it is," Sylvie said, after giving the matter serious consideration. "Wait! Turn to the side. Yes, as it is. That pale blue color makes your hair shine like sunlight, Griselda. Is Darlington meeting us at the box?"

"Yes, he is. But I do wish you hadn't invited him. I've already taken care of the other thing."

"I know," Sylvie said, "and I'm so sorry that I unnecessarily invited him. I didn't realize, and then I saw him look at you."

"Indeed," Griselda said wryly.

Darlington did look at her. And she couldn't help it; she kept looking at him as well. That had never happened before. In the case of the trysts she'd had since Willoughby died, she had experienced a reasonable *frisson* on deciding to engage in the evening's pleasure, had enjoyed herself during the appointment, and felt absolutely no desire to repeat the experience.

It was different with Darlington. She woke up in the middle of the night, her body tingling with a dream that she couldn't remember, although she instinctively knew the subject. It was embarrassing. She had to excise this uncomfortable reaction and devote herself to finding a spouse. After all, she wanted a child, didn't she? Of course she did. She wanted a little Samuel of her own.

She'd never lacked for confidence, but her *affaire* with Darlington had steadied any nerves she might have felt in that area. After all, she'd seduced one of the most handsome young men in the *ton*.

"What is Darlington's age?" Sylvie asked, as if she could read her thoughts.

"I have no idea," Griselda managed, shrugging as if the question was of little interest.

"We can look in that book of people," Sylvie said.

"You meant *Debrett's*?" Griselda had thought of that, and discarded it as conventional and anxious. As if she were a young girl, pining for a duke's son and looking up his birthday.

"But surely you must know, Griselda," Sylvie persisted.

"Men are not like women. Since they don't debut, they tend to appear in London on their own schedule."

"Do you have any idea when he first appeared?"

She did, as it happened. 'Twas an embarrassing thing, but she did. There weren't many tall men with his rakish air appearing each year. Griselda shuddered. God forbid she should grow to be like one of those matrons who sat in the corner of the room and giggled over the young men coming down from university.

"Griselda?" Sylvie asked. There was an amused little smile in her eyes.

"I believe he first appeared in London around four years ago. If he came directly from university, that would make him around twenty-four." It was appallingly young.

"And you cannot be thirty yet. It's hardly a difference at all."

"Flatterer! I have passed that birthday, as you must well know."

"Then you must be at most a year past thirty," Sylvie said. There was a sincere ring in her voice that soothed Griselda's spirits. "Darlington looks as if he would like to gobble you up."

Griselda smiled uncertainly.

"I could never countenance such passion," Sylvie said, taking out her fan at the very idea. "His eyes actually look hot when he watches you. You do know that he watched you quite a bit at Lady Mucklowe's, don't you?"

Of course, she'd seen him leaning against the wall. "Making a cake of himself."

"Men are so prone to that," Sylvie said, and hesitated. "Griselda, do you mind if I ask you a question about Mayne?"

"Of course not. Although if you're going to bemoan the fact that he makes a cake of himself over you, I already know that. My poor brother is absolutely ravished with love."

"Yes," Sylvie said. "But I wish to speak to you about his discontent. He is not a happy man, you know? Perhaps he has always been like this, with a touch of the restlessness with his life?"

"No indeed," Griselda said, startled. "Mayne was a cheerful boy, and he certainly seemed to be enjoying himself—" She stopped. "But you are right in that he has changed in the last year or so. "He used to race around the *ton* making little scandals wherever he went and—to my mind—enjoying himself greatly. But then he fell in love."

"Ah," Sylvie said, leaning forward. "I should have known there was a lady at the heart of it. Tell me."

"There's nothing to tell," Griselda said, wondering if she were breaking a promise.

"No fidelity between brothers and sisters," Sylvie said, with that uncanny ability she had to know what someone was thinking. "The only true loyalty is between female friends. You must tell me, Griselda, if only so that I know what is causing his agitation."

"Her name is Lady Godwin," Griselda said reluctantly.

"A very, very slender woman with a great passion for music?"

"Is there anyone in the *ton* whom you have not met?"

"Yes, of course. I have not been presented to Lady Godwin, for example. But I like to know as much as I can about people; it is what makes life interesting. So he fell in love with this Lady Godwin, did he?"

Griselda looked carefully at Sylvie, but there wasn't even a shadow in her bright eyes. Truly, she *was* a Frenchwoman. "Mayne did fall in love with her," she admitted. "I believe the countess briefly flirted with the idea of having a tryst with him, but she ultimately decided to remain with her husband. They are very happy together and I heard that she is having a second child. Or perhaps she's already had the child; I can't remember and I haven't seen her recently. She's likely in the country."

"In that case, she must be *enceinte*," Sylvie pointed out. "If the child were already born, she would be here for the season."

"Perhaps," Griselda said, wondering a little at Sylvie's dispassionate tone. "I believe she is a very fond mother."

"Even so, one might bring an infant to London," Sylvie said. "So Mayne experienced a great unrequited passion, is that it?"

"Something of the sort," Griselda said. "And since then, he has not engaged in *affaires* of any kind."

"How long ago was this entanglement with the countess?"

"Two years?" Griselda said doubtfully. "At least that long. Rafe hadn't started his guardianship of the Essex girls yet, as I recall."

"Mayne has not taken a mistress in *two years*?" Sylvie seemed greatly struck by this. "Of course, you may simply be unaware of his interests."

"It's possible," Griselda said. "But I've seen a great deal of him. You know, he was engaged to Tess Essex, who married Felton. And then he acted as something of a companion to Imogen Maitland, who just married Rafe."

"I find it extraordinary that a duke wishes all and sundry to call him by his first name," Sylvie remarked. "Holbrook asked me to call him Rafe as well. Can you imagine?"

"Yes," Griselda said.

"I am worried that Mayne has fallen into a melancholy," Sylvie stated. "While I am all that is sympathetic, naturally, I must tell you that I have a natural antipathy to dismal people. My father suffered terribly after the death of my mother. We fled shortly after her burial, and then we were so far from his relatives and friends. You can imagine."

"I can only try."

Sylvie sighed. "The reason I did not come to London until now, when I am truly at an advanced age myself—all of twenty-six—was because my poor papa could not spare me. He was very despondent most of the day. It is only last year that he met a nice widow, married her, and is feeling much more cheerful. Even so, he spends most of his day in a way of which I cannot approve."

"What does he do? He lives in Northhamptonshire, doesn't he?"

"Yes, in Southwick. He has bred a great many dogs there.

And he allows several of them into the house, you understand."

Griselda nodded.

"This is not just a house," Sylvie said. "He built it along the lines of one of the great French country houses, Château des Milandes. It is beautiful—but full of *dogs*." Her dismay was evident.

"Oh dear," Griselda said.

"He lets them out, and then he goes outside to see where they are, and he brings them back in. Mind you, we have footmen who could very well do this work, if the dogs must come in the house. But my father has such a fondness for these animals that he thinks to read their mind." Sylvie sighed again. "I could not persuade him to come to London for the season. Luckily, my godmother is kind enough to chaperone me, but I think Papa should leave those dogs occasionally."

"You don't like dogs?"

"I had a little poodle as a child. Of course, I am fond of a well-behaved animal. But these have large tails. They bark, they smell, and sometimes they swim in the lake. Luckily, the widow whom he married is quite fond of animals. I was so grateful to her for taking over my father, I cannot tell you. I was beginning to see myself wasting away in that château, with no one for company but my father, my sister, and the dogs! My little sister, you understand, takes after my father and does not—" she paused impressively—"mind dog hair!"

"It sounds miserable. And very unlike you, Sylvie."

"Precisely. At any rate, I do have something of a dislike of being around people who are despondent in the way of my father."

"Mayne does not like dogs, as far as I know," Griselda hastened to say.

"No, but—"

"He will cheer up. He merely needs to settle down a bit. Once you are married, it will be different."

"Perhaps I should allow him to set a wedding date," Sylvie murmured. She looked rather unconvinced.

Griselda had a flash of panic. She couldn't watch her darling brother's heart be broken twice. "Certainly you must. I expect Mayne is dejected because he hasn't anything to look forward to. Once you have a family, of course everything will be different."

They crossed into the Ascot grounds and the carriage slowed sharply. Everywhere, carriages were pulling up and young girls in fluttering dresses and flirty little bonnets were clambering out. They looked like moving peonies, all heading toward the racetrack. Even in the carriage, Griselda could hear the muffled roar from the track.

"Shall we have to walk a great way?" Sylvie asked.

"Oh no," Griselda said. "We'll be dropped directly at our box."

Sylvie smiled.

Griselda sat back, feeling a qualm of true anxiety. Sylvie wasn't entirely happy. What would Mayne do if he were jilted, for the second time, by a woman whom he loved so tenderly? It made her feel ill just to think about it.

21

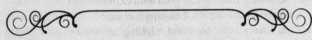

From The Earl of Hellgate,
Chapter the Seventeenth

I name her, Dear Reader, after one of Shake-speare's fairies, for she was as elusive and sweet to me as one of those sprites. You will loathe me for the truth of it . . . but when I beheld her gentle countenance, I burned with the desire to possess her. And yet marry her I could not . . . she was married to a worthy burgher. I tremble as I write the words:

The bonds of matrimony did not stop me.

Lucius Felton's box at Ascot was, without doubt, the most luxurious on the grounds. The King's box was a rather simple structure, lined in red velvet, and boasting chairs that were uncomfortably thronelike. But Felton had decided to take a box at Ascot only after he married, and he had a particular fondness for enclosed racing boxes. Since there wasn't one to be had at Ascot, he bribed the manager of the racetrack a fabulous amount—some said it was enough to run the entire operation for the next year—and built himself an elegant little box, with a roof to keep off the sun and rain. It was open along the track, naturally, but it extended far enough back so that there were a few little rooms off it, necessary to a lady's comfort when her husband (like Mr. Felton) was a devout enthusiast of the track.

There was, Josie discovered with extreme pleasure, a small retiring room for ladies, boasting a chaise longue. "Tess does have a lovely life," she said, sighing at the beauty of it all. The retiring room was an oasis of calm luxury, papered in silk the color of a spring beech leaf. When she walked in, Sylvie was already there, carefully turning her pink lips to a more intense peony color.

"Your Tess is indeed a very lucky woman," Sylvie agreed. "I am sorry that I did not see Mr. Felton before she did."

Josie smiled at Sylvie's frank assessment. "You might not have liked him."

"I would like anyone with his resources. And may I say that I am glad to be out of the marriage market before you appeared?" she remarked, looking Josie up and down. "Now that you have shed those strange undergarments, you are a rival."

Josie burst into laughter. "No one can say that you aren't generous, Sylvie."

"I speak a truth," she said, with her little French shrug. "I am of course slimmer than you, and I think that my nose is a trifle smaller, but I have not that air of"—she waved her hands—"*séduisant,* that you have."

"Unfortunately, I don't speak French," Josie said, rubbing a little bit of lip color on her lips as well.

"It means you look like a good bedfellow," Sylvie said baldly. And at Josie's giggle, "Did I say it wrongly? I work hard at this English, but it is difficult."

"I am sure that you look like an entrancing bedfellow yourself, Sylvie!"

"Oh no," she said. "I don't because I won't be. I'm not

very interested in that sort of thing. But luckily for me, there are men who feel as I do."

"Mayne?" Josie said, suddenly horrified by the turn in the conversation.

"Precisely." Sylvie put down her lip color, picked up a small enameled box and began powdering her nose.

"Are you sure," Josie said hesitantly, "that is, Mayne is not known for . . ."

"Oh, I know that his reputation is of the worst," Sylvie said, waving her hands again. "But men do not look for the same thing in their wives that they desire in a casual companion. Unless I am very mistaken, my fiancé would be taken aback by an expression of carnal interest on my part. And since I feel no such interest, we are well matched."

Josie bit her lip. Sylvie saw her face and smiled kindly.

"You must not color people with your brush," she said. "Does that make sense?" And at Josie's shake of the head, "Ah well. What I mean is that Mayne falls in love only with the women who are unattainable. It is a common type of man. In fact, from something Griselda told me, he has been in love only once before, and the lady in question was happily married." She closed her powder box, clearly considering her opinion on the subject final.

Sylvie tripped out of the room, and Josie sat staring at the mirror, her heart wrenched by the idea that Mayne could only fall in love with women who were unattainable. Surely after they married, Sylvie would grow more—more carnally interested, to use her own word.

Or she wouldn't, Josie thought, picturing Sylvie's cool little profile. Given that Sylvie was engaged to Mayne, and yet uninterested in him . . . what could change her mind?

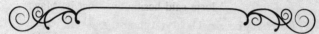

22

From The Earl of Hellgate,
Chapter the Seventeenth

I assure you that she came to no harm from our
frolicking. I persuaded her, Dear Reader, that
my blemished soul could be healed only by her
ministrations, and she, lovely Peasblossom,
adored sprite, believed me. She soothed my
soul . . . and other parts of my anatomy, in my
carriage. One afternoon that I shall never forget
I met her in the ruins of a lovely chapel, and
there amongst the wildflowers and fallen stones,
we . . .

The Ascot

If Darlington was supposed to be looking for a spouse, he
certainly wasn't going about it in a very productive way,
to Griselda's mind. Instead, he was hanging around their
party and seizing every opportunity to say scandalous things
to her. This made life interesting, but, of course, virtue suggested that she send him away.

"You must go off somewhere else," she scolded him. They
were all walking toward the royal enclosure, because
Griselda had heard that the new Duchess of Clarence had

arrived. Somehow they had drawn slightly ahead of Mayne, who had Sylvie and Josie on either arm.

"I shan't," he said into her ear. "I can't."

"You should be finding a young lady to court," she said. There was something in his eyes that made her feel groggy and quite unlike her capable self. Hadn't she decided to find a spouse for herself as well?

"I will stay here and help you choose your future spouse," he said, as if he could read her mind. "Lord Graystock appears to be wandering in our direction, for instance."

Griselda looked obediently. True enough, Graystock was ambling toward them. He was a shaggy fellow with a cheerful face and a sharp nose.

"He resembles nothing more than an amiable badger, given that white streak in his hair," Darlington said. "The two of you could settle in the country and set up a badger run."

Graystock was bowing now and saying hello in a determined fashion that showed that he, at least, would find the idea of a badger run with Lady Griselda quite acceptable.

But Griselda eyed his rather yellow teeth and withdrew her hand quickly.

"He's not so terrible," Darlington said, after Graystock had taken himself away. "There are those who would find Lady Griselda Graystock a less than salubrious sobriquet, but I'm sure you would get used to it."

"You are very unkind," Griselda pointed out.

"Always," Darlington said with a grin. "Are there any more of your suitors about?"

"After all, I must marry a worthy man, just as you must marry a worthy woman," Griselda said, tipping back her parasol and looking up at him.

"Must your spouse exhibit a badger-like worthiness?"

She smiled at him. He wasn't as sharp-tongued as he liked to pretend; in his eyes she could see the kind of disappointment that her brother used to display, back in the days when he had a toy he didn't wish to share. She changed the subject. "Have you read Hellgate's *Memoirs*?"

"That piece of rubbish? Absolutely not."

"I am finding it fascinating. Did you know that most people consider my own brother to be the basis for the book?"

"So you told me."

"I wish that the book hadn't been based on my brother," she said with a sigh. "It makes him seem so paltry, do you know what I mean? Mayne had these little attachments over a twenty-year period, but reading them all at once makes him seem despicably puerile."

"I don't see why you are certain your brother is the model," he said, looking as confused as men always did when one tried to explain the finer points of literature. "I was under the impression that Hellgate married, for example, and your brother is unmarried, is he not?"

"You will simply have to take my word for it," Griselda said. "Hellgate quotes the poet John Donne, and I promise you that my brother could spout poetry from morning to night if he wished to."

"Unexpected depths," Darlington murmured. "Aren't you feeling rather hot and weary? Perhaps ready to retire to a more secluded spot?"

"Not at all."

"You look quite hot."

Griselda blinked for a moment. She didn't *feel* hot. Was he really saying that her face was unattractively flushed? To her mind, there was nothing more pedestrian than a lady checking her face in a small glass. "I am absolutely comfortable," she said, though there was a bit of an edge in her voice.

"I beg to differ," he said, staring down at her with such an alarmed face that she actually began to wonder what could have gone wrong. Could her carefully applied face paint have smeared in the sun? Surely not. She wore only the slightest touch. "Oh dear," he said, peering into her face.

Griselda's heart was beating quickly and it wasn't from fear of a facial disaster. "Really?" she asked weakly. He was only an inch or two from her mouth. But he couldn't, he couldn't possibly kiss her here, with crowds of persons about and—

"You are *ill*."

"I am?"

"You are quite ill. Don't you feel rather odd?"

Griselda had to admit that perhaps she did. Her heart was racing alarmingly, and her knees felt quite weak. And now she thought about it, her cheeks were warm. She opened her mouth.

"Don't try to speak."

She began to speak anyway but her attention was caught by the color of his eyes. They really were extraordinary: a beautiful cool gray color that shaded into blue.

"You are about to faint. I can see it in your pallor."

Pallor? Griselda thought. How could I be pale? Visions of herself delicately patting on a small amount of Virgin's Blush that morning drifted through her head.

She frowned at him, just as something clipped her behind her knees and her right foot skated out from under her.

With a startled gasp, she dropped her parasol—but there he was. She was scooped into his arms, for all the world like the heroine of a melodrama. "Don't worry," he said to her with such a sweet, anxious expression that her heart thumped even harder. "I'll take care of you.

"It's just heat," he said to Josie, who had turned and was looking concerned. "Nothing to fear," he told Mayne. "I shall accompany Lady Griselda to her home, since she has grown faint."

Her brother was obviously torn between brotherly devotion and his horse. "I'm fine," Griselda said, not struggling to get down. After all, since Darlington deliberately tipped her off-balance, he might as well strain his muscles holding her above the ground. Who was she to cavil about the fact that she felt no faintness whatsoever? In fact, perhaps she was dizzy. She certainly felt wildly happy.

Mayne must have glimpsed her face because his eyes narrowed and he started to say something, but Darlington had already turned and was plowing through the crowd. Griselda put her head against his shoulder. He must be terribly strong to carry me along like this, she thought.

"You will put me down if you're about to fall over, won't you?"

"Why would I fall over?"

She glanced up, and sure enough, his face had the utterly wicked look of joy that a boy gets when he hides his favorite toy rather than share it. "You," she said, "ought to be ashamed of yourself."

"I so frequently am that I'm afraid the emotion has lost some of its punch. I will take you to my house."

They were almost at the hackney enclosure now. His long legs were carrying her through the crowds at top speed. "I can't go home with you," Griselda said. He put her on the seat, but then he stopped, arms braced on either side of her, and leaned toward her. His body blocked the light coming in the carriage; surely no one could see.

"You certainly can," he said. "I'll put a blanket over your head and pretend you're a potted plant."

"I can't!"

"You can."

Griselda pushed herself up, ready to do battle even though it brought his lips within an inch of hers. Sure enough, he dipped his head. Some moments later she came out of a daze to find that she was clutching his shoulders. "I don't do this sort of thing," she said wonderingly.

"Neither do I." She met his eyes and knew it was true.

"I don't sleep with women, and in fact, I've never invited a woman other than my mother into my apartments. But I would like you to come, Ellie."

"Ellie is a servant's name," she said, pushing her bottom lip out, just because she wanted to make him look.

Of course he did more than look, and by the time that kiss was over, she would have gone with him anywhere. And he knew it. He looked down at her with a slumbering little smile in his eyes and then finally pulled himself entirely into the carriage.

Griselda fell back, feeling as if her heart were going to pound its way out of her chest. "And what do you think the driver thought of the way you were stuck halfway in and halfway out of this hackney?" she said, hearing the gasp in her own voice.

He just grinned at her.

"Lord knows, *anyone* could have walked by the carriage," she said, fussing with the bodice of her dress because it had become slightly disarranged.

"Have you ever been in a gentleman's lodging?"

"Of course not!"

"A first for both of us, then."

23

From The Earl of Hellgate,
Chapter the Nineteenth

Now I come to the darkest chapter in my lurid career, Dear Reader, and I must beg of you again to close the pages of this book . . . set it to the side and take out your Prayerbook instead. Within you will find verses to nourish your inner spirit and true life, whereas here . . .

Oh Reader, Beware Indeed!

Mayne was conscious that he ought to be the happiest man on earth. Gigue had won her heart. Not only was he the richer by some thousands of pounds, but Rafe's entry had been soundly beaten. There's nothing like trouncing a dear friend to make one's joy complete.

What's more, he had his exquisite fiancée on his arm, and she was showing every sign of enjoying the Ascot. He glanced down at Sylvie. She was wearing a daring French coat of imperial satin in a lavender-blossom color. She had informed him of the particulars; in fact, he felt he knew her costume down to the color of its thread: the lilac color, bordered at the waist, the brocade ribbon of a shaded jonquille color (whatever that was), the scalloping around the feet, and the *pièce de résistance*, an Indian turban cap with a white sarsenet parasol with Vandyke floss fringe.

It wasn't that he didn't appreciate the picture she made, tripping along in her Indian turban. She looked dainty, French, and charmingly *au courant*. Perhaps it was just that he wasn't a turban sort of man. Or it might be the way the French coat pressed Sylvie's front so that she looked (a thought never to be revealed) as flat as a plate in the front. There were moments when women's fashion was inexplicable from a man's point of view.

Josie's costume was altogether more simple. She was wearing a walking dress in a scarlet color, very simple, rather than trimmed and fringed and *au courant*. She'd taken off her bonnet, and was swinging it from the hand that wasn't tucked under his elbow. And she was paying no attention whatsoever to Sylvie's observations, but kept craning her neck to watch horses thunder by on the track.

She looked as fascinated by the racetrack as if she'd never seen a horse run before, whereas Sylvie showed little interest in the sport. It was probably just that Josie was practically still in the nursery, though you'd never know it now that she'd discarded that hideous corset. She presented an entirely delicious picture of curvy womanhood. No garment in the world could make Josie flat as a plate, not even that horrendous corset. In fact, Mayne had noticed that every man who passed them was ogling her greedily.

"Mayne!"

He turned and looked down at his fiancée, who was looking up at him inquiringly.

"Boots of scarlet cloth trimmed with velvet," she said pointedly.

Mayne prided himself on quick recoveries. "Yes indeed,"

he said, with all the experience of years of talking to Griselda.

"But the gold and pearls—blended, you understand," Sylvie said, wrinkling her nose. "Entirely overdone, don't you think?"

"Yes, indeed." His attention wandered away again. Josie had stopped and was standing on tiptoe, watching as a group of horses thundered past them. "Look!" she cried, pulling his arm. "Unless I'm mistaken, one of Rafe's horses has won!"

Mayne peered over to the final line, and sure enough, it seemed that the winning horse was wearing Rafe's colors. He supposed he could allow Rafe a victory now and then.

"Divided on the forehead, like horns," Sylvie said to him.

"Of course." Surely they had seen enough? He was longing to return to the box where he could watch the races from a decent vantage point.

"Mayne!" Sylvie was laughing at him, he realized with a start. "You're not paying the slightest bit of attention, are you? I just observed that the Duchess of Piddlesworth was wearing a horn of pearls on her forehead and you agreed!"

"I do apologize," Mayne said, although he felt rather irritated, to tell the truth. "Would you like to return to our box now? It is rather difficult to see the races from here."

Sylvie would never do anything quite so graceless as to pout . . . but there were those who might call her expression a pout. "How tedious," she said, frowning at him. "I would much prefer to continue to look for Countess Mitford. I promised her that I would tell her something of the French way of arranging a drawing room."

Mayne felt a sudden, mad desire to get away from her. "Yes, let's look for Countess Mitford," he said. "I'm sure she is waiting for you with bated breath."

Sylvie's eyes narrowed slightly but she said nothing. She was, Mayne realized, far too well-mannered to engage in something as undignified as brangling in a public arena. "I apologize," he said, looking down at her again.

But she smiled at him. "I was just thinking that you are akin to my father." She wrinkled her nose. "He is, you understand, quite obsessed with the fate of his dogs. Are they well, are they strong, do they need a constitutional dose of barleywater?"

"Barleywater?"

She nodded. "The poor animals dare not show a yellow eye or he puts them on a special diet of steamed broccoli and barleywater."

Mayne shuddered. "I fail to see any connection between myself and your father." Josie had let go of his arm and was standing just beside the fence, watching as another heat of horses made their first sweep around the turn.

"Josie!" Sylvie cried. "Do back up. You'll become quite dusty."

But Josie didn't hear her. She was clapping as a slender chestnut broke from the pack and swept forward, her little ears cocked far back. Even from here Mayne recognized the stride of a winner.

"Who is she?" Josie called back to him.

He shook his head. "Palmont's colors—"

A gentleman moved next to Josie and was eagerly talking to her, and then they watched, shoulder-to-shoulder, as the horses swept about again. A tall, gaunt gelding was gaining on the inside . . . gaining . . . gaining.

"No, no!" Josie screamed wildly.

Sylvie made a small sound of disapproval. "Who is that *man* whom Josephine is standing beside?"

"Lord Tallboys," Mayne said. Tallboys was watching Josie more closely than the horse. But she was completely swept into the excitement of the race, her cheeks pink, gloved hands gripping the railing tightly. "Rafe introduced him to Josie at the Mucklowe ball."

"Is he respectable?"

Mayne frowned down at her. "Do you think that I would allow Josie to be in his presence were he not? He's a good man with an excellent estate."

"Unmarried?" Sylvie asked in a hushed voice. And then: "Excellent!"

Just then the brown horse seemed to gather herself and stretch her neck, and before the crowd could even take a breath she swept past the winner's post. Josie was screaming and waving her discarded bonnet; Tallboys gave a roar of approval. Then Tallboys was dancing Josie around in an exuberant circle.

Sylvie laughed, watching them. "I think little Josephine just made a conquest."

"Indeed," Mayne said, watching how Josie's curls were flying as Tallboys swept her around. She was laughing and laughing. Tallboys was a bit young for her. Couldn't be more than four-and-twenty.

Which was just the right age.

Sylvie moved forward and Tallboys instantly came to a halt and gave a boyish bow. "You must forgive me," he said, "I'm afraid that Miss Essex and I were overcome by the exuberance of the occasion."

Sylvie dimpled at him and Mayne watched, expecting him to get an eager glint in his eye on hearing Sylvie's charming accent. "An enchanting show of enthusiasm," she was saying. "Perhaps you had made a feather on the race, hmmm?"

"Took a flutter," Mayne corrected her. "Tallboys, your servant."

Tallboys didn't seem to have understood Sylvie. He had turned back directly to Josie and had pulled out his race book. "You see," he said, "her name is Firebrand. It's a good name, isn't it, Miss Essex?"

"I think she was too delicate to be a firebrand," Josie said.

"Did you see how she flicked her ears after she slowed down? As if she knew she had won and was laughing."

"She certainly knew she won; a good horse always does."

"Some of my father's horses became quite dejected when they lost." And then they were off, talking of Josie's father's stables.

Sylvie turned back to Mayne. "I think Lord Tallboys has found a new passion in life," she whispered. "He will give Skevington some stiff competition."

"Do you think so?" Mayne felt as crotchety as a man of sixty. "He's quite young."

"They can play together, like two kittens."

To Mayne's mind, the way Tallboys was looking at Josie had nothing to do with kittens. "We must return to the box now," he said, pointedly not issuing Tallboys an invitation.

Tallboys was an inane fool, though he'd never noticed it before. It was a wonder that Josie had laughed at his pitiful comments. She sounded as delighted as if she were talking to Prinny himself.

It was irritating to find oneself behaving like as much as a fool as Tallboys. He'd never liked it in others, and he was too honest not to notice the same stupidity in himself. The truth of it is, Mayne told himself, that you are engaged and yet you don't *feel* quite engaged. He always thought that engagements were a matter of stolen kisses and sudden meetings of eyes.

Of course, he'd done all the business of stolen kisses in the past, and he didn't want a wife who was as light-skirted as the women he'd slept with. He had to make up his mind. Either he wanted to exchange kisses with his fiancée or he didn't.

Josie was trailing along behind Sylvie and Mayne, who seemed to be in a rather irritable mood, when suddenly a voice in her ear said, "Miss Essex?"

And when she turned in that direction, there was a portly

young man smiling down at her as if he knew her very well.

She knew his face but she couldn't place it, so she said, "Good afternoon, sir."

"We met at a ball last week. I'm Mr. Eliot Thurman. May I take your arm?" he asked.

Mayne was continuing without her, so she did take his arm. And then before she knew it, they had wandered off in quite a different direction than Tess's box, toward the tents where they were serving refreshments.

She went along rather listlessly. After all, did it matter? Mayne was in love with his passionless fiancée, to whom Josie was beginning to take quite a dislike. Griselda had left with Darlington, and if Josie thought that there should be limits to how close one grows to the enemy, well, Griselda had not asked her.

If only Annabel had come to Ascot! But Annabel didn't want to bring Samuel into these crowds; Imogen was on her wedding trip; Tess was in Northumberland with her husband . . . Josie sighed. Then she roused herself. She might as well try to be polite.

"Do you have a horse entered in a race, Mr. Thurman?" she asked.

"No, I have not," he answered. "My mother says that a gentleman must have an occupation. I'm a little too lazy for something as strenuous as smoking tobacco, so I devote myself to betting." And he broke into a great peal of laughter: "Haw, haw, haw!"

Josie felt as if she must have missed something. "Your mother thought you ought to smoke tobacco . . . as an occupation?"

"It's a jest," he said to her with a shading of disapproval in his voice.

Last time she heard it, jests were supposed to be funny. Or at least make sense.

They had walked quite beyond the tents, into the formal gardens that ringed the stables and the racetrack. "I suppose we should return," she said, stooping to examine the primroses. But someone had made a mistake and planted evening primroses and most of them were shut up against the sun.

But Mr. Thurman paused and made an odd little noise with his throat. Josie looked at him. He did it again. Suddenly Josie had the alarmed thought that he might be having a fit of some kind. People who had that sort of sodden red color high in their cheeks were prone to seizures of the heart, or so she'd heard. She frowned at him. Surely she knew that face, and in some unpleasant context too—

A second later she realized that Thurman was having an attack of a different kind, as he pulled her into his arms and pressed his lips to hers. They were surprisingly cool and rather flabby. For a moment Josie was frozen in surprise, but then he forced a plump tongue between her lips and she began struggling to get loose.

He was surprisingly strong. Before she realized it, he had backed her under the overhanging roof of the stable. Josie felt as if she were watching from the outside: watching another girl—some other girl, not herself—struggle against the man who had her pinned against the wall. He was rolling his tongue in her mouth so that she was almost choking. Suddenly she felt her dress catch on a spur in the boards behind her and rip. She started struggling, kicking him over and over in the shins, but she was wearing slippers, and he had his feet planted solidly. She tried to kick higher, but her dress was narrow and confined her movement. She managed to wrench sideways, away from him.

He pulled back for a moment and said, "You're a feisty one." His voice was thick, as if he were drunk. Josie filled her lungs to scream but he clamped his mouth over hers again and she almost suffocated. And then she realized to her horror that the rip in her gown was widening. If she didn't get away it might fall clean off her body.

If she didn't—

So she did.

She raised her leg in one quick and smooth motion and planted her knee squarely in the groin that had been rubbing itself all over her dress. His hands loosed her arms instantly and she staggered to the side, hearing her dress rip on the rough boards again so that she could feel air on her back.

He staggered back, bent over, his voice coming in a high wheezy rasp. "You damned—damned—"

Josie turned to run—of course she should run!—but then her eye caught the back door of the stables. In order to keep the stalls clean and sweet-smelling for the visitors who would be wandering through the stables, the grooms had been diligently throwing refuse out the back door. Presumably someone would haul it away in the morning, but now—

There was a spade leaning against the wall and a mound of ordure as high as her knees. It was the act of a second to dig the spade into the heaping brown mess and swing around in his direction. She couldn't lift it over her waist, but she didn't need to. As the shovel swung about it gained momentum, and just as Mr. Thurman raised his head, doubtless to say something despicable, the steaming, dripping pile of horse dung flew off the shovel and slammed against his face. The last glimpse Josie got before she turned and ran through the door into the stables was his wide-open eyes and his even wider open red mouth, both obscured a moment later by a mass of wet, brown muck.

She darted into the stables and started running down the long aisle. It was the noon hour, and no races were scheduled until the afternoon. Even the stable boys must be loitering in front of the building. There was no one to help. He would see her; he would catch her. Any moment she would feel his beefy powerful hand on her shoulder.

Then she caught sight of red blankets with Mayne's crest, slung over the side of a stall. She glanced behind her, and the wide aisle of the stables lay clear, with nothing more ominous than particles of straw dancing in the sunlight. Without pausing for breath, she unlatched the door of Gigue's stall, darted around her sleek side and threw herself down in the yellow straw at the back of the stall. And held her breath.

She couldn't hear anything. No sound of steps. Nothing but the snorting breath of the filly as she stamped uneasily.

"Hush," Josie whispered. "Hush, please."

The horse whickered a little in response and switched her tail so it lashed Josie's face with stings like a flock of tiny wasps. Josie's eyes filled with tears. She'd lost her reticule somewhere, her bodice was ripped, and when she pushed herself into the corner of the stall, she discovered that her bare back was against the boards. That rip she heard had gone straight through her chemise and gown.

Once she started crying, she sobbed so hard that her body shook all over. Finally, she collected herself, ripped off a section of her chemise and used it as a handkerchief and began thinking about how to leave the stable. She could hear the voices of stable boys filtering down the aisle. It was only a matter of minutes, a half hour at most, before someone would be along to check on Gigue. Billy would return from his midday meal.

There was a wooden ladder nailed to the wall, leading up to the hay loft. She could climb the ladder and simply wait until everyone went home for the day.

Gigue, meanwhile, had managed to turn herself around in the narrow space of her stall and was snuffling at Josie's face in a comforting sort of way. "I'm so glad you won today," Josie whispered to her. "Oh, how am I to get out of here?"

The enormity of her situation was growing on her.

Obviously, Mr. Thurman had decided to make the best of a bad situation and taken his malodorous self off to his lodgings to change. Of course he hadn't followed her. She knew now that she had been safe the moment she darted through that open door: the last thing Thurman would want was to marry her. He was the horrid friend of Darlington who had made fun of her at Imogen's wedding ball. And yet if anyone—particularly Rafe—ever found out what just happened, she would be forced to marry Thurman.

She was ruined, and the only solution for ruination that Josie had ever heard of was marriage. Well, she wasn't precisely ruined. But the memory of Thurman's clutching hands brought on another shuddering fit and she had to tear off more of her chemise to mop up her tears.

Why was it that her sisters managed to get themselves ruined with handsome gentlemen who were poised to fall in love with them? Whereas she had to wander off with a disgusting turnip of a man whom she'd kill before she'd agree to marry. It just wasn't fair.

Gigue suddenly raised her head, pricking up her ears. Likely, Billy was coming. He would send for Mayne, and Mayne could pull his carriage around the back of the stables, or perhaps he could just throw a blanket over her and pretend she had fainted.

Except he wouldn't be able to carry her out of the stables, given her weight. If she were covered up by the blanket, she wouldn't have to see his face grow red with the exertion, or hear him panting. Tears started to slip down her face again, and Josie wiped them away impatiently.

She sat up in the corner, brushing off some straw. Gigue had turned about again and was reaching her head out of the stall and whickering. Josie took one look down at her gown. If she were seen in this situation, explanations would have to be made. And if those explanations *were* made, she would have to marry Thurman.

A second later Josie was clambering up the ladder into the hayloft. It was a huge, open space that stretched above all the stalls. Golden straw was heaped in large forkfuls on the floor. She would be safe here until she could find her way home later.

Unless she told Mayne? For that was surely Mayne's voice. She knelt next to the hole and tried to peer down and sideways, but all she could see was Gigue's twitching coat. Mayne was crooning to her in his deep voice, and to Josie's horror, the very sound of his voice made warmth prickle over her body.

The last thing she wanted was to develop a *tendre* for Mayne! He was so far above her reach that it was as if he were the god Apollo himself. What's more, he was in love with another woman.

Even as she told herself all these things, Josie laid herself flat so she could better peer through the hole. Yes, there was Mayne. It was comforting just to see him: his careless elegance that must have taken hours to achieve. His hair fell over his brow in a sleek and shining curl that fell in a perfect tumble. From the angle of the hayloft, she could just see his shoulders as he caressed Gigue. His coat sat on his broad shoulders as if a wrinkle wouldn't dare to alight.

What a contrast to herself! Her clothes were ripped and soiled; she had been half mangled by a loathsome man. It would give her a great deal of pleasure to see Mayne mussed. Crumpled. Muddy. Perhaps dressed in rags. A little smile curled her lips. Perhaps in a loincloth!

But then she suddenly realized that she wasn't thinking about a dandy's comeuppance, but the dandy's legs. Below her, his back moved down. He was bowing.

"She's not here," he said. "Damn it, I wish Griselda hadn't succumbed to the heat." He must have come to the stables to look for her, Josie. And Josie knew instantly Mayne was accompanied by Sylvie. There was no mistaking the change in

Mayne's voice. It made her feel palpably ill, the way his voice got syrupy and lovesick when he spoke to his fiancée.

"She has very large teeth," Sylvie was saying. "And they are so *yellow*."

"Not for a horse," Mayne replied.

"You should arrange for one of your persons to wash her teeth. I am certain she would be more comfortable."

Mayne didn't even laugh, which Josie took to be a sign of his smittenness. She could just glimpse the top of Sylvie's turban. It was as alluring as Sylvie herself.

"Sylvie," Mayne was saying, and there was something about the tone in his voice that made Josie swallow. "You're so beautiful. Do you know that?"

If Sylvie didn't have a precise understanding of her own worth, Josie would eat her hat. Not that she had a hat, for she'd lost her bonnet with her reticule.

"Thank you," Sylvie said, without a trace of the abject pleasure that Josie would have felt at that compliment.

"I cannot restrain myself around you," Mayne said. Though it was really *Garret* talking, not Mayne. It was the private man, a man in love. A tear fell down Josie's cheek and she absentmindedly brushed it away. All she could see was the corner of his shoulder now, but he was reaching out, drawing Sylvie to him.

Josie shivered. If he ever pulled her into his arms, she would—she would fall into them like a tree toppled in a lightning storm.

Sylvie was of a different caliber. Ashes where Josie would be fire. "Mayne, I scarcely think this is a proper moment for—"

He swooped. Josie held her breath. That's what he would do, of course. He would sweep Sylvie into his embrace, and she would melt against him, just the way all the heroines of the Minerva novels did. Then Sylvie leapt back into her view.

Her voice was colder than a February Sunday in Lent.

"How dare you! How dare you maul me in such a fashion, Lord Mayne!"

Kiss her again, Josie thought. She wants to be seduced. You were too fast. Or she's too shy.

"It seems we must clarify our relations," Sylvie stated, her voice frigid. "I am never to be approached, or mauled, in any fashion."

It's because she's French, Josie thought. An English-woman could never resist Mayne. Oh God, if only he would speak to her with half the longing he poured into one word to Sylvie, she—she—

"I am fond of you, and I shall certainly allow you your marital rights."

Josie instinctively gasped and then clapped her hand over her mouth.

"Did you hear me?" Sylvie asked impatiently. "I wish to make certain that you understand me, Mayne. I realize that you have lived in England, and have absorbed some regret-table customs here. But I must ask you to give me every consideration that you would give your own mother."

"My mother," Mayne said, finally.

Josie's heart sunk. He didn't have that liquid note of happiness in his voice anymore.

"Of course!" Sylvie replied. "Surely I needn't tell you that the most important women in your life, those deserving of the most respect, are your mother and your wife. Pooh! This conversation is quite foolish, is it not?"

"I think it is remarkably interesting."

"I do not believe for a moment that you would treat your mother with anything less than the most delicate and filial respect. She is a holy sister of the Church, is she not? I fail to see why you should treat me with any less courtesy."

"My mother did indeed retire to a convent," Mayne said. "But you, Sylvie, are no nun."

"I deserve precisely the same courtesy," Sylvie said. "A

lack of decorum led to the downfall of the French monarchy."

"I meant you no discourtesy."

There was a moment of silence and then Sylvie said, painstakingly, "I find this subject rather distasteful, but I have always believed that it is better to be quite clear in matters such as these."

Josie was gripping the edge of the hayloft opening so hard that her fingers were white.

"I agree," Mayne said.

Of course, she shouldn't be listening. No one should listen to this. For Sylvie was explaining in her ravishing French accent that she would dislike it of all things if Mayne took it in his head to manhandle her whenever he felt the wish. In fact, she would prefer that perhaps an amicable schedule could be—

Josie had to bite her lip. She wasn't sure whether she wanted to laugh or snort. Annabel would die laughing when she heard this.

Not that she would ever disclose that she had done such an ill-mannered thing as listen to a private conversation of this nature. She edged a bit farther away, and some strands of hay fell onto Gigue's back.

"Sylvie," Mayne said, interrupting her lecture. "Darling, you simply don't understand how things are between a man and a woman, *chérie.*"

"I assure you—" Sylvie said. From where she was, Josie could just see the curve of Mayne's cheek as he cupped Sylvie's face in his hands. His fingers were long and strong. He leaned toward Sylvie and Josie almost gulped. He had the longest eyelashes she could imagine on a man. No wonder—

No wonder Sylvie was silent in his arms. Josie felt pricks in her eyes again, and now she really felt ill-mannered, watching. They were so clearly in love, so beautiful together.

Mayne would persuade Sylvie to kiss him, and years from now they would laugh at her reluctance. Laugh surrounded by their *children*.

Josie shut her eyes tightly so that she couldn't see his bent head, the tenderness in his fingers, the passion in the way his shoulders bent toward Sylvie. She never would be a woman like Sylvie, a woman whom a man like Mayne would worship, the way he did Sylvie. Tears slid hotly over her fingers. She was the sort of woman whom a man felt he could maul with impunity. She was the sort of woman who ended up behind the stables, being pushed against the wood, while Sylvie, delicate, beautiful Sylvie, was adored by Mayne.

Her body was rocking with sobs now, but she didn't make a sound, just pressed her hands over her mouth.

All the exhilaration of watching Thurman's face disappear behind brown sludge was evaporating. How was she to get home? How could she bear to—

Her eyes flew open.

The slap startled Gigue too, and she kicked the wall in protest.

24

**From The Earl of Hellgate,
Chapter the Nineteenth**

I know no better name to give her than that of
Shakespeare's fierce Amazon queen, Hippolyta.
In mourning because the lovely Peasblossom had
flown back to her little nest, I wandered down
the streets of London, scarce knowing where I
was. This particular day I had visited Hampton
Court, and although drained by sorrow, I had
been to King Henry VIII's tennis court and
taken three very fair sets from a certain gentleman of my acquaintance . . .

I t's rather disconcerting to bring a woman to my house,"
Darlington said as the hackney slowed to a close.

He couldn't be as disconcerted as Griselda was. After a
lifetime of appropriate behavior, she was throwing all cau-
tion to the winds and actually entering a gentleman's house?
And yet . . .

She looked at Darlington's strong, lean body and his un-
settling beauty. She was going to his house. She would think
about propriety, spouses, and other unpleasant topics tomorrow.

"Aren't all young bachelors accustomed to bringing fe-
males into their dwellings?" she asked, shaking off the sense
that she was like one of those women, who were for hire,
presumably.

"I don't think so. My mother visits occasionally, but she
sends a footman to fetch me to her carriage rather than enter
the house herself."

"Why doesn't she enter? Or request that you visit her?"
Griselda asked.

"Have you met the duchess?"

"We have been presented."

Darlington grinned at her. "Then you know that my
mother is charmingly irresolute."

"I'm afraid I don't know her well enough to make that
judgment."

"My father ordered the entire family to avoid me at all
costs, at least until I had set myself up in a decent marriage."

"How very—very—" But she couldn't think what to say.

He didn't seem to mind. "My mother is fond of me and so
she comes to visit, nimbly making her way around my father's commandment. He knows, but turns a blind eye."

"I'm sure you are a trial to him."

"He despairs, he despairs." The door to the carriage
swung open.

Darlington lived in a small house on Portman Square.
Griselda didn't know what she expected: an apartment, probably. After all, he was the third son of a duke, and penniless,
by all accounts. But it was a sweet little house with an elabo-
rately carved arch over a black walnut door. It wasn't as
large as her own house, but it was more charming.

As they walked up the path, an elderly man with stern
eyes opened the door and bowed stiffly.

"Thank you, Clarke," Darlington said, taking Griselda's
pelisse himself and handing it to the butler.

Griselda felt more and more confused. *Did* young bachelors have butlers? Apparently so.

"We'll have tea in my study," Darlington told Clarke.

Did young bachelors serve tea to women who had entered their house for a less than respectable purpose? Apparently they did, because she found herself walking sedately before Darlington, for all the world as if she were going to tea with a duchess.

The walls of Darlington's study were painted a dark crimson color. There were no pictures on the walls, for the simple reason that every wall was covered with books. Griselda's mouth almost fell open. Of course, she'd seen books. Rafe had a reasonable number of books in his study, though she'd never seen him actually reading one. And certainly there were books in her house. But here books lined the walls, and stacks sat on the floor. There were books on the large desk and books on the armchairs.

"I gather that you are a great reader?" she asked.

" 'Tis one of my faults," Darlington said.

Griselda trailed a gloved finger over the spines of the books closest to her. They weren't the sort of books she would have expected. Rafe had rows of classics in his study, all bound up in leather and dating back a few centuries, if the dust that fell from them was any indication.

Darlington had rows and rows of . . . how to put it? Books that the servants read. Books that *she* read with secret pleasure. Books from lending libraries. The kind that had titles like *Nocturnal Revels* and the *Malefactors' Bloody Register.* Books about murder. His desk had stacks of the same. She picked one up.

"I read this," she said, glancing over her shoulder as she opened the flyleaf of Herbert Croft's *Love and Madness.* "A most affecting story. All those letters between Martha Ray and her murderer."

"Cross made them up," Darlington said, coming to her shoulder.

"That's hardly the point, is it? Of course the author made up the letters. But they were so affecting."

"How so?"

Griselda tucked herself into a chair. He was standing entirely too close to her, and it made her pulse race. "The argument that the murderer—what was his name?"

"James Hackman."

"That's right. When he was trying to convince Martha to leave her lover, the Earl of Sandwich, he was remarkably convincing in saying that she wasn't Sandwich's *property*. Of course," she added hastily, "it's all remarkably scandalous and she was a loose woman."

Darlington came over and leaned on the back of her chair. She felt him pick up a strand of her hair. "Loose women," he said dreamily. "How we love them. Of course, Hackman fell so much in love that he grew to hate her."

"You imply that he killed her from hatred," Griselda said. "I think he killed her because he couldn't bear to have her in the world, and himself not in a room next to her. I think he simply couldn't countenance their separation any longer."

"You have a romantic soul."

"No. But I have spent a great deal of time watching people in the *ton* create indiscretions."

"While creating none such yourself."

Until today, Griselda thought, wondering again at herself. She tilted back her head and looked up at him. There he was: all tawny masculinity, that lean face and eyes that looked older than he was. "People make fools of themselves when they're in love—or in passion."

"Are you?"

"That's a blunt question. I do not consider myself a fool."

"Thus you are not in love."

She almost shut her eyes against his beauty. "Certainly not!"

"I begin to believe that I am."

Griselda blinked at him. "You are—"

"In love. With you. Not that you need fear that I shall take a pistol to your heart as poor Hackman did."

"You are as mad as Hackman, then," Griselda said. He bent over the chair, and his hair fell over his brow. She couldn't stop herself and reached a hand up to his cheek.

"Do you know what Martha looked like?" he asked.

"No."

"Not like you. She was a member of the *demimonde*, the notorious mistress of an earl. She had a cleft chin."

"I don't."

He tapped a finger on her chin. "No, you don't. That's a perfectly round little chin that I see before me. And Martha had dark hair."

Griselda couldn't help smiling. It was an odd thing to know that the gentleman before you was as aware as you were that your hair was fair by nature . . . because it was fair all over her body.

"It's said that she had bright, smiling eyes and a warm, open countenance."

"Who said that?" Griselda asked.

"*Westminster Magazine*. April of 1779."

"How on *earth*—"

"Would you believe me if I told you I was a scholar?"

"Not for a moment," Griselda said, smiling at him. She knew scholars. Why, Rafe's own brother was a scholar, and a Cambridge professor at that. "Can you read ancient Aramaic?"

"What's that?"

"I believe it's the language the Bible was written in," Griselda said.

"I had the sort of education that leads me to believe the

Bible was written by an Englishman, in an Englishman's language." He dropped her hair and was just sliding a warm hand down her arm when the door opened and his butler arrived with a tea tray.

"It feels odd to be serving tea to you," Griselda said a few seconds later. "Rather as if I am a maiden aunt on a visit." They were sitting opposite each other, and she was pouring from an exquisite blue teapot.

He bellowed with laughter at that. "You don't look like a maiden aunt of my acquaintance," he said wolfishly.

She felt herself turning pink, but still had to say it. "Yet I'm so much older than you are." She put a lump of sugar in his cup and handed it to him. "I truly feel as if my age makes this both remarkably improper and, in some odd way, more proper. After all, I am far too old to be having an impetuous affair."

"With a younger man," he said, his eyes teasing her over his teacup.

"One hates to think what people would say about me." It was a relief to say it, rather than have the niggling silent shame of it under her breastbone.

"I expect they'd say you were desperate."

She wrinkled her nose. "Distasteful."

"Desperate, with an appetite for beauty."

Griselda put down her teacup a bit sharply. "Worse and worse."

"Oh, I can do better than that," he said. "This *is* like Martha and Hackman, you know. He was much younger than she."

"I begin to feel as if I should flee this house to save my life," Griselda said, making a rather vain attempt to change the subject.

"Seven years they had between them," Darlington said, putting his teacup to the side.

If he was fishing for her age, she certainly was not going

to tell him. In fact, she really ought to leave now. All that exuberant impetuosity she felt earlier had disappeared.

"How surprising that you know so much of that ancient murder case," she said.

"I know about any number of curious old stories," he said, not seeming to notice the little *froideur* in her voice. "But tell me, Griselda, what do you find most surprising about Martha's love affair with Hackman? That he was younger, or that he killed her?"

"Murders are alarmingly commonplace," Griselda observed.

There was a little smile at the corner of his lips that made her take a lemon biscuit, although she wasn't in the least hungry.

"So you would find their age difference to be the most interesting aspect of the case?"

"Surely we can talk of something else?" she asked. "I do think we have said all there is to say on the subject."

"Indeed, I would like to show you the disposition of my house," he said, rising when she did.

Griselda had already made up her mind that she wasn't going upstairs. True, she had had wild thoughts earlier . . . but they were quite quelled now, and she had returned to her senses. "*Is* it your house? I'm certain that someone told me you were penniless. Do you live here on your father's sufferance, then?"

He took her arm. "Getting your own back, are you?"

"I'm sure I don't know what you mean. This is a charming room," Griselda said, pausing on the threshold to a small dining room. The furniture was excellent, old comfortable pieces in black walnut. She waved her hand at the paper, which was a light gold color, marked with small birds: masculine yet delightful. "Did your mother choose this?"

"No, my sister Betsy."

"Oh, of course." And then, as he was opening the door to

a small sitting room, "But you haven't a sister Betsy! Your father has three sons."

He grinned at her. "Perhaps you looked me up in *Debrett's*? Before sleeping with me, I mean. Surely every matron makes sure that bloodlines are in order before skipping off to a hotel."

"You, sir, are a terrible conversationalist," Griselda said tartly. "Do you always say precisely what comes into your mind?"

"I am known for being an uncomfortable companion for that very reason," he said.

"So who is Betsy?"

"There is no Betsy."

She turned to look, and he was leaning against the doorjamb, looking at her in that oddly intense manner of his. "I told you. The only woman who has entered my house is my mother, and that rarely."

"So . . ."

"I chose the paper myself. I am used to taking care of myself. And I think that you are much the same, are you not? Who takes care of you, Lady Griselda? As I understand it, your mother lives a retired life, does she not?"

"I have no need of anyone to take care of me. But if I have need of something, my brother has always sufficed."

"Mayne?"

"He's the only brother I have, and unlike Betsy, he actually exists."

"Mayne does not strike me as a particularly caring person."

Griselda's eyes narrowed. *No one* insulted her brother—unless, of course, that person was discussing adultery. "He has always watched out for me. And now, I really must be going."

"You haven't seen the upstairs yet."

"That would be quite improper."

"All the more reason," he said, smiling at her. "I think, Lady Griselda, that you need someone to take care of you."

"I—"

Two seconds later he had scooped her into his arms, as if she were nothing more than a fainting heroine. "You're making a practice of this," she said, not struggling to get free, as that would be inelegant.

"I hope to," he said, carrying her up the stairs.

"Is your butler watching us?" Griselda asked.

"I told him to go home. He's not really a butler. He doesn't live here."

"If he's not a butler, what is he?" Griselda asked, struggling to keep her tone casual. He smelled faintly spicy, with an overlay of ink. For some reason she found it intoxicating.

"He was accused of murder," Darlington said. "But he didn't do it, I assure you."

Griselda opened her mouth, but then they were in Darlington's bedchamber, and she suddenly realized that—that—

"There's no use in complaining," he said.

"You can put me down," she said with dignity.

"As long as you promise not to turn around and trot down the stairs."

"I *never* trot."

So he let her down, but the moment her feet touched the ground he caught up her face in both his hands and kissed her. One minute they were talking, and the next he was taking her mouth with a kind of savage desperation that had nothing to do with light conversation about butlers and murders. Because that must have been a joke, Griselda thought dimly, but thoughts were sliding away now, and a sort of delicious fog descended on her mind in which the only things that mattered were the taste of him, the smell of him, and the sound of his breathing.

It took her maid at least fifteen minutes to disrobe Lady

Griselda Willoughby. It took Darlington approximately fifteen seconds. The hooks seemed to fly apart at his fingers
and he kept kissing her all the while, kissing her so that she
didn't think about what was happening. It was as if Griselda
threw away the "lady" part of her with every garment that
fell to the ground. By the time he took her chemise, she felt
as wild as any thoroughly debauched concubine. Her hair
swirled around her shoulders, and she didn't feel like a
maiden aunt any more. Not seeing the way that his fingers
trembled when he touched her. Or the way he stood still
when she touched him, his breath quick, eyes dark.

"God, you're beautiful," he said.

Griselda felt beautiful.

25

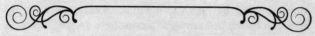

From The Earl of Hellgate, Chapter the Nineteenth

She was statuesque, and carried herself as if she were one of King Henry's unfortunate wives. Such is my weakness, that although I had sworn to eschew the fair sex, and I was in the black days of mourning . . .

Josie crept down the ladder about half an hour after Mayne and Sylvie left. She'd found a grain sack to wear over her shoulders so the rip in her gown didn't show. Her plan was to wait for one of Mayne's stablehands and ask him to show her a back way out so that she could find a hackney.

She came down as hurriedly as she could and then hid in the front corner of Gigue's stall, where she couldn't be seen from the aisle. People kept strolling by, even though the races were over, until at last the trickle of feet stopped. She stood, shivering, overcome by exhaustion, fear and distress. Her mind was revolving in unhappy circles.

Finally, she heard footsteps coming that stopped before the stall; that must be one of Mayne's stablehands. Gigue had been bending her neck and nosing her trough, as if hopeful that food had somehow landed there since she searched the last time. Josie had formed a very low opinion of her intelligence.

Sure enough, the stocky figure of Mayne's stablemaster, Billy, pushed open the door to Gigue's stall. "Good evening," she said, as quietly as possible, so as not to startle the man. But he jumped anyway. "I must look a sight," she said, trying a little smile.

"Aye, and you do, miss," the man said, blinking at her. "What in the love of God happened to ye, then?"

Josie bit her lip before it could start trembling again. "I should like you to find me a hackney," she said, "if you please. And then bring me to it. I must go home."

His eyes skittered up and down, from her face to her gown, to the brown burlap clutched over her shoulders.

"I know I look awful. Please help me get home. I shall be glad to pay handsomely for your aid."

"I won't need any payment. Sit down, miss. You look as if you're about to fall down. I'll fetch you a carriage, but it will take a moment, as there's a mite of traffic."

Josie looked down at the straw around her feet. Of course, she could sit down. She was terribly tired. "Don't you think someone might see my knees from the aisle? I cannot be seen."

"Not a bit of it. I'll just fetch a few more burlaps from next door, and throw them over your knees and there's naught a thing to see."

Gratefully, Josie slid down until she was sitting in the corner, and a second later Billy piled a few more burlaps about her. They smelled like grain. She opened her eyes a little blearily. "You didn't feed the horses with this grain, did you? It smells green."

He stared at her with an odd frown. "You're right about

that, miss. We had three sacks that were tossed for being too green."

Josie closed her eyes again.

By the time Mayne appeared at the door, she was fast asleep. He stood for a second, looking down at her and feeling a swell of rage in his throat such as he had never experienced before. Billy was right. Even from here he could tell that Josie had been violated. Her face was dead white and all streaked with tears. Her hair was falling around her shoulders, and her gown was splattered with brown mud, as if she'd been pushed down and tried to fight back. For a second he couldn't breathe.

Billy stood at his shoulder. "You've got to get her home," he said.

That made his limbs move.

He pushed open the gate and entered the stalls, crouching down before her. All her beautiful brandy-colored hair was falling to the side. Her dress had been torn off; he could see a bit of creamy white shoulder through the fabric. And her gown was covered with brown splotches of mud. She must have been thrown onto the ground. He pulled his cloak off his shoulders and draped it over her so she couldn't be recognized when he carried her out, and then in one swift movement he scooped her up and stood.

One moment he was holding her, and the next she had slugged him so hard in the eye that he dropped her unceremoniously.

"It's his lordship," he heard Billy say.

But with the one eye that was still open, Mayne was staring at Josie's dress, which was literally ripped from her back. He almost retched. "How did this happen to you?" he said hoarsely, his voice coming out with the growl of a dog. *"Who?"*

"I'm so sorry," she said. "You put that cloak over my eyes and I thought—"

"Who?"

"I—I—" Her eyes filled with tears. Billy pulled the cloak back over her shoulders and pushed her gently to the side of the stall at the sound of footsteps.

"Better to talk later," he said to Mayne.

But Mayne didn't think he could talk. He'd just realized that there was blood on Josie's skirts. Not much, but enough. The world literally blackened in front of him, and he swayed for a moment. He didn't think he could do anything. Then he wrenched his eyes away and forced his stomach to calm.

"Mayne?" Josie said rather uncertainly. "Could you please take me home? Is Sylvie waiting for you?"

He swung around. "Put the cloak over your head," he ordered. She pulled it up obediently.

"There's no one in the corridor," Billy reported.

Mayne didn't breathe until she was in his carriage. Even there, he couldn't find words, other than one: *"Who?"*

Josie was huddled in the corner, looking like a girl of fourteen. Mayne felt his gorge rising again. She showed no signs of answering him.

"Oh God," he said slowly. "It wasn't—Josie, was there more than one?"

She shook her head, and now he saw a tear sliding down her cheek.

He came to his knees beside her and took her hands. They were wet with tears and felt tiny and cold. "Just tell me his name, Josie. I'll take care of you." And him, he added to himself silently.

She shook her head again. "I will not marry him."

"Of course you won't!" The words choked from his throat. He almost said that whoever the man was, he wouldn't be alive for a wedding, but caught it back.

"If I say who it was, I'll have to marry him," Josie whispered, pulling one of her hands free so that she could scrub the tears from her cheeks. "I can't."

"I'll kill him first."

An odd little smile trembled on her lips. "And eat his heart in the marketplace?"

Mayne got off his knees and sat on the seat, pulling her into his lap. It was all improper, but she was ravished, and she was quoting Shakespeare, and she was so much Josie that his heart was full. "Beatrice wished that she were a man; I am that man," he said into her hair. "I'll kill him first, and we'll worry about the disposal of his organs after."

She leaned against him. But: "I'd rather no one knew about it, not even you, Mayne."

Mayne stopped himself from shaking her. She'd been through an ordeal. "You must tell me his name."

"Killing is a stiff penalty," she said. "I shall have to think about it." And that was the most she would say, except that halfway through his tirade she began to cry, and so he shut his mouth and thought about death by hot oil.

When they reached Tess's house, he carried her in. The butler took a look at his rapidly swelling eye and opened his mouth to say something, but Mayne pushed by him. A second later he put Josie down, and she ran to her sister. The cloak fell off and he met Felton's eyes over the embracing women. Josie was crying again, and Tess was saying frantic, incoherent things and tracing Josie's back with unsteady hands.

Felton was beside him in one stride, his eyes as cold as a viper's. "Who," he stated.

Mayne shook his head. "She wouldn't tell me. There wasn't"—he said it with difficulty—"more than one. I found her in the stables."

Felton looked over his shoulder. Tess had drawn Josie

onto the settee and was talking fast, in a low voice. "How did she become separated from you?"

"I don't know. Griselda felt faint and left the grounds. Josie was just behind me, and then she wasn't. We searched everywhere; Sylvie and I even went to the stables."

Josie was shaking her head.

"She will never tell," Mayne said. "She's afraid we'll make her marry him." Lucius Felton moved suddenly, and Mayne read the movement. "She doesn't understand that." Their eyes met with the truth of murder between them.

"Tess will find out who did it," Lucius said.

"How do you know?"

"I'm married to her."

Mayne nodded. "I'll go home and fetch Griselda." Between them, Tess and Griselda would take care of Josie. If that were possible.

26

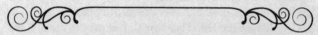

From The Earl of Hellgate's Memoirs,
Chapter the Nineteenth

Before I had my wits about me, Dear Reader, the fair Hippolyta had—I blush to say it—tied me to the wall by means of some ingenious hooks and the scarf from her hair. You will chastise me for not breaking these fragile bonds, but I fancy that anyone of the male persuasion who happens upon these words will understand my hesitation. For I could not offend her sensibilities, and presently she began to engage in such bewitching activities . . .

For the fourth time, Griselda said that she must leave. She didn't want to. The problem was Darlington. How dare he look at her with that rapt expression, as if he found what she said—no matter how inane—madly interesting? And how dare he make a sheet look so elegant?

"Just imagine if all your lady friends could see you now!"

She shuddered at the thought. "Don't even mention it," she implored.

A shadow crossed his eyes. "It's not so bad, is it?"

She rolled to her side as well, and then up on one elbow, so they lay facing each other. The sheet had slipped to his waist, leaving a broad chest and broader shoulders, tousled blond hair, and those arrogant cheekbones. Every inch of his ancient lineage spoke in those cheekbones.

"You look like a sugarplum," Darlington said. "I could eat you for breakfast, and every meal after that."

Griselda laughed, and her hair slid across her chest. It felt wickedly decadent lying in bed with the sheet at her waist, her breasts not pinned in, or corseted, or even covered . . . just there. And his eyes devouring them.

"How can you stand being so beautiful? I think I'd be like Narcissus and just admire myself all day long."

"You are quite lovely yourself," she said, memorizing his face.

He shrugged. "The better to buy myself a wife, I suppose."

"Do you have anyone in mind?"

"I can't think about such a disheartening subject when I have you with me."

"What about Miss Mary Parish?" she asked.

"The girl with spots?"

"She only has a few, and they won't last over a year."

He shook his head. "No."

"You mustn't be so attached to physical beauty." She reached out to trace a path across the muscles of his chest. His skin felt warm and slightly roughened with hair. "Lady Cecily Severy. The daughter of a duke."

"And since it's her third—or is it fourth?—season, she can't be choosy about marrying a penniless third son," he said.

She heard the faintest ring of sarcasm in his voice and flattened her palm into a caress. "You have a great deal to offer."

"In reality, no. I have a clever way with a phrase, but when

I lose my temper I'm a veritable bastard. I have few skills, thanks to my father's errant belief that I would go into the Church, all evidence to the contrary."

"They must maintain some standards," Griselda said, smiling at him.

But he didn't smile back. "Once my father accepted that the Church would likely never have me, he began bringing home lists of debutantes. Young girls of an appropriate family, with a large dowry. Of course, they couldn't be of the very best quality, or they would never wish to marry one such as I. It had to be a nicely calculated mix: a girl with means, but one whose parents would be sufficiently dazzled by their new son-in-law's relation to the Duke of Bedrock that they would overlook his impoverished status, his lack of skills, and his general uselessness."

Griselda's hand went to her mouth. "The Wooly Breeder," she breathed.

His eyes were bleak with self-dislike. "That poor girl ended up without a match for a whole season."

"But she did marry happily last year," Griselda said.

"She would not have been happy married to me, for all that her father and mine thought they had sewed it up beautifully."

Griselda was staring at him. "You weren't only making yourself known with clever phrases. You were getting rid of your father's choices. I suppose that Josie was unlucky enough to attract your father's attention."

"A perfect choice, from his point of view. Miss Essex's birth is impeccable. Her dowry was also known to be quite large. At the same time, she was fatherless and reputed to be rather less than perfect in form. Just the sort of young woman who might be persuaded to accept me."

"He didn't say that!"

"Actually, he did."

"You should never have called Josie a sausage, even so."

"I am telling you only so that you despise me as much as I despise myself," he said, his voice steady. "I ruined those girls' lives—your ward among them—merely so that my father could not promote them as appropriate brides."

There was no point in pretense. "That was shabby of you," Griselda said, "if understandable." She hesitated. "But you're not going to do it again . . . you are planning to marry now, aren't you?"

"Marry a debutante?"

"Yes."

"I shall not."

"But I thought—"

"I changed my mind. Recently."

Griselda's heart was beating to the tune of all the questions she had. Why—why—why. She said nothing. It was not her business why—

"Don't you want to ask me any questions?" He lay before her, a golden symphony of muscle and silken hair.

Absolutely not.

"Do I wish to talk about your future nuptials?" she said, feeling a smile curve on her lips that was as old as Cleopatra herself. "I do not. But I can think of some very important questions . . . I'll ask you those instead, shall I?"

He was grinning at her through the hair over his eyes, so she brushed it back.

"First question," she said, "and pay close attention, if you please. What do you like best about *this* part of my body?"

Darlington's answer involved a demonstration of friction and physics . . . and somehow she never reached her second question.

27

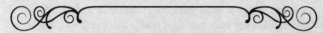

From The Earl of Hellgate,
Chapter the Nineteenth

She drew off my clothing, Dear Reader, while I stood transfixed, as silent as any block of marble not yet kissed into life. How can I say this without a blush? I allowed her to have her way with me, and if it were her pleasure to call me to her side in the midst of a rondeau, I came to her. And if it were her pleasure to request that I disrobe even in the very midst of the *ton*—in Almack's, Dear Reader, I faint to write the words, I . . . my pen falls from my despairing fingers . . .

Griselda wasn't home. At first Mayne just stared at the butler who informed him that his sister was at the races. She wasn't at the races! She'd gone home hours ago with Darlington . . . she'd felt faint . . . Darlington had—
Darlington.

But just to make sure, he took his carriage around to Griselda's little town house, for all that she hadn't lived there for two years, since agreeing to act as chaperone to the Essex girls. It was dark and the knocker muffled.

Then he sat in his carriage, ignoring the fact his driver

was waiting to be told where to go. He felt as if the world had crashed around his shoulders.

His sister was having an *affaire*.

His fiancée had just handed back his ring in no uncertain terms. In fact, he had no fiancée. Sylvie was gone.

And little Josie had been ravished.

He felt like the hollowed out inside of a gourd. Of these three events, the only one that really mattered was the last.

Griselda . . . well, he supposed that he was hardly one to chastise someone for *affaires*. Lord knows, he'd had more than he could count. Almost.

He loved Sylvie. But was he really capable of loving anyone? Probably not. Because he'd feel more anguish at her rejection, if that was the case.

But Josie. Josie. Tears almost came to his eyes. He blinked hard and shouted to Wiggles.

"Where to?" came the shout back to him.

"Felton." Because suddenly it was all clear to him. Josie was ravished. She was ruined. She might even carry a child from this day.

Unless he married her.

Of course he was a devil's bargain, soiled as he was with the reputation of a roué and the tired soul of a degenerate. But he was better than nothing, and if she didn't want to marry the father of her child, she could damn well marry him.

As Mayne sat in the carriage, the fixed truth of it only grew firmer in his soul. For the first time in his miserable, misbegotten life, someone needed him.

A block or two later he shouted at Wiggles, and redirected the carriage to the bishop's palace where his uncle lived. His uncle had written him a marriage certificate once before. Felton had snatched that out of his hands and married Tess himself.

But there was no one to step forward and marry Josie. She was the laughingstock of the *ton,* and now she would never be a marriage prospect, no matter the size of her dowry. What did women *do* with a child born of such a union as she had endured?

But he couldn't seem to think that far, because every time he considered what had happened to Josie a black cloud came over his eyes and he broke out in a sweat, finding a moment later that his fists were curled and he was breathing heavily.

There, in the darkness of the carriage swaying down St. James's Street, Mayne made an oath to himself.

He'd marry Josie and then he'd find that bastard, whoever he was, and kill him.

Slowly.

It was the first time he'd smiled in hours.

28

From The Earl of Hellgate,
Chapter the Twentieth

She was my queen, my paramour, and my agony.
I would have done anything for her, even lay
down my life at her feet. Slowly our relations
changed. She grew less commanding and more
amorous.

Rather than commanding my caresses, she caressed me. Reader . . .

"D o you know what I like most about this story?" Annabel
asked. She was sitting on Tess's dressing room stool,
her hair falling about her shoulders, just as she had looked
when she received Tess's summons. "I love the fact that his
mouth was *open* when you slung all that manure at him."

"I would have swung the shovel, not the manure, against
his face," Tess said tightly.

Josie was just out of a hot bath scented with jasmine. It was
all beginning to feel like a nightmare passed by. After all, no
one had seen her; Mayne had taken care of that. "Mayne led

me straight to his carriage," she said, knowing she was repeating himself. "After I knocked him to the floor!"

"Poor Mayne," Tess said thoughtfully. "It does seem that his life is oddly entwined with ours. As if he were our possession. First I was to marry him, although Annabel, you wanted the privilege. Of course, Imogen never wanted to *marry* him." She was sitting on the edge of the bed, and had thrown her hair forward and was brushing, so that her voice emerged, rather muffled, from behind a chestnut-colored waterfall of hair.

Josie could feel that Annabel was looking at her. She pretended to be adjusting the belt of her dressing gown.

Tess continued, oblivious to the undercurrents in the room. "And I don't think that Josie ever expressed such a wish. Josie, didn't you expressly say that you wouldn't take a man over twenty-five?"

There was silence in the room. Josie could feel herself turning pink. Annabel's eyes were narrowed.

Meanwhile, Tess kept brushing. "I can't imagine any woman *not* wanting to marry Mayne. I was perfectly happy to do so. He's magnificent looking—"

"If tired," Annabel interjected.

"With a good estate."

"Not like your husband's."

"Pooh!" Tess said, throwing all her hair to the side and straightening up. Her face was pink. "Lucius would be the first to say that he owns far more properties than he has any use for."

"I would applaud your ambition," Annabel said to Josie, "but there's the unfortunate problem of his fiancée."

"What!" Tess yelped. She turned to Josie. "Are—"

"Of course not!" Josie said. "Could we return to a more reasonable subject?"

"Well, I don't understand exactly how you ended up

walking alone with that despicable young man," Tess said. "Where was Griselda?"

Annabel frowned at her. "That's irrelevant. If you haven't noticed that Josie is showing every sign of having fallen in love with Mayne, I'm not so unobservant."

"I have not!" Josie said hotly.

Tess put down her hairbrush. "For all the level of obliviousness you credit me with, Annabel, I think it is you who is showing a singular obtuseness. Mayne has a fiancée. Moreover, he is infatuated with Sylvie. If our Josie has indeed taken a fancy to him—and who wouldn't, given his obvious attributes?—it can do no good for us to refine upon the subject. He is marrying Sylvie."

"Well, as to that . . ." Josie said.

Her sisters' heads snapped in her direction.

"No!" Annabel gasped.

Josie couldn't help grinning. "She slapped him."

"Slapped him?" Tess echoed. "Sylvie? Sylvie de la Broderie slapped Mayne?"

"What on earth did he do?" Annabel said. "I'm sure he deserved it."

"He didn't!" Josie said. "He didn't—"

"How do you know?" Tess asked.

"I could hear."

"You were eavesdropping!"

"Of course she was eavesdropping," Annabel said, exasperated. "You're starting to sound like an old biddy, Tess. Are you telling me that you would tiptoe away if you happened on a scene during which Mayne was being slapped and . . . are you saying that she broke off their engagement altogether, Josie?"

And, at Josie's nod, *"Fascinating!"*

"But perhaps I shouldn't tell the details to Tess if she disapproves," Josie suggested.

Tess rolled her eyes. "The deed is done. Feel free to divulge the details."

"He kissed her," Josie said.

Annabel frowned. "And?"

"And she slapped him."

"That was *it*? One kiss and she decides she'd rather not be a countess? You must have missed something, Josie."

"What are you suggesting?" Tess asked.

"Perhaps he grabbed her breasts," Annabel said with relish. "Frankly, I cannot imagine Sylvie enjoying a grab and tickle."

"He didn't," Josie said. "He would never do something like that."

"Oh, you'd be—"

"No, I wouldn't!" Josie snapped. The very suggestion made her think about Thurman and the way he pawed her front, for all the world as if he were an elk trying to uncover grass from the snow.

Annabel looked at her narrowly. "All the more reason why Thurman deserved that shovelful of manure."

"Did he paw you?" Tess exclaimed.

Josie wrinkled her nose. "It wasn't terrible. Just—"

"Terrible," Annabel said. "There is a reason why young women are supposed to stay with their chaperones, you know."

"It seems to have been a remarkably wanton afternoon," Tess observed. "Where on earth did Mayne manage to kiss Sylvie in such a way that you observed her?"

"We were in the stables," Josie admitted. "But they couldn't see me."

"What did she say after she slapped him?" Annabel asked. "I always meant to slap someone for the impertinence of kissing me, but somehow I generally forgot."

"Well, Mayne kissed her, and then there was a terrible crack when she slapped him."

"And then?" Tess said, obviously fascinated despite herself.

"I probably shouldn't—"

"Tell or we'll have your guts for garters," Annabel said.

"You can't tell your husbands," Josie said.

They both nodded.

"Well, Mayne said something like, 'Sylvie, what devil's game are you playing?' His question might have included an expletive or two," Josie said. "I was so surprised, you understand."

"Yes, yes," Annabel said, waving her hand. "And Sylvie?"

"Sylvie said, and I know I have this right: 'When I decide to be manhandled by a *canard,* I will know where to come, Mayne. I thought you were putting your degenerate life behind you—but obviously you wish to drag me into the muck with you.' " Josie finished with fine dramatic flair.

"Canard?" Annabel said. "Isn't that French for a duck?"

"Well, perhaps I got that word wrong, then, because I'm sure she didn't mean duck," Josie said. "She really sounded quite violent. Or rather, not violent so much as disgusted. She was revolted. You could tell. She was shaking."

"Not to be pedestrian," Tess said, "but perhaps Mayne has bad breath. It comes from bad teeth, as I understand. Lady Dayton told me—"

"He doesn't," Josie said firmly.

"It's a question of teeth," Tess began, but Annabel waved her into silence.

"Josephine Essex," Annabel said, "do you care to tell us precisely when Mayne kissed *you*?"

After a second of silence, Josie said, "It was only one kiss."

"One kiss?" her sisters said in chorus.

"Not even a real kiss. It was just a kiss to show me how to walk right."

"What?" Tess said.

"Did you enjoy it?" asked Annabel.

Josie could feel herself growing pink. "Not so much," she said. "It was just a kiss, after all." She tried to give a casual shrug. The kind of shrug that indicated she certainly had not been dreaming of that kiss every single night since it happened.

"Just a kiss," Tess said. "Do you know what is most interesting about this, Annabel? Mayne kissed me once."

Josie transferred her scowl to her eldest sister.

"I did not enjoy it, and I don't believe he did either. We shared one extremely tepid kiss when we decided to marry, and I distinctly remember thinking that all the talk of kisses must be wildly over-estimated, as it was nothing special."

"Not like Lucius's kisses, hmmm?" Annabel said mischievously.

"Hush. *And* I happen to know that Mayne kissed Imogen as well."

Josie swallowed. Apparently she was just the last in a long line of Essex women whom Mayne had graced with his attentions.

"She didn't enjoy it either. In fact, to hear her tell the tale, Mayne kissed her only so that he could convince her that there was no point to their having an *affaire* since there was no desire between them."

"And now we have a third woman, Sylvie, who has described Mayne as a lackluster kisser," Annabel said. "Poor Mayne! He really must be handicapped in that area."

"That's absurd!" Josie said hotly. "He—He—" She floundered to a stop.

"He what?"

"Stop clowning about like that," Tess said to Annabel. "If Josie enjoyed Mayne's kiss, it's all for the best, but if you think about it, the man has really suffered a trail of disappointment. Didn't he fall in love with Lady Godwin before she rejected him?"

"In love with Lady Godwin? Mayne?" Annabel repeated. "I don't think so. I think he's in love with Sylvie, more's the pity for him."

Josie bit her lip. "I know he's in love with Sylvie. He told me himself."

"Before or after he kissed you?" Annabel asked.

"After. And before. He wanted to make certain that I didn't take the—it—too seriously."

"Wasn't that generous of him?" Annabel asked. "That man deserves a fall more than any gentleman I've heard of lately. How dare he warn you that he's in love with another woman and then kiss you?"

"He was only trying to help," Josie said. "And he *has* had the fall, Annabel. He lost Sylvie."

"Will she go back to him?"

"I don't think so. It's hard to explain but she was truly *revolted*. I could hear it in her voice."

"Poor Mayne," Tess said.

"Fie on that," Annabel said briskly. "We know of four women who disliked his kisses: Lady Godwin, Tess, Annabel, and now, Sylvie. But we know of one who enjoyed them."

Josie felt her blush getting hotter. "That has nothing to do with it," she managed.

"That has everything to do with it," Annabel said. "If you wish to marry him, then your sisters are just the ones to make sure it happens."

"Are you cracked?" Josie cried. "I can't marry Mayne. It's madness even to say that aloud. I'm young and he's—and I'm—I'm *fat*."

"You are *not* fat," Tess snapped. "I am tired of hearing that, and I'm tired of seeing in your eyes that you're thinking it. You are beautiful. Have the past few days taught you nothing? Why do you think that loathsome Thurman stole his loathsome kisses? Because you are beautiful, and since you gave up the sausage corset, the men are slavering over you. And if you think Mayne hasn't noticed that, you're cracked. I saw him look at you myself."

"Nonsense. Mayne wouldn't ask me to marry him in a million years."

"Why not?"

"I have made a study of marriage. You know that. I've catalogued every single novel published by the Minerva Press in the last few years. Men ask women to marry them, as far as I can see, because they are struck by reverence for their delicate beauty. Or because they are somehow forced into the marriage by a ruse. Mayne shows no interest in my delicate beauty, even if I had it, and ruses are not as easy to pull off as one would think."

"What do you mean by a ruse?" Annabel said, looking interested.

"A trick. A stratagem. The word covers a multitude of sins," Josie said. "Every marriage that didn't happen in a conventional way. Your marriage, for example. You married due to a scandal."

"And mine, I suppose," Tess put in. "Since I married Lucius after he engaged in just such a ruse to get Mayne out of the way."

"Imogen's second marriage was conventional—"

"In some ways," Annabel said, laughing.

"But her first came about due to a ruse."

"The evidence seems to be heavily weighted in favor of such stratagems," Tess pointed out. "I suggest that we approach Mayne and the question of marriage with that in mind."

"Easier said than done," Josie said. "Ruses are all very well if one is as delectable as the two of you. But I—"

"No more of that," Tess said. "I agree with Annabel. If

you want Mayne—and God knows, you're the only one who seems to want him—then you shall have him."

"I didn't mean to encourage you," Josie said, feeling alarmed. "Truly, I wouldn't wish to marry in such a harum-scarum way. The fact that your marriage is a good one doesn't mean that the end result will always be so favorable. I'd hate to take such a risk."

"Even if it were to marry Mayne?" Annabel asked, with interest.

Josie opened her mouth and then hesitated.

"Our way is clear," Annabel said to her sister.

"No," Josie said despairingly. "No!"

"Watch us," Annabel said.

29

From The Earl of Hellgate, Chapter the Twentieth

Dearest Reader, you know me now as well as I know myself. And I'm sure you understand that as her passion for me sweetened, so did mine wane. Before long, I was no longer her faithful swain, and . . . ah, darling Hippolyta . . . forgive me. The tempests of our early relations were such that I could not be happy in the Paradise that you later offered me.

Smiley had spent the last twenty years as Mr. Felton's butler in town (a distinction necessary, he felt, to distinguish himself from Mr. Felton's three other butlers, all of whom presided over establishments situated, regrettably for them, in the depths of the country). He was accustomed to a quiet life. After the master married, the household certainly became more lively, but the mistress was as calm as her husband. They did not keep late hours.

But tonight! Here it was ten of the clock, and Smiley was conscious of a faint feeling of resentment. First the Earl of

Mayne brought the young Miss Essex to the house. Then the Earl of Ardmore and his wife arrived. They were family, of course, but Smiley felt that family had its place.

It was time for him to retire to his snug little sitting room, where Mrs. Smiley would have a pan of hot water ready for his feet. Powerful trouble it was, standing on his feet all day long, and much of that on marble floors.

Not an iota of his thoughts showed on his face as he opened the front door yet again. "Your lordship," he said, bowing to the Earl of Mayne.

"Smiley," the earl said. "Would you be so good as to announce my arrival, and that of my uncle, the Bishop of Rochester?"

Smiley took the earl's many-caped greatcoat and the bishop's velvet cloak and ushered them into a sitting room. Suddenly his feet didn't hurt as much as they had earlier. Could it be that his house was about to be party to a wedding?

What other reason could there be for tumbling a bishop out of his bed? Smiley opened the study door just as the Earl of Ardmore said something about kisses.

"The Earl of Mayne and the Bishop of Rochester," Smiley intoned, with some satisfaction. So it was about kisses, was it? In his experience, there were kisses and kisses. The kind of kisses that led to a bishop appearing in the house at a late hour of the clock went along with a tumble . . .

He moved to the right of the door, doing a fine imitation of a marble statue. Sure enough, the Earl of Mayne launched into speech without waiting for him to leave.

"I've brought along my uncle—"

"Much to my disapprobation," put in the bishop, who collapsed onto the sofa as if he were a marionette without strings.

"There's only one solution to this disaster."

"There is—" intoned the bishop but shut his mouth when his nephew flashed him a look.

Smiley would have closed his mouth as well. The normally pristine earl looked like a rough customer tonight. Like the kind of man one avoided down at the docks. His hair wasn't an elegant tumble: it was pulled straight back from his forehead, as if he'd dragged it back with a hasty hand. His face was shadowed with beard, and there was a black circle around one of his eyes.

But it was really the set of his jaw and his shoulders that gave Smiley pause. Mayne looked like a man bent on murder, rather than marriage.

Yet marriage it was. Because Mayne was explaining that the bishop was there to marry him to Miss Essex. And no protests changed his mind, not even the bishop's protests that he was supposed to marry people between the hours of eight A.M. and noon.

Mayne just turned around and gave his uncle a look from those shadowed eyes that would have befitted Beelzebub himself. "I suggest you pretend the sun is shining." He said it softly, but Smiley, still standing by the open door, heard every word. "Because otherwise, I shall be forced to tell Mama."

"Ah, your mother?" the bishop said with a gulp.

As it happened, Smiley knew about the Earl of Mayne's mother. She was the abbess of one of the few nunneries left in England, and by all accounts, she was a powerful woman, who controlled hundreds of acres and had the ear of the Queen herself.

The prudent thing to do at this point would be to summon Mrs. Felton. After all, Mr. Felton wasn't doing much more than stand there, rocking a bit on his heels with that quiet little smile of his. Which told Smiley nothing more than that the master thought the marriage wasn't such a bad idea. The Earl of Ardmore was looking properly thunder-struck; those Scottish types were always a bit slow on the uptake, to Smiley's mind.

He retreated into the hallway and sent a footman to fetch

the mistress's own maid, Gussie. Gussie's eyes grew wide when she heard his terse statement. Two seconds later Mrs. Felton and her sister, the Countess of Ardmore, came flying down the stairs in a flutter of silk.

Smiley opened the study door again, but Mrs. Felton wasn't nearly as imperceptive as her husband; she smiled at him in a way that said he should retire.

A good butler knows that a footman spinning champagne bottles in a vat of ice will chill the wine quickly.

The baize door closed with a slap behind him.

30

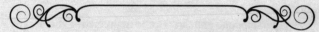

From The Earl of Hellgate,
Chapter the Twenty-first

The time had come for marriage. I steeled my-self for the end of my amorous activities. From henceforth I would be confined to my wife's bed-chamber alone. Or so I told myself.

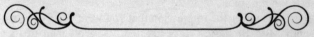

I f you would just summon Josie," Mayne was saying again, trying to instill even the slightest bit of civility into his voice, "my uncle will perform this ceremony and the entire business will be over."

"But Mayne," Tess said, "while my sister and I certainly appreciate your gallantry, aren't you engaged to be married to Sylvie de la Broderie?"

Mayne's jaw clenched. "Miss Broderie changed her mind. Earlier today," he clarified.

"I doubt that Mayne would offer his hand in marriage if it were still promised to another," Felton said. "Yet is his sacrifice necessary?"

"It is," Mayne snapped. Damn it, hadn't they *talked* to Josie? Hadn't they seen the state she was in, and the condition of her clothing? He had no wish to discuss the ins and outs of what happened to Josie with anyone. Ever.

"We are grateful for you coming to Josie's rescue," Annabel said, looking sweetly at him. "She needs someone to rescue her. Of course it will be hard for her to allow a gentleman to press his addresses after such a distressing experience."

Finally someone appeared to be appreciating the gravity of the situation. "Right," he said. "So could you please ask Josie to come downstairs—or I will go upstairs and fetch her myself."

"As long as you are quite certain that you don't wish to mend fences with Sylvie?" Tess asked.

"She returned my ring," Mayne said, hearing a cold knife-edge in his voice.

"I was under the impression that you were deeply in love with Miss Broderie," Tess insisted. "A gentleman in that situation may well weather a small disagreement, and win his way back into his lady's graces by the following evening."

"Even if I weren't marrying Josie," Mayne said impatiently, "I haven't the faintest interest in chasing after Sylvie de la Broderie like a tame lapdog. What happened was between the two of us, and suffice it to say that Sylvie has made up her mind that I am not to her liking. My feelings in the matter are quite irrelevant."

"Except they are not because you are marrying *our* sister," Tess said.

Mayne's lips drew back and he almost snarled at her.

Annabel stepped forward and put a hand on his arm. "Do forgive Tess's sisterly anxiety," she cooed. "Tess did not mean to imply that you would marry Josie if you still cared for Miss Broderie."

"I don't," Mayne snapped.

Annabel smiled at him. "It is such a kind thing of you to

do, to offer to marry Josie in this way. Almost chivalric, in fact."

Mayne couldn't even think what to say about that piece of idiocy. How could she twinkle at him when such a dreadful thing had just happened to her sister? His jaw clenched before he could tell her exactly what he thought of her smiling face.

Instead he bowed, turned around and opened the door. They were all a pack of weaklings, sitting around and talking of love and honor when Josie had been ravished. Why, they should be out beating the streets for the perpetrator. They should be holding Josie's hand as she wept.

Josie wasn't weeping.

She walked out of a bedchamber door just as he reached the top of the stairs. He came to a halt instantly.

"Josie." Which was a stupid thing to say, but his mind seemed to have sunk into a bog. She looked pale, but composed and very beautiful. She was so beautiful that it struck him like a blow that anyone would touch her. Even looking at her made him feel like a madman.

"I came to marry you." That didn't come out right, Mayne thought. He was looking at her skin, what he could see of her neck, to see if there were bruises. Because he intended to repay the bastard, bruise for bruise . . . before he killed him, of course.

"To marry me?" If anything she turned even paler.

He cleared his throat. Josie may not have thought through the consequences. The possible child. Although surely women . . .

"Why would you want to marry me? Unless my sister—did you talk to Annabel?"

He scowled at her. "What the devil has Annabel to do with it? You need a husband. I intend to marry you. My uncle is here and he'll do it."

She was just staring at him, so he dragged a hand through

his hair. "Look," he growled, "I know I'm not the best bargain in the world. Sylvie just dropped me. In fact, I'm a pretty soiled piece of goods, if you want the truth." A second later he was cursing himself. How could he bring up the question of *soiling*?

But she didn't burst into tears, just stood regarding him silently. He squared his shoulders. "You need to marry, Josie. You are—are ruined."

"I am? Are you sure?"

Of course, she was so innocent she probably didn't even know what was entailed in being ruined. She probably didn't even have the language to describe what happened to her. Mayne raked his hand through his hair again. "Yes."

She seemed to shrivel a bit. Then her eyes narrowed. "Did my sisters tell you I was ruined?"

"Josie," Mayne said, "there's no need for your sisters to confirm the circumstances. It must be tremendously painful for you to talk about."

"I'm not the same kind of person as Sylvie," she said after a moment. "Sylvie is beautiful—" She held up her hand when he would have spoken. "If we marry, it would be because you are struck with the wish to serve as a knight in shining armor. But you thought to marry Sylvie because you were in love with her. You told me so yourself. Would you not wish to look for that same emotion elsewhere?"

"No."

"I won't be a very good hostess. You are sophisticated and urbane; I do not understand the *ton* very well, and as you know, I have not been a success."

"You will be," he said stubbornly, "if you want to be." They were talking about things that didn't matter a fig, not with the huge yawning grief burning a hole in his chest because of what had happened to her. To Josie. His Josie, now. "If anything, I'm too old for you."

She smiled a little at that and Mayne's heart lightened.

Because he'd been reading women's eyes for years, and Josie, young though she was, didn't think he was too old. He could tell that.

"We are going to marry now," he said, taking her hand and turning around. He didn't wait to see if she said yea or nea. She was going to say yes. He'd never known, with more surety in his life, that this was the right thing to do.

They reentered the library to find that his uncle was sleeping on the sofa. Josie's sisters and their husbands swung around to look at him, almost with alarm, Mayne noticed with some disdain. Not Felton, of course. Felton had been his friend for years now, and Mayne could read his every nuance. In Felton's steady gaze was approval. He, if no one else, understood exactly why this marriage had to happen tonight.

The rest of them were fools, but Felton was a man of honor who clearly grasped, with his usual logic, that Josie was utterly ruined and in need of a husband.

Mayne shook his uncle until he came awake with a tumble of expletives quite unsuited to a man of the cloth.

"If it weren't for your mother, I wouldn't do this for the King himself," he roared.

"Mother will be grateful," Mayne said.

A moment later he had everyone where he wanted them. His uncle was yawning over a book of common prayer and fumbling with a special license. Annabel was holding hands with her husband, and Felton stood beside Mayne.

"Where's Griselda?" Tess asked suddenly. "Oh Mayne, you can't marry without your sister's presence. Griselda will never forgive us."

"She's busy at the moment," Mayne said. "I'll tell her what happened."

He nodded to his uncle, who obediently began, "Dearly beloved, we are gathered here today . . ."

Mayne didn't hear any of the rest of it. He just looked

down at the dark chestnut of his almost-wife's hair. She was looking down at their hands.

"In sickness and in health," intoned the bishop. Mayne tightened his hands on Josie's. I'll take care of you, he promised silently. I'll protect you, and no one under God's great earth will ever hurt you again.

After the ceremony Josie suddenly looked up at him. Mayne's heart was pounding violently; he hardly knew why. She was terrifyingly beautiful, this wife of his. Her dark hair was carelessly bundled on her head and still damp from a bath. Her skin had the glow of pearls seen by candlelight. But Mayne knew it wasn't physical beauty that made his heart pound.

It was the Josie-heart of her, the intelligence and wit that she had so often used against him on their trip to Scotland. What had happened to her was all his fault. Not only did he lose her at the racecourse, but he took off her corset, and taught her how to kiss. She transformed before his eyes, and those of the male half of London. It was mesmerizing, seeing that erotic beauty come to the surface.

It was his fault that some bastard raped her. The words, the grim truth of it, steadied him.

Was he supposed to kiss her? No! After her experience . . . He raised her hand to his lips and kissed it.

Something crossed her eyes, disappointment perhaps, but then she was turning to her sisters. Annabel was crowing with delight. Felton was at Mayne's shoulder, smiling at him.

"It had to be done," Mayne said in a low voice, because he was feeling a queer need to justify himself.

"For many reasons," Lucius said, taking him in a rough—and wholly uncharacteristic—hug.

"An interesting night," the Earl of Ardmore said, contenting himself with bowing to Mayne.

"In some ways," Mayne said. He glanced over at the

women. Annabel was laughing at something Josie had said, laughing so hard that she was shaking. He'd have to get used to that: laughter followed Josie wherever she went. "Has anyone discovered who the man in question was?"

Lucius's face stilled instantly. "It may be that Josie has confided in my wife; Tess hasn't yet told me."

Mayne's fists clenched involuntarily. "Tomorrow, then. I should accompany my uncle back to his lodgings." The poor man had collapsed back onto the sofa with his eyes closed, and Mayne had to admit that he looked rather gray.

"Your uncle tells me that he drank three bottles of claret with his supper," Ardmore said genially. "It's remarkable that he's on his feet at all. I think I should accompany him, don't you?"

"Absolutely not," Mayne said, and then the words dried in his mouth. Both men were looking at him with mockery in their eyes. "I collect that I was about to drive into the night without my wife."

"One quickly grows accustomed to the state," Ardmore said.

"Such a pity that Rafe isn't here," Lucius said.

"No doubt my mistake would have given him rare pleasure," Mayne said. He turned to his wife. His wife! Could it be that he really had a wife?

And yet there was a young woman, shining chestnut hair, wide-flung eyebrows, laughing eyes, lovely lips: and the world would know her as the Countess of Mayne. The idea was so dumbfounding that he took the champagne thrust into his hand and drank it without thinking.

31

From The Earl of Hellgate,
Chapter the Twenty-first

We married in a simple ceremony, attended by
my family and hers. I thought to break the news
to the *ton* that a notorious rake was tamed by
matrimony after the fact. It wasn't until we were
in the silence of our matrimonial bedchamber
that I realized . . .

Oh Dear Reader, I failed my dearest little wife
when she most needed me.

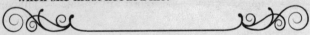

Annabel couldn't stop laughing all the way up the stairs,
and saying in a low, wicked voice, "Don't ever challenge one of the Essex sisters!" But Josie was beginning to
feel a deep, swelling sense of panic.

Mayne was downstairs.

The *Earl of Mayne*.

And he had married her. Or she had married him, one or
the other. Because— But she couldn't think about *because*
at the moment.

As soon as they reached Tess's bedchamber, Josie turned

to Annabel. "I have to ask you something terribly important. Did you tell Mayne I was ravished? Is that what he means by ruined?"

The laughter fell out of Annabel's face. "Thank God you weren't ravished."

When Josie escaped from her hug, she asked it again. "But where did Mayne get the idea that I was, Annabel?" She looked to Tess. "*Did* you two tell him that so that he felt he had to offer marriage?"

"Darling, we would never do such a thing," Tess said, with all the authority of an elder sister. "Never. That would be an untruth."

Josie narrowed her eyes. "Then why does he think I'm ruined? Unless I am ruined, just because of that kiss. I was under the impression that there was a great deal more to ruining than a kiss."

"Men," Annabel said, "exist primarily to make mistakes. They don't know it's true, but it is. It seems that Mayne made a little mistake. He overestimated the unpleasantness of your experience. The truth is that he would never have married you unless he wanted to do so."

But Josie was having trouble breathing. Couldn't a marriage be annulled under these circumstances? Wouldn't Mayne feel that the whole thing had been a hoax to trick him?

Tess wrapped an arm around her shoulder. "None of us married in a conventional way, Josie. And we're all quite happy."

But Josie was launching into full-fledged panic. "I must have lost my mind! He really thinks—he thinks I've been *ravished*. Oh my God. I married under false pretenses."

"He'll be ecstatic to find that is not the case," Annabel said, obviously trying in vain to school her face to gravity.

"The two of you are quite blithe when it comes to morality!" Josie cried. "What was I thinking?"

"You were thinking that you wanted to marry Mayne—what is his given name?" Annabel asked.

"Garret," Josie said.

"There! I collect you are the only woman other than Griselda who knows his real name. The truth is that you wanted to marry Garret, and he wanted to marry you. And never mind what excuse he offered for the business."

"Lucius put forward the excuse that Mayne had jilted me," Tess said.

"It just doesn't seem the same level of seriousness," Josie said with a gulp. "I lied—well, in so many words—I lied to my *husband*. In order to get him to marry me."

Annabel gave her a hug. "It'll be all right by tomorrow morning. I promise."

"I have to make him fall in love with me. By tomorrow morning!"

Annabel sat down on the bed. Tess was curled into an armchair by the fire, but Josie couldn't calm herself enough to sit down. She just stood in the middle of the room, feeling panic roaring through her like a tidal wave.

"I wouldn't discuss the question of your ravishment until *after* the wedding night," Annabel said, after a moment.

"That's what I need to know about," Josie said tightly. "The wedding night. I understand the mechanics of the situation."

"There's really not much more to it," Annabel said. She was on the verge of giggling again.

"Don't ignore me," Josie hissed. "I'm not a baby anymore. I'm about to marry—no! I just married a man who has slept with a great many women, and I need—I need—" She couldn't put into words what she needed. Some trick, some stratagem to make him think that she was a better bed partner than all those others.

Tess smiled at her, and there wasn't mockery in her eyes. "Just enjoy yourself."

"That's right. Enjoy yourself," Annabel affirmed.

Josie had never felt more rage toward her sisters in her life. "I don't want to seem presumptuous, but I'd like you to be specific."

"There are some things that can't be spelled out," Annabel said.

Josie turned on her. "Spell them out anyway."

"Use your imagination," Tess suggested.

"My imagination," Josie said, stunned by the enormity of what she couldn't visualize. "Where does imagination come into it? As I understand it, the man climbs on top of his wife and—and does what he has to do. I don't see any room for imagination. From what I've heard, it's painful. Mrs. Fiddle, in the village, said there might be blood." She made a face.

"Oh, as for that first time," Tess said, "don't worry about it. I hardly felt it."

"I was exactly the same," Annabel said, nodding. "A tiny pinch, and no blood. I think Mrs. Fiddle must have been rather hysterical on the subject."

"You still don't understand. You don't seem to grasp what I'm facing. Mayne has slept with the most beautiful and seductive women in London. And I am—what I am. I need some sort of special technique." She felt desperate. "Annabel, you must know something!"

Annabel frowned at her. "There aren't any special techniques. That is, perhaps there are, but they're something you have to discover on your own. Between you and Mayne."

"Don't be fearful," Tess put in.

"That's wonderful," Josie snapped. "I'm going into this situation blind, and you tell me not to be fearful. Tell me something helpful!"

"The most helpful thing I can tell you is to allow your husband to give you pleasure," Annabel said. "I never understood that before I was married. What will drive him mad with pleasure is if *you* are overcome by the same emotion."

Josie sat down and tried to think about that one. Whether that was enough to keep Mayne at her side when he had fled the beds of so many other women, doubtless all of whom were overcome by pleasure.

"I wish Griselda was here," Annabel said. "She would know the precise details, but I do think that Mayne has never managed to keep a relationship with a woman going above a week. Or is it two? Tess, do you know?"

Tess made a face. She hated this sort of gossip as much as Annabel loved it. "My understanding is that it has been a question of a week, if that."

"So, Josie," Annabel said. "All you have to do is keep your husband in your bed over a week, and you've won the battle."

Josie thought about that.

Annabel came and perched on one side of her armchair. "I think that you and Mayne will be very happy together," she said, smiling.

Tess sat on the other side and stroked Josie's hair. "Mayne has just won the greatest Ascot of them all."

Josie managed a wobbly smile. They seemed to have forgotten that Mayne was in love with another woman. She didn't have the heart to bring Sylvie up. It was one thing to contemplate a victory, if one could call it that, over all of Mayne's married lovers. It was another to imagine ever dislodging his love of Sylvie from his heart.

"I'm going to be the best wife he ever has," she said in a little stony voice.

"Of course you will be! And luckily, you're his first and only wife, so you needn't even worry about competition," Annabel said.

"I'll have to be—" she gulped "—well, *nice*."

"You are nice," Tess offered.

But Josie wasn't interested in compliments. "Not most of the time," she said, looking at her sisters. "I'm a bad-tempered beast, just as you've called me so many times. I really am. I'm horrible." Her face started to crumple and she caught herself. "You don't understand just how much I *hate* all those people who called me a sausage. Or who laughed along with it. In fact, sometimes I think I hate most of the population of London."

"You might wish to disguise that a bit," Annabel suggested.

"I'm going to be much, much nicer than I really am," Josie stated. "Sweet. Honey-sweet, like all the heroines in my books."

Tess was looking doubtful.

"Don't you think I can do it?"

"Of course you can do anything you wish—"

There was a knock at the door. It was Lucius, who put his head around the door and said, "My lord bishop is begging leave to return to his house."

Josie rose to her feet, feeling the comforting presence of her sisters at her sides. "I am ready," she said.

It seemed that Lucius was accompanying the bishop to his house, and that meant—that meant she and Mayne were free to leave. To go to his house.

"I have no nightgown," Josie whispered to Tess in a moment of pure terror.

"My maid already gave a bag to the footman," Annabel said, giving her a warm hug. "I'm so happy for you, darling."

Tess came too, and the three of them stood in a wreath of arms and kisses. "I just wish that Imogen were here."

"I love you both," Josie said a bit damply.

"You'll be all right," Annabel whispered in her ear. "Just—"

"I know!" Josie said, panicked that Mayne would hear her sister's advice about pleasure and the rest of it. Or worse, advice about her temper. Because there he was at her elbow:

the man who had, according to gossip, slept with virtually every beautiful woman in London—and left them a week later. And she thought to keep him as a husband?

He didn't look like a seducer at the moment. There was something wild and dark in his eyes, a note of anguish that Josie didn't like. "I'm all right," she said to him, before she even knew she spoke.

"Shall we . . ." He hesitated.

How could she go with him? She couldn't! But before she even knew what was happening, she was being wrapped in a pelisse. She couldn't even find her voice when they were in the carriage, so they sat in silence for at least five minutes while she sank deeper into a morass of embarrassment. If she told him the truth, what would he do? What would he say? He only—

"I just want you to know, Josie, that I would never force you into any sort of intimate experience that you are not prepared for," Mayne said suddenly.

She could hardly see his face, but then he leaned forward and the light from the small lamp hanging at the side of the carriage fell on him. He looked so earnest, kind, and resolute that her heart dropped into her toes. She didn't deserve him.

"I cannot imagine a more terrible experience for a woman." He took her hand, and even though Josie knew she should be writhing in guilt, her heart started beating more quickly. "I'll do anything I can for you. And if there's a child—"

She shook her head.

"You can't know." He said it so gently that her heart turned over and she pulled her hand away.

"Garret—" But somehow her confession died on her lips. She wanted to be married to him. At the base of it all, there was nowhere on earth she wanted to be other than in this carriage, able to call him by his first name. And if she was going to go to hell for the blackness of her crimes . . . He was so beautiful, with his straight brows and serious eyes.

"Of course neither of us have been in this situation before. Our marriage may have begun in a bungling fashion, Josie, but it will be as serious to me as if we'd wed in Westminster Abbey. I know I have a poor reputation, but I said farewell to that life a while ago. I will not betray you."

"No," she said. "Nor I you."

"I shall guard you a bit more fiercely than I did at the racetrack," he said, turning her hand over. "I suspect it will take some time for you to countenance the idea of intimacies. I want you to feel at ease. We can wait for those matters as long as you wish. A year even."

Josie swallowed. The only thing that came to mind was a forlorn line of Desdemona's when Othello was sent off to war: *the rites for which I married him are bereft me.* A fancy way of asking the governor not to send her husband off to war before they consummated their marriage. But how could she say such a thing? With Mayne thinking that she was devastated by Thurman's disgusting advances?

Of course, if she were a more ladylike person, she probably would be distraught. After all, Thurman certainly made an attempt to grab her breast, the loathsome muckworm.

Something must have showed in her face, because all of a sudden Mayne was sitting beside her.

"Who was it?" he asked. His voice echoed queerly around the carriage.

Josie's breathing missed a hitch. How could she tell him? He'd probably murder poor Thurman, and all the man did— albeit with a singular lack of grace—was kiss her. Well, maul her. Still . . .

She was quite aware that if the upshot of being mauled by Thurman was being married to Mayne, she would endure it all over again. "I took care of it myself," she said.

"What?"

Josie gulped. There was no help for it; she'd have to tell the truth. "We were behind the stables."

He wrapped an arm around her and it felt so good that she let herself lean into his shoulder.

"Why were you behind the stables?"

"I didn't really notice where we were going," Josie confessed. She could hardly say that she had been tired of watching Sylvie's darling little turban and her slim little figure and the way she clung to Mayne's arm.

His arm tightened. "So he took you behind the stables and—"

"He started to kiss me and—things of that nature. My dress ripped." He made a muffled sound and Josie said: "I wrenched free at one point and he came back toward me, and there was a pile of manure." She stopped.

"A pile of manure?"

"And a shovel."

"Oh, my God," Mayne said.

"I slung it at him," Josie told Mayne's coat.

"Where'd you hit him?"

"In the face."

There was a moment of silence. "The man still needs to die, but I'm proud of you. Now who was it?"

How could she answer that? She looked at him instead. They hadn't been so close to each other since the time he kissed her in his turreted room. Her heart was going so quickly she could feel it against her gown. She looked at him, at the eyelashes that were longer than hers, and his eyes, and the beautiful, weary look of him. A wave of heat swept over her body. Heat and hunger.

She swallowed and felt the ripple in her throat. In fact, she felt every inch of her skin, as if it belonged to someone else.

There was something in his eyes. It was as if the sound of

the horses had died away and they were both holding their breaths, or perhaps only she was . . .

"Josie," he said, after what seemed like a century.

"Yes?" She whispered it.

"You're my *wife*." He looked almost comically surprised.

Josie could tell that this was the moment to make a clean breast of it. Not that it was really her fault that he had decided she was ravished, but she hadn't clarified the matter. "Do you mind being married?" she asked, losing her courage.

"I hardly know." The carriage was drawing to a halt. "Do *you* like being married? To me?"

"Yes," she said. And she let it all sweep over her again, the masculine, warm smell of him, the beauty of him, the broad shoulder she leaned against, his blatantly seductive, beautiful eyes. "I do like being married to you," she said, rather shakily.

His eyes searched hers, just long enough so that she quivered with anxiety. Then the door swept open and the step was out. She moved down into the crisp night air, and she wasn't Josephine Essex any longer.

She was the Countess of Mayne.

32

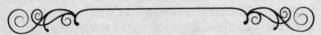

From The Earl of Hellgate,
Chapter the Twenty-third

Dear Reader, have you guessed that I am not designed for the state of matrimony? My poor darling Mustardseed, to name her after another of Shakespeare's fairies. I shall not say much of her, for our life together was short, and sometimes sweet.

Thurman was not having a good night. He had arrived home in a malodorous state and grumblingly washed himself up. He consoled himself with snapping at his man and sending his dinner back twice to be remade.

It wasn't until the middle of the night that he sat bolt upright in his bed with an oath on his lips.

He'd suddenly realized that he might find himself at the cold end of a long sword on the morrow. He stared at the gray light filtering into his room, his fingers gripping the coverlet.

"Bloody hell," he whispered out loud. If the Sausage went back to all those brothers-in-law of hers and told them his name, he'd be married to a fat Scottish woman before he turned around. He threw off the covers and tottered out of bed, his bare legs cold under the skirt of his nightdress.

"No," he groaned. "No, no, no."

His father wouldn't support him, not in this. What had he been thinking? He got a little carried away when she fought him. It was her fault, really. If she had just recognized what an honor he was paying her by deigning to kiss her, none of this would have happened.

The last sight he had of her, her dress torn and her hair falling about her shoulders, flashed before his eyes. No one would believe him when he said he didn't tear her dress. Because he didn't. He didn't even know how that happened. All he did was get a handful of her breasts, just to see if they were as large as they seemed.

He couldn't stop a little grin at that. You can't keep a Thurman down, not when he's got a hot spell on him. We're all the same, and 'ware the village maidens when—

But she wasn't a village maiden, that was the problem. And he—he almost felt like retching at the thought—he might find himself married to that great cow of a woman. Even the thought of how his brothers would laugh at him made him feel like killing someone.

Finally he splashed cold water on his face. He managed to dress himself only after his man, Cooper, asked twice, and after he realized that he was foolishly thinking that her brothers-in-law wouldn't attack an unclothed man.

By ten in the morning he had walked a circle in his study a hundred times. Of course she would tell them. She would leap at the chance to marry the eldest son of a squire. Damn, damn, damn.

She did have a dowry, he kept telling himself. And her breasts weren't so bad. In fact, a woman in the dark is the same as any other woman. He could—

He couldn't! He wanted to howl at it. The idea that he— one of Darlington's friends, his intimates—marrying a woman called the Scottish Sausage made his gorge rise.

It was almost a relief when Cooper appeared and announced a visitor. "Tell them to come in!" he snapped.

Cooper blinked. "It isn't more than one. It's a man called Harry Grone."

Not a gentleman. Not a brother-in-law. Thurman nodded. Could he be some sort of intermissionary, a lawyer, perhaps?

He positioned himself in front of the fire, legs well apart. "What do you want, then?" he barked, the moment the door closed behind Cooper. He had to be aggressive and manly. He had decided to deny everything. It was worth a try.

But this was no lawyer to an earl. In fact . . .

"I've come to ask a small favor," the man said. He was a dried-up old prune of a thing who looked as if he had few teeth and less wits. Thurman couldn't stand old people. They smelled and pissed in their trousers.

"The answer is no."

"I'm prepared to pay magnificently for your generosity," the man said. He drew out a bag of sovereigns.

Thurman could feel his heart slowing back to normal. His father kept him well-stocked with everything a young heir-about-town needed. "Get out of my house," he snarled.

"And all I wanted was a bit of information from your family's printing house. Just a wee bit of information. Wouldn't take the young master more than a moment to find it out."

The idiot didn't think that he, Thurman, actually entered the premises of the printing press, did he?

" 'Tis a powerfully expensive life," the man crooned. "Perhaps you might use this small gift to pay a gambling debt . . . or a tailor's bill?"

"I don't gamble." He started walking toward Grone. It would feel absolutely right to take this bounder apart, limb from limb. Grone was questioning his honor. He *deserved* to be beaten.

The man jumped back faster than Thurman could imagine a bald-pate could move. "I'll leave my card," he squeaked, throwing something on the table. "The offer is good, sir." And he was gone before Thurman could grab him.

Thurman satisfied himself with picking up the entire table with the card on it and throwing it against the wall. It flew to pieces with a great splintering of wood. Bloody Hepplewhite furniture was made of toothpicks.

33

From The Earl of Hellgate,
Chapter the Twenty-third

**She came to me on a Monday, and she died on
Friday, in a most lamentable series of events. I
like to think that she flew from my arms into
God's bosom, although in a less poetic vein, she
ate a bad piece of eel pie and died soon after.**

They were sitting around a scrubbed white table in Darlington's little kitchen. "Have you ever eaten in a kitchen before?" he asked, handing her an apple he'd polished.

"Never." Griselda was perched on a kitchen stool, hugging a bowl of cocoa.

"I have a kitchen maid and a cook," he explained, "but they live in their own houses."

"I am rather confused," Griselda observed. "You are not a penniless man."

"Luckily, no." Darlington was cutting perfect squares of cheese, and handing them to her to eat with the apple.

"You know perfectly well what I mean," Griselda said.

"Does your father make you an allowance? It must be very generous."

"Nosy, aren't you?"

She grinned at him, feeling her hair down her back and the pure deliciousness of knowing that there were only the two of them in the whole house. She'd never been alone in a house in her life. She and Willoughby lived in a house populated by at least fifteen other souls at any given time. But this house was quiet. The only thing that could be heard was the distant rumble of a carriage passing now and then. "In my house," she said, "one can always hear the sound of someone walking down the corridor, or building up a fire, or washing dishes."

"I like to live alone." He handed her another piece of cheese, balanced on an apple. "There are servants' quarters in this house, small though it is, but I still send everyone home."

"Why do you have so many books?"

"I enjoy them," he said, putting the knife away. "What do you read for pleasure? Have you read Canto IV of Byron's *Canto Harold*? It was just published."

"At the moment I am absolutely absorbed by Hellgate's *Memoirs,* as I told you the other day. I think I've figured out every single one of his *amours*. I know without question, for example, who Hermia is, and no one else seems to have figured that out."

"You do?"

"Hellgate says that Hermia is a duchess; he met her at court, and she made love to him in a broom closet. Well!" Griselda leaned closer. "I myself spied the Duchess of Gigsblythe emerging from just such a broom closet a year or two ago. I was in St. James's Palace, on my way to the Chapel Royal. You know that monstrous long passage that leads from the Office of the Treasury? She sneaked out of the closet ahead of me!"

"How on earth did you know it was a closet?" Darlington said, looking amused and not at all dazzled at the wonderful piece of gossip she had just handed him.

"I opened the door and checked, of course!"

"My goodness, how enterprising of you. What if her *amour* had been still there, perhaps wearing only his smalls—or not even that?"

"There was nothing but a small room with a few buckets and the like. You could stop cutting cheese and apple if you wish; I am no longer hungry."

Darlington looked almost surprised as he looked at the plate full of wafer-thin cheese and apple slices before him. He pushed it slightly to the side. "But Griselda, what *would* you have done had you surprised one of the Royal Dukes straightening his stockings?"

She giggled. "The truth is that it hadn't even occurred to me that the room was used for such encounters . . . not until I read Hellgate's memoirs. Then of course I knew who he was talking about. She must use the room on a regular basis. I would never have thought it of her."

"Fibster," Darlington said. "There's not a person in the *ton* who wouldn't have imagined Gigsblythe using such a room if it struck her fancy."

Griselda laughed.

"The more interesting point is how do you know that she ever met Hellgate in that room? There may be many who know of that convenient closet."

"Did you?" Griselda demanded.

"I did," he said. "And yet I have an unblemished history that is quite the opposite of Hellgate's. I do believe that useful little closet, and one or two others like it, are known to most of the *ton*. You, my dear"—he reached out and tapped her nose—"are a virtuous woman. There are few of you."

"I'm not virtuous," Griselda protested. "How can you say

such a thing when I am sitting opposite you, in your own house? And nary a chaperone in sight!"

"Nor a chemise either," he said, his eyes catching hers.

"No corset," she whispered, feeling the brush of soft cotton against her breasts.

"No servants."

Griselda couldn't quite sort out how it happened . . . whether she laid back on the table of her own accord, or whether he picked her up. The only thing she could do was think that whatever virtue she had possessed before that night was gone indeed.

For a man who claimed slim experience, Darlington had a powerful imagination. For once she was there, on the table, her dressing gown wrenched open so that she was all creamy curvy flesh, Darlington didn't leap on her.

No, he carefully placed moist, cool wafer-thin slices of apple about her body, "As if you were an apple tart of the French persuasion."

And Griselda, caught between laughter and trembling, argued that she was an apple pie, but never a *tart*.

But then he braced his arms on the scrubbed table and announced a wish to bite each piece of apple without biting her.

And what began with laughter amid nips—he proved to be terribly awkward and was constantly missing the slices of apple—turned into something quite different by a half hour later.

It was entirely the fault of the apples.

The cheese . . .

Well, that was another story.

34

From The Earl of Hellgate,
Chapter the Twenty-fourth

To say that I was cast into despair is to underestimate the height of my agony. Darling Mustardseed was to save my tarnished soul, keep my eyes from all other women, and put my feet on the path of righteousness. Instead, she died before, in all honesty, Dear Reader, I had managed to persuade her to do more than fumble about under the bedclothes. In short, she died without experiencing a woman's pleasure; 'tis a burden that will stay with me until my benighted and much-desired death.

It was her wedding night, and Josie was unable to sleep. Never had she felt like more of a failure. When she attempted to tell Mayne the truth of her unravished state, she lost her nerve, and consequently, he still thought she had been ravished.

If there was any woman in the world capable of being blunt about an embarrassing subject, it was she. Josie knew herself well enough for that. She could have said—there were a million things she could have said.

She could have said it elegantly: *I am untouched by that loathsome viper.*

Bluntly: *After I struck him with a shovel of manure, the gentleman in question left with haste.*

Even more bluntly: *My person is untouched and there is no need for you to marry me.*

The most bluntly of all: *I am a virgin. Still.*

Sentences she could have said to Mayne kept tumbling through her mind. *I am not ravished* would have worked. Or this one: *The man never touched me intimately, beyond a few fumbling grabs at my chest.*

The truth was that she spent years thinking about how to trick a man into marrying her, and now that she'd done it, the enormity of her mistake was choking her. Minerva Press novels were just that—*novels*. No one worried about what the heroine said to the hero once she'd tricked him into marriage.

Her mind reeled, thinking about the enormity of her crimes, to give the act its proper due. She had married under false pretenses. She had allowed Mayne to sacrifice himself, thinking that she was unmarriageable—while really she was unmarriageable because she was a conniving, horrible jade.

But it wasn't as if she'd stolen Mayne *from* someone. Josie was certain that Sylvie would never take him back. Not after the way she'd spoken to him with loathing.

Though, of course, Mayne might have wished to marry someone with Sylvie's exquisite little figure. Josie kept swallowing back tears. Compared to Sylvie, she was a great galumphing beast, all curves and flesh.

Sometime later Josie sighed and rubbed her forehead. She was in a strange house belonging to a man who would likely annul their marriage on the morrow. She had a headache that wouldn't stop, and no matter how she thought about it, the mortification she faced in the morning would be unlike anything she had experienced before.

Over the breakfast rolls, if not earlier, she was going to be absolutely clear. She would simply tell Mayne that she was *virgo intacto*. It would be much more comfortable to say such a thing in a foreign language. If there were footmen in the room, they wouldn't follow her reference. The only problem was that she wasn't entirely sure of the phrase.

Virgo immaculata also sounded familiar. Immaculate certainly meant untouched by a man. So maybe that was it. She kept going back and forth between the two: was she immaculate or intact?

A half hour later Josie was sure she was going out of her mind. If only she were in Rafe's house, she would check his Latin dictionary. Finally she made up her mind to go down to Mayne's library and find the proper words. She just could not bring herself to say *I am a virgin* in English.

The house was silent as a grave when she crept out of her door. Mayne had a very pretty upper floor, with a curved hallway that belled gracefully over the antechamber below. Presumably, the door just at the top of the stairs was his bedchamber. Josie held her breath and tiptoed. It went without saying that she would die of embarrassment if he woke.

She sneaked down the stairs in the cool wash of moonlight coming through the front door, clutching her dressing gown around her. Still she heard nothing. The antechamber was a wide circle of marble floor, the walls lined with portraits.

A painting of a woman who was likely Mayne's mother was positioned just in a splash of light. She was colorless in the glow from the moon, but Josie's eyes flew to the Dowager Countess's tiny waist. She probably didn't even need a corset; she was that small. On her face was the utter confidence of a perfect woman, the kind of woman who never experienced a blemish or felt a traitorous desire for another buttered muffin.

The very sight of Mayne's mother strengthened Josie's resolve. His mother was French, and Sylvie was French.

Everyone knew that Frenchwomen were all slender. Mayne's house was the sort of house for which Sylvie was an appropriate mistress.

The door to the left surely led to a sitting room. If Mayne's house were laid out in the same fashion as Rafe's town house, the second door would be to a dining room, and the third . . .

She pushed it open softly. The room was dark as pitch. She groped forward into the darkness, stumbling her way to the wall. The first thing her outstretched fingers encountered was a row of books, the cool feeling of their leather bindings unmistakable. Relief flooded her chest.

She felt sideways until she encountered the soft velvet of a curtain. She pulled it back, shivering at the rattle of curtain hangers above her. A French window looked onto a stone railing that glowed oddly silver in the moonlight. Beyond the railing the garden looked magical and rather frightening, as if it were a place where wishes came true and fairies danced.

"Ridiculous," Josie whispered to herself.

The moon was so bright that it was almost like daylight, except that daylight is a bright amber, and moonlight is a wilder, shimmering light. The whole lawn looked as if it were underwater.

Entranced, Josie stepped forward. The handle of the French door turned in her hand, and she walked outside. For a moment she froze, looking up at the windows of the house. But Mayne was undoubtedly asleep, dreaming the just sleep of a charitable man, a man who treated marriage as a mission by which to rescue maidens in distress. She couldn't hear a sound from the house behind her.

The path of moonlight lay across the lawn like a broad band of silver, except it was silver that looked alive to the touch. At the bottom of the garden trees sprang up and the moonlight played over fragile green leaves as yet unburned by summer sun. The little grove looked like a fairy city, a fairy forest, stretching up from the lawn to a sky studded with stars.

Josie blinked across the lawn. There was something she didn't understand about those trees. That was a little hawthorn, and there an oak tree. Next to it an apple and perhaps a mock pear. It looked almost as if faint lights caught for a second in the trees and then winked out.

It should have been frightening, she thought. She never believed in fairies, after all, not even when she was small. Some part of her still didn't believe in them, and never would, not until she was face-to-face with an elfish creature. Preferably with wings.

Yet somehow she couldn't be frightened, and even all her worry and misery over the marriage and Thurman's horrid groping fell away. It was warm outside, the kind of sweet spring warmness that makes you feel overdressed in a dressing gown. Josie felt suddenly comfortable in her skin and her bones and her body, the way she used to feel when she was a child, before she understood that she'd been born with the wrong shape.

She almost laughed out loud. But instead she ran forward, leaving her slippers on the threshold to the house. She hadn't been barefoot for years, and yet it felt exactly right to curl her toes into the soft grass. Before her moon path cast its wavering, underwater light and the grass turned to an ocean. It was intoxicating, the way the broad band of light invited one to dance. Though of course she wouldn't dance. She was a grown lady now . . .

Perhaps just a swinging, running step here and there.

Across the lawn, and in the shade of a young hawthorn, she turned to look back at the house. Nothing was stirring. The house was sleeping, each window blank, and not even the dim glow of a candle could be seen.

She caught another flicker from the corner of her eye, like a fairy twinkle. So she reached up into the tree, feeling her hair catch on a branch. She had to untie her hair ribbon and shake her hair free to come away from the branch. But then she reached up again and caught hold of one of the little objects hanging from the branches, pulling it hard.

She took it back out in the moonlight to examine it.

No fairy, this.

It was a glass ball. A perfectly round glass ball that hung by a ribbon from the branch. Josie frowned over it. She couldn't imagine why such an ornament would be hanging on a tree. Could Mayne have done such a thing?

There were etchings on the glass, but she couldn't see them well in the moonlight. Yet how beautiful it was! When she held up the globe, it caught the moonglow and threw it back on her hand. For a moment she just held it, turning it so the watery light of the moon danced over her hands and her arms, catching the rumpled darkness of her hair. There were glass balls in all the trees, big ones and little ones, casting a lovely confusion of light and shadows over the lawn.

Josie danced a little bit farther. All her misery was gone, all the grief and self-loathing and hatred washed away in the moonlight. Tomorrow was another day. That thought felt like a blessing, as if there were indeed fairies dancing in Mayne's woods.

The thought made her laugh. Her husband was a man known to have slept with most of the married women in the *ton* . . . was he a man to have a fairy wood in his backyard? His fairies would be small lascivious nymphs, playfellows of Bacchus.

The inside of the woods beckoned like a dark dream. There were early roses growing somewhere; she could smell their faint, rather ragged smell. Their perfume beckoned too, and so without another glance back at the sleeping house, Josie drifted into the wood, holding her drop of moonglow in her hand.

* * *

Mayne stayed on the threshold of the library until he was quite certain that Josie was finding her way to the rose bower and wouldn't reemerge from the wood. Then he walked after her, feeling queerly as if he didn't believe his own eyes.

Was that truly his young wife—the words echoed in his chest with an odd resonance—his young wife who had danced into the woods with a swirl of midnight hair? She held one of his glass globes up to the moonlight as if she were an ancient pagan priestess in some sort of act of moon worship.

Perhaps she was a pagan goddess, a distilled intoxicating version of womanhood. He had frozen there, watching the sweet panel of her cheek, icy cream in the moonlight. Even from the other side of the lawn he could feel the force of Josie's capacity for joy.

She was wearing nothing more than a sturdy dressing gown, tied at the waist, and yet Mayne discovered his heart beating wildly, as he watched the line of her flank, the intoxicating way that she curved in at her waist. She looked like a painting by the great Raphael, one of those he painted for his adored mistress. Josie had the same soft arms and rounded breasts as the lavishly beloved Renaissance paramour.

Every inch of Mayne's body burned to run across the lawn and snatch her into his arms. She didn't look like a subdued, ravished maiden any longer. She was enthrallingly sensual, with her bare feet and unbound hair.

A deep certainty settled in his chest, and with it a gladness so profound that he almost laughed aloud. Josie had not been ravished. Whatever had happened to her, his darling girl had not been thrown onto the ground and taken. More likely, she left the man in question on the ground. In fact, now that he thought about the manure story . . . he could hardly stop himself from laughing.

Instead he stopped for a moment on the stone portico and pulled off his boots. He hadn't retired to bed; he had just been sitting by the fire in his bedroom, brooding over what to do with an injured wife . . .

Who wasn't injured.

The joy of it flooded his body. She was *his,* and she wasn't hurt. Every pulse of blood in his body was informing him exactly what to do with that exquisite nymph who just danced her way into his woods.

Mayne ran across the grass in his bare feet, feeling a hedonistic pleasure that he never experienced in all his tawdry meetings by candlelight with women tired of their marriages. When he reached the wood he cast an experienced eye over the glass balls. They all appeared to be sturdily moored to their branches, swaying a bit in the rustling wind, but just as beautiful as they'd been since Aunt Cecily first envisioned them.

He walked quietly through the few trees, heading to the rose arbor. That's where she would be, of course. It all had a queer sense of inevitability, as if all the terror and upset of the last twenty-four hours came down to this moment of walking toward his new wife. The rose arbor was in the very back of his garden, sheltered on two sides by the ancient stone walls that separated his house from that next door. The roses had grown and grown until they hung in great tattered sheets over the walls.

Josie was sitting in the middle of the arbor, not on the stone bench, but with her back against the statue of a leaping dolphin, caught in mid-flight. Her lap was full of cascades of roses, their sweet and delicate smell strong in the night air.

"Didn't you scratch your hands plucking those roses?" he said, drifting silently to the wall and then remembering, too late, that he should have given her some indication of his presence.

But she didn't scream.

She just looked up and smiled. His breath burned in his chest at her wide-spaced, arched brows, tip-tilted eyes, the swirl of her hair.

"How extraordinarily odd," she said. "For a moment I thought that Dionysus had appeared in his woods."

Mayne ran a hand through his hair. Lord knows, from her point of view, he likely was as old as any Greek god. "I'm not sure that's a compliment; isn't Dionysus the Greek name for Bacchus, the god of wine?"

"The god of wine and nature, the one who carries a staff wound with ivy, and whose maenads dance through the night."

He walked forward, his trousers brushing roses and releasing a rich burst of flavor into the air. "I have no doubt but that you are one of the maenads. Will you dance all night?"

"I am a terrible dancer," Josie said with a chuckle. "I believe you noticed?"

He sat down next to her on the flagstones. The ballrooms of Almack's seemed a different world. Above them the dolphin cast his arched shadow across the paving stones.

"This was your aunt's rose arbor, wasn't it?" she asked him.

"It was," he said. "According to my father, she loved this place next after her turret. She planted the roses before she grew very ill. Even when she was extremely frail, she would have the servants carry her to the arbor in fine weather."

"It's enough to make me believe in fairies. And I assure you that I am the kind of person whose imagination is decidedly impoverished."

"I don't believe that. Not with all the novels you read."

"It's the truth. When we were young, we would all play house, of course. Annabel was brilliant at making up stories, and Imogen would chime in. I haven't a shard of imagination myself; I like things to be very clearly explained."

Mayne leaned his head back against the pedestal and

looked up at the sky. It looked close enough to touch, like soft velvet, so worn that stars shone through. "Cecily truly believed there were fairies living here, in the woods. She hung the glass balls to delight them."

"I thought that must be it. How lovely that you've kept up the tradition."

"My father would have wished it," Mayne said. "He died quite suddenly, but I know he would have asked me to do it."

She said nothing, but she picked up his hand. To Mayne's horror, his throat felt a bit tight. Her hand was soft and warm, curling around his.

"Would you dislike being left a widow, Josie? We seem to be rather short-lived in my family."

"That's absurd."

"I'm much older than you are."

"Women die far more often than do men," she said. "In childbirth, for one."

"A melancholy thought."

"And you're not *so* much older than I am. How old are you?"

"How old are *you*?"

"Eighteen."

"When I was eighteen," Mayne said after a moment, "I had seduced two married women and been spurned by three."

"I have been spurned by most of the *ton*," Josie said cheerfully, "and if I seduce you, you will be my first married man."

He turned his head and looked at her, all devil in his eyes. "I'm not certain I heard you correctly."

"I'm quite certain that you did."

"An angel's face," he said, "but a devil's tongue."

"An expression of desire within the bounds of matrimony is a virtuous thing to do. Besides, I always meant to seduce someone and then marry him."

"It's too late for that."

"Actually, this marriage can be annulled."

He was silent, looking at her. Her nightgown unbuttoned down the front with tiny pearl buttons that shone faintly in the moonlight. Holding his gaze, she reached up to the first button and undid it.

"Josie," he said.

"I always planned to scheme my way into marriage with an impudent act," she told him. "In truth, I hadn't intended to be quite so impudent"—she undid another button—"but I can see quite well that you will annul this marriage on the morrow, saying that you are too old."

"I am too old for you."

"Are you fifty years old?"

He made a sound like a startled laugh. "No."

"Forty?"

"Not yet."

"How many years past thirty?"

"Almost five."

"Thirty-four is a very good age for a man."

If Mayne were indeed Dionysus, she thought, he would seduce her, of course. Dionysus was no respecter of maidens and their maidenheads.

The annoying thing was that Mayne was just holding her hand, as if she were a child of seven.

Yet something about the wild, underwater night had clarified everything for Josie. She wanted Mayne. It was a terrifying kind of hunger, the sort of embarrassing emotion that leads one into tricking a man into marriage.

"Mayne," she said, making up her mind.

"Garret," he said. He had let go of her hand and was strewing rose petals around their feet in an absentminded fashion.

"I am," she said, pausing to make the statement impressive, "a *virgin immaculata.*"

Mayne responded in a very gratifying way. His mouth fell open and he blinked at her like a village idiot. "You are?"

Josie grinned at him. "Isn't that wonderful?"

"It is?"

"Well, I think it is."

"You mean, like Mary, *Virgin Immaculata*?"

"I suppose so," she said uncertainly.

Mayne's face had an odd expression, as if he were about to burst into laughter. "Are you distressed by this . . . development?"

She frowned at him. "So what did I just tell you about myself?"

"Let's see," he said. "I believe you just said that you're a sanctified virgin. Along the lines of being a living holy tabernacle. My mother, being French, is Catholic and quite fond of Mary. *Virgin Immaculata* is a reference to Mary, who was born without original sin."

There was a moment's silence.

"I always thought that I would marry a saint," Mayne said. Now she could see the deep amusement on his face. "And how happy my mother will be. You do know that she's an abbess, don't you?"

And it was funny. Before she knew it, Josie was giggling, and then, when Mayne started laughing, howling along with him.

"*You* marry a saint!" she gasped, laughing helplessly.

"Stranger things have happened." He picked up a handful of rose petals and sprinkled them over her hair. "Though you look particularly pagan this night." There was something in his eyes that made Josie want to laugh and fall silent all at once. "Of course, I would be most disconcerted to discover that a deity had reserved you for his own child."

Her laughter died. A silken rose petal slipped past her cheek.

"I've a mind to reserve you for my own enjoyment."

"But you didn't," Josie said. This was the moment for the greatest clarity of all. Perfect candor was called for. "You married me thinking that I wasn't a virgin, Garret. And— And I am."

"Because you tossed a shovelful of manure over the man before he forced you."

She nodded. "You didn't have to marry me. We can annul the marriage." Although she had no intention of allowing him to do such a rash thing. But from what she'd seen of men, it was best to allow them to think things through slowly.

"You would do better to marry someone along the lines of young Skevington," Mayne said. "Or Tallboys."

If she allowed Mayne to slip away tonight, he would never be hers. The truth of it was in her heart, along with a deeper truth about the way she felt, a truth that she refused to examine at the moment.

It would have been horribly unnerving, in the darkness of a bedchamber, to think of exposing herself in such a way. But in the warm evening air, her body felt sleek and beautiful, curved in a dangerous, potent way. And Mayne's eyes seemed to make a promise to her again and again.

"How warm it is tonight," she said, and undid another button on her nightgown.

Mayne's eyes fell to her hands and then moved back to her face. There was a look in his eyes, a very small smile, that made her remember for one second how much experience *he* had with seducing and being seduced, and how little experience she had in the same arena.

But it was as if Dionysus himself were whispering in her ear. She uncurled herself and stood up, walking over to the low wall. Then she turned.

Mayne had risen to his feet, of course. He would never stay seated in the presence of a woman. But he didn't follow her. He stayed where he was, leaning against the dolphin. His black curls were falling over his eyes like rumpled silk. His eyelashes shadowed his eyes so that she couldn't see anything but the long clean lines of his cheeks, the restless aristocratic beauty of him. Somehow even that wasn't terrifying, just entrancing.

Josie felt as if she were wearing nothing more than gossamer cobwebs.

"You resemble a maenad more by the moment," Mayne said. And yet he made no move in her direction.

The key, Josie thought to herself, would be to say something that would make it absolutely clear that if he wished to seduce her, perhaps now would be the time.

"If you felt inclined to make an advance to me," she told him, "you could do so."

Definitely that look in his eyes was laughter.

"But Madame Countess, if I made an advance to you, *and* if that advance were successful, we would no longer be able to annul our marriage," he pointed out.

Josie was gaining more courage every moment, from the look in Mayne's eyes, from the stillness around them, from the oddly curious sense of power she felt. "I would not wish you to feel obliged to do anything to which you were not naturally inclined," she said, allowing laughter to steal into her voice. For in truth, she felt like laughing. Laughing and . . . something else. She felt fluid and seductive, as unlike her normal self as possible.

She walked back to him, feeling her hair on her shoulders. Feeling the sway of her hips and the tilt in her lips. Knowing that she was walking toward him with precisely the kind of promise that he had taught her.

He didn't say anything, just looked at her, all shadowed eyes and secret smile, and it was as if the whole world held its breath.

Josie reached up and pulled his mouth down to hers.

One had to suppose that kissing Mayne was like drinking aged brandy, that golden liquor Rafe used to be so fond of.

After all, he was older than she, and more knowledgeable, and surely he knew everything about kissing?

But somehow she felt as if she were the one with experience. He tasted startled and uncertain, whereas she was absolutely confident. She poured herself into that kiss, winding her arms around his neck and rejoicing in the feeling of her breasts against him. She was a pagan goddess, curved, beautiful, a perfect shape in every way.

He groaned against her lips.

"Garret," she whispered, feeling as if small sparks might be flying in all directions. "That small building in the corner was your aunt's, was it not?"

"Josie, are you absolutely certain that you wish to seduce me?" he said, sounding drunk and responsible at the same time. "Skevington is planning to ask for your hand in marriage. My uncle can wipe the record of our marriage from his books as if it never happened. You do not have to marry a man like me."

"What do you mean by a man like you?" she asked, genuinely curious.

He pulled back and looked at her. "A man of thirty-four. A man who has slept with many, many women. I don't have any diseases, Josie, but that's by the grace of God. I do nothing and I am nothing, Josie. You must understand that. I lost my way, a few years ago, and I haven't found it. If there is a way to find."

"Not to deflate your tale of woe, but I can find your way for you."

He raised an eyebrow.

"All you have to do is worship at my feet," she said smugly, trying to choke back her giggle.

"I gather you think I'm bleating like a sheep?" Mayne said, a little smile playing around the corner of his mouth.

"You're a born horseman," she told him. "You have stables,

and horses, and more than enough money. Of course I think you're being a fool." Then she added: "Not to be harsh."

"Skevington will worship at your feet," Mayne said.

"Actually, I don't want to be worshipped."

He waited.

"Do you know what I want most, Garret?" She pulled his shirt free from his trousers. "I want to be *desired*."

"You are that." He said it a bit hoarsely.

"You often look bored," Josie told him. "You drift about, looking discontented and bored with life. But then, one day, you looked at *me*. As if I really were me."

"And?"

"You suddenly looked like a wolf," she whispered. His shirt felt like warm velvet under her fingertips. She wanted to run her hands under it. "You flared into life, and it was me who made you feel that way."

"It's foolish, grotesque in a man my age," he said. But he wasn't pushing away her hands.

"Stop being a fool and talking of your age," Josie said. "I'm tired of that and it has no place between us, don't you see? What's between us made me follow you to Cecily's turret, had you wearing my dress and kissing me when you were engaged to another woman, made me marry you, though I knew full well that I wasn't ravished. I *took* you."

Something was changing in his eyes. She shivered like an aspen in a storm as he touched her. "You took me," he stated.

"You thought you were rescuing me, but that was just your man's foolishness."

He was a stubborn one, this husband of hers. She could see him steeling himself to make one more attempt. So she contented herself with stepping even closer, so that she could smell the clean male scent of him.

"I'm not going to fall in love." He said it desperately, with the fervor of a man who knows he's lost a battle but won't quite give up. "We have to be honest with each other, Josie. I was in love with Sylvie. I don't believe I have more of the emotion in me."

A whisper of chill wind touched Josie's back. "You were in love . . . or you still are? Would you prefer to win her back, Garret? Because if you have that hope in your heart, we should not continue." And she looked at the ground, because she couldn't bear to see love for another woman in his eyes.

"Sylvie and I have no future together," he said.

So he was still in love with her. But Josie took the pain of that and pushed it away. She, Josie, wasn't in love with *him,* so why should she care?

"All right, then. You can take the mementos of your brief engagement and put them in a box. In the attic."

She could feel him laughing before she heard his response: "Would I be allowed to visit them now and then?"

"Yes," Josie said. "I'll find you occasionally, in the twilight of the attic, turning over a faded blue ribbon that Sylvie wore in her hair."

"What a lovely picture," Mayne said.

"Actually," Josie said, getting into the spirit of the thing, "you might want to take a ribbon of hers, perhaps the one she wore the night you first kissed her, and wear it next to your heart, Garret. Then when you die and we're laying you out in state, I'll find the ribbon, and almost throw it away, but then—"

"With sobs that would break the heart of Beelzebub himself, you'll tuck it back next to my heart and go to your grave knowing that your husband loved another."

"I like that," Josie said, thinking about it. "Especially the part where I almost throw your ribbon away but stop myself."

He pulled her a little closer and she could feel his body, hard against hers. "There is one problem."

Josie was rethinking about the heartrending scene at the coffin. "I think I will throw away that ribbon, Garret, so be warned. I may even burn it."

"I don't have any ribbons," Mayne pointed out. "Not even from the first night I kissed Sylvie."

"You must have something."

"Nothing."

"A shame," Josie said. He was looking at her now, and there was something in his eyes that made nonsense of the idea of Sylvie's ribbons. Yes, he was in love, but . . .

"I've often thought that desire and love are very similar," she said, telling him because he might as well know now how scandalous she was. "Who's to say that desire is not the same as love?"

"I've felt many a stroke of desire, Josie, and only a few of love."

She shook back her head, letting her hair fall behind her, free and wild. "I suppose you're right. If desire were love, there'd be no unmarried streetwalkers."

He laughed, but she could feel him drawing even closer. His hands were spread on her back, their bodies just a hair's breadth apart.

"Do you desire me, Garret Langham, Earl of Mayne?"

His eyes were dark in the moonlight. "You're no street-walker, Josephine Langham, Countess of Mayne."

"If I were, I would be more practiced at seduction," she said. "Shan't you give me lessons?"

"In seduction?"

"You are an expert." She raised her hands to her hair again, feeling as pagan as any fairy queen. "If you return to the house, I will take it that you do not desire me enough for this marriage."

She turned her back and began walking toward the small house nestled into the corner of the garden.

"Josie!" His voice was like liquid velvet, wild and sweet.

She turned, knowing that her breasts were completely visible through the light fabric of her gown, and understanding for the first time in her life that their sweet, unsteady weight was no drawback in a man's eyes.

"What if I were a fairy queen?" she said.

"What then?"

"I would command you to stay. *Out of this wood do not desire to go. Thou shalt remain here, whether thou wilt or no.*"

"I feel a donkey's head descending onto my shoulders," he muttered. But he was walking after her.

She didn't look back, just walked up the step to the little house and pushed open the door.

"That's supposed to be locked," he said. But he was following her.

It was a small room, with nothing more than a sofa in the corner. The moon streamed through the small window.

"If I remove your donkey's head, will you kiss me?" she whispered.

He stood by the door, large, shadowed. She couldn't see his face.

"There's no going back from this."

"I don't want to." Exhilaration was running through her veins. For her, there had only been this man, from the moment he kissed her and showed her how to be a woman. Garret turned her, with his desire, from shapeless to shapely. From undesirable to desired.

She would never want anyone else in her bed, or in her life.

35

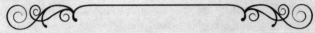

From The Earl of Hellgate,
Chapter the Twenty-fourth

For weeks I haunted my Mustardseed's grave, weeping silently and refusing nourishment. For was I not some sort of pariah, as damaging to a woman's soul as the gaze of a basilisk? I expect, Dear Reader, that you think I quickly recovered my spirits and felt the flame of lust raise again in my soul.

No! I assure you that days passed . . .

I must return to my house."

"No." He said it sleepily, but with such satisfaction that she almost laughed. But still she struggled to a sitting position.

"I'm sore, and I'm tired, and I'm far too old for this sort of gallivanting," she told him.

He propped himself up on one arm.

"Marry me?"

Griselda was bending over to pick up a stray stocking that lay abandoned on the bedroom floor. The words drifted over to her slowly, as if they'd been whispered. She straightened, stocking in her hand, and turned. "There's no need for that," she said, smiling at him with all the gladness she felt in her heart that her lover was a man of honor. "I am so grateful for you asking the question, though. It always struck me as utterly demoralizing that people carry on *affaires* when—"

She broke off. What she saw on his face wasn't the polite relief of a man who has asked the requisite question and been offered a reprieve. She froze in the middle of the room. "Don't say that," she said. "Don't."

"I must. I can't think of anything but you, Griselda. I dream of you. I smell you when you aren't with me. I can't make clever remarks, because the only person I want to speak to is you."

"You—" she said, and swallowed. "You are suffering an infatuation. It happens to young men." She said that briskly, to remind herself that he was young. *Very* young.

He didn't look very young as he got out of bed and walked toward her. "Age has nothing to do with it."

"It has everything to do with it," she retorted. "Everything! I wish I'd met you when I was younger, or you were older, or . . . or whatever was needed. Truly, I do. I would have pursued you so fiercely you couldn't see another woman without me smiling over her shoulder. I would have done anything—anything!—to marry you."

"Then have me."

"To have is not to *take*. I won't take you, with your life ahead of you. You'll find a wife who's your age or younger, and she'll bear you a dozen babies." She reached out and brushed back a lock of his hair. "I will dance at your wedding, darling, and that gladly. But I will never be your bride, for all that I am honored beyond all measure by your request."

His eyes burned into hers. "You love me."

Griselda raised her chin. This was getting entirely too personal. "I do not love you," she said, keeping her voice steady and gentle. "I appreciate you. I am proud of you."

He flinched. "Proud of me? For *what*?"

She saw what he meant and blinked. And almost laughed. "Not that! Pride is not the emotion that comes to mind when I think of your prowess!"

"Then you have no right to feel proud of me, as if—as if you were my mother." He spat it out.

Griselda reminded herself that young men have fierce passions, but she could feel her own temper rising. "I am not your mother, but I might as well be."

"Stubble it!" he said, his voice slapping her. "How old are you, Griselda Willoughby? What right have you to act as if you were eighteen years my elder?"

"Perhaps not eighteen years," Griselda said, trying to remain calm.

"Perhaps not ten," he said, and there was a distinct edge to his voice. "Perhaps not five."

"Nonsense!" Griselda said.

"Then I ask you again: how old are you?"

He had kissed her body in its most intimate places. Still Griselda stood motionless, her jaw set. She never talked of her age. Never.

"Griselda," he said, low and clear. And she could see that he was enraged.

Then he turned away, as if tired of waiting for her to answer. "You, Griselda, are thirty-two. You have more than enough years, if you wish, to present me with half a dozen children. And I am twenty-seven, almost twenty-eight. There is, at the moment, five years between us."

"You knew," she whispered. And then: "Twenty-seven?"

"You thought I was, what, eighteen? You knew that wasn't the case."

"I didn't look you up."

"I looked you up. And had you been thirty-nine, my question would be the same. And if you'd been forty-nine. But as it is, Griselda, you can hardly claim to be my mother, given that you were all of four years old when I was born."

"Five."

He shrugged. "There are things far more important about me—to me—than my age. In fact, there are many reasons why you may not wish to marry me, and my age is probably the least of it."

She stared at his back. "Why would I not wish to marry you, Darlington?"

"I am a writer."

"What?"

She felt disjointed, as if she'd missed part of the conversation.

"I am a writer," he repeated, turning around. "You asked how I support this house? I write."

"Novels?"

"No. I write in a lesser genre altogether. I write stories of crimes that have really happened. I have written sensational pamphlets; I have written gallow sheets; I have written accounts that purported to be the confessions of a murderer. I have in fact written down those confessions on occasion."

"How do you hear the confessions?"

He shrugged. "I have friends among the constabulary. I am generous with guineas when I find a good story. It's a business that pays remarkably well. I can afford to marry you, if you would even consider such a thing."

Still she stared at him, until his mouth twisted and he turned away. "I entirely understand that my means of living is not reputable. I am a laborer. In truth, I find it shameful myself, and my family finds it abhorrent. My father literally cannot bring himself to mention my work at all. It's one of the reasons he is so frantic about my marital prospects. Since I am already prostituting my honor, as he sees it, I might as well engage in a more honorable version of the same."

Griselda took a deep breath. This was all becoming far too annoying. How dare he act as if she were so shallow as to cavil at the idea of marrying a writer? Was not she the one who confessed to reading those very books? And how dare he consider her such a despicable person as to read and enjoy the genre and not honor its authors?

Meanwhile Darlington was still talking. "I write all that sensationalist prose that we were talking of last night. The murderer's mother invariably swoons on hearing of his capture; the victim's mother swoons on hearing of the incident. I turn all my victims into sturdy young men who would have made excellent husbands and fathers, no matter how despicable they were in real life." He stopped.

She still hadn't replied. It broke his heart that Griselda had nothing to say to him. He stared down at the polished surface of his dressing table, waiting with tense shoulders for the sound of the door opening and shutting again. But no: Griselda was too well bred for that. Too much a gentlewoman. She would make some excuse, she would—

A faint sound was the only thing that alerted him. He turned around to find that Griselda's hand was on her forehead and she was swaying back and forth, clearly about to faint.

She swooned into his arms with a faint sigh that went straight to his heart. "Griselda!" he shouted. And then realized that he shouldn't shout at her.

What the hell was going on? Could he have horrified her so much that she fainted? He looked around desperately. One was supposed to apply smelling salts when women fainted, but he didn't have anything like that around. Could any strong smelling object work? There were onions in the kitchen.

He laid her on the bed. She was limp and still, lying there with her eyes closed. She looked stark white. It must have been a worse shock than he had imagined.

"Griselda," he commanded, "open your eyes."

She lay still as death. Water! That's what he needed. He should dash water in her face. Lord knows, he'd described that scene enough. Of course there wasn't any water in his bedchamber, so he ran through the door and down to the kitchen.

When he came back, clutching a pitcher, his guest was still limp. Weren't women supposed to come out of it after a second or two? He began to hoist the jug in the air.

Griselda judged it was time to wake up and uttered what she considered to be an entirely fetching sound of distress. Darlington put down the pitcher, somewhat to her relief.

"Griselda," he said. "How are you feeling?"

She allowed a slight moan to pass her lips and threw her hand up to her brow in a dramatic gesture. "Oh, can it be?"

He rubbed her hands and she could hear him swearing under his breath. She had to take a deep breath to prevent a smile from erupting. "Can you have said what I thought I heard? Surely . . . no! It cannot be!" That was a little repetitive, but for someone who wasn't a writer, she was doing fairly well.

"Griselda," Darlington said, "I am truly sorry to have caused you distress, but—"

"My lover," she said, opening her eyes and looking up at him, "my lover is nothing more than—than a *common laborer*!"

"Well—"

But she didn't let him continue. "Oh, slay me now!" she cried. "I have soiled myself. My life is ruined. My reputation, my life, my body, my . . ." She paused and considered whether to faint again. Instead she peeped up at him.

He was grinning down at her, all the boyish roughness of him that she loved. Because she did love that side of him.

"I gather you think you're an actress?"

"I can write a scene as well as you can," she told him.

"Clichéd," he said contemptuously.

"Pot calling the kettle black!"

"*My* fainting women never moan," he said.

"More fools they," she said. "I am hugely enjoying this faint, and I am only sorry that I had to cut off my performance before you drenched me with water."

"Call me a fool," Darlington said. "But Griselda, why did you faint?"

"To see if you had any experience of fainting women," she said, sitting up comfortably and patting her hair. "You haven't, have you?"

"Well, no."

"In fact," she went on, "I'd lay a guinea to a shilling that you simply make up most of what you print."

"Not *most* of it."

"But you embroider it."

"Well . . ."

She smiled at him. "Do you think that I am a fool? That I didn't surmise your career from our conversation?"

"But don't you—aren't you—"

"Am I embarrassed to find that my lover is a writer of lively prose, enjoyed by hundreds, if not thousands of people? That he has managed to make himself rich, so he needn't depend on his father nor marry a young woman for her dowry?" She met his eyes directly. "Had you bowed to your father and married, Darlington, we would never have known each other."

"Knowledge in the Biblical sense? Yes." Before Griselda quite knew what had happened, he was on his knees by the bed and he had her hands in his.

"Marry me, Griselda. Neither of us will be good for anyone else after this; you know that."

"You're saying I should marry you just because I'm not good for anyone else?"

"I ruined you," he said, his eyes holding hers and not

letting her make another foolish comment. "You're mine, and no one else's, Griselda."

"Oh—"

But he was kissing her, and it seemed that he didn't need an answer that very moment.

And perhaps they both knew the answer in her heart.

36

From The Earl of Hellgate,
Chapter the Twenty-fourth

It was all of a week or more before I left my Mustardseed's grave, and at least a week after that before my faltering steps took themselves to any sort of entertainment. Tho' I was clad, as you can imagine, in the most immaculate black. Therein lay my downfall, Dear Reader.

For I, poor I, have always looked my best in black.

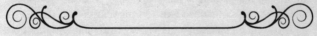

I don't know what comes next," Josie said, laughing a bit. "My novels always stop at the bedchamber."

He walked over until he stood just before her.

She kept talking because she felt nervous, and that made her want to chatter. "Of course, you would make a prime hero."

"Really," he drawled. "Do you think you could write me?"

"After reading so many novels, I could write *anyone*," she said with conviction.

He laughed. "Then write me. Go ahead. Describe me in the lush prose of one of those novels you love so much."

She reached out a hand and touched his eyebrow. Mayne felt a little shudder, as if he were a mere youngster again, faced by his first woman. But somehow in this particular night, it felt like that, as if they were the only man and woman in the world.

"Two eyebrows, midnight black," Josie said, her finger lightly stroking him. "Eyelashes that are too long for a man, and oh! Eyes dreadfully tired . . . exhausted by the debauchery of centuries."

"Centuries?" Mayne said, laughing. "I'm not really a Greek, you know."

"Centuries," Josie said, nodding. "A nose, quite noble really, in its original. One cannot but look at it mournfully, to see the gothic greatness with which it was once endowed, but now—dear reader, alas—faded to a mere nose."

"A mere nose!" Mayne was starting to feel slightly insulted. "What should it be, pray? And what do you mean faded? It's the same nose I've had for years."

"Lips of a melancholy dark cherry tint," she said, her eyes laughing at him. "Even with the beams of the moon falling on them, they retain a hint of wildness . . . a bacchanalian hint that speaks to the—to the—"

He was leaning forward now. He felt as if every inch of his body was alive, every cell urging him toward her. "Those lips," he said, "are indeed bacchanalian. But what do nice young ladies know of Bacchus? My turn to paint your face. You'll have to help me, though, for I haven't read many novels."

"No," she said, grinning. "I expect you'll describe me like one of those horses you're always reading about."

"And what a lovely filly that would be." He felt like Bacchus himself, drunk on the moonlight and his beautiful young wife. "There are horses with as long lashes as yours, Josie. Did you know that?"

She nodded.

"And horses with a mane of black silk, like your hair."

"It isn't black," she pointed out. "You appear not to know the color of my hair."

"When we were in the coach on the way to Scotland," he said, "it would take on a deep ruby glow if the sun was shining in the window. But in moonlight it looks as deep and mysterious as the night sky." He wrapped a lock around his finger.

"Your lips," he continued conversationally, "have not the faded glory you give my nose, but a deep red. The kind of red that makes a man feel weak with desire. Do you know why, Josie?"

She shook her head, not taking her eyes from his.

"Because they are plump and luscious," he said, very close to her now. "Because to look at them is to want to taste them. To look at them is to want to taste you."

She almost said something about being plump all over, but the words died in her throat. Somehow her disdain for her own body seemed ridiculous in light of the way he looked at her. When he looked at her . . .

"You look like a fairy queen, Titania from Shakespeare's play," Mayne said.

She laughed at that. "A queen!"

"Titania is no ordinary fairy, after all. And you are no ordinary woman."

"Honesty compels me to admit that I am a terribly ordinary woman," Josie said. "I'm plump, addicted to novels, and afraid of riding horses."

"Dear me," Mayne said, enjoying himself hugely. "Have you *no* redeeming qualities to offer a spouse? Perhaps I should rethink this."

"I am fairly cheerful," Josie told him. "I can be funny if I have a clever moment. I'm very honest, and I'm told that's a virtue, although it sometimes works to my disadvantage."

"No beauty?" he said mournfully.

She shook her head. "Not in comparison to other women."

"Shall I tell you how I see you?"

"Not if you're going to tell me lies. I really dislike lies, Garret."

"I won't bother with your lips, or your hair, your eyes or your skin—though it is the most beautiful skin I've ever had the pleasure to be near, Josie. Let's just start here, shall we?" He pulled her closer. Then he said: "Feel what I'm thinking with my hands."

She frowned at him.

"You don't need words for everything," he told her. "I'll tell you with my hands."

He put his fingers on her cheeks, a touch as sweet as a baby's kiss. His hands slid down her cheeks with deliberate slowness. She shivered a little. A thumb traced the plump curve of her lower lip and then she knew, she knew what he was doing. It was as though his thumb told her everything. It paused on her lip for a moment and she closed her lips around him. He tasted strange and male. Heat flooded her body.

"Do that again," he said, his voice rough, "and—"

Her lips closed around his thumb again, teasing him with a little bite. He made a sound in his throat and then continued downward. Over her throat, hands leaving trails of fire.

"Watch me," he said. She was watching his face, of course, his beautiful eyes. But she looked down, obediently.

There in the moonlight his hands looked huge and male. The edge of her nightgown was wide and lined with Belgium lace. His spread fingers came warm down her neckline and then just to the neckline, the open buttons.

Josie held her breath. What would he do? His hands slid

down her arms, arms that under his fingers felt perfectly curved, soft and beautiful. "Have you ever seen Raphael's paintings of his mistress?"

She looked up, knowing her cheeks were flushed, telling herself it didn't matter. He was circling her wrists now, his hands twice the size of her bones.

"No," she whispered.

"She has your figure," he whispered back. "The kind of curves a man could drown in, could never leave."

Those fingers were moving back up her arms, and Josie almost didn't hear him in the fever dream caused by his caress. She was holding her breath again, but he was slow and sweet in his time, smiling a little. He hooked his thumbs under the neckline of her gown and rubbed a circle.

She just stopped herself from moving with him. Then he was pulling, pulling the neckline down.

She whimpered and her mind flared with embarrassment, and then rational thought skittered away again. He was inching the gown down over her arms and her breasts. His palms were warm against her evening-cooled skin. Warm and possessive. One wrench, and the gown fell to her hips and clung there.

"Look down," he said, his voice a siren's call. So she did. But then every rational thought fled.

His hands were golden, dark against her skin, which gleamed with the same pearl of the moon. He slid his hands down her front as if he were discovering a new land, and she looked up, saw him swallow hard, and understood.

He was holding her breasts as if they were gifts from the gods. Looking down, she saw them through his eyes: pure desire, soft, unsteady, overflowing from his hands, her nipple peaked where his thumb rubbed it. She was biting her lip to stop herself from rolling her hips toward him, when his hands started moving down again, silkily tracing the way her waist curved in and then out into the generosity of her hips.

He paused and met her eyes, but he must have seen what he wanted there because with a flick of his fingers the nightgown slid down her thighs and fell to the ground. Then his hands were everywhere. Running over the curve of her bottom, and suddenly she felt the deliciousness of its roundness, felt it as if she were the one comparing it to a bony behind. Felt the curve of her waist out to her hips, and understood for the first time how a man might want to sink into softness.

"But," Josie gasped. "All your women, those women—"

"*Not* my women," he growled.

But she stood her ground. "All those women with whom you—you had trysts with—were slim. Very slim. And you fell in love—" But she stopped.

His fingers were curving around her thighs, perilously close to the heart of her. She reached out and he gathered her in with one arm so she was leaning against him, her skin startlingly white against his clothing, but his other hand didn't move.

She could feel her heart beating, beating faster and faster. And then she felt a soft touch between her thighs.

He started talking just when her mind blurred and heat was licking at her stomach in a way guaranteed to make her light-headed. "They were skinny," he said into her ear. *"Out of these woods do not desire to go."*

"Humph," she said. She was the one who was the reader; it was rather disconcerting to find herself with someone who apparently knew his way between the pages of a play. *"Thou shalt remain here, whether thou wilt or no,"* she told him, leaning against his shoulder so that he could do as he wished with her body.

"I am a spirit of no common rate, the summer still doth tend upon my state. Mmm, Josie, you're so soft there. Do you like that?"

She gasped a bit.

"What's the matter?" he teased. "Can't you remember the next line?"

She was *not* going to utter the next line.

His eyes were laughing at her, and then he said it instead, but of course he was just joking. *"And I do love thee: therefore, go with me."*

"Oh, piffle," she said, with another little gasp at something he did with his thumb. "There have been so many you've loved."

"Not true," he said. "I'm not sure that I'm capable of the emotion."

Josie leaned against him, and let him continue touching her, playing her as if she were a delicate instrument whose every note he was learning.

"Neither of the women I thought I loved ever looked at me the way you do," Mayne said into her ear.

Josie knew without question that she looked desperate. Sylvie, for one, never looked that way. She was too beautiful to be desperate.

"It's shameful to admit it," Mayne said, "but when you look at me I feel beautiful."

She should stop him; she should really stop him. Except she couldn't. She was gasping now.

"When I look at you," he said, "I feel out of control. Which is likely why I never, ever approached any woman who made me feel the way you do, and since I'm still not exactly sure how we got married—"

"We aren't married, not really."

"We will be in about ten minutes."

"Oh," Josie whispered.

Then he had her in his arms and he was putting her on the sofa.

"You want to be here, or you wouldn't have gone along with this marriage in the first place," he said. He stood beside her, pulling off his clothes, and Josie didn't even bother to arrange her limbs in such a way to minimize her curves, because she couldn't breathe. Not when she saw all those muscles, and the way his chest tapered to his hips, and then . . . below that . . .

Mayne followed her eyes. "I've never slept with a virgin," he said, a little pucker between his brows.

"Neither have I," Josie said, reaching out for him. "But I'm willing to give it a try."

But he didn't fall onto her directly. Instead he lay beside her and kissed her eyes and her cheek, while she shivered. Until finally she slowly came to realize that making love— with Mayne at any rate—was a sensual feast that would likely take hours.

It took time, and kisses, and little whispers, and a giggle or two, but finally Josie found herself no longer lying beside him, but touching him greedily. It was all, she thought groggily, a matter of imitation. He kissed her cheek, and then the curve of her neck, and then her shoulders . . .

So she kissed his lip, and felt the roughness of a coming beard, and then kissed him lower, on his shoulders and chest.

And all the time, he was whispering to her, and his hands were wandering over her body, making her tremble and even cry out until—until she said, rather desperately, "Garret, it's not that this is unenjoyable, but do you think that you—that we could—that you could stop kissing my shoulder now?"

A little laugh broke from his chest and he came over her, on his knees, looking down. "What would you like to do next?"

Josie was shivering all over with excitement, and trying in vain to think of something witty to say.

"I'm no virgin, Josie," he said. He had a hand in the patch of curly hair between her legs, and now she was finding it hard to hear, let alone think.

"I guess not," she mumbled.

"But damned if I don't feel like one at this moment," he

said, lowering his head to her breast so she couldn't see his eyes. Which she would have liked to do. He sounded rather bewildered.

"You do?" she managed.

But whatever response he might have thought to make was muffled because he was kissing her breast. She had trouble understanding words when he was worshipping her with his mouth. Even more so when he kissed down over her tummy, and left little nip marks on her hips, and then . . .

By then nothing he said was making much sense anyway, although she was dimly aware that he had kept talking. About how he felt like a virgin, and as if she was different.

Josie heard him, and threw it away. She didn't need words. What she needed was just what he was doing with his hands, and then with his mouth . . .

Her toes were curled, and her back was arched, and she was whimpering for lack of air, and trying to keep it to a ladylike level. Except she couldn't, not after he brought his hands to play as well. She was making all sorts of unladylike noises, and she couldn't stop rising toward him, but she didn't care.

He pulled her knees apart, and rose over her, and she had one startling moment, one picture that she never forgot, her whole life long, of Garret Langham, Earl of Mayne, his face rigid and his eyes wild, his shoulders braced, and a look in his eyes . . .

Suddenly she believed him. Believed that he felt new, as new as she did. Believed that for some strange reason it all felt as new to him as it did to her. Because she watched the ragged breath escape from his lips as he rocked against her. And heard the guttural sound that came from his lips as he entered her.

One of the reasons she remembered everything so vividly was that from about two seconds after that first nudge—which felt pretty good, she had to admit—the rest of it *didn't* feel very good. In fact, that feverish heat evaporated from her legs as quickly as it had come, and instead of wanting to rise toward him, her only instinct was to get away.

Within another second the only things going through her mind were thoroughly unromantic swear words, things she'd heard in the stables, anything that would describe the awful stinging, painful stretching. It wasn't at all the way Annabel had described it. It hurt like—like *hell*. That was the worst phrase she knew, and she wasn't even sure it covered the situation.

Mayne was braced on his arms over her, looking down, and of course he could tell, so she gave him a tight little smile. "Is it almost over?" she asked, trying not to sound too hopeful.

His voice came out funny and hoarse. "Not quite. Should I make it faster rather than slower, Josie?"

"God, yes," she said, wondering if it was still too late to annul. No, she didn't mean that. But it was unfortunately true that unlike her sisters, she didn't—

"Ow!" she cried. And then, on the verge of outrage she actually burst out with the unsayable: "Hell!" Because he had lunged forward and something broke inside her.

"I'm sorry, Josie," he panted.

She wiggled. "It feels slightly better now," she offered, ignoring the fact that she was indisputably ruined for life.

"Good," he said with that odd strangled sound to his voice, "because I don't think I could stop, so bear with me, please?"

Josie pulled her mind back to the business at hand.

And when she didn't answer immediately: *"Please."*

"Of course," she said, trying to put a gracious tone in her voice. "Go right ahead." Now she realized that Sylvie had been given better information than she had, though Sylvie's offer of once a week sounded like a lot. Perhaps once a month.

It didn't seem to hurt quite as much now. Garret's shoulders were sleek and bulged with muscle in a way that she never would have believed, looking at his elegance in a coat. She would have thought his muscles would be all lean and ropy, but instead he had the kind that bulged, and rippled under pressure.

It was an odd thing they were doing. Or he was doing to her. Because once it stopped hurting so much, she could feel the heat trickling back into her legs. And then she started running her hands over his shoulders, because they were so beautiful and muscled in such a clean shape, and the heat increased.

In fact, once Garret lowered his head to her breast, well, she had to admit that it wasn't half bad. The intimacy of it was—

But she lost that thought, because he changed position somehow, and now he was coming into her lower and slower, and it did something funny to her stomach, and pulses of fire were sparking through her again.

She gripped his arms.

"It doesn't hurt as much, does it, Josie?" he asked.

The odd, guttural sound of his voice, so far from Mayne's usual polished tones, that made her heart speed up as well. And then he said, "Because you're mine now, Josie, *mine*." Her heart started going so quickly that it did something to her body, because she started rising to meet him, just a little lift of her hips.

He readjusted again, and now there was something in what he was doing that made her feel rather crazed, and those whimpers started again, except she didn't have time to worry about staying ladylike. He was pulling her up and she realized that his big body was sweaty and for some reason his sweat made her feel wildly excited. And then she happened to look down where they were joined.

It was as if lights exploded in her head and now she was

crying out every time he came against her. And clutching him hard, pulling him back. And he wasn't kissing her breasts anymore, he was ravaging her mouth, and all the time he was talking, saying things about her sweetness, and her taste, and the softness of her, and what he wanted to kiss, and bite and taste, and finally it came like a forgiving wind in the summer heat, rushing up from her curled toes and making her convulse against him again, and again, and again, crying his name in a bewildered kind of way.

Later she was never quite sure what he said, but she thought it was something to do with mercy and perhaps a deity or two, because a second later he let out a strangled groan and then took her mouth in the sweetest kiss she could have imagined.

37

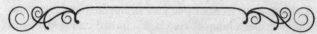

From The Earl of Hellgate,
Chapter the Twenty-fifth

Doubtless, Dear Reader, you believed the flames of my lust had been quenched by despair and grief. And so they were, for a time. I had made up my mind to take another wife. Clearly, it was the only way to keep myself from damnation, and I felt all the agony of my failed relation with Mustardseed. Thus after a decent period of mourning, I came to London again, determined to find a wife.

And then I saw her.

Sun was coming in the window, so Josie rolled over in protest, intending to bury her head under the pillow. Except her arm was caught in the coverlet, so she pulled. And then like a fawn noticing the watchful eye of a fox, she suddenly came awake.

Her arm was pinned down by a male arm. A muscled golden-skinned male arm. She stared at it, while the night before poured back into her memory like water into a jug. She was no virgin now, *immaculata* or otherwise. Not anymore.

They had sneaked back into the house in the middle of the night after Garret swore he couldn't sleep on a sofa. Josie blushed to even think about what happened on that sofa.

He was sleeping. Hardly daring to breathe, Josie inched closer. He was *hers*. And oh . . . he was beautiful. In his sleep that weary look was gone from his face and he looked happy. His curls were so black that they shimmered in the morning sunlight, like a lump of coal if you turned it toward a lamp. Even glancing at his lips made Josie's stomach squeeze, and her toes curl reflexively . . . it was new, this feeling of hot desire. She had a feeling it would become commonplace.

Her new husband was something of a will-o'-the-wisp . . . which meant that she should enjoy him as much as she possibly could, while he was still interested. Though how he ever grew tired of the sort of pleasure they shared last night, she didn't know. Couldn't imagine.

Of course when he opened his eyes she was smiling like a fool. Josie snapped her lips together. "Good morning."

He propped himself up on his elbows, looking utterly bewildered. The sheet slid all the way down to his waist in a most enticing fashion.

"I'm your wife," Josie prompted him, pushing the heavy weight of her hair back over her shoulder. "Josie? Otherwise known as Josephine?"

The bewilderment disappeared from his face and a bleak look passed over it instead. "Damn me to hell," he said, flopping backward and putting an arm over his eyes.

At least he didn't damn *her* to hell. "I gather that you do remember me?"

"Of course I remember you."

"Gracious of you."

"I damn well went and slept with a woman who is barely old enough to be my niece, although I had made up my mind to annul the marriage. What in the bloody hell came over me?"

"Me?" Josie asked hopefully.

He groaned.

"Although it was more like I was under you than you were over me," she said, coming up on her knees. He couldn't get away now. Not for years and years.

"Oh God, you're even talking like a Bartholomew babe," he groaned. Without removing his arm from his eyes, he reached out with the other one and pulled her down to him.

She fell against his chest with all her usual grace. Probably other women had cuddled against him like lithesome kittens but she was taken off guard and thumped down on top of him. He smelled wonderful, spicy, with a flavor of the outdoors. She took another deep breath. He had a hand in her hair, untangling it.

"Why are you snorting into my chest?" he inquired.

"I'm not," she said, her lips muffled by the roughness of his chest hair. "I'm tasting you, not snuffling you. And"—she touched him delicately with the tip of her tongue—"you taste very good."

"Ah," he said.

Garret tasted a little salty, a little like soap, a little like something else . . . essence of Man. Or essence of Mayne? He shivered when she kissed his flat little nipple, so she did it again. And again.

He wasn't saying anything, but Josie had heard about men in the morning. They were bears. Everyone knew that. Sulky. Sullen. Fine. He could simply lie there and sulk, and allow himself to be used. So she . . . used him.

She trailed her fingers and sometimes her lips all over his broad chest. Muscles, Josie discovered, weren't hard the way they looked, but warm and rather silky to the touch. And if she put her lips against his skin, tasted him, even nipped him with her teeth, he shuddered again, a tiny shake, as if a chill wind blew over his skin.

His heart was beating harder and faster, and she smiled

inside herself. He had almost no chest hair, which was, she thought, rather unusual for a man. At least . . .

"Why don't you have chest hair?" she asked. She had just discovered that when her hair trailed across his chest he made a tiny sound. A good sound, she thought.

When he answered, his voice was slow and dark, and the smile inside her grew. "I don't have chest hair because . . . I don't have any." He wasn't making a lot of sense, but she could forgive him that.

He deserved a bit of punishment, though, for saying that she spoke like an infant. "Of course, I don't know why you *should* have chest hair," she said, drawing her hair across his chest again, and enjoying the little puff of air that came out between his teeth. "I would look very odd with chest hair." She looked down at her chest and then looked up to meet his eyes.

Her nightgown was caught under her knees, and her breasts stood out against the light fabric as if she were wearing nothing at all. One thing that was good about her breasts was that they didn't sag down toward her waist, the way women's breasts sometimes did. He seemed to like them too.

"What do you think?" she said.

He blinked at her.

"Of my breasts?" she prompted him. "I think they're rather cheerful."

He cleared his throat. "Cheerful?"

"Well, I would prefer to have a smaller version because they go so well in gowns. I have my mother's figure, as I understand it. But anyway, I've always thought that my breasts were . . . cheerful. They stand up, see?"

His lips parted.

She was really enjoying herself. Of course, she was playing a part. But wasn't she always playing a part? Wasn't everyone always pretending to be something they weren't?

And didn't he deserve it for acting as if she were a brainless little twit, too young for marriage?

So she pulled her nightgown even tighter against her chest. Her breasts were rather lovely, if she said so herself. Now that she'd got over the idea they were too large.

"Well," she said, "perhaps I should go find a bowl of porridge . . . in the schoolroom, don't you think?" She narrowed her eyes at him. "Isn't that where we babies belong?"

He was reaching out for her like a man in a desert. "Stupid of me," he said, his voice sounding rather choked.

"Yes, well," Josie said, swinging her legs over his as if to leave the bed, which caused her nightgown to fall back on her thighs.

"Come here, you dastardly infant," Mayne said, and then he moved so suddenly that she didn't even sense it happening, and she was pinned beneath him. "Make fun of me, will you?" he growled at her.

"You're the one who called me a Bartholomew babe," she taunted, loving the weight of his body on hers. "Perhaps I'm just too young for marriage?" To prove her point she arched her back just a bit, just so that her breasts rubbed against his bare chest.

"Vixen," he muttered, bending his head.

But she twisted away from his kiss. "Why did you look so surprised to see me when you woke up? Tell the truth. Had you forgotten who I was?"

"Did I look surprised?" His head moved lower and he began doing the oddest thing: kissing her breast through her nightgown . . . Josie moved her legs restlessly. It felt wonderful.

"Yes, you did," she said, gathering her thoughts together. "I do believe you had no idea who I was."

"I knew who you were," he said, drawing her nightgown off her shoulder.

"Then why the confusion?"

"Because I've never woken up with a woman," he said. His lips skated along the skin of her shoulder, leaving a little path of fire.

"Nonsense," she said rather breathlessly. "We don't have the sort of marriage where you must ladle on the fibs, Garret. I know you've woken up in beds all across London."

He made a muffled sound that seemed to be a negative.

He was kissing her breast, and the rough feeling of it washed over her like a wave, drawing her into someplace where she couldn't seem to think of a clever retort.

When Mayne raised his head he found that his wife was lying in an attitude of pure, boneless pleasure. He pulled her nightgown down even farther, over her other shoulder. There was a small sound of cloth ripping and Josie opened her eyes. He rubbed his thumb across her nipple and she closed her eyes again.

There was no doubt in his mind that she had the most beautiful breasts he'd ever seen. The women he'd slept with had high, hard breasts, like small apples. Josie's were soft and abundant, spilling into his hands like a gift. Her nipples were as exquisite as the rest of her, pink and delicate.

He couldn't help thinking about the first woman he fell in love with, Lady Godwin. She was slim and straight, and held herself very erect. He knew what her breasts were like, because she affected the gauzy floating materials of the day. If he ever found Josie wanting to wear those gauzy kinds of dresses, he'd lock her up before he'd let another man see her breasts.

Josie's breasts made his heart ache just to look at them. They made his loins burn with a desire to sink into her softness, her womanliness that was so very different from the hard planes of his own body.

Josie's mouth was open slightly, all lush crimson lips and

sweet mouth. He couldn't wait so he pulled her toward him. "Josie," he said.

She was pulling him down onto her, panting a little.

"I don't wake up with women . . . ever."

"Mumph," she said, and then, "Oh, oh—*oh*."

Mayne felt as if he had received a benediction. Her legs curled naturally around his back and she was coming to meet him, her eyes open now.

"That's so wonderful," she said. But then: "No—*ouch*—stop now!"

He choked on a laugh and stopped, as commanded.

"Perhaps you might come a bit closer now," Josie commanded.

"Do you like it?" he asked, wondering why he felt like laughing. He never laughed during bedroom intimacies. After, perhaps. Or before. Never during.

"When it doesn't hurt. But I preferred what you were doing last night."

Mayne paused for a moment. "What?"

"What you were doing last night," she said, smiling up at him. "That was lovely. This is—" she wriggled under him "—not quite as perfect. Very nice, but—"

The laughter was growing and growing. No woman ever corrected him in bed. In fact, generally speaking, they had no complaints.

But he readjusted, pulled back, and then lunged forward. As his lady commanded. And she let out a little shriek that wasn't the least bit ladylike.

So he decided that he had the desired angle, as she put it. And then he decided to try another angle. She approved. A third: she didn't like it. In fact, she got quite cross and reached behind him and pulled him toward her.

Which made him start shaking all over and then he stopped thinking about angles, because her hands were on his ass, shaping him, pulling him into her, closer and closer. He could hear her panting, little unladylike pants, and urging him on.

The sunshine was pouring over both of them, and whereas all the slim women of his acquaintance had hidden their bodies from view, Josie was there, every creamy inch of her. So he forced himself to stop, pulled away even though his little cat of a wife grew almost abusive, and feasted on her, all the curves and deliciousness of her. Let himself learn every dimple. Ended up kissing that poor part of her that hurt so much last night.

It didn't seem to hurt anymore, though, and really, his young wife had quite a temper when aroused. In fact, she was threatening all sorts of things by the time he came back up and silenced her with a kiss that left her boneless in his arms.

Whereupon he slipped back into her, found the angle she loved as naturally as if it were breathing, and then put her exactly where he wanted her, clinging to him, her hair tousled and her eyes soft.

Looking at him as if he were the only man on earth, the only man for her, the only one.

Which he was.

"What do you mean, you never wake up with women?" Josie asked sometime later. He knew the question was coming. She was cuddled against his side, all boneless soft silken skin, and he was grinning up at the ceiling and reminding himself that there was a reason to live. He'd just discovered it.

"I always leave during the night," he said, settling her more comfortably into his shoulder. "That is, I left."

"You *do*? What do the ladies say when you leave?"

"Not very much."

"Don't they wish you to stay? I quite enjoyed waking up in

this fashion." He glanced down at her to see if she were trying to shock him, but apparently she wasn't, because she had one cheek against his chest and she looked utterly content.

"So did I," he said.

"Well, didn't they?"

"I never gave anyone the chance."

"Why not?"

He moved a little, uncomfortable, until he realized that he'd lost contact with her hip and he wanted her right next to him, so he pulled her tight again. "I suppose it felt too intimate."

She was smiling. "You *are* a virgin," she announced.

"Not that I noticed."

"A morning virgin."

"As long as I'm not immaculate," he said wickedly, and turned on his side so he could see her face.

" 'Tis a sad thing to lose one's virginity," she said, her eyes dancing with laughter.

"Is it?"

"I shall never call a unicorn to my side now, you realize."

"Are you acquainted with a good many horned quadrupeds?"

"There was a bull in my father's pasture one year who was monstrously ferocious," Josie said. "His name was Bumble, but you could hardly say we were acquainted, for all he almost gored me from behind."

"More the fool you to go into his pasture," Mayne said.

"How did you know I did that?"

"Because I know you, Josephine. You will always go into the bull's pasture, and I suspect I shall spend the rest of my misspent life keeping you safe."

"No you won't."

"I won't?"

"You'll be too busy," Josie said. "With your stables. You know, I had an idea about that."

He hated talking to other people about his stables, but he was so comfortable that though he waited for the little chill of disfavor to settle over him, it didn't.

"What do you think would happen if you bred Manderliss with Sharon?"

"Nothing much," he said. "Sharon has that bent hock, you know."

She was silent for a moment. "But she also has those gorgeous long withers."

"And if you put them together with Manderliss's speed and stamina, it would be splendid," Mayne agreed, tucking her even closer. "The pair I was thinking about is Sharon and Seaswept."

"Really?" Josie sounded doubtful. "Didn't you tell me that Seaswept has a slight sway back?"

He loved the fact that she had never forgotten even the tiniest details he'd told her about his stables. He told her that a year ago.

"You know who else would be a good match?" Josie said. "Rafe's Hades."

"His withers are too short."

"But Sharon's withers are long, so perhaps it will all work out. I think it's tiresome the way people only mate horses within their own stables, unless they pay extraordinary amounts to stud a champion who won a race or two. The best champions come from lively mixtures," Josie said with conviction.

Mayne thought that over. "Actually, Rafe has a young mare in his stables who might be a brilliant match with Seaswept."

"In that case, you could trade with him, and mate Manderliss with his Lady Macbeth. Because I can just imagine the colt they would produce."

Mayne could too: a gorgeous, flowing-maned bronze horse.

"We'll have to live on your estate," Josie said rather sleepily. "You can't let someone else play about with a colt from Manderliss and Lady Macbeth."

"Of course," Mayne said, knowing that he had meant to all along. He was tired of being an absentee horse manager. Tired of reading the breeding magazines, and arranging things, and then leaving for the season, even though it was foaling time.

"Won't you miss London?" he asked.

"Absolutely," Josie said. "I'll have to leave you on your own in the country while I gallivant at balls."

The surge he felt in his chest stunned him and he was silent.

"I'm just joking," Josie said, with a gurgle of laughter in her voice. And then she was asleep.

So he lay there and resorted his priorities. There were the stables and the season and London. All those tawdry days and nights lost at Almack's and less savory places fell to the bottom of the list. His stables rose to the top.

But perhaps . . . not quite to the top.

There was something else too.

But he didn't want to explore that thought; it felt too frightening to explore.

38

From The Earl of Hellgate,
Chapter the Twenty-fifth

**From the moment I saw her, I knew that she was
the One ... the One to complete my soul, fill in
all the rough, unpolished edges that had formed
during my years of depravity, preying on the im-
pure desires of married women. I saw her on the
other side of the street ... delicate, pure and
clear as a shaft of sunlight. I saw her ... and I
loved her.**

It was embarrassing, waking up again to find that afternoon light was streaming in the windows. But her maid
didn't seem to think it amiss when she finally climbed out of
the bath, dressed, and wandered downstairs. In fact, Josie
was rather shocked by how kindly everyone was, until she
realized that she was now the mistress of the house.

In truth, she felt like a guest. How could she be married to
Mayne? Josie, Countess of Mayne? It did not ring true. Perhaps this was all a dream.

And yet ...

She'd *done it*!

She probably looked like a complete idiot, smiling to herself. But wasn't a woman allowed a moment of triumph? Josie walked straight past the dining room and out the glass-paned doors leading to the side garden. She knew where her husband would be on a fine morning—well, afternoon—and he wouldn't be indoors.

"It's all quite straightforward," she said aloud to herself, the laughter bubbling up inside, "Tess married, and then Annabel married, and then Imogen married—

"And then *I* married!"

It sounded like a fairy tale, it really did. All four of them married. Happy.

She was going to be the best wife that Mayne ever imagined. She would be sweet and loving to him at all times. Not that it would be any great sacrifice. She actually caught herself skipping on her way to the stables around the back of the house.

She knew perfectly well what kind of women men fell in love with. Honey-sweet women. Since she would never be angry or sharp-tempered, he was as good as hers.

She found Mayne leaning against a stall talking to Billy. He looked up at her with a smile.

"Good morning to you, Billy," Josie said, ignoring her husband for the moment. "And how are you keeping yourself since the Ascot? Have there been any more problems with those devilish nuts?"

"Not a bit of it," Billy said. "I used the recipe you sent me, your lady. And may I say that all of us here in the stables are that happy about your marriage to his lordship? We don't think he could have found a better match for hisself in all of England."

Josie could feel herself going a little pink.

"What do you think of Selkie?" Mayne asked. Selkie

was a big, rangy chestnut with plenty of bone in his leg.

"He's lovely," Josie said, holding out her hand so Selkie could lip her palm.

Mayne reached over and scratched Selkie between the eyes. "He did very well for me. He won a few small races and then was cut out at the Derby. He doesn't quite have the heart for racing; if he feels as if he's losing, he just settles back and accepts his place. I'm retiring him to stud."

"Is he an Arabian?"

"Exactly. By way of the Byerley Turk."

"Byerley was all the way back in the 1600s, wasn't he?"

"What a pleasure to have a wife with such extraordinary knowledge of horses."

It was all so companionable and pleasant that Josie could never have believed what happened next. But however it happened, within a few minutes she and Mayne were bellowing at each other. Bellowing!

It was all Mayne's fault. He had picked up the idea somewhere that the sire, the male horse, introduced to his sons the characteristics of his own father, but passed on to his daughters the characteristics of his mother.

"I don't agree," Josie said quite reasonably. "In fact, that's absurd. You're saying that characteristics are qualified by the gender of the animal."

"Precisely," Mayne said. "You see it all the time. If you put a stallion to stud who has a well-ribbed body, you'll find it in a colt. If the result is a filly . . . no. Characteristics pass on through the male line to the male. And the reverse."

"Absurd," Josie said again, warming up to her subject. "Let's take a really famous horse as an example. Where do you think that Eclipse's offspring got all that temperament they exhibit? Not from Eclipse. It comes through the mares they put him to stud with. What's more, Eclipse's sire was Marske, and yet Eclipse's broad chest came from his dame, Spilletta. Everyone says that!"

"You can't know that something as ephemeral as temperament came from the maternal side," Mayne said.

"I certainly do," Josie said. "And I'm not alone in that opinion. *Racing Journal* noted that Eclipse's offspring follow their mother more readily than their father. Why do you think that none of them were as great a racer as he was?"

"Because some combinations tend to highlight defects in the line," Mayne pointed out. His eyes were narrowed a bit and he didn't look quite as lazy as he usually did. "And frankly, how can you say that King Fergus wasn't as great a racer?"

"Because he wasn't."

"His sire line has some of the greatest horses in this country!"

"Eclipse's offspring were temperamental—vicious even—because he was put to stud with twitchy mares. Every single one of them!" Josie stated. "The fact is that you can't dictate what qualities will come from where. We had Nectarine, a lovely bay, brownish red with white feet and a white blaze. He was fifteen hands at the least. Our broodmare Gentian had shown that she could throw a winner, but every single colt he sired on her had a short pelvis. And *that* came from the bay's mother."

"There are always exceptions," Mayne persisted. "As I said, some combinations highlight defects. Who knows whether that short pelvis really came from the bay's mother? Your Gentian might have had a whole family of hobbling sires in her line. After all, record keeping was hardly adequate in Scotland twenty years ago."

With a little cough, Billy scooted sideways and out the door of the stable.

"As a matter of fact, we *were* keeping record books," Josie said, scowling at Mayne. "My grandfather detailed every horse that passed through his hands. I can tell you without hesitation that Gentian didn't have a short pelvis anywhere in her line."

"There will always be exceptions to any case, but a breeding program has to be organized around a principle. I've seen enough evidence for this idea that I've designed next year's program around it." .

Josie rolled her eyes. "No wonder you haven't had a solid win in two years."

"An unjust observation. After all, I haven't even started this breeding program."

"May I see it?"

"Are you going to be kind?"

"Do you want kindness or a win? Don't be an—" She caught herself.

"I suspect my new wife was about to call me a name," Mayne said.

"Never," Josie said, although she was guiltily aware that husbands didn't like to be called *asses*. She'd almost forgotten about being honey-sweet.

But a moment later, reading his breeding program, she forgot it again. "You're dreaming if you think that you'll get a good match from breeding Selkie with Tisane. You forget that I know Tisane. She raced against one of my father's horses two years ago at the Kelso races. She would have won, except that she didn't care enough."

"That wasn't the reason," Mayne protested.

"Yes, it was," Josie stated. "I had the distinct impression that Tisane was a little afraid of being run over. That is *not* something that you want to redouble by breeding her with a stallion who has no spirit." She stroked Selkie's nose to apologize for the insult.

"You can't expect the characteristics of the parents to transmute perfectly into the sire line. I'm not worrying about these horses having poor performances because it's *their* parents' qualities that will skip into their progeny."

"Absolutely absurd," Josie said again. "I'd think you'd been out in the sun too long if you were standing before me. Do you really think that children take after their grandparents only? What about you? Are you expecting our daughter to look like your mother? I think not!"

"I hope not," Mayne said. "I adore my mother, but she has a voice like a bullfrog."

"According to you, our daughter will inherit a bullfrog's temperament, then," Josie said. "Luckily for her, your theory is utter drivel."

Mayne burst out laughing. "Now I'm going to start praying that our daughter's temperament doesn't take after her mother's!"

Josie blinked at him and then realized she'd forgotten. Utterly forgotten that she was a honey-sweet wife.

Mayne was still laughing at her when she saw something change in his eyes. He glanced down the long, empty corridor of the stables. No one was there except for a few horses drowsing in their stalls as flecks of straw floated through the shafts of sunlight. "I'll show you the lofts," he said, taking her hand.

"The lofts?" Josie questioned, and then reminded herself to be nice. Very nice. "Of course, darling," she said. "Whatever you wish."

He took her over to the ladder against the wall. Then he paused. "Are you able to climb a ladder?"

Josie rolled her eyes and then nipped up the ladder so that he wouldn't have time to examine her bottom. As a consequence, she went up the rungs so quickly that her slipper caught at the top and she fell sprawling into a pile of hay.

Laughter sounded behind her and she had the prickly sense that he was gazing at her bottom, so she flipped over.

Sure enough, he was standing at the opening, legs spread, looking about as delicious as any man had the right to look. His pantaloons clung to his legs as if they were painted there. It just wasn't fair, to Josie's mind, that he came by that body of his naturally, and she . . .

He didn't bend down and pick her up; instead he squatted down next to her, just as if she were a small girl who'd fallen in the grass. "What are you thinking about?"

"Your legs," she said honestly.

He snorted with laughter. "You're thinking about my legs. Legs? What's there to think about?"

Suddenly she was feeling *it* again, that lovely sweet singing low in her belly, and the racing in her blood that made her feel just right in her body, not plump, not awkward—just right. She turned on her side and put her hand on his knee. "Don't you know?"

"No."

"You've probably heard symphonies of praise about your body. I don't want to make you any vainer than you already are."

He laughed again, a dark soft sound deep in his throat. "Believe it or not, among those women to whom you refer so casually not a single one mentioned my legs."

"They must have been blind," she said. It was hard to ignore the muscles bunched in his thighs. They made her want to dance a little waltz, right here in the straw. And by the look of his eyes, he knew it.

"Now you," he said slowly, "you didn't have the hundred lovers that I was lucky enough to experience."

She pouted, the kind of pout that pushed out her lips. His eyes caught there and she felt more like dancing than ever. "One of the many unfair things about being a woman rather than a man."

"You missed nothing by it. That's what I wanted to say. Nothing. Not a single woman praised my legs."

"Well, what did they praise?" she asked, surprised out of her haze of desire for a moment. "This is a most improper conversation," she added, looking at his grin.

"You, Josie, are quite often improper," her husband said. "I think it's a congenital trait. In fact, I would guess that our daughter will be at risk of getting herself thrown out of the *ton* for impropriety if we don't watch her closely."

He had given in, albeit silently, on the breeding program, Josie realized. He had listened to her and he meant to change his program on the basis of her logic. No one ever had done such a thing before, surely not her father, who laughed at her every suggestion until she stopped making them.

"Your legs are beautiful," she said, with a shaky little catch in her voice. "I—" But she couldn't think how to phrase what she meant. Something about the muscles and the hardness of him and the way he was everything she wasn't: powerful and yet graceful, with no unnecessary bits or blobs about him.

"The odd thing is that I would say the same to you, but never of myself," Mayne said, and he really did sound puzzled. His hands were stealing up her skirts and she let it happen.

"My legs—" she said, and broke off. There was no point in detailing her feelings about that.

"Soft and curvy," he said, his fingers discovering just that softness. The dancing feeling was back, so strong that she almost twitched her hips. "Your skin is as white as a petal. I know that's not very original." His hands were on her thighs now. He was over her, and she closed her eyes because there was something in his face that made her feel . . .

Odd.

"I think I like you here the best of all," he whispered. His fingers were under her, shaping her bottom. The very bottom she had scampered up the ladder so that he couldn't see. "It's got the kind of curve that could make a man burst into tears, you know, Josie?"

"No," she whispered.

He was kissing her neck. "Your thighs make a man want

to sink into you, sip you, taste all the sweetness you're hiding."

"Oh," Josie breathed. She had her hands in his rumpled dark hair, but his head slipped away and then he was there, tasting the sweetness, and the muddled pleasured joy of it spread through her body.

It wasn't all that much later when she was shuddering, her dress around her waist, and she didn't even care that the sunlight was there and he could see everything, not when his eyes were wild and dark, and telling her—

"If even one of those hundred women, Josie—"

It hurt a little bit, so she squirmed. But it hurt and felt good at the same time.

"What about the hundred women?" she said. "Not that you should be bringing up such insensitive subjects— Ouch!"

"Does that hurt?"

"No, I just enjoy pain— Bloody hell!"

He stopped, and a stricken look crossed his face. "It's too soon. I'm an idiot. I'm so sorry, Josie, I—"

She stopped him before he started babbling. "Just stay there," she ordered him. He froze. She wiggled a little, letting her body get used to the intrusion of him. "All right," she said.

"All right what?"

"You can—" She waved her hand. "You know."

He looked as if he were frozen in place.

"Come in a bit more," she said ungraciously. "Isn't there any language for this sort of thing?"

He choked on a laugh, and then slowly inched forward. Hair fell over his face and he looked so dear that she smiled and didn't even notice that he was stealing forward again.

"Are you extraordinarily large?" she asked a second later.

He seemed to have trouble getting his voice, but then he said, "I don't really know."

"Well, all those women must have told you, although I do think that we should stop talking about them," she observed.

"I was trying to tell you, Josie, that if even one of those women—not that there were a hundred, because there weren't—but if even one of them had . . ." He gave a funny little sound in his throat. "Are you sure you want to do that?"

Josie arched her back again. "It feels good."

He angled his hips in a different way.

"That," she gasped, "feels better than good."

So they enjoyed that for a bit, until they had a rhythm. It was almost like dancing, to Josie's mind, except that she was terrible at dancing, and she seemed to be all right at this. In fact, she didn't think that Mayne had any complaints. She was discovering all sorts of things about him that she liked. The two little hollows on the side of his hips, for example.

"I like your ass," she told him, clutching him there.

He gave that choked kind of groan again and arched up, bracing himself on his arms so that he could look down at her. Josie knew her hair was all damp with sweat but she didn't care. He'd ripped her gown so he could kiss her breasts, and so she arched up toward him in invitation. He laughed, and panted, and tasted her again, and then said: "Just what sort of a lady uses the word *ass*, Josephine?"

"Did you want to marry a lady?" she said, not caring about that because she could feel all her moorings to the earth starting to float away. Waves of delicious heat were rolling from her toes to her fingertips and she didn't really care what he said as long as he kept thrusting into her in just that way.

Mayne looked down at her and forgot to answer the question. Because when Josie looked like that, all cream and roses, panting and sweaty and sweet, clutching his ass with both hands and wrapping herself around him, he didn't want to marry a lady.

But he didn't forget the other thing he had to tell her; he just waited until they had collapsed into a sweaty little heap. Then he pulled Josie on top of him so the straw wouldn't give that gorgeous cream skin of hers a rash, and said it into her hair.

"If one of those hundred women had had your body, Josephine My Wife, I wouldn't be married to you, and that's the truth."

"Huh?" She sounded startled, so he said it again.

"I wouldn't have been able to leave her. I probably would have had a duel with her husband, and killed him, and then had to leave the country."

"Well, I'm glad that didn't happen," she said, sounding skeptical. "You must be blind so I'm sure you would lose in a duel."

He smiled into her hair. "You're the blind one." She smelled like a saucy woman, everything he'd ever dreamed of. Not that he'd had enough brains to dream about someone as intelligent as Josie.

"Just think. I might have ended up married to someone who really understood horse breeding," she said.

"Vixen."

"I'm not a vixen. I'm your honey-sweet wife."

He snorted. "Must have got yourself mixed up with my other wife."

Josie lay on top of him, face buried in his shoulder and thought about how sweet she was going to be to him. Just as soon as he stopped saying stupid things. "You don't have any other wife," she observed. "You've been too busy bounding from skirt to skirt like a jackrabbit looking for a carrot."

He gave her a little pinch. "I think I was looking for a rabbit hole."

The enjoyment in his voice cued her in. "That's debauched!" she said. "I'm no rabbit hole for your pleasure."

"Hmmmm," he said, sounding a bit sleepy. "And I have a carrot for you . . ."

It was all so ridiculous that she couldn't even bring herself to point out how debauched his language was, and that clearly he'd learned his odious jokes from all that hell-raking behavior. Instead she just stroked his hair because it sounded as if he might be going to sleep.

And she didn't want to wake him.

39

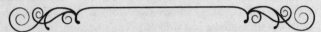

I saw her . . . and I wanted her. And yet she was everything I was not: clear and beautiful in soul and body, as chaste as the snow and as virtuous as an angel. Would she—could she—marry me? That was the challenge I set myself now. Not to soil an angel, but to marry her. To win her heart, win her hand, win her place next to mine.

Ah, Dear Reader, what do you think of my chance of success?

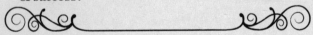

One week later
Whitestone Manor, Surrey

Josie awoke and grinned at the ceiling of the matrimonial suite of Whitestone Manor. Otherwise known as the seat of the Earl of Mayne. And that of his countess.

As of this morning, Josie had officially kept the Earl of Mayne in her bed for seven nights. And seven days, if you counted what happened in the library yesterday. She moved her legs experimentally and winced a bit. Unfortunately, the pain persisted. Of course, it didn't persist all that long.

Every time Mayne . . . well, every time they began, she said *ouch,* and had to resist an impulse to push him off. But he was always slow and sweet in the beginning, and whispered apologies in her ear, and did other things with his hands. And before she knew it, her body would decide that she didn't mind the invasion after all.

In fact, the very thought of what her body liked and didn't like made her blush.

The door swung open. "His lordship thought you might prefer breakfast in your bed," her maid said cheerfully. "And a package has arrived for you from London."

"My book!" Josie said, sitting up and reaching for it. It wasn't just any book either. It was Hellgate's *Memoirs,* that depraved story that everyone in London had read except herself. Now that she was married, she ordered it straight from Hatchard's.

It was a beautiful edition, bound in red leather, stamped in gold. She opened up the first page. *I have lived a life of immoderate passion,* she read. Delicious! A little too florid for Mayne, but . . .

When she reached for her hot chocolate a few seconds later, it had gone stone cold and apparently an hour had passed.

Mayne had no idea how much gossip about his life she knew. She knew everything. *The Tatler* had reported in detail the *affaire* that he and the beautiful actress, Octavia Regina, engaged in. From what she could see, Octavia was detailed under the name Titania in Hellgate's *Memoirs.* It made it a bit odd that they were both quoting *A Midsummer Night's Dream* the previous night . . . but that was the nature of coincidence. Odd.

An hour later she was absolutely sure. She was holding in her hands a florid, but detailed, record of her husband's various escapades over the past twenty years.

Josie took Hellgate's *Memoirs* with her into the bath, after her maid inquired the second time about hot water. She couldn't identify all the women. The story of Hellgate's short marriage was clearly a tarradiddle, placed there to disguise the fact that Mayne's life was laid bare on the page.

The morning dwindled into luncheon, and when her maid brought word that his lordship was going into Chobham and wished to know if she would accompany him, she merely shook her head.

It was five in the evening before Josie stopped reading. She had reached a terrible chapter, one that had her fingers trembling a little. Hellgate had met an angel, chaste as the snow.

Sylvie.

And he was in love with her, of course.

I cannot live without her... I dream nightly of her exquisite form. Dear Reader, you are thinking that I am a tawdry person indeed. And it is true! I first caught sight of her from the opposite side of the street, and she looked as delicate as any angel, as slim and frail as a piece of china. It has ever been so with me: robust women bounce past me without any notice, but—

Josie stared blankly into space. Sylvie had an exquisite form, all right.

Not that he would ever speak in such a florid fashion. He expressed himself simply. That night when Mayne taught her how to walk, he told her twice that he was in love with Sylvie.

After being called a Scottish sausage by most of London, she hadn't thought that anything *could* cause her more pain than her figure. But it seemed there were depths of sorrow which she hadn't thought about.

Because the truth was that her husband thought of her as a bouncing, robust woman. And he thought of Sylvie as a delicate, fragile angel.

*No man alive could not fall in love with her, with her
charming air that called to every masculine impulse
to care for her. Women are indeed the frailer sex, and
there is no firmer way to a man's heart than to remind
him of his duty toward the fair sex.*

Frail? Frail? No one could say she was frail. She glanced
down at her thighs, a tear chasing the first down her cheek.

If only she could get consumption and almost die, perhaps
Mayne would love her. He would pull her into his arms. Josie
could almost see the scene before her. She would raise her
delicate, fragile hand to his cheek—so slim that the light
shone through her fingers—and press a trembling caress to
his face.

He would cry then. And he would be sorry that he ever
thought he loved a spindly Frenchwoman.

Of course, there was that other woman he loved as well,
Lady Godwin. Another spindly, insubstantial type.

Other than wishing savagely that both Sylvie and Lady
Godwin would get the opposite of a wasting disease, Josie
couldn't think what to do about the women Mayne had
loved. Presently her maid brought a tea tray. "His lordship is
just changing his clothing," she said, bustling about. "I'll
ask him to join you for tea, shall I? It's not good to spend the
day on your own, my lady."

She took herself out the door without waiting for a yea or
nea. Josie sighed. She should probably scrub her face in case
Mayne realized she had been crying, but he probably wouldn't.
Even with the Argand lamp lit, the room was hardly bright
enough for that.

The truth was that she had to stop being so tiresome. So
her husband wasn't in love with her, but in love with a brittle
Frenchwoman who didn't have any thighs at all. Josie thought
about that. Mayne liked her body. He said so.

Even if it would make Mayne fall in love with her, she didn't really want to dwindle down to a fragile little set of bones who could drift along the street like an angel. For one thing, what about her breasts?

Mayne liked them as they were.

The door opened and the man himself entered. He stopped and bowed. "You needn't bow to me," Josie observed. "We are husband and wife."

"The day I neglect to treat you with the respect you deserve is the day I shall count myself a base ingrate," he said, sitting down opposite her and inspecting the teapot.

Josie poured him a cup and found herself leaning forward so he could take a glance at her bosom—should he desire to do so.

Apparently he did, because when she handed him a teacup his eyes had a particular darkness that she was coming to know quite well. And yet, Josie thought to herself, my breasts are not delicate or insubstantial.

"What have you been thinking of all day?" Mayne asked.

"I've been reading Hellgate's *Memoirs*."

There was a moment of silence.

"And what, precisely, is your relation to Hellgate?" she asked, when he said nothing.

"I'm not sure," he said slowly. "I only read about half of the book before I threw it away. I couldn't read past the chapter where I was supposedly tied to the wall, a pleasure which I am not eager to experience."

"I am reluctant to think that my husband may have been such a fool as Hellgate."

"A fool? All of London admires him."

"A fool," Josie said. "Who could possibly write a sentence as foolish as that piffle he wrote about wanting not to soil an angel, but to marry her?"

"You're a harsh critic," Mayne said, reaching out for another cucumber sandwich.

"Leave me one of those," Josie said, suddenly realizing there were only two left. "So did you write that sentence?"

"You must be joking."

Relief flooded Josie's heart.

"But there's no avoiding the fact that the author seems to have played ducks and drakes with my life," Mayne said. "He must be a devoted reader of the gossip columns."

Josie felt a sick, churning jealousy in her stomach. "He caught the nuances of your engagement to Sylvie," she said.

"I didn't read past the middle," Mayne said. "It's surprising how tedious one's life becomes turned into puerile prose."

"He says that you fell desperately in love on glimpsing her slender figure on the other side of the street," Josie said. "And that her delicacy brought out a masculine wish to protect and honor."

"Well, Sylvie does play a fragile womanhood role very well."

Josie pushed away the sick, churning jealousy in her stomach. What could she do? Her husband was in love with Sylvie. But he was married to her, and there was nothing worse than a woman who sat about moaning about things that couldn't be helped.

Mayne didn't seem to be on the edge of tears at the thought of his former fiancée. In fact, he had managed to eat the last cucumber square while she wasn't watching. His face was carved, degenerate, just like one would imagine a man named Hellgate to look.

But then he flipped back the lock of hair over his eyes and smiled at her, and Josie forgot everything she was thinking. Hellgate or not, when he smiled, she would do anything for him.

Yet he was a fool. All men were fools.

"What are you thinking?" he asked, watching her so intently that she felt as if he were undressing her.

"That men are fools," she told him.

He reached out and took her hand.

"True," he said, and with a twist of his wrist, she ended up on his lap, so he said it into her ear. His palm spread across her breasts, spanning her. "Alas, so true. Tell me, do you think I am particularly foolish, or is it a general characteristic?"

"I don't know very many men well enough to categorize them," Josie said, thinking about it. "I think you are certainly remarkably foolish to have—well—" She shrugged.

"Wasted my life?"

"Not your life, your substance."

"As a matter of fact," Mayne drawled lazily, "my estate is about the only thing I haven't wasted."

"I didn't mean that. Your—Your spirit. Like that Shakespeare poem, about spending his spirit in a waste of shame."

He was smiling at her. "I always thought he was talking about semen. Nothing spiritual about it."

"I know that," she said tartly. "He's talking about spending spirit in a *waste of shame*. Frankly, I can't help but think that someone as tedious as that Mustardseed is a waste of shame. Or a shameful waste."

He was nuzzling her neck. "You're right."

"What?"

"You're right," he repeated. "It was a waste of spirit and a shameful waste, and anything else you want to call it."

Josie felt that kind of queer urge, as if one of her teeth was aching and she couldn't stop touching it with her finger. "And when Hellgate fell in love? Was that a waste?"

"Falling in love is never a waste," Mayne said. His hands were straying now, making her squirm in his lap. But she couldn't not ask.

"Do you still love Mustardseed, then?" she asked.

"Who?" He raised his head. His hair was disheveled,

falling around his face, and his eyes had that intense blackness she was coming to love.

"Is love a feeling that just disappears, like desire?" she
persisted.

For a moment he looked confused and then he said,
"Love, no. Love stays. Don't you agree?"

She stroked his hair. "Yes. Love stays with you. It's irritating but persistent."

"Are you in love?"

She couldn't see his eyes and so for a moment she toyed
with the idea of telling him she had a hopeless passion for
someone. It would even the scale so he didn't feel sorry for
her. Being as she was in love with her husband, she meant.
The husband who was in love with someone else. "Absolutely not," she said, steadying her voice. "I'm not the sort to
fall in love."

He grinned at her. "All honey-sweet wives are in love
with their husbands."

"No, they're not." The more she thought about it, the
more annoyed she felt. What had he been doing, scrambling
from bed to bed like some sort of tomcat on the prowl?
Didn't he have anything better to do with the last twenty
years of his life?

"Why not?" he asked. His voice was a little guarded now,
though.

She didn't feel like anyone's honey-sweet bride. She felt
like a woman stupid enough to fall in love with a man who
was in love with a Frenchwoman. Everyone knew that
Frenchwomen were perfect—and Sylvie was a prime
example—so she had no chance of shaking that image free
from his heart. "I just wish that you had made some better
choices."

His jaw tightened. "Hellgate's life is not mine, for all
there may be resemblances."

Josie stood up and looked out the window, her back to him. "Did you or did you not trot from the bed of one married woman to the bed of another, for all the world like a child looking for sweets?"

"That seems unnecessarily critical," he said.

"I don't think so." She turned around again. "I married a man whose inability to stay in one bed is notorious enough that a version of it becomes a best seller. I think it's quite a fair, if not gentle, description. A mean description would—" She stopped.

"Would be what?" he snapped.

"Would describe you like some sort of untamed dog, hopping onto one woman for a sniff and then wandering off to another!"

"Truly vulgar," he said slowly.

She slapped the red leather book. "And this isn't? Vulgar?" She couldn't read his eyes at all, but her blood was racing through her veins. "You know what I think the most vulgar thing of all is?"

"Do inform me."

"That when you fell in love, you fell in love with such *angelic* women, to use Hellgate's words. Chaste. Nothing like yourself."

"True."

"It makes it worse, somehow."

"Because they were so chaste that I shouldn't have touched their palms with my debauched kiss?" His voice sounded perfectly even but he was obviously angry.

"That's not it exactly," she said. "It's that you liked bedding women enough that you—you had your hundred women. But when you decided to fall in love, you fell for women who weren't even interested in the act."

"Chaste doesn't mean—"

"I don't know about Lady Godwin," Josie cried recklessly, "but I do know about Sylvie. I *know* that she didn't feel desire for you. All the women who did feel desire for you were only good enough for a week, and then you left them. You saved your emotion for the women who never wanted you at all."

He just stared at her.

"You told me that about Lady Godwin. You said that she wanted her husband, not you." She was beginning to feel bitterly ashamed; sweet wasn't a word she could ever apply to herself.

Mayne cleared his throat. "I suppose you could be right."

"I am right," Josie snapped. "I suppose you played the voluptuary's role because you enjoyed it."

"One does."

"According to Hellgate's *Memoirs,* all those women lusted after you. Why did you fall in love with a chaste angel figure? Why didn't you just marry one of those hurly-burly Jezebels?"

"I rather think I did," he said silkily.

She looked away. If he didn't know that she wasn't akin to those married woman who played their debauched games with him . . . there was nothing more to be said. She couldn't think how to begin the conversation over, to stop what had started, to take back her own words.

"You're right," he said suddenly. "I haven't had an *affaire* in two years because I came to the same conclusion you did. I threw away years of my life on tawdry little encounters with doxies, married or not. I'd even agree with Shakespeare about *the wasteland of shame,* or whatever that phrase was."

She pressed her lips together. What sort of victory was this?

"But you oughtn't to make fun of my love for Sylvie, nor for Lady Godwin either," he said. "Probably they were too chaste for the likes of me, but they showed me a way out of the dissipation. Desire is always there, after all. There's always another pair of beautiful eyes, or an alluring smile . . ."

He was talking more to himself than to her. Josie had a

metallic taste in her mouth that suggested she might lose the tea she just drank. One could only suppose it was her own future he was describing, married to a man who found the world full of alluring smiles and endless desire.

"But after I fell in love with Lady Godwin, I suddenly saw how stupid all that pleasure was. How pleasureless, in a way. And then it was the same with Sylvie." That wasn't anger in his eyes; it was self-loathing.

"Don't you think you're exaggerating?"

"In what way?"

"Honestly, I don't think *pleasureless* is the right word to describe your experiences. Or for that matter, the experiences of your inamoratas."

"What?"

She had to chase away that look in his eyes. "I don't think bedding you is pleasureless or stupid. I could easily become addicted to the practice. I can see why you spent twenty years doing it. The truth is that I would probably throw away my life doing exactly the same, were it only permitted for women."

He threw up his head and stared at his young wife, startled. She looked unbearably young and desirable. "You don't understand," he said slowly.

"For the kind of pleasure you've given me in the last week, Garret . . . I would do anything for that. Throw away my life, my reputation, anything you asked for. Partly, I got so angry because I am so jealous of all those other women."

"You are?"

She nodded. "I want you to make love to *me* in secret chambers at the palace. And in the kitchen garden at a ball. And—"

"I never made love to anyone in a kitchen garden," he snapped. "That was made up by the author."

"Wherever. The truth is that I hate every one of those

hundred lovers you had. I covet every moment they spent with you."

A harsh laugh came from his chest. "You were likely in your cradle when I made love for the first time."

"I do have to take into account that it's a good thing all those women came before me, because I'm sure they taught you many things about pleasuring a woman."

The bleakness was out of his eyes. "So what you're saying is that there was a good side to all my debauchery."

"Am I thinking too much of myself?" she asked, sinking back onto the bed.

He followed her, of course. "A woman has to look out for her own pleasure."

"A thought I've had many a time," she said with satisfaction.

"You're making a mistake, though," he said. "There's a difference between the kind of pleasure you and I share and that—"

But she was tired of this conversation. It made her heart stop when she saw that look of self-hatred in his eyes. So she covered his mouth with her hand and told him, quite severely, that men should always obey their wives without the slightest objection. She didn't take her hand away until she was quite certain he understood what she was saying.

And then she lay back against the pillows and told the Earl of Mayne precisely what it was that he should do.

He seemed to understand all right, because he said in a jaded tone, "I'm sure I've seen this bedchamber before. It's time for me to flit on to another bed."

Josie smiled at him and then put one finger under the little sleeve of her afternoon gown. It was a pale lemony yellow, with a glorious strip of lace running just under the breasts. She played with the little scrap of fabric as if it were too tight. "I might let you go tomorrow," she said.

His eyes were getting that wild look again, so she snuggled

even farther back against the pillows, which meant that the delicate yellow fabric strained over her breasts. She didn't need to look down to know that her nipples were framed against the fabric. She could feel them longing for his touch.

"No lady can hold a rake for long." But his voice didn't sound convinced.

She felt as if someone should be caressing her breasts, and he wasn't, so she did it herself. She could hear his breathing. "But I'm no lady," she told him. "Not an angel."

"No," he breathed.

"Not a chaste scrap of the cloud either."

For a moment he was distracted and frowned at her.

"As Hellgate describes his dearest love," she clarified.

"I can't see a cloud in this room," he promised.

"In fact, I'm a bit of a reprobate," she said, coming up on her knees. "A strumpet."

A strumpet would take her own pleasure, and Josie was enjoying that. In fact, her own hand felt almost as good as Mayne's—

But maybe he saw that thought in her eyes, because a second later he pushed her hand away, and then . . .

40

**From The Earl of Hellgate's Memoirs,
Chapter the Twenty-sixth**

I realized then that I had mistaken the nature of
love. Love has nothing to do with desire; it's the
quest for the divine, found on earth. It's finding
a woman whose soul preserves a shard of heaven,
and worshipping her . . . worshipping at her feet.
I was a new man.

Thurman had never seen his father looking like this. He
looked . . . *old*. Tired. Even desperate. Thurman felt
like curling his lip, but he didn't. He bowed and offered his
father a cup of tea. "An unexpected pleasure."

Henry Thurman sat down heavily and waved Cooper out
of the room. Then he braced his hands on his knees in that
way Thurman always hated, because it just wasn't something a gentleman did. His father still had a smell of the
printing press around him, for all his grandfather was the
one who started the enterprise.

"There's no way to put this easily," he said.

Thurman sat down opposite him. He had just been about
to go for a drive in Hyde Park, and he wanted nothing more

than to lope out of the room and leave this perspiring, heavy man behind.

"We're ruined."

"What?"

"Ruined. I borrowed some money, and thought it would come through in the percents . . ." The story tumbled out. One name kept drumming through the flood of miserable language from his parent. Felton. Felton. Felton.

"Who is Felton?" Thurman finally demanded.

His father broke off and blinked at him. "Lucius Felton. Runs most of London, on the financial side anyway. He closed the loan . . ." And he was off again.

Thurman had the gist of it. Lucius Felton had ruined his family. Lucius Felton was responsible for the loss of the house in Kent—for that was what his father was saying now—and the loss of his allowance, obviously, and the loss of his racing curricle.

Lucius Felton.

The man responsible for giving the Sausage her dowry.

The man married to the Sausage's sister.

He'd never felt sicker in his life, just sitting there and watching his father's red face as he said that his mother's jointure was secure, of course, and so they would be retiring into the village where she grew up because there was a small house. One of his brothers was entering the Church.

"Mr. Felton," his father said, and the words filtered through the haze in Thurman's brain, "has been kind enough to buy your youngest brother a commission in the army."

He stopped.

Thurman just waited. Surely there was more. Surely Felton had told him? Had told his family what he had done?

But Felton hadn't, because his father was looking at him with a horrible expression of pain and pity and despair. "I'm the saddest about you," he said. "Your mother and I will be happy in the village. You know we like a simple life. But you . . . I shouldn't have played ducks and drakes with your inheritance, son."

"No, you shouldn't have," Thurman said sharply. "How could you get yourself into the hands of someone like Felton?"

"I didn't know . . . he was always most kind, but then . . ." In five minutes Thurman saw it all. In the last week, Felton had bought up all of his father's outstanding loans. He had taken over the printing press. He had kindly "spared" his mother's jointure, and given them, as an act of charity, the money to buy his brother a commission.

"So there's only you," his father said.

"Me?" Thurman replied, still not quite following.

"There's no money, lad. This house—" He glanced around. "Well, the rent is paid for the next week. You'd best tell your man to leave immediately. And what are you to do then, Eliot? Have you an idea of a profession, lad? You must have learned a great deal off at those schools of yours."

Thurman was silent.

"I'm trying not to worry about you," his father said. "Not you, with all your friends from Rugby. They'll help you out of this tight spot. Get you a position somewhere. Perhaps you could be a secretary to a great man. You were always clever with a pen."

Thurman could barely make his lips move. "Out," he said.

"Well, now—"

"Out! You've taken my inheritance and destroyed my life. The only good thing about this is that I won't ever have to listen to the foolish ravings of an imbecilic old man like yourself any longer! We were never of the same stock, *never!*"

Henry Thurman rose slowly. "You'll always have a home with us, Eliot. We know you've grown above us. But you'll always be able to come home."

"Never," Thurman spat. "Never."

Henry Thurman stumbled out of the house, feeling as sick

as a man could. Of course, he had ruined young Eliot's life. Eliot was raised to be the hope of the family, the young gentleman who was going to move into the aristocracy. He was friends with all those lords. Surely he'd fall on his feet. His fine friends would help him. That Darlington, for instance, whom Eliot always talked of.

Inside the house, Thurman was bellowing at Cooper. "The card," he said hoarsely. "The card!"

Cooper had listened at the door just long enough, and then ducked into the back to wrap the silver in a cloth. He knew where the card in question was. "I'll look for it, sir," he said, heading to the back of the house so he could wrap up the silver teapot and a pair of candlesticks he'd always fancied.

After a reasonable period of time, when he had everything he wanted crated and tied in two large boxes, he brought Thurman the card.

Just as he expected, Thurman glanced at the inscription, HARRY GRONE, THE TATLER, and banged out of the house. That gave Cooper more than enough time to whistle for a hackney, load up the two crates, and hop into the carriage.

He left the front door swinging open, just in case anyone cared to enter.

As it happened, two gentlemen did choose to enter. They strolled into Thurman's sitting room and glanced around at the furnishings.

One of them, the Earl of Ardmore, stripped off his coat.

The other, Lucius Felton, flipped through the meager invitations ranged on the mantelpiece. Then he walked to the window and drew back the curtain just a trifle.

They had to wait until evening.

Thurman did Grone's little errand, sweeping into a printing press that was all sixes and sevens as the news was out that it had a new owner. He bullied his way into the files and left.

But Thurman hadn't gone home directly with the bag of sovereigns Grone handed over. He'd taken it to the Convent, and bought everyone round after round of drink. He couldn't stop thinking that by tomorrow the news would be everywhere. By tomorrow it was all over.

But for one last, golden evening he could still be a rising young gentleman, an heir with plenty of the ready. He threw a sovereign on the counter as the tapsters curled their lips in a semblance of smiles. He threw a sovereign in the air when a barmaid perched on his knees. He pretended Darlington and Wisley and the rest were with him . . . even though they weren't.

When he finally staggered home, the remnants of Grone's bag in his pocket, he was no longer worrying about the day to come. He'd deal with that tomorrow.

He fell out of the hackney, giving the driver a sovereign when he asked for eight pence. The curtains in his sitting room twitched, though he didn't notice.

He banged through the front door and just stood there, sodden with beer and gin, shaky and drunk. He threw back his head like a wolf howling at the moon. "Cooper!" he bellowed. "Cooper!"

Cooper didn't come, but the door to the sitting room slowly swung open, so Thurman lurched through that door.

41

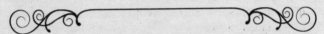

From The Earl of Hellgate, Chapter the Twenty-sixth

Not every man is lucky enough to fall in love with a woman of this sort. I know I don't deserve her . . . and yet, Dear Reader, I am lucky enough to carry her promise in my heart. She will marry me. I will roam no further . . . the empty places in my heart are filled by her goodness and sweetness.

I will spend my life cherishing the ground she walks on.

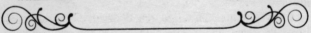

Somehow she'd ended up falling asleep in Darlington's arms again. It was all too easy, now that Josie was married and she had returned to her own little house. He came for tea, and before she knew it, she was in his hackney . . .

Why shouldn't she marry him? Griselda asked herself. People would make jokes. They would make fun of her. They would say she was baby-stealing. She looked at the tumble of hair next to her again.

Sometimes he seemed older than she. There were people like that, people who were old before their time.

And he needed her. She would lead him to a happier relation with his father, and stop him from being spurned by his family. She would celebrate his writing.

Perhaps she should wake him and tell him her decision?

It would do him no harm to worry. She swung her toes out of bed as quietly as she could. Thank goodness he didn't have servants, the way every other person did. Her clothes were in a crumpled heap in the entryway; Griselda had to stop and press her hands to her hot cheeks once, from the pure shame of it.

She wasn't quite certain how to get home. She would have asked a footman to fetch her a hackney, but Darlington had told the servants not to return until noon.

She almost woke Darlington up, but now she was wedded to the idea of making him beg a few more times. It was all so . . . delicious. Why shouldn't she be courted, like other women? He should bring her roses, and a poem or two. The idea of a poem written by Darlington made her giggle.

She didn't know his neighborhood all that well, but surely Fleet Street lay just to the right? Within a moment of walking she glimpsed the large thoroughfare where she would certainly be able to call a hackney.

When a carriage slowed to a stop next to her, she turned to it gladly. She hadn't welcomed the idea of hailing a carriage—rather vulgar, to wave her hand for all to see— and it was far better that one had . . .

That was not a hackney.

In fact, it was a carriage she knew quite well, almost as well as she knew her own. A footman leaped from the back and held open the door.

There was nothing for it, so she entered.

"Lady Blechschmidt," Griselda said, sitting down with as

much dignity as was possible. Her hair was bundled into a simple knot. She had done little more than wash her face. If Emily Blechschmidt glimpsed her dinner dress being worn in the morning, it would be instantly apparent that she hadn't been home since the previous day.

"Lady Griselda."

Emily Blechschmidt was at least six years older than she. As always, she was dressed with the kind of sober elegance that invited no untoward glance.

I was getting to be like that, Griselda thought to herself. I could have become like Emily, who isn't even forty, but is one of the fiercest moralists in the *ton,* quite as sharp-tongued as an old maid of eighty.

For a moment the carriage was utterly silent. Griselda's mind was racing. Why did it have to be Emily whose coach drove by, Emily, who was known far and wide for her fierce and dogmatic views of unchaste behavior and loose women?

For her part, Emily had taken one swift look at Griselda Willoughby and known exactly how Griselda had spent her night. After all, Emily had spent her entire life watching the *ton* from the sidelines, watching as men and women fell into each other's arms, danced into the garden together, gave each other secret smiles from the chaperone's corner. It made her angry; it made her feel sick with longing; it made her feel small. She prided herself on her sharp tongue when it came to loose women, on her sizzling pronouncements when it came to hurly-burly debutantes.

To Emily, Griselda's imperfect hair and sleepy eyes meant that she should, of course, spurn her friend. Even if they had been friends for years.

But there were times when a woman had to put aside morality and ethics.

"You never asked me why I was at Grillon's Hotel when you saw me there last year," she said finally.

Griselda was staring down at her hands, but she looked up. "It wasn't my place."

"I think it should be," Emily said. "If we're to be friends."

Griselda's smile was a little lopsided. "I rather thought we were friends."

"We have been acquaintances," Emily told her. "You would be horrified by what I was doing at the hotel."

Griselda's smile grew wider. "I promise you that I won't be."

"You will be." Emily was silent for a moment. But she was tired of all the silence, and besides, that *affaire* was over. "I'll never do such a thing again."

Griselda nodded. "Unless you wish to."

"I don't wish to. I'm bitterly ashamed of myself."

Griselda didn't seem to share her feelings of shame, so Emily realized that Griselda probably had a wedding in her future. "You couldn't understand."

"Actually, I do," Griselda said. "I really do. After all, Emily, I myself . . ." Her voice trailed off.

"I would gather that you just spent a night with a gentleman."

"I believe," Griselda said, "that I shall marry the gentleman in question, Emily. I believe I shall."

There was silence between them again. But Emily felt—had felt for weeks—that if she didn't tell someone, her heart would crack open. "I too had an *affaire,*" she cried, hearing the wildness in her own voice.

Griselda smiled at her. "I guessed that."

"But I've been so moralistic, so disparaging of others," Emily said. "You have always been chaste in your behavior, but you have rarely passed judgment on others. Do you loathe me?"

"No," Griselda said without hesitation.

"You will," Emily said. "You will."

Griselda blinked. "A married man?" she asked.

"Worse," Emily said.

"Worse?"

Emily couldn't look at her anymore. "Much worse," she whispered.

"I can't think," Griselda said. "A servant?"

"Servants are just *men,* married or unmarried; they're just *men!*"

"Then—" Griselda's mouth fell open. "You—"

"Gemima," Emily said, and her voice was hard, saying it. "Lady Gemima."

"She's enchanting," Griselda said after one gaping second. "Are you and she . . ."

Emily could feel the tears boiling up in her throat, all the tears that she couldn't shed because no one—*no one*—could know the terrible things she'd done. "No!" She couldn't even look at Griselda. But a moment later a soft handkerchief was put in her hand, and Griselda's arm wrapped around her shoulders.

"Don't cry, Emily," Griselda said, and it didn't sound as if she were going to throw open the carriage door and jump out from pure disgust. "Don't cry. Gemima is lovely. If I—if—well, she's so funny, and nice."

"She's—She's *not* nice," Emily wept. "She—She—" She broke down and after that she didn't even understand the things she tried to say because they were so mortified and despairing that they couldn't be put properly into words.

After a while the carriage stopped. Somehow they ended up in Griselda's snug little drawing room, and the whole story came out in bits and sobs, and Griselda rocking Emily against her shoulder, just as if she weren't the most immoral woman on the face of the earth.

"You see," Emily said, her voice a little hoarse from the crying, "she's going abroad. And she's—she's taking her new friend with her, and that's all there is to it."

"I'm so sorry," Griselda said. She handed her a cup of tea. "Gemima has made a terrible mistake."

"Why shouldn't Gemima fall in love? And with such a perfect woman in every way," Emily said despairingly. "Perfect!"

"As are you. But who can tell why these things happen?"

"It's because I've been so unsympathetic to others. I've thought and thought about it in the last fortnight, and I know why this has happened, why Gemima fell in love with someone else. It's my just desert. Fate has dealt me a blow because I deserved it."

"Nonsense," Griselda said. "Sympathy follows experience, Emily. I'm sure you could never be indifferent to the foibles of others. But you were never heartless. You're being far too harsh on yourself."

Emily sniffed, and put away her handkerchief. Crying was such an odd thing. She'd wet her pillows every night, but it only made her feel weak and ill. But one good cry into Griselda's shoulder and she felt it might be possible to face tomorrow. "Whoever he is, he doesn't deserve you," she said damply.

Griselda laughed. "That's a given. As you wisely pointed out, he is a *man*."

Emily had to smile a bit at that. "Oh," she said, "I do have some news for you too, Griselda."

Griselda looked up from the teapot.

"It's about Hellgate."

"They've discovered who wrote the *Memoirs*?" Griselda asked.

"Exactly. It's so fascinating: Mayne can't have more than the slimmest acquaintance with the author."

"What sort of person is he?" Griselda asked, carefully refreshing the hot water. "We decided that he must be a devout reader of the gossip pages."

"It's much more interesting than that," Emily said, accepting a pyramid cream. "This looks absolutely delicious! How does your cook make it?"

"It's her own recipe," Griselda said, "and she guards it fiercely. I do know that it takes hartshorn shavings and blanched almonds. I think the prettiest part is the way she cuts up the lemon peel into the shape of leaves."

"Yes, and stacks them up so neatly. My cook could never do this. She's quite good at ordinary things, you know. Like fricassee of turnips." She made a face and Griselda laughed. "But really, you won't believe who wrote that book."

Griselda frowned.

"You've forgotten what we were talking about," Emily accused. Griselda turned pink again. "That's because you're in love. Ah well, I shall dance at your wedding."

Griselda's smile had a deep happiness that would have made Emily bitter, except she didn't feel bitter any longer. "Now listen," Emily said. "This is the most fascinating *on dit* I've heard all season."

"Better than Count Burnet's divorce petition? I must say that I find it difficult to forget the details of Burnet's home life, at least as the servants described it."

"I didn't believe the half of those stories," Emily said. "No, this is fascinating because he was one of *us,* Griselda!"

"Who? Hellgate?"

"Hellgate was your own brother, as we all believe. No— the author!" She leaned forward. "His name was discovered by a most enterprising reporter working for *The Tatler.*"

Griselda pulled her thoughts away from Portman Square and the blond man who had undoubtedly risen from his bed by now.

"Fascinating," she said. "Surprise me!"

42

From The Earl of Hellgate, Chapter the Twenty-seventh

It was a new experience for me to speak from my heart, rather than from my loins, Dear Reader. Only then did I realize how little my heart had been concerned with my many relations, even with my dearest wife. But now . . . how I yearned! And yet it was no physical lust, but a heart-filled, earnest love. I wanted the best for her, in her life, at all times.

So I had to face the truth: was I the best for her?

The letter arrived along with all of the mail, except that the butler, Cockburn, handed it to her instead of Mayne by accident.

Josie stared down at it, her fingers suddenly cold.

Neatly printed on the upper left was the name of the writer: *Sylvie de la Broderie.*

Sylvie was writing to Mayne? Why? What could she possibly wish to say? He was married.

The possibilities raced through Josie's mind. She barely caught herself before she cast the letter into the fire.

The sick, muddled feeling beat at her stomach and at her heart too. She would like to kill Sylvie and her slender figure.

"Unladylike," Josie muttered to herself. But when had she ever cared for ladylike activities? Ladies never read other people's mail.

She wouldn't do that.

Ladies never eavesdropped.

Some rules are meant to be broken. Likely Mayne would rip it open and read the note quickly. Likely Sylvie was writing to ask for advice, or to wish him the best on his marriage. That must be it. Of course. Sylvie had exquisite manners.

If she betrayed even the least interest in her husband's letter, she would seem gauche and ridiculous. There was only one way to achieve unconcern.

By stealth.

When the Earl of Mayne returned to his study that afternoon, he found three letters waiting for him, precisely squared in the center of his blotting paper. He was still chilled from watching his most promising filly, Argent, canter around and around the training yard, so he scooped up his letters and strolled over to the fire.

Which allowed his wife, cozily seated on the floor behind the great velvet curtains, a perfect view of his face and hands.

He ripped open Felton's letter first. *It's done,* he read to himself. *Ardmore took to the task with an enthusiasm likely resulting from his personal experiences with this sort of mongrel. We finished the business by offering Thurman's services to the crew of a slow whaler on its way to Newfoundland. They needed a scrub hand for the deck.* Mayne grinned. He owed Felton one. And Ardmore. It was a good feeling to have brothers-in-law. Men to watch your back.

The second letter he opened was from Griselda. He raised

an eyebrow. His sister rarely took a hysterical tone, and yet there was a definite trace of hysteria in her words.

He must return to London at once. He must make all haste, in fact, he must leave that very night. He must give her deepest apologies to Josie, but he must return. That last word was underlined three times, and he thought he could even see the blur of a tear. What the devil was that about?

He turned over the sheaf of foolscap only to see that Griselda had apparently realized that he would wish for more information. *About Hellgate,* she'd scribbled. *Those infernal* Memoirs. *Come at once and say nothing about my letter. I must ask you to say nothing to your wife as well.*

Mayne sighed. The only good thing about all of this was that he didn't have to make the two-hour coach ride by himself, bouncing along on the indifferent springs. He was married now. He and Josie could . . . amuse themselves for a few hours.

He tipped Griselda's note into the fire and turned to his other missive. Why in the hell was his former fiancée writing him? Not that he didn't wish her well, because of course he did. But there was no question in his mind that if he never saw Sylvie de la Broderie again, it wouldn't grieve him.

He leaned against the fireplace and opened the letter. It was scented, an affectation he found unappealing, so he held it away from himself.

But then, reading her delicate French hand, he felt himself easing into all the charm and loveliness that was Sylvie. He hadn't loved her for nothing, after all, although it was hard to remember the reasons when Josie was around.

For a moment he stared blindly over the sheet. Compared to Sylvie, Josie was everything warm and sensual and delicious. His love for Sylvie—if one could even call it that— seemed a paltry, brittle thing in contrast, based on nothing more than her charm.

Because she was charming.

My dearest Mayne, Sylvie wrote. *I wish to write you to assure you that I am not désolée over your marriage to little Josie.*

Little Josie? Compared to Josie, Sylvie was a spindly, scrawny thing. I'd be bedding that frosty twig, but for the luck of the devil, he thought to himself. And couldn't help grinning.

I am exhausted by the constant round of parties in London, the letter continued. Mayne could just imagine. Sylvie couldn't say no to an invitation; there were nights when they had attended three parties in a row, one after the other. *I have decided to take a small trip with my close friend, Lady Gemima. She has persuaded me that Belgium is as delicious as France, and we are determined to recover ourselves. To be honest, Mayne, I am hesitant, but I do long to leave London for a short time. Somehow, I miss my Paris more than ever these days, and a change will be beneficial.*

Mayne thought about that for a moment. Gemima was a great gun, as everyone called her. She would take care of Sylvie. Or rather, all those attendants she carried about with her would do the chore. In fact, Sylvie would likely have the time of her life.

I did not want to leave without saying farewell to you, best of friends. But I am saddened by the thought that you might have suffered some loss of esteem that drove you into a hasty marriage. I have come to believe that I myself am not made for marriage. But I shall always carry the greatest regard for you in my heart, dearest Mayne. You are the only gentleman of my acquaintance with whom I could have countenanced such an undertaking, and I am only troubled at the thought that you might carry a lingering sense of insult, given the graceless way by which I ended our affections.

She was a good little thing, was Sylvie. A good, sweet lady who didn't want him—or anyone else, as it seemed. But loving her hadn't been a *shameful waste,* as Josie described his *affaires.* In fact, it had been a fairly decent thing to do, on the whole. He wasn't always a fool. Just once in a while.

Adieu, she wrote. *I wish all the greatest happiness for yourself and Josie. I think you shall find it together.* At that, a ghost of a smile touched his lips.

He raised the letter to his lips and smelled, one more time, the complicated French scent that symbolized Sylvie— all her femininity, her delicacy, her Frenchness. Her wrongness for him.

Then, with one sharp twist of his wrist, he threw her letter in the fire.

And walked out of the room to find Josie. He had a mind to make Josie laugh. To see her crinkle her nose at him and maybe—just maybe—he would snatch her up and throw her on the bed, just to hear her deep chuckle, the one she gave when she was excited, and giving in, and about to kiss him as if she would never stop.

43

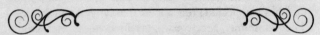

From The Earl of Hellgate, Chapter the Twenty-seventh

I lay awake at night, Dear Reader, wrestling with the fragments of my conscience. All that was good in me told me to let her continue to walk in the pure and delicate light of her chastity. But my heart sobbed and wept for her. Finally I decided to ask for her hand. How did I ask, you may wonder? I used Shakespeare, of course.

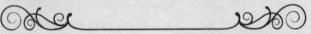

Josie sank to the floor as if her knees were made of water. She'd known it, hadn't she? She knew Mayne loved Sylvie. He'd *told* her that he loved Sylvie, back when he first made love to her. He'd told her again, in so many words, when he offered marriage and said that love wasn't important.

But it was more cruel to see him kiss a letter from Sylvie. What had she done? *Oh, what had she done?*

It wasn't just Mayne's feelings for Sylvie that she'd overlooked when she married Mayne under false pretenses. Apparently she'd underestimated Sylvie's feelings as well, because otherwise why would she write him?

Perhaps Sylvie was the sort of woman who fought with

her loved ones, who threw rings back at her fiancé, and didn't mean it. Now she thought of it, Frenchwomen were notorious for that sort of drama. Sylvie probably thought that Mayne would come around in the morning, ring in hand, and beg for her hand again.

And she, Josie, with her foolish notebook full of schemes about how to win a husband, and how to arrange a marriage: she'd overlooked the most important thing of all. That a husband who loves another, no matter how enthusiastic he is in bed, is a heartbreaking companion.

None of her quips and her cleverness mattered in the face of this. She could make Mayne laugh. She could make him pant in bed. But she could never supplant the sweetness of the love he felt for Sylvie.

She could no more imagine him kissing a letter that she wrote him than she could imagine him kissing a saddle. Which was probably about where she mattered in his life: as a lusty, buxom saddle that he could ride on at will.

Josie rose, but discovered that her knees were weak, and she had to cling to the curtain for support. Finally she straightened up feeling ragged and destitute, like an ancient beggar woman.

How could she have been so stupid as to think that she wanted a husband under any circumstances? Her heart was burning like a coal in her chest.

Outside of the room she was greeted by Cockburn, who informed her that his lordship wished to leave for London within the hour.

The letter. Sylvie must have summoned him.

She walked into her bedchamber and allowed her maid to change her into a traveling costume. Blood thudded in her ears. Her eye fell on the little crimson book in which she had so carefully written down the complicated and fascinating ways by which heroines of the Minerva Press found their husbands.

Useless. She had a husband, and none of those books told

how to make someone *fall in love*, or more important—fall *out* of love. For that she needed the drug Shakespeare talked about in *A Midsummer Night's Dream*. Love-in-idleness, it was called. The fairy dropped it in a gentleman's eyes, and he promptly fell out of love with Hermia.

How could Mayne truly love Sylvie? Truly? She was lovely, of course. But he thinks my body is lovely too, Josie thought. Sylvie didn't care for horses. And she didn't, really, care for *him*.

I do, Josie thought, with every drop of longing in her body. Oh, I do. I love my husband.

She was clutching the book so hard that her fingernails made marks in its leather cover.

There was a scratch at the door. "His lordship is ready to leave for London, my lady, whenever you're ready."

Josie got up numbly. Tess would help. Annabel was presumably on her way back to Scotland with her husband and child, and Imogen was on her honeymoon, but Tess would help.

As she left the house, Mayne came toward her. "I received a note from Sylvie," he said, smiling as if it was of little import. "She's leaving at five o'clock on the *Excelsior,* so I thought we might see her off."

She almost choked. "Perhaps you might say farewell for both of us. I would like to be taken to Tess's house, if you please."

He bowed. "Of course."

"I have a terrible headache," she told him.

He bowed again. "My condolences."

She climbed into the carriage, snuggled into the corner and closed her eyes. She had all of two hours on the way to London to figure out what to do.

Since no King Oberon was likely to offer her a handy dose of *love-in-idleness,* she would have to come up with Mayne's cure by herself.

44

From Hellgate's Memoirs,
Chapter the Twenty-eighth

I knelt at her feet. "I burn for you," I told her. "I
pine for you. I perish . . . thinking of you. If you
will not have me, I shall throw myself into the
frigid Thames and die, thinking of you. To me,
you have the purity of a cloud, the clarity of ice,
the whiteness of snow.

"Marry me."

Don't argue with me," Josie snapped. "I know it's a complicated plan, but it's the only one that I can think of."

Tess's eyes were wide. "Complicated? It's utterly *insane,*
Josie!"

"It is not insane. In fact, it is well-designed."

"You must be joking. Tell me you're joking."

Josie's eyes narrowed. "If you won't help me, I'll simply
hire those who will."

Tess was shaking her head. "No. You can't do this!"

"Yes, I can."

"No, you can't! You can't drug Mayne."

Josie waved her hand. "It's the mildest drug in the world. We give it to horses just to calm them, and Peterkin gave it to the stable boys all the time when they had to have a tooth pulled. It will simply make him sleepy and malleable."

"You're talking about your *husband*," Tess said, half horrified and half laughing. "How can you possibly plan something like this?"

"It's necessary," Josie said stubbornly. "He really thinks he's in love with her, Tess."

"Yes, but he'll come to realize—"

"No, he won't. I didn't think about it clearly until I saw him kiss her letter. I can't live with him, knowing that he loves someone else. I can't."

"I don't believe he does love Sylvie," Tess said, much more seriously.

"Neither do I."

"Well, then—"

"He *thinks* he loves her."

Tess gave a helpless little laugh. "I just don't see how—"

"Sylvie is sailing to Belgium. That's at least two nights on board ship, perhaps more." She leaned forward. "Neither of us have been aboard ship, but you know what Mr. Tuckfield told us about his trip around the Horn of Africa with his wife."

"He said that he almost threw her overboard three times," Tess said. "But Josie, Mr. Tuckfield is a Scottish horse breeder."

"When Mayne is on board ship with Sylvie, he'll discover that he's not in love with her. He won't throw her overboard—"

"I should hope not!" Tess interjected.

"But he'll stop kissing her letters and thinking about her."

"You don't know that he thinks about her."

"I don't know that he doesn't."

"Ridiculous!" Tess cried.

"Oh? How would you feel if you thought that Lucius was thinking about someone else when he made love to you?" Josie met her sister's eye. "If he looked thoughtful, and you didn't know whether he was remembering a woman he lost? If he murmured something while he was kissing you, and it sounded like a woman's name to you?"

Tess frowned.

"It will poison us. It already is, a little bit. I can feel it."

"You are so dramatic. I honestly think you've read too many novels, Josie. You never would have come up with this crazy scheme if you hadn't read all those books."

"I have always thought a plan of action is the best way to tackle problems."

"That's true enough," Tess said reluctantly. "But I don't see why this plan has to be so complicated. And involve drugging Mayne!"

"It is actually quite simple. I shall give Mayne a drink that will make him cheerful and sleepy, and then I will send him to the wharfs."

"You will *send* him? Like a parcel?"

Josie thought for a second. "I'll inform the footmen that Mayne wishes to board the *Excelsior*. That's the name of Sylvie's ship."

"I don't see why you have to drug him."

"He won't get on the ship otherwise."

"True."

"You see," Josie said. "This will *work,* Tess. And I don't need your help in the least, so you needn't worry about it."

"You do need my help," Tess said. "*Your* footmen are Mayne's footmen, may I remind you. They are not going to drag their sleepy, drugged master onto a ship and leave him there."

Josie frowned.

There was a moment's silence and then Tess said reluctantly: "But my footmen will do it."

"*Will* you?"

"I don't approve!"

"Of course not. But will you? Tess"—and there were tears glimmering in her eyes now—"I can't live knowing that he loves Sylvie. Whether he loves her or not, I mean. I can't bear the idea that he thinks he loves her."

Tess gave her a hug.

Griselda was waiting for her brother in her sitting room. "You came!" she cried, jumping to her feet.

He walked in, looking as elegant and unconcerned as ever. Which had to mean that no one else had the chance to inform him before she did. The words started tumbling out: Darlington . . . Hellgate . . . the *Memoirs* . . .

Mayne dropped into a seat before the fire and sat there frowning. He looked outraged. Griselda's heart dropped into her slippers. He was going to threaten Darlington. Challenge him to a duel. Perhaps kill him.

"You can't!" she squeaked.

"Can't what?"

"Call him out."

"Why the devil would I do that?"

She stared at him. "Aren't you outraged? You look—"

"Something's wrong with Josie," he snapped. "So you're telling me that Darlington wrote Hellgate's *Memoirs*. And you've been having an *affaire* with him. The same Darlington who called my wife a Scottish sausage?"

"Yes," she whispered.

There was a moment of silence. "I was thinking of killing him for that," he said slowly.

"You mustn't."

"I suppose not. Could you have possibly chosen a more likable fellow to bed?"

"I—" Griselda swallowed back her tears. "I like him a great deal. And he will never say anything as cruel again. He's terribly sorry about the anguish he caused Josie."

"Given his abominable prose, I hate to think about the intimacies he's whispered to you in private."

"Darlington is not an abominable writer! You—You—"

Mayne's laugh was that of an infuriating older brother. "Piffle, given his inability to put together an articulate sentence. I would have thought better of you."

Griselda swallowed hard. "Would you stop funning and *think* for a moment, you ass!" She never swore. In fact, she could hardly believe it when she heard the word fly out of her mouth.

"Think about what?" Mayne said, a little quieter. "Obviously you're planning on marrying him."

"What if he's merely doing it to turn me into a book?" Griselda shrieked at him. "Have you thought of that?"

There was a moment of silence. "Then I would kill him," Mayne said.

Griselda met her brother's eyes.

He came over to her and put a hand on her cheek. "Just because he can't write doesn't mean that he's suicidal, Griselda. I assume that he is proposing marriage?"

She nodded jerkily.

"Yet another reason he might live to walk the aisle," he said, turning around and scooping up his gloves.

"Don't you—don't you care that he wrote that book?" she choked.

"In a word: no. I thought the *Memoirs* was remarkably foolish. I do care that he wants to marry you, but I think by far the more interesting point is that *you* wish to marry him. You do, don't you?"

She smiled at him, through a veil of tears. "I think so."

"I know so." He dropped a kiss on her nose. "He doesn't deserve that. I'll tell him myself, once I get things worked out with Josie."

"Oh—" Griselda said.

But he was gone.

45

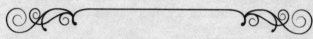

From Hellgate's Memoirs,
Chapter the Twenty-eighth

I knew she loved me when her eyes filled with
tears. She loved me . . . She loves me. Dear
Reader, know this: there is nothing like that
sweet emotion to change a man's life, nay his
entire character. She is Mine, she is Mine.

Dear Reader, rejoice. I am remade.

I t was all much easier than Josie would have thought.
Mayne came to fetch her at Tess's house and she handed
him a cup of tea, mentioning that Tess would return in a moment.

He started to tell her something about Darlington and
Hellgate—could it be that Darlington wrote the *Memoirs*?
But Josie couldn't keep her attention on the subject because
he was drinking the tea.

And then . . . before she even drew a breath, he was
asleep, leaning into the corner of his chair, his eyelashes
shadowing his cheeks. She couldn't help it: she knelt in
front of him and brushed his face with her fingers. "Because

I love you," she whispered to him. "It's only because I love you so much."

He sighed and smiled. After she had a molar pulled, she woke up with just that delicious sense of having had a happy dream.

Then she pulled herself upright, went out and carefully closed the door behind her. Tess was waiting for her. "Do you have the letter?"

"I need to write it," Josie said, fighting back her tears.

"Are you *certain*?"

"Of course I am! It's just that he looked so defenseless, lying there. He didn't even know that I'd drugged him."

Tess shook her head. "I think it's a foolish scheme. But write your letter." She pushed her toward the writing desk.

Josie sat down with a piece of fresh foolscap. It would be no good to make the letter flowery. That wasn't like her. Of course, she couldn't tell him the truth either.

Dear Garret,

I know you will be surprised to find yourself on board ship. What I didn't understand when I married you is that love is the most important thing—not marriage, but love. You love Sylvie, so you ought to be with Sylvie. Even if she won't accept your hand in marriage, it is a terrible thing to be separated from the person you love, and I can't bear the idea that I am responsible for it.

Josie

She was crying so hard that she left the letter where it was and collapsed onto the bed.

"Don't worry, darling," Tess said, helping her to stand up and then wrapping a cloak around her. "I'm going to take you back to your house while Lucius takes care of everything else."

"You *told* Lucius?"

"Of course I told Lucius," Tess said, looking surprised. "How could I get Mayne out to the wharf? Lucius is just the right person. You know he's very good at getting things done correctly, Josie."

"I didn't want anyone to know," she said, wiping away her tears with the sheet. "I didn't want *anyone* to know!"

"Lucius is necessary for your scheme," Tess said soothingly. "Up with you."

When they walked down the stairs, the door to the sitting room was still closed. "He will only stay asleep for four hours at the most," Josie said, suddenly anxious. "He has to be at the docks by five o'clock when the tide turns. What if the *Excelsior* leaves without him?"

"It won't," Tess said. "You know that Lucius never makes mistakes."

Josie thought about that as they trundled along the London streets. It was true that Lucius Felton was just the sort of man who was never late. Probably the tide would wait for him, if for no one else.

"What did he say?" she asked.

"Who?"

"Lucius! What did he think of my scheme?"

"He thought it was utter poppycock," Tess said. She saw Josie's mouth open and held up her hand. "Until I reminded him that I myself was originally engaged to Mayne. And what if I were holding out a hopeless passion for Mayne?" She smiled to herself. "He didn't seem to like that idea."

"You were both very lucky," Josie said, knowing that her voice was surly.

"True."

They didn't speak again until they were inside the house, Mayne's house. "You need a bath," Tess said, ringing the bell. "You need a bath, and supper in your room, and then bed. You are exhausted. Why, Josie, your face looks all thin and drawn."

Josie thought about it. Sure enough, she hadn't been eating much in the last few days, and nothing at all today. Tess pushed her before the glass. "Look at yourself!"

Josie touched her cheeks. There were hollows there. Almost like cheekbones.

"You look awful," her sister told her.

And suddenly, as if the mirror had cracked before her, Josie saw what she meant. Those weren't tempting hollows in her cheeks, but the signs of weariness. She didn't look beautiful, she just looked oddly gaunt. She sighed. Apparently her face was not the sort that would look good slim.

By now Mayne must be on the boat, discovering that she'd given him up. Turned him over to Sylvie. Set him free.

The thought made her nauseous, so she listlessly climbed into the bathtub.

"I'm going home now," Tess said, popping her head in sometime later. "I've ordered you a light supper in your room."

"Thank you," Josie said.

"I'll be over first thing in the morning," Tess said, blew her a kiss and was gone.

But Josie didn't want to eat in her room. When she climbed out of the bath, she put on Mayne's robe, the sleek silk one he lent her after she threw away her corset, that very first night when he rescued her at the ball. Then she spoke briefly to Ribble and climbed the stairs to Cecily's turret.

There it was, as shadowy and sweet and magical as it had been the first night Mayne brought her there. The unicorn danced along his vine, and the little boy who looked like Mayne swung by one hand.

Josie crumpled into the big chair from which she'd watched Mayne prance around in her dress, but she didn't cry.

She knew, with a bone-deep certainty, that she was right. He didn't love Sylvie, for all he thought he did. Up here, in the turret room, she even dared to whisper the truth of it.

"He loves me," she whispered. Who was she telling? His Aunt Cecily's spirit, perhaps. "He does. He loves me."

Ribble came up with a glass of wine and some supper. Josie had brought only one thing to the room with her: the Earl of Hellgate's *Memoirs*. She sat there in the guttering light from the lamps, rereading the long passionate adventures of a man she loved more than life itself. The wine was deep red, and felt as magical as the walls. Reading the book made it almost as if *she* had been all those women Mayne loved . . .

And yet, did he love them?

He said that he never laughed in bed with them. The stories seemed thin and anxious now, full of desire but also tedium. She paused at the story of Hippolyta and how she bound Hellgate to the wall of the garden house. Mayne said he threw down the book when he reached that chapter, said that he had never engaged in such an activity.

But Josie could quite see tying Mayne to the bed. In fact—she smiled and drank another sip of wine—once he returned from his little voyage that was just what she would do.

He might be a little angry at first.

But once he got over it . . .

There was a noise at the door, and Josie didn't even look up, just turned the page. Now Hellgate would discard his Amazon mistress as if she were no more important than a cast-off slipper, and turn to—

She looked up.

There in the shadows of the door was—Mayne. Drops of water were streaming from his shoulders, from his hair. His eyes were rimmed by dark circles.

"Joooosie," he said hoarsely. "They dropped me from the

rowboat . . . I was bound and couldn't swim . . . I had to come say farewell to you . . ."

Josie didn't say anything. The air went dark and thick around her, as if there was no air in a world without her husband. She couldn't speak. She couldn't breathe.

She fainted.

Mayne walked into the room and looked down at his wife, shaking himself like a dog after a good rain. She was out like a snuffed candle. He picked up her glass of wine and took an appreciative draught. She was drinking the Château Margaux 1775 that his father laid down. Very nice.

Then he sat down on the footstool before her chair and looked at her.

Too many novels, that was the truth.

"Josie!" he said. And then: "Josie!" She didn't stir, so he ran a hand along her cheek. She was so beautiful that his heart turned over, and yet he schooled himself to be firm.

"Josephine, you wake up now," he told her.

So she did. Her eyes opened and she stared at him. "Garret?" she asked.

"Ghost of," he said promptly.

She grabbed his hand. Looked at him for one moment, at his damp hair (thanks to a quickly administered glass of water), and then lunged out of her chair and shook him. "How could you? How could you do such a thing to me? I thought you were dead!"

He would have defended himself more, but he was laughing too hard.

"You—You—I'll make a ghost of you," his little wife shrieked.

Finally he managed to stop her from beating him around the shoulders and caught her hands in his. "You deserved it, Josie," he said, fighting back another great swell of laughter.

But there were tears in her eyes, and the laughter died in his throat. For a moment he saw everything in her eyes: a love that would last their entire lives, a vulnerability that would never go away, and, where he was concerned, a deep selflessness that made her the most wonderful, funny, intelligent woman he knew.

Then her eyebrows snapped together. "Bastard!" she snapped.

"You deserved it."

"I never should have trusted Tess. Never."

"Woke up to find Felton chortling at me," Mayne admitted. "Mind you, he did hand over that letter you left for me."

"Oh."

"Damned if I'm not surrounded by terrible writers," he said. "First Darlington—and that bounder looks to be becoming my brother-in-law—and now my own wife. 'Love is more important than marriage.' Purple prose! Fluff and feathers! It could have been written by Hellgate himself."

"I'm sorry that my writing wasn't up to your standards," Josie said with dignity.

"Not only did you write me a fluffy letter, but you drugged me and tried to get rid of me," he said remorselessly.

"I didn't!" She struggled against his hands. "I never wanted to get rid of you."

"You wanted me thrown onto a boat with a Frenchwoman whom I hardly know."

"It was Sylvie! If you remember, you were going to marry Sylvie!"

"God yes, it was Sylvie! How could you think that I would want to spend several days trapped aboard ship with Sylvie?"

"Because—Because—"

But it was time to stop the foolishness, so he sat down and pulled her straight into his lap, looked her in the eye and said, "You'll never get rid of me, Josephine."

"Never?" she whispered.

"Not by drugging me, nor sending me to sea either."

"I didn't want to."

But he wanted to hear it, so he waited.

"I love you," she said. "I love you too much to keep you away from Sylvie."

His smile came straight from his heart. "We can leave Sylvie out of this, though how you came to think I loved her—"

"Because you told me so repeatedly? Because you were going to marry her? Because you kissed her letter?"

"I never kissed any letter of hers!"

"You did, you—"

"If you loved me," he said, cutting through the piffle, "how could you let me go?"

"That's why. I had to give you to her, if that's what you wanted."

He cupped his hands in her face. "I will *never* let you go, Josephine, my wife. Not if you fall in love with Hellgate himself."

She was laughing and crying at the same time. "But, Garret, I *am* in love with Hellgate, didn't you know?" She pushed her fingers into his damp curls.

Then he was kissing her, fiercely, as if he could drink her in and make her his. Except she was already his.

"I never knew what love was," he said, feeling the words piling up inside him. "I thought I was in love with Sylvie . . . how could you not have known what an ass I was to even imagine such a thing?"

"Well . . ." she said. And kissed him.

"I gather you wanted me on that boat precisely because you knew better?"

"I thought," Josie explained, "that you might be in love with me, and you just hadn't realized it yet."

"Oh, I realized it." He kissed her, hard.

"You didn't say—"

"I would have. You are my countess, and the only woman I have ever loved. In the whole of my misbegotten, Hellraking life."

Her laughing eyes were a little teary, so he worked his hands into that dressing gown of hers. It was a damned useful garment, the way the tie gave at the waist, and then it fell open to show him a feast of creamy flesh and beautiful breasts.

He couldn't stop kissing her, though. He'd stray onto her breast, and have her crying with the pleasure of it, but then he had to kiss her mouth again. And again.

"I'm not the same around you," he told her at some point. "I'm never bored, Josie. I'm not—I'm not myself."

"Yes, you are," she said, as bossy as ever. "Could I possibly suggest that you go back to what you were doing?" Because his hand had stilled with the need to tell her, to make her understand.

"You're not listening," he whispered, even as he caressed her again, watching her eyes close and an enchanting little pant come from her lips. She was all sweet plump welcome, but he still wanted to say it.

"With you, I'm not Hellgate," he told her, knowing she wasn't really listening. "I'm not some dissolute rake, sleeping with anything with two legs. I'm going to turn the Mayne stables into something people remember for decades. And I'm going to—"

"For God's sake!" she said, her eyes snapping open. "Garret Langham, are you actually talking about your stables—*now*?"

He looked down at her. Her lips were pouting a dark cherry color from all his kisses. He had one hand curved around her breast and the other between her legs, and her eyes were wild and loving and desperate with need, all at once.

"Well," he told her, easily picking up her hips and positioning her just so. And then letting her slip down on him, inch by inch. "I thought we could—" he had to take a breath "—talk about our breeding program."

"You're lucky to have me," Josie told him against his lips. Then she nipped his lower lips and wound her arms around his shoulders.

"I know it," he said.

She was setting the pace, making his blood race, making him feel as untamed as a tiger. Her hair tumbled down her back, unruly and soft. She cupped her hands around his face. "I should kill you for that water trick."

"Don't," he gasped. "I don't think that . . . ghosts have—" But he was done talking. So he just kissed her into silence, his own sweet Josie, his beloved, his wife.

46

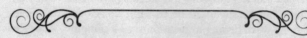

From The Earl of Hellgate's Memoirs,
Chapter the Twenty-eighth

As I say *adieu* to you, my Dear Readers, I can
only wish with all my heart that you might sail
on the same clouds of happiness as do I . . . reach
the same summit of bliss as I have.

Adieu, Adieu!

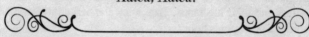

The party to celebrate the debut of the book that everyone
said would be the publication of the century had already
been going on for two hours when the Regent stamped to the
front of the room to make a few remarks. He was holding a
signed copy, bound in crimson leather and studded with pearls
(the printing press operated by Lucius Felton had moved into
luxury bindings with great success).

Harry Grone was hurriedly scribbling notes for *The Tatler.*
The Regent's speech brought a tear to every eye, he wrote.
*The way he talked of his beloved daughter, Our Mourned
Princess, was deemed most affecting. The Regent then did
the inexpressible honor of giving the memoir's author, Dar-
lington, a royal embrace. As our readers remember,* Grone

noted, *Darlington was knighted a few weeks ago for his work on the Princess's biography.*

Sir Charles Darlington took the stage and thanked the Regent in the most fulsome of terms. He then turned to his wife, Lady Griselda . . . Grone paused. He didn't approve of the fact that her ladyship was in company while visibly *enceinte,* but he supposed he had to change with the times. Still, he wasn't going to mention such a thing in *The Tatler. Darlington said he'd written the memoir for his wife, and that she was*—What did he say? "The possessor of his heart"? Grone sighed. His hearing wasn't all it could be, and he'd rather Darlington stuck to simple Anglo-Saxon words.

Everyone was most affected by his obvious devotion for his wife, he finished.

Perhaps if Grone had glanced to the back of the room, he might have changed his mind. For there stood four Essex sisters and their husbands. True, they clapped wildly to celebrate Darlington's book.

But Josie, the Countess of Mayne, was giggling madly during Darlington's speech. Her husband had his arms around her waist and he kept whispering in her ear, clearly trying to hush her into silence.

"Be still, you minx!" Mayne whispered.

"It's just such twaddle," she whispered back.

"Yes, but did you hear how many leather-bound copies Felton is printing?" Mayne asked her. "Darlington's twaddle is beloved by thousands."

She leaned back against him, loving the fact that she could feel his enthusiasm straight through the floating silk of her gown. "Garret . . ." she whispered, wiggling against him.

"Do you want to make a sight of me?" he growled in her ear.

She leaned her head back on his shoulder, bringing her lips just under his. The Earl of Mayne was never a man who cared much about cleaning up his black reputation. And he couldn't ignore an invitation like that.

He whisked his wife about and began kissing her as if they weren't in a room full of her sisters, as if the Regent wasn't just before them, as if newsmen weren't making notes for gossip columns, as if the world wasn't going to end someday.

Because none of that mattered, not when Mayne had Josie, his own delicious, laughing Josie, just where she needed to be.

In the circle of his arms.

Epilogue

Three years later

"Bloody hell," Josie gasped. "This is awful. This is—This is worse than anything. I'm done. Done! Done, I tell you!" She was shrieking now.

Tess wrapped an arm around her shoulder. "You'll be all right, darling, I promise it. Just calm down."

"Calm down. Calm down!" Josie swung around. "Stop laughing!"

"I'm not laughing," Annabel said, straightening her mouth quickly. "I was just remarking to Imogen that—"

"There's no call to remark anything!" Josie snapped. "I truly—" She broke off. "Oh—oh—oh—*bloody hell*!"

There was a knock on the door and Annabel opened it. "Hello, Mayne!" she said cheerfully.

"I heard her shouting." His face was stark white and his eyes looked haggard. "Is she in much pain? May I see her?"

"I don't see why not. There's nothing much happening yet. It's far too early. We keep telling her that nothing will happen for hours and hours, but you know Josie. She's not patient."

Annabel swung open the door to reveal Josie bent over, clinging to Tess as if her elder sister were a raft in the middle of a storm.

"Josie," Mayne said hoarsely, striding over to her. "Are you all right?"

She turned around and swept the hair out of her eyes. "Of course I'm not all right. I'm dying here. Dying!"

Tess stepped back and Mayne wrapped his arms around his wife. "I would do anything for you. Would you like me to rub your back?"

Imogen grinned at Annabel. "Don't you love it when men forget to be the lord of the castle for a moment or two?"

Annabel actually lived in a castle, and her deep chuckle was infectious. "After each of our children, Ewan has sworn that he will never put me through such a thing again."

"Good thing you have that huge bar on your bedchamber door," Imogen said with a little snort. "Although I can't think why you're looking so round, Annabel, if you've taken up a life of chastity."

Annabel grinned. "It's my natural state," she said. But the hand she curved over her tummy said something different.

Mayne was feeling much better now that he had Josie in his arms. It was pure agony pacing the corridor and knowing she was in pain. "I'm here now," he said into her ear.

"I don't like this," Josie said, leaning her head against his shoulder. "I'd like it to be over now."

"Well, it won't be," Tess said. "We have hours left. Mayne, you really ought to leave."

"I'm not leaving," Mayne said. "If Josie has to endure hours more of this, I'm not going anywhere." There was a mulish, frantic look to his eyes. "There are too many people in here."

Without another word, Mayne whisked his wife into the luxurious little dressing room off the master bedchamber and closed the door behind them.

"Well, for goodness' sake," Tess said. "Should we allow that?"

"There's a bed in there," Annabel said. "Perhaps he can talk her into having a little rest."

Griselda entered the bedchamber. "Where on earth has Josie gone?"

"Oh, Mayne took her into the dressing room for a bit of a cuddle," Annabel said comfortably. "Have a seat, darling."

"I'm not the one in labor," Griselda objected. But she had a golden-haired cherub asleep in the crook of her arm, so she sank into a chair with a happy sigh.

Behind the door they could hear Josie's voice rising to a shriek. She was swearing again. "I was far more ladylike during my first labor," Annabel told them.

Imogen laughed outright.

"No, it's true," her sister protested. "I only swore . . . once in a while."

"I didn't have time to swear," Imogen said. "I was too breathless generally carrying on. Once was enough, to my mind. And Rafe's. I thought he had aged ten years when I finally was allowed to see him."

"How long were you in labor with Samuel?" Griselda asked Annabel. "I still feel terrible that you were off by yourself in Scotland. Imogen and I should have stayed with you."

"I had Nana," Annabel said. "She was of the opinion that a laboring mother's mind should be kept off the subject, so she told me ribald jokes. I did try telling one of Nana's jokes to Josie a few minutes ago, but she just grew abusive. In fact, we had to send the midwife downstairs, as she was looking quite shocked at Josie's language."

At that moment they all heard Josie's voice snapping something from behind the dressing room door. Tess started to rise, but Annabel grabbed her arm. "Josie is doing so much better with Mayne there, and she does have hours to go. Her labor only just started. She would do better if she didn't waste so much energy swearing about it."

At that moment Josie was lying on the little cot in her dressing room, wiggling around to try to make her back stop hurting so much. Even inbetween the contractions—not that there seemed to be much time inbetween anymore—her back hurt like the devil.

"Is it unbearable?" Mayne croaked. He was sitting beside her, holding her hands as hard as he could. His hair was tossed every which way, and if she wasn't in such pain she would have laughed at him.

"Not quite," she said through clenched teeth. For some reason she felt like arching her back, so she did that. "But another five hours of this will be intolerable."

"Perhaps it won't take so long," Mayne said, his face growing even whiter.

Josie felt as if she couldn't quite keep her mind on the conversation. It was as if her body was turning itself inside out. Really . . . how could this go on for another five hours? "Griselda was in labor for *ten* hours," she gasped, holding her husband's hands so tightly that she felt as if his bones were shifting.

"I'm here with you," he said. His eyes were so beautiful, looking down at her, that Josie would have smiled, except she couldn't. All she could do was arch her back again and pant a little.

"I thought there was supposed to be a break between the pains," she said a moment later.

"Do you want to speak to your sisters?" Mayne said, not moving.

She could read his eyes as well as she knew her own heart. If Tess, and Imogen, and Annabel entered the room, they'd make him leave, and it wouldn't be the two of them anymore.

"They said it would take hours," she said. "But I just— just—" She broke off.

Mayne swept the hair off her face. "What, darling?"

"I forgot. I—I—"

Mayne leaned over her. "Darling, *what*—"

A second later Mayne instinctively jumped to his feet, but Josie still had hold of one of his hands. "No!" she panted. She had instinctively planted her legs on the bed. She arched her back again, clinging to his hand with all her strength.

"Tess!" Mayne bawled, looking down at his beautiful, sweaty wife. "All of you! Get the midwife!"

He heard laughter outside the door, and then he dropped Josie's hand, whether she wished it or not.

The door opened and Annabel's voice said, "Now, Mayne, you have to understand that it takes—"

But that was one moment too late. Because what Annabel saw when she opened the door was the earl holding a small, messy baby who opened her eyes, blinked her foolishly long eyelashes (she took after her father), and let out a bellow of rage (she took after her mother as well). And Mayne, the sophisticated, urbane Earl of Mayne, looked down at his little daughter and began to cry. Josie was sitting up and holding out her hands.

Annabel closed the door again.

She said, "Imogen and Tess."

They looked up. They were playing with Griselda's baby's toes. "You know how we assured Josie that labor lasted hours and hours?"

Tess started to her feet. "You don't mean—"

"Would you please ring that bell?" Annabel asked. "Because there's a baby in there."

"Oh Lord!" Tess shrieked, pulling the rope so hard that it came off in her hand.

The midwife grandly swept them to the side and entered the dressing room. They almost crowded in after her, but Tess stopped Imogen at the door. "Give them a moment," she whispered.

Griselda took her baby back to the nursery, but finally

they couldn't wait any longer, and Annabel opened the door again, Imogen and Tess at her shoulders.

Josie was propped up against the back of the small bed, looking as beautiful as only a woman whose labor lasted exactly forty minutes can look. Snuggled in her arms was a scrap of a baby, looking up at her with an expression of fascinated indignation, as if she didn't quite know what to make of her mother. And seated on the edge of the bed, with one arm around Josie and his hand on their daughter, was Garret Langham, Earl of Mayne.

He looked so happy that Annabel's heart turned over to see him.

Without saying a word, she wreathed her arms around Tess and Imogen, and the three of them stood together and smiled . . . and cried a little bit too.

"She's so beautiful," Josie told them, her eyes glowing. "She's the most beautiful baby I ever saw. She looks just like Garret."

"No, she doesn't," Mayne said, trailing a finger over his daughter's cheek. "She's the spitting image of her mother."

"What will you name her?" Annabel asked. Her newest little niece began sucking on her fist with a kind of intensity that suggested she might be interested in learning how to nurse.

"Cecily," Josie said, "after Mayne's aunt."

"This is the best gift that anyone has ever given me," her husband said, and his eyes were suspiciously bright again.

"I wish Mother were here," Tess said. They were all clustered around the baby now, plumped on their knees. Little Cecily had curled her hand around Annabel's finger, and Imogen looked as if she were rethinking her one-baby rule.

"I'm sure she's watching us," Annabel said softly.

"While I would be happy to have met our mother, it was

the three of you who raised me," Josie said. "I always felt safe and loved. And"—she was crying now, tears sliding down onto Cecily's blanket—"I can never thank you enough. Because somehow I ended up with everything I most wanted in the world. I don't think anyone's ever been as happy as I am at this moment."

Cecily was encased in a circle of arms, tears, and hugs. She peered about blearily, and then realized that *she* wasn't happy. And if *she* wasn't happy, then why were all these people laughing, acting as if the world was a perfect place? Something was wrong . . . Something was terribly wrong. And no one had noticed.

She filled her lungs with a sense of righteous indignation.

She aimed to teach a lesson that Josie and Mayne, like every new set of parents, had yet to learn. When one turns over one's life to a small scrap of a tyrant, pure happiness is fleeting.

And yet its deeper cousin, joy, stays with you for life.

A Note About Sisters and Shakespeare Plays

More than any of my previous novels, this story owes a debt to Shakespeare. The interweaving between my novel and Shakespeare's *A Midsummer Night's Dream* go from the enchanted wood and its fairies, to the drug, *love-in-idleness*, to the characters' names, used by Darlington in Hellgate's *Memoirs*. But underpinning these structural links is a deeper thought. In Shakespeare's play a man believes himself in love, and under the drug of moonlight, an enchanted forest, and a measured dose of *love-in-idleness*, he changes his mind and discovers true love. The same is true for my novel's hero. Mayne was so muddled in his thinking about women that he wasn't able to think clearly until he had lost his rational sense altogether. And Josie (plus a little *love-in-idleness*) was just the one to do that service for him.

At one point Josie quotes from another bit of Shakespeare, talking of a *wilderness of lust*. This is not from *A Midsummer Night's Dream*, but from an altogether harder-edged source, a sonnet written (as far as we know) for Shakespeare's private pleasure, and from his most private feelings. "The expense of spirit in a waste of shame/Is lust in action," he writes, talking of sexual intercourse undertaken purely from motives of desire. Mayne knew the landscape of Shakespeare's sonnet. He had lived in that wasteland of shame for years. I knew it would take an extraordinary woman to drag him into heartfelt life again, but Josie could be trusted to do it.

One final note on Hellgate's *Memoirs*. I made them up, obviously, but I had a bit of help with Hellgate's exuberant, overwrought language. At various points Hellgate borrows from the letters of Sarah Bernhardt (a French actress from the 1800s) and from those of Napoleon Bonaparte to Madam Marie Welewska in 1807. If you would like more exact information on Hellgate's bits and pieces, Marvell's poem quoted by Josie, the Minerva Press, or references to Shakespeare, please visit my website at *www.eloisajames.com*. For each of my books, I put up pages giving you an inside scoop on characters, history, and anything else I find interesting. Do stop by—and while you're there, wander by my Bulletin Board and join the discussion about this novel!

A prelude to
Desperate Duchesses
Coming in April 2007

Overheard at a ball, Melbury House,
Northampshire

Laetitia-Matilda Edgeworth to Lady Hester
Vesey, at 9 P.M. sharp:

"I know that the lobster patties are terrible,
Hester; they always are. Did you hear that the
Duchess of Beaumont has definitely returned to
London? I heard it from an impeccable source:
Kendal. You must admit, he knows everything,
and even more interesting, he described himself
becoming *dear friends* with the duchess while
in Florence last summer . . . Of course it means
scandal, but I am so tired of virtue. We old women
must have something to amuse us. Do you know, I
might return to London for the season as early as
next week to get a look at her myself . . ."

Lady Hester Vesey to Lady Webster, at 10:13 P.M.:

"I just heard from an *unimpeachable* source

that Beaumont's wife is in London. Apparently she fell desperately, in love with Lord Kendal last summer after a romantic intrigue in Florence of all places. I myself found the city most unaccommodating, and the lack of drains disconcerting. What? You think so? Oh, no, we can expect nothing from her but gambling and gallantry; there is no point in asking her to be a patroness of the hospital."

From Lady Wister to Lady Leveson-Gower, at 12 A.M.:

"Two people have told me the most intriguing *on-dit* about the Duchess of Beamont, have you heard it yet? My dear, where have you been all evening? Apparently she is carrying a child! It can't be Beaumont's, though I suppose there is a remote chance that he made a trip to France during the Christmas season. It would depend on whether Parliament was in session. Was your husband in town through December? Wister always remarks that Beaumont rarely misses a day in Parliament. No, I can't remember either. At any rate, everyone says it is Kendal's child, so I suppose it was prudent of her to return to London. God knows, if it's a boy, Beaumont will face a dilemma. But then, as Wister remarked to me last night at supper, Beaumont hasn't managed to produce an heir himself, so perhaps he'll be grateful. Beggars can't be choosers, as they say."